Paul Laurence Dunbar

THE COMPLETE POEMS

OF

PAUL LAURENCE DUNBAR

WITH THE INTRODUCTION TO
"LYRICS OF LOWLY LIFE"

BY

W. D. HOWELLS

NEW YORK
DODD, MEAD AND COMPANY
1913

DEDICATIONS

LYRICS OF LOWLY LIFE

TO

MY MOTHER

• , •

LYRICS OF THE HEARTHSIDE

TO

ALICE

• , •

LYRICS OF LOVE AND LAUGHTER

TO

MISS CATHERINE IMPEY

• , •

LYRICS OF SUNSHINE AND SHADOW

TO

MRS. FRANK CONOVER
WITH THANKS FOR HER LONG BELIEF

INTRODUCTION TO LYRICS OF LOWLY LIFE

I THINK I should scarcely trouble the reader with a special appeal in behalf of this book, if it had not specially appealed to me for reasons apart from the author's race, origin, and condition. The world is too old now, and I find myself too much of its mood, to care for the work of a poet because he is black, because his father and mother were slaves, because he was, before and after he began to write poems, an elevator-boy. These facts would certainly attract me to him as a man, if I knew him to have a literary ambition, but when it came to his literary art, I must judge it irrespective of these facts, and enjoy or endure it for what it was in itself.

It seems to me that this was my experience with the poetry of Paul Laurence Dunbar when I found it in another form, and in justice to him I cannot wish that it should be otherwise with his readers here. Still, it will legitimately interest those who like to know the causes, or, if these may not be known, the sources, of things, to learn that the father and mother of the first poet of his race in our language were negroes without admixture of white blood. The father escaped from slavery in Kentucky to freedom in Canada, while there was still no hope of freedom otherwise; but the mother was freed by the events of the civil war, and came North to Ohio, where their son was born at Dayton, and grew up with such chances and mischances for mental training as everywhere befall the children of the poor. He has told me that his father picked up the trade of a plasterer, and when he had taught himself to read, loved chiefly to read history. The boy's mother shared his passion for literature, with a special love of poetry, and after the father died she struggled on in more than the poverty she had shared with him. She could value the faculty which her son showed first in prose sketches and attempts at fiction, and she was proud of the praise and kindness they won him among the people of the town, where he has never been without the warmest and kindest friends.

In fact from every part of Ohio and from several cities of the adjoining States, there came letters in cordial appreciation of the critical recognition which it was my

INTRODUCTION

pleasure no less than my duty to offer Paul Dunbar's work in another place. It seemed to me a happy omen for him that so many people who had known him, or known of him, were glad of a stranger's good word; and it was gratifying to see that at home he was esteemed for the things he had done rather than because as the son of negro slaves he had done them. If a prophet is often without honor in his own country, it surely is nothing against him when he has it. In this case it deprived me of the glory of a discoverer; but that is sometimes a barren joy, and I am always willing to forego it.

What struck me in reading Mr. Dunbar's poetry was what had already struck his friends in Ohio and Indiana, in Kentucky and Illinois. They had felt, as I felt, that however gifted his race had proven itself in music, in oratory, in several of the other arts, here was the first instance of an American negro who had evinced innate distinction in literature. In my criticism of his book I had alleged Dumas in France, and I had forgetfully failed to allege the far greater Pushkin in Russia; but these were both mulattoes, who might have been supposed to derive their qualities from white blood

vastly more artistic than ours, and who were the creatures of an environment more favorable to their literary development. So far as I could remember, Paul Dunbar was the only man of pure African blood and of American civilization to feel the negro life æsthetically and express it lyrically. It seemed to me that this had come to its most modern consciousness in him, and that his brilliant and unique achievement was to have studied the American negro objectively, and to have represented him as he found him to be, with humor, with sympathy, and yet with what the reader must instinctively feel to be entire truthfulness. I said that a race which had come to this effect in any member of it, had attained civilization in him, and I permitted myself the imaginative prophecy that the hostilities and the prejudices which had so long constrained his race were destined to vanish in the arts; that these were to be the final proof that God had made of one blood all nations of men. I thought his merits positive and not comparative; and I held that if his black poems had been written by a white man, I should not have found them less admirable. I accepted them as an evidence of the essential unity of the human race, which does not

INTRODUCTION

think or feel black in one and white in another, but humanly in all.

Yet it appeared to me then, and it appears to me now, that there is a precious difference of temperament between the races which it would be a great pity ever to lose, and that this is best preserved and most charmingly suggested by Mr. Dunbar in those pieces of his where he studies the moods and traits of his race in its own accent of our English. We call such pieces dialect pieces for want of some closer phrase, but they are really not dialect so much as delightful personal attempts and failures for the written and spoken language. In nothing is his essentially refined and delicate art so well shown as in these pieces, which, as I ventured to say, described the range between appetite and emotion, with certain lifts far beyond and above it, which is the range of the race. He reveals in these a finely ironical perception of the negro's limitations, with a tenderness for them which I think so very rare as to be almost quite new. I should say, perhaps, that it was this humorous quality which Mr. Dunbar had added to our literature, and it would be this which would most distinguish him, now and hereafter. It is something that one

feels in nearly all the dialect pieces; and I hope that in the present collection he has kept all of these in his earlier volume, and added others to them. But the contents of this book are wholly of his own choosing, and I do not know how much or little he may have preferred the poems in literary English. Some of these I thought very good, and even more than very good, but not distinctively his contribution to the body of American poetry. What I mean is that several people might have written them; but I do not know any one else at present who could quite have written the dialect pieces. These are divinations and reports of what passes in the hearts and minds of a lowly people whose poetry had hitherto been inarticulately expressed in music, but now finds, for the first time in our tongue, literary interpretation of a very artistic completeness.

I say the event is interesting, but how important it shall be can be determined only by Mr. Dunbar's future performance. I cannot undertake to prophesy concerning this; but if he should do nothing more than he has done, I should feel that he had made the strongest claim for the negro in English literature that the negro has yet made. He has at least

INTRODUCTION

produced something that, however we may critically disagree about it, we cannot well refuse to enjoy; in more than one piece he has produced a work of art.

W. D. HOWELLS.

INDEX OF TITLES

INDEX OF TITLES

INDEX OF TITLES

[xiii]

INDEX OF TITLES

[xiv]

INDEX OF TITLES

INDEX OF TITLES

[xvi]

INDEX OF TITLES

INDEX OF TITLES

INDEX OF FIRST LINES

INDEX OF FIRST LINES

INDEX OF FIRST LINES

[xxii]

INDEX OF FIRST LINES

[xxiii]

INDEX OF FIRST LINES

INDEX OF FIRST LINES

[xxv]

INDEX OF FIRST LINES

[xxvi]

INDEX OF FIRST LINES

INDEX OF FIRST LINES

INDEX OF FIRST LINES

INDEX OF FIRST LINES

INDEX OF FIRST LINES

[xxxi]

INDEX OF FIRST LINES

ERE SLEEP COMES DOWN TO SOOTHE THE WEARY EYES

ERE sleep comes down to soothe
     the weary eyes,
  Which all the day with cease-
     less care have sought
The magic gold which from the
     seeker flies;
  Ere dreams put on the gown
     and cap of thought,
And make the waking world a
     world of lies,—
  Of lies most palpable, uncouth,
     forlorn,
That say life's full of aches and
     tears and sighs,—
  Oh, how with more than dreams
     the soul is torn,
Ere sleep comes down to soothe the
     weary eyes.

Ere sleep comes down to soothe the
     weary eyes,
  How all the griefs and heart-
     aches we have known
Come up like pois'nous vapors that
     arise
  From some base witch's caldron,
     when the crone,
To work some potent spell, her
     magic plies.
  The past which held its share of
     bitter pain,

Whose ghost we prayed that Time
     might exorcise,
  Comes up, is lived and suffered
     o'er again,
Ere sleep comes down to soothe the
     weary eyes.

Ere sleep comes down to soothe the
     weary eyes,
  What phantoms fill the dimly
     lighted room;
What ghostly shades in awe-creat-
     ing guise
  Are bodied forth within the
     teeming gloom.
What echoes faint of sad and soul-
     sick cries,
  And pangs of vague inexplicable
     pain
That pay the spirit's ceaseless en-
     terprise,
  Come thronging through the
     chambers of the brain,
Ere sleep comes down to soothe the
     weary eyes.

Ere sleep comes down to soothe the
     weary eyes,
  Where ranges forth the spirit
     far and free?
Through what strange realms and
     unfamiliar skies
  Tends her far course to lands of
     mystery?

To lands unspeakable — beyond
surmise,
  Where shapes unknowable to
  being spring,
Till, faint of wing, the Fancy fails
and dies
  Much wearied with the spirit's
  journeying,
Ere sleep comes down to soothe the
weary eyes.

Ere sleep comes down to soothe the
weary eyes,
  How questioneth the soul that
  other soul,—
The inner sense which neither
cheats nor lies,
  But self exposes unto self, a
  scroll
Full writ with all life's acts un-
wise or wise,
  In characters indelible and
  known;
So, trembling with the shock of
sad surprise,
  The soul doth view its awful
  self alone,
Ere sleep comes down to soothe
the weary eyes.

When sleep comes down to seal the
weary eyes,
  The last dear sleep whose soft
  embrace is balm,
And whom sad sorrow teaches us
to prize
  For kissing all our passions into
  calm,

Ah, then, no more we heed the sad
world's cries,
  Or seek to probe th' eternal mystery,
Or fret our souls at long-withheld
replies,
  At glooms through which our
  visions cannot see,
When sleep comes down to seal the
weary eyes.

THE POET AND HIS SONG

A song is but a little thing,
And yet what joy it is to sing!
In hours of toil it gives me zest,
And when at eve I long for rest;
When cows come home along the
bars,
  And in the fold I hear the bell,
As Night, the shepherd, herds his
stars,
  I sing my song, and all is well.

There are no ears to hear my lays,
No lips to lift a word of praise;
But still, with faith unfaltering,
I live and laugh and love and sing.
What matters yon unheeding
throng?
  They cannot feel my spirit's
  spell,
Since life is sweet and love is long,
  I sing my song, and all is well.

My days are never days of ease;
I till my ground and prune my
trees.

[4]

PAUL LAURENCE DUNBAR

When ripened gold is all the plain,
I put my sickle to the grain.
I labor hard, and toil and sweat,
    While others dream within the
        dell;
But even while my brow is wet,
    I sing my song, and all is well.

Sometimes the sun, unkindly hot,
My garden makes a desert spot;
Sometimes a blight upon the tree
Takes all my fruit away from me;
And then with throes of bitter pain
    Rebellious passions rise and
        swell;
But — life is more than fruit or
        grain,
    And so I sing, and all is well.

RETORT

" Thou art a fool," said my head
        to my heart,
" Indeed, the greatest of fools thou
        art,
    To be led astray by the trick of
        a tress,
By a smiling face or a ribbon
        smart;"
    And my heart was in sore dis-
        tress.

Then Phyllis came by, and her face
        was fair,
The light gleamed soft on her
        raven hair;
    And her lips were blooming a
        rosy red.

Then my heart spoke out with a
        right bold air:
    " Thou art worse than a fool, O
        head!"

ACCOUNTABILITY

Folks ain't got no right to cen-
        suah othah folks about dey
        habits;
Him dat giv' de squir'ls de bush-
        tails made de bobtails fu' de
        rabbits.
Him dat built de gread big moun-
        tains hollered out de little
        valleys,
Him dat made de streets an' drive-
        ways wasn't shamed to make
        de alleys.

We is all constructed diff'ent,
        d'ain't no two of us de same;
We cain't he'p ouah likes an' dis-
        likes, ef we'se bad we ain't to
        blame.
Ef we 'se good, we need n't show
        off, case you bet it ain't ouah
        doin'
We gits into su'ttain channels dat
        we jes' cain't he'p pu'suin'.

But we all fits into places dat no
        othah ones could fill,
An' we does the things we has to,
        big er little, good er ill.
John cain't tek de place o' Henry,
        Su an' Sally ain't alike;
Bass ain't nuthin' like a suckah,
        chub ain't nuthin' like a pike.

[5]

When you come to think about it,
how it 's all planned out it 's
splendid.
Nuthin 's done er evah happens,
'dout hit 's somefin' dat 's in-
tended;
Don't keer whut you does, you has
to, an' hit sholy beats de
dickens,—
Viney, go put on de kittle, I got
one o' mastah's chickens.

FREDERICK DOUGLASS

A HUSH is over all the teeming
lists,
  And there is pause, a breath-
space in the strife;
A spirit brave has passed beyond
the mists
  And vapors that obscure the sun
of life.
And Ethiopia, with bosom torn,
Laments the passing of her noblest born.

She weeps for him a mother's
burning tears —
  She loved him with a mother's
deepest love.
He was her champion thro' direful
years,
  And held her weal all other ends
above.
When Bondage held her bleeding
in the dust,

He raised her up and whispered,
"Hope and Trust."

For her his voice, a fearless clarion,
rung
  That broke in warning on the
ears of men;
For her the strong bow of his
power he strung,
  And sent his arrows to the very
den
Where grim Oppression held his
bloody place
And gloated o'er the mis'ries of a
race.

And he was no soft-tongued apolo-
gist;
  He spoke straightforward, fear-
lessly uncowed;
The sunlight of his truth dispelled
the mist,
  And set in bold relief each dark
hued cloud;
To sin and crime he gave their
proper hue,
And hurled at evil what was .evil's
due.

Through good and ill report he
cleaved his way
  Right onward, with his face set
toward the heights,
Nor feared to face the foeman's
dread array,—
  The lash of scorn, the sting of
petty spites.

PAUL LAURENCE DUNBAR

He dared the lightning in the
lightning's track,
And answered thunder with his
thunder back.

When men maligned him, and
their torrent wrath
In furious imprecations o'er him
broke,
He kept his counsel as he kept his
path;
'T was for his race, not for himself he spoke.
He knew the import of his Master's call,
And felt himself too mighty to be
small.

No miser in the good he held was
he,—
His kindness followed his hori-
zon's rim.
His heart, his talents, and his
hands were free
To all who truly needed aught
of him.
Where poverty and ignorance
were rife,
He gave his bounty as he gave his
life.

The place and cause that first
aroused his might
Still proved its power until his
latest day.
In Freedom's lists and for the aid
of Right

Still in the foremost rank he
waged the fray;
Wrong lived; his occupation was
not gone.
He died in action with his armor
on!

We weep for him, but we have
touched his hand,
And felt the magic of his presence nigh,
The current that he sent throughout the land,
The kindling spirit of his battle-
cry.
O'er all that holds us we shall triumph yet,
And place our banner where his
hopes were set!

Oh, Douglass, thou hast passed
beyond the shore,
But still thy voice is ringing o'er
the gale!
Thou 'st taught thy race how high
her hopes may soar,
And bade her seek the heights,
nor faint, nor fail.
She will not fail, she heeds thy
stirring cry,
She knows thy guardian spirit will
be nigh,
And, rising from beneath the
chast'ning rod,
She stretches out her bleeding
hands to God!

[7]

LIFE

A CRUST of bread and a corner to
    sleep in,
A minute to smile and an hour to
    weep in,
A pint of joy to a peck of trouble,
And never a laugh but the moans
    come double;
        And that is life!

A crust and a corner that love
    makes precious,
With a smile to warm and the
    tears to refresh us;
And joy seems sweeter when cares
    come after,
And a moan is the finest of foils
    for laughter;
        And that is life!

THE LESSON

MY cot was down by a cypress
    grove,
    And I sat by my window the
    whole night long,
And heard well up from the deep
    dark wood
    A   mocking-bird's   passionate
    song.

And I thought of myself so sad
    and lone,
    And my life's cold winter that
    knew no spring;
Of my mind so weary and sick and
    wild,
    Of my heart too sad to sing.

But e'en as I listened the mock-
    bird's song,
    A thought stole into my sad-
    dened heart,
And I said, "I can cheer some
    other soul
    By a carol's simple art."

For oft from the darkness of
    hearts and lives
    Come songs that brim with joy
    and light,
As out of the gloom of the cypress
    grove
    The   mocking-bird   sings   at
    night.

So I sang a lay for a brother's ear
    In a strain to soothe his bleed-
    ing heart,
And he smiled at the sound of my
    voice and lyre,
    Though mine was a feeble art.

But at his smile I smiled in turn,
    And into my soul there came
    a ray:
In trying to soothe another's woes
    Mine own had passed away.

THE RISING OF THE STORM

THE lake's dark breast
Is all unrest,
It heaves with a sob and a sigh.
Like a tremulous bird,
    From its slumber stirred,
The moon is a-tilt in the sky.

PAUL LAURENCE DUNBAR

From the silent deep
The waters sweep,
But faint on the cold white stones,
And the wavelets fly
With a plaintive cry
O'er the old earth's bare, bleak
    bones.

And the spray upsprings
On its ghost-white wings,
And tosses a kiss at the stars;
While a water-sprite,
In sea-pearls dight,
Hums a sea-hymn's solemn bars.

Far out in the night,
On the wavering sight
I see a dark hull loom;
And its light on high,
Like a Cyclops' eye,
Shines out through the mist and
    gloom.

Now the winds well up
From the earth's deep cup,
And fall on the sea and shore,
And against the pier
The waters rear
And break with a sullen roar.

Up comes the gale,
And the mist-wrought veil
Gives way to the lightning's glare,
And the cloud-drifts fall,
A sombre pall,
O'er water, earth, and air.

The storm-king flies,
His whip he plies,
And bellows down the wind.
The lightning rash
With blinding flash
Comes pricking on behind.

Rise, waters, rise,
And taunt the skies
With your swift-flitting form.
Sweep, wild winds, sweep,
And tear the deep
To atoms in the storm.

And the waters leapt,
And the wild winds swept,
And blew out the moon in the sky,
And I laughed with glee,
It was joy to me
As the storm went raging by!

SUNSET

THE river sleeps beneath the sky,
    And clasps the shadows to its
        breast;
The crescent moon shines dim on
        high;
    And in the lately radiant west
        The gold is fading into gray.
    Now stills the lark his festive
        lay,
    And mourns with me the
        dying day.

While in the south the first faint
        star
    Lifts to the night its silver face,

[9]

And twinkles to the moon afar
  Across the heaven's graying
    space,
Low murmurs reach me from the
    town,
As Day puts on her sombre crown,
And shakes her mantle darkly
    down.

THE OLD APPLE-TREE

There's a memory keeps a-run-
  nin'
  Through my weary head to-
    night,
An' I see a picture dancin'
  In the fire-flames' ruddy light;
'Tis the picture of an orchard
  Wrapped in autumn's purple
    haze,
With the tender light about it
  That I loved in other days.
An' a-standin' in a corner
  Once again I seem to see
The verdant leaves an' branches
  Of an old apple-tree.

You perhaps would call it ugly,
  An' I don't know but it 's so,
When you look the tree all over
  Unadorned by memory's glow;
For its boughs are gnarled an'
  crooked,
  An' its leaves are gettin' thin,
An' the apples of its bearin'
  Would n't fill so large a bin

As they used to. But I tell you,
  When it comes to pleasin' me,
It 's the dearest in the orchard,—
  Is that old apple-tree.

I would hide within its shelter,
  Settlin' in some cosy nook,
Where no calls nor threats could
    stir me
  From the pages o' my book.
Oh, that quiet, sweet seclusion
  In its fulness passeth words!
It was deeper than the deepest
  That my sanctum now affords.
Why, the jaybirds an' the robins,
  They was hand in glove with
    me,
As they winked at me an' warbled
  In that old apple-tree.

It was on its sturdy branches
  That in summers long ago
I would tie my swing an' dangle
  In contentment to an' fro,
Idly dreamin' childish fancies,
  Buildin' castles in the air,
Makin' o' myself a hero
  Of romances rich an' rare.
I kin shet my eyes an' see it
  Jest as plain as plain kin be,
That same old swing a-danglin'
  To the old apple-tree.

There 's a rustic seat beneath it
  That I never kin forget.
It 's the place where me an'
    Hallie —
  Little sweetheart—used to set,

PAUL LAURENCE DUNBAR

When we'd wander to the orchard
So's no listenin' ones could hear
As I whispered sugared nonsense
  Into her little willin' ear.
Now my gray old wife is Hallie,
  An' I'm grayer still than she,
But I'll not forget our courtin'
  'Neath the old apple-tree.

Life for us ain't all been summer,
  But I guess we've had our share
Of its flittin' joys an' pleasures,
  An' a sprinklin' of its care.
Oft the skies have smiled upon us;
  Then again we've seen 'em
    frown,
Though our load was ne'er so
    heavy
  That we longed to lay it down.
But when death does come
    a-callin',
  This my last request shall be,—
That they'll bury me an' Hallie
  'Neath the old apple tree.

A PRAYER

O Lord, the hard-won miles
  Have worn my stumbling feet:
Oh, soothe me with thy smiles,
  And make my life complete.

The thorns were thick and keen
  Where'er I trembling trod;
The way was long between
  My wounded feet and God.

Where healing waters flow
  Do thou my footsteps lead.
My heart is aching so;
  Thy gracious balm I need.

PASSION AND LOVE

A MAIDEN wept and, as a com-
    forter,
Came one who cried, "I love
    thee," and he seized
Her in his arms and kissed her
    with hot breath,
That dried the tears upon her
    flaming cheeks.
While evermore his boldly blaz-
    ing eye
Burned into hers; but she uncom-
    forted
Shrank from his arms and only
    wept the more.

Then one came and gazed mutely
    in her face
With wide and wistful eyes; but
    still aloof
He held himself; as with a rev-
    erent fear,
As one who knows some sacred
    presence nigh.
And as she wept he mingled tear
    with tear,
That cheered her soul like dew a
    dusty flower,—
Until she smiled, approached, and
    touched his hand!

THE SEEDLING

As a quiet little seedling
  Lay within its darksome bed,
To itself it fell a-talking,
  And this is what it said:

"I am not so very robust,
  But I 'll do the best I can;"
And the seedling from that
    moment
  Its work of life began.

So it pushed a little leaflet
  Up into the light of day,
To examine the surroundings
  And show the rest the way.

The leaflet liked the prospect,
  So it called its brother, Stem;
Then two other leaflets heard it,
  And quickly followed them.

To be sure, the haste and hurry
  Made the seedling sweat and
    pant;
But almost before it knew it
  It found itself a plant.

The sunshine poured upon it,
  And the clouds they gave a
    shower;
And the little plant kept growing
  Till it found itself a flower.

Little folks, be like the seedling,
  Always do the best you can;
Every child must share life's
    labor
  Just as well as every man.

And the sun and showers will
    help you
  Through the lonesome, strug-
    gling hours,
Till you raise to light and beauty
  Virtue's fair, unfading flowers.

PROMISE

I GREW a rose within a garden
    fair,
And, tending it with more than
    loving care,
I thought how, with the glory of
    its bloom,
I should the darkness of my life
    illume;
And, watching, ever smiled to see
    the lusty bud
Drink freely in the summer sun to
    tinct its blood.

My rose began to open, and its
    hue
Was sweet to me as to it sun and
    dew;
I watched it taking on its ruddy
    flame
Until the day of perfect blooming
    came,
Then hasted I with smiles to find
    it blushing red—
Too late! Some thoughtless child
    had plucked my rose and fled!

PAUL LAURENCE DUNBAR

FULFILMENT.

I GREW a rose once more to please
　　mine eyes.
All things to aid it — dew, sun,
　　wind, fair skies —
Were kindly; and to shield it
　　from despoil,
I fenced it safely in with grateful
　　toil.
No other hand than mine shall
　　pluck this flower, said I,
And I was jealous of the bee that
　　hovered nigh.
It grew for days; I stood hour
　　after hour
To watch the slow unfolding of
　　the flower,
And then I did not leave its side
　　at all,
Lest some mischance my flower
　　should befall.
At last, oh joy! the central petals
　　burst apart.
It blossomed—but, alas! a worm
　　was at its heart!

SONG

My heart to thy heart,
　　My hand to thine;
My lip to thy lips,
　　Kisses are wine
Brewed for the lover in sunshine
　　and shade;
Let me drink deep, then, my
　　African maid.

Lily to lily,
　　Rose unto rose;
My love to thy love
　　Tenderly grows.
Rend not the oak and the ivy in
　　twain,
Nor the swart maid from her
　　swarthier swain.

AN ANTE-BELLUM SER-
MON

WE is gathahed hyeah, my
　　brothahs,
　　In dis howlin' wildaness,
Fu' to speak some words of com-
　　fo't
　　To each othah in distress.
An' we chooses fu' ouah subjic'
　　Dis — we'll 'splain it by an'
　　　by;
　　"An' de Lawd said, ' Moses,
　　　Moses,'
　　An' de man said, ' Hyeah am
　　　I.' "

Now ole Pher'oh, down in Egypt,
　　Was de wuss man evah bo'n,
An' he had de Hebrew chillun
　　Down dah wukin' in his co'n;
'T well de Lawd got tiahed o' his
　　foolin',
　　An' sez he: "I'll let him
　　　know —
Look hyeah, Moses, go tell
　　Pher'oh
　　Fu' to let dem chillun go."

[13]

"An' ef he refuse to do it,
I will make him rue de houah,
Fu' I 'll empty down on Egypt
All de vials of my powah."
Yes, he did — an' Pher'oh's ahmy
Was n't wuth a ha'f a dime;
Fu' de Lawd will he'p his chillun,
You kin trust him evah time.

An' yo' enemies may 'sail you
In de back an' in de front;
But de Lawd is all aroun' you,
Fu' to ba' de battle's brunt.
Dey kin fo'ge yo' chains an'
shackles
F'om de mountains to de sea;
But de Lawd will sen' some
Moses
Fu' to set his chillun free.

An' de lan' shall hyeah his thun-
dah,
Lak a blas' f'om Gab'el's ho'n,
Fu' de Lawd of hosts is mighty
When he girds his ahmor on.
But fu' feah some one mistakes
me,
I will pause right hyeah to say,
Dat I 'm still a-preachin' ancient,
I ain't talkin' 'bout to-day.

But I tell you, fellah christuns,
Things 'll happen mighty
strange;
Now, de Lawd done dis fu' Isrul,
An' his ways don't nevah
change,

An' de love he showed to Isrul
Was n't all on Isrul spent;
Now don't run an' tell yo' mas-
tahs
Dat I 's preachin' discontent.

'Cause I is n't; I 'se a-judgin'
Bible people by deir ac's;
I 'se a-givin' you de Scriptuah,
I 'se a-handin' you de fac's.
Cose ole Pher'oh b'lieved in
slav'ry,
But de Lawd he let him see,
Dat de people he put bref in,—
Evah mothah's son was free.

An' dahs othahs thinks lak
Pher'oh,
But dey calls de Scriptuah liar,
Fu' de Bible says " a servant
Is a-worthy of his hire."
An' you cain't git roun' nor thoo
dat,
An' you cain't git ovah it,
Fu' whatevah place you git in,
Dis hyeah Bible too 'll fit.

So you see de Lawd's intention,
Evah sence de worl' began,
Was dat His almighty freedom
Should belong to evah man,
But I think it would be bettah,
Ef I 'd pause agin to say,
Dat I 'm talkin' 'bout ouah free-
dom
In a Bibleistic way.

But de Moses is a-comin',
An' he 's comin', suah and fas'

PAUL LAURENCE DUNBAR

We kin hyeah his feet a-trompin',
   We kin hyeah his trumpit blas'.
But I want to wa'n you people,
   Don't you git too brigity;
An' don't you git to braggin'
   'Bout dese things, you wait an'
      see.

But when Moses wif his powah
   Comes an' sets us chillun free,
We will praise de gracious Mastah
   Dat has gin us liberty;
An' we 'll shout ouah halleluyahs,
   On dat mighty reck'nin' day,
When we 'se reco'nised ez citiz'—
   Huh uh! Chillun, let us pray!

ODE TO ETHIOPIA

O Mother Race! to thee I
      bring
This pledge of faith unwavering,
   This tribute to thy glory.
I know the pangs which thou
      didst feel,
When Slavery crushed thee with
      its heel,
   With thy dear blood all gory.

Sad days were those — ah, sad
      indeed!
But through the land the fruitful
      seed
   Of better times was growing.
The plant of freedom upward
      sprung,

And spread its leaves so fresh and
      young —
   Its blossoms now are blowing.

On every hand in this fair land,
Proud Ethiope's swarthy children
      stand
   Beside their fairer neighbor;
The forests flee before their stroke,
Their hammers ring, their forges
      smoke,—
   They stir in honest labour.

They tread the fields where
      honour calls;
Their voices sound through sen-
      ate halls
   In majesty and power.
To right they cling; the hymns
      they sing
Up to the skies in beauty ring,
   And bolder grow each hour.

Be proud, my Race, in mind and
      soul;
Thy name is writ on Glory's scroll
   In characters of fire.
High 'mid the clouds of Fame's
      bright sky
Thy banner's blazoned folds now
      fly,
   And truth shall lift them
      higher.

Thou hast the right to noble pride,
Whose spotless robes were purified
   By blood's severe baptism.
Upon thy brow the cross was laid,

[15]

And labour's painful sweat-beads
made
A consecrating chrism.

No other race, or white or black,
When bound as thou wert, to the
rack,
So seldom stooped to grieving;
No other race, when free again,
Forgot the past and proved them
men
So noble in forgiving.

Go on and up! Our souls and
eyes
Shall follow thy continuous rise;
Our ears shall list thy story
From bards who from thy root
shall spring,
And proudly tune their lyres to
sing
Of Ethiopia's glory.

THE CORN-STALK FIDDLE

WHEN the corn's all cut and the
bright stalks shine
Like the burnished spears of a
field of gold;
When the field-mice rich on the
nubbins dine,
And the frost comes white and
the wind blows cold;
Then it's heigho! fellows and hi-
diddle-diddle,
For the time is ripe for the corn-
stalk fiddle.

And you take a stalk that is
straight and long,
With an expert eye to its
worthy points,
And you think of the bubbling
strains of song
That are bound between its
pithy joints —
Then you cut out strings, with a
bridge in the middle,
With a corn-stalk bow for a corn-
stalk fiddle.

Then the strains that grow as you
draw the bow
O'er the yielding strings with
a practised hand!
And the music's flow never loud
but low
Is the concert note of a fairy
band.
Oh, your dainty songs are a misty
riddle
To the simple sweets of the corn-
stalk fiddle.

When the eve comes on, and our
work is done,
And the sun drops down with a
tender glance,
With their hearts all prime for
the harmless fun,
Come the neighbor girls for
the evening's dance,
And they wait for the well-
known twist and twid-
dle —

More time than tune — from the corn-stalk fiddle.

Then brother Jabez takes the bow,
  While Ned stands off with Su-
    san Bland,
Then Henry stops by Milly Snow,
  And John takes Nellie Jones's
    hand,
While I pair off with Mandy
  Biddle,
And scrape, scrape, scrape goes
  the corn-stalk fiddle.

"Salute your partners," comes the
  call,
  "All join hands and circle
    round,"
"Grand train back," and "Bal-
  ance all,"
  Footsteps lightly spurn the
    ground.
"Take your lady and balance
  down the middle"
To the merry strains of the corn-
  stalk fiddle.

So the night goes on and the dance
  is o'er,
  And the merry girls are home-
    ward gone,
But I see it all in my sleep once
  more,
  And I dream till the very break
    of dawn
Of an impish dance on a red-hot
  griddle

To the screech and scrape of a
  corn-stalk fiddle.

THE MASTER-PLAYER

An old, worn harp that had been
  played
Till all its strings were loose and
  frayed,
Joy, Hate, and Fear, each one
  essayed,
To play. But each in turn had
  found
No sweet responsiveness of sound.

Then Love the Master-Player
  came
With heaving breast and eyes
  aflame;
The Harp he took all undismayed,
Smote on its strings, still strange
  to song,
And brought forth music sweet
  and strong.

THE MYSTERY

I was not; now I am — a few
  days hence
I shall not be; I fain would look
  before
And after, but can neither do;
  some Power
Or lack of power says "no" to all
  I would.
I stand upon a wide and sunless
  plain,

[17]

Nor chart nor steel to guide my
    steps aright.
Whene'er, o'ercoming fear, I dare
    to move,
I grope without direction and by
    chance.
Some feign to hear a voice and
    feel a hand
That draws them ever upward
    thro' the gloom.
But I — I hear no voice and touch
    no hand,
Tho' oft thro' silence infinite I
    list,
And strain my hearing to supernal
    sounds;
Tho' oft thro' fateful darkness do
    I reach,
And stretch my hand to find that
    other hand.
I question of th' eternal bending
    skies
That seem to neighbor with the
    novice earth;
But they roll on, and daily shut
    their eyes
On me, as I one day shall do on
    them,
And tell me not the secret that I
    ask.

NOT THEY WHO SOAR

Nor they who soar, but they who
    plod
Their rugged way, unhelped, to
    God

Are heroes; they who higher fare,
And, flying, fan the upper air,
Miss all the toil that hugs the sod.
'Tis they whose backs have felt
    the rod,
Whose feet have pressed the path
    unshod,
May smile upon defeated care,
    Not they who soar.

High up there are no thorns to
    prod,
Nor boulders lurking 'neath the
    clod
To turn the keenness of the share,
For flight is ever free and rare;
But heroes they the soil who 've
    trod,
    Not they who soar!

WHITTIER

Nor o'er thy dust let there be
    spent
The gush of maudlin sentiment;
Such drift as that is not for thee,
Whose life and deeds and songs
    agree,
Sublime in their simplicity.

Nor shall the sorrowing tear be
    shed.
O singer sweet, thou art not
    dead!
In spite of time's malignant chill,
With living fire thy songs shall
    thrill,

And men shall say, " He liveth
   still ! "

Great poets never die, for Earth
Doth count their lives of too great
   worth
To lose them from her treasured
   store;
So shalt thou live for evermore —
Though far thy form from mortal
   ken —
Deep in the hearts and minds of
   men.

TWO SONGS

A BEE that was searching for
   sweets one day
Through the gate of a rose garden
   happened to stray.
In the heart of a rose he hid away,
And forgot in his bliss the light of
   day,
As sipping his honey he buzzed in
   song;
Though day was waning, he lin-
   gered long,
   For the rose was sweet, so
   sweet.

A robin sits pluming his ruddy
   breast,
And a madrigal sings to his love
   in her nest:
" Oh, the skies they are blue, the
   fields are green,
And the birds in your nest will
   soon be seen ! "

She hangs on his words with a
   thrill of love,
And chirps to him as he sits above
   For the song is sweet, so sweet.

A maiden was out on a summer's
   day
With the winds and the waves
   and the flowers at play;
And she met with a youth of
   gentle air,
With the light of the sunshine on
   his hair.
Together they wandered the flowers among;
They loved, and loving they lin-
   gered long,
   For to love is sweet, so sweet.

———

BIRD of my lady's bower,
   Sing her a song;
Tell her that every hour,
   All the day long,
Thoughts of her come to me,
   Filling my brain
With the warm ecstasy
   Of love's refrain.

Little bird! happy bird!
   Being so near,
Where e'en her slightest word
   Thou mayest hear,
Seeing her glancing eyes,
   Sheen of her hair,
Thou art in paradise,—
   Would I were there.

[19]

I am so far away,
    Thou art so near;
Plead with her, birdling gay,
    Plead with my dear.
Rich be thy recompense,
    Fine be thy fee,
If through thine eloquence
    She hearken me.

A BANJO SONG

OH, dere 's lots o' keer an' trouble
    In dis world to swaller down;
An' ol' Sorrer 's purty lively
    In her way o' gittin' roun'.
Yet dere 's times when I furgit
        em,—
    Aches an' pains an' troubles
        all,—
An' it 's when I tek at ebenin'
    My ol' banjo f'om de wall.

'Bout de time dat night is fallin'
    An' my daily wu'k is done,
An' above de shady hilltops
    I kin see de settin' sun;
When de quiet, restful shadders
    Is beginnin' jes' to fall,—
Den I take de little banjo
    F'om its place upon de wall.

Den my fam'ly gadders roun' me
    In de fadin' o' de light,
Ez I strike de strings to try 'em
    Ef dey all is tuned er-right.
An' it seems we 're so nigh heaben
    We kin hyeah de angels sing

When de music o' dat banjo
    Sets my cabin all er-ring.

An' my wife an' all de othahs,—
    Male an' female, small an'
        big,—
Even up to gray-haired granny,
    Seem jes' boun' to do a jig;
'Twell I change de style o' music,
    Change de movement an' de
        time,
An' de ringin' little banjo
    Plays an ol' hea't-feelin' hime.

An' somehow my th'oat gits choky,
    An' a lump keeps tryin' to rise
Lak it wan'ed to ketch de water
    Dat was flowin' to my eyes;
An' I feel dat I could sorter
    Knock de socks clean off o' sin
Ez I hyeah my po' ol' granny
    .Wif huh tremblin' voice jine in.

Den we all th'ow in our voices
    Fu' to he'p de chune out too,
Lak a big camp-meetin' choiry
    Tryin' to sing a mou'nah th'oo.
An' our th'oahts let out de music,
    Sweet an' solemn, loud an' free,
'Twell de raftahs o' my cabin
    Echo wif de melody.

Oh, de music o' de banjo,
    Quick an' deb'lish, solemn,
        slow,
Is de greates' joy an' solace
    Dat a weary slave kin know!

PAUL LAURENCE DUNBAR

So jes' let me hyeah it ringin',
  Dough de chune be po' an'
    rough,
It 's a pleasure; an' de pleasures
  O' dis life is few enough.

Now, de blessed little angels
  Up in heaben, we are told,
Don't do nothin' all dere lifetime
  'Ceptin' play on ha'ps o' gold.
Now I think heaben 'd be mo'
    homelike
  Ef we 'd hyeah some music fall
F'om a real ol'-fashioned banjo,
  Like dat one upon de wall.

LONGING

IF you could sit with me beside
    the sea to-day,
And whisper with me sweetest
    dreamings o'er and o'er;
I think I should not find the
    clouds so dim and gray,
And not so loud the waves com-
    plaining at the shore.

If you could sit with me upon the
    shore to-day,
And hold my hand in yours as in
    the days of old,
I think I should not mind the chill
    baptismal spray,
Nor find my hand and heart and
    all the world so cold.

If you could walk with me upon
    the strand to-day,

And tell me that my longing love
    had won your own,
I think all my sad thoughts would
    then be put away,
And I could give back laughter
    for the Ocean's moan!

THE PATH

THERE are no beaten paths to
    Glory's height,
There are no rules to compass
    greatness known;
Each for himself must cleave a
    path alone,
And press his own way forward
    in the fight.
Smooth is the way to ease and
    calm delight,
And soft the road Sloth chooseth
    for her own;
But he who craves the flower of
    life full-blown,
Must struggle up in all his armor
    dight!
What though the burden bear him
    sorely down
And crush to dust the mountain
    of his pride,
Oh, then, with strong heart let
    him still abide;
For rugged is the roadway to
    renown,
Nor may he hope to gain the en-
    vied crown,
Till he hath thrust the looming
    rocks aside.

THE LAWYERS' WAYS

I 'VE been list'nin' to them lawyers
  In the court house up the street,
An' I 've come to the conclusion
  That I'm most completely beat.
Fust one feller riz to argy,
  An' he boldly waded in
As he dressed the tremblin' pris'ner
  In a coat o' deep-dyed sin.

Why, he painted him all over
  In a hue o' blackest crime,
An' he smeared his reputation
    With the thickest kind o'
    grime,
Tell I found myself a-wond'rin',
  In a misty way and dim,
How the Lord had come to fashion
  Sich an awful man as him.

Then the other lawyer started,
    An' with brimmin', tearful
    eyes,
Said his client was a martyr
  That was brought to sacrifice.
An' he give to that same pris'ner
  Every blessed human grace,
Tell I saw the light o' virtue
  Fairly shinin' from his face.

Then I own 'at I was puzzled
  How sich things could rightly
  be;
An' this aggervatin' question
  Seems to keep a-puzzlin' me.
So, will some one please inform
  me,
  An' this mystery unroll —

How an angel an' a devil
  Can persess the self-same soul?

ODE FOR MEMORIAL DAY

DONE are the toils and the weari-
  some marches,
  Done is the summons of bugle
  and drum.
Softly and sweetly the sky over-
  arches,
  Shelt'ring a land where Rebellion is dumb.
Dark were the days of the country's derangement,
  Sad were the hours when the
  conflict was on,
But through the gloom of frater-
  nal estrangement
  God sent his light, and we welcome the dawn.
O'er the expanse of our mighty
  dominions,
  Sweeping away to the uttermost
  parts,
Peace, the wide-flying, on untiring
  pinions,
  Bringeth her message of joy to
  our hearts.

Ah, but this joy which our minds
  cannot measure,
  What did it cost for our fathers
  to gain!
Bought at the price of the heart's
  dearest treasure,
  Born out of travail and sorrow
  and pain;

PAUL LAURENCE DUNBAR

Born in the battle where fleet
  Death was flying,
    Slaying with sabre-stroke bloody
      and fell;
Born where the heroes and mar-
      tyrs were dying,
    Torn by the fury of bullet and
      shell.
Ah, but the day is past: silent the
      rattle,
    And the confusion that followed
  .   the fight.
Peace to the heroes who died in
      the battle,
    Martyrs to truth and the crown-
      ing of Right!

Out of the blood of a conflict fra-
      ternal,
    Out of the dust and the dimness
      of death,
Burst into blossoms of glory eter-
      nal
    Flowers that sweeten the world
      with their breath.
Flowers of charity, peace, and
      devotion
    Bloom in the hearts that are
      empty of strife;
Love that is boundless and broad
      as the ocean
    Leaps into beauty and fulness
      of life. ·
So, with the singing of pæans and
      chorals,
    And with the flag flashing high
      in the sun,

Place on the graves of our heroes
      the laurels
    Which their unfaltering valor
      has won!

PREMONITION

Dear heart, good-night!
Nay, list awhile that sweet voice
      singing
    When the world is all so bright,
And the sound of song sets the
      heart a-ringing,
    Oh, love, it is not right —
    Not then to say, "Good-
      night."

Dear heart, good-night!
The late winds in the lake weeds
      shiver,
    And the spray flies cold and
      white.
And the voice that sings gives a
      telltale quiver —
    "Ah, yes, the world is bright,
    But, . dearest heart, good-
      night!"

Dear heart, good-night!
And do not longer seek to hold
      me!
    For my soul is in affright
As the fearful glooms in their
      pall enfold me.
    See him who sang how white
    And still; so, dear, good-
      night.

[23]

Dear heart, good-night!
Thy hand I 'll press no more forever,
And mine eyes shall lose the
light;.
For the great white wraith by the
winding river
Shall check my steps with
might.
So, dear, good-night, good-
night!

RETROSPECTION

WHEN you and I were young, the
days
Were filled with scent of pink
and rose,
And full of joy from dawn till
close,
From morning's mist till evening's
haze.
And when the robin sung his
song
The verdant woodland ways
along,
We whistled louder than he
sung.
And school was joy, and work was
sport
For which the hours were all too
short,
When you and I were young,
my boy,
When you and I were young.

When you and I were young, the
woods
Brimmed bravely o'er with every
joy
To charm the happy-hearted
boy.
The quail turned out her timid
broods;
The prickly copse, a hostess
fine,
Held high black cups of harmless wine;
And low the laden grape-vine
swung
With beads of night-kissed ame-
thyst
Where buzzing lovers held their
tryst,
When you and I were young,
my boy,
When you and I were young.

When you and I were young, the
cool
And fresh wind fanned our
fevered brows
When tumbling o'er the scented
mows,
Or stripping by the dimpling
pool,
Sedge-fringed about its shim-
mering face,
Save where we 'd worn an en-
t'ring place.
How with our shouts the
calm banks rung!

PAUL LAURENCE DUNBAR

How flashed the spray as we
  plunged in,—
Pure gems that never caused a
  sin!
  When you and I were young,
    my boy,
  When you and I were young.

When you and I were young, we
  heard
  All sounds of Nature with de-
    light,—
  The whirr of wing in sudden
    flight,
The chirping of the baby-bird.
The columbine's red bells were
  rung;
The locust's vested chorus
  sung;
  While every wind his zithern
    strung
To high and holy-sounding keys,
And played sonatas in the trees —
  When you and I were young,
    my boy,
  When you and I were young.

When you and I were young, we
  knew
  To shout and laugh, to work
    and play,
  And night was partner to the
    day
In all our joys. So swift time
  flew
  On silent wings that, ere we
    wist,

The fleeting years had fled un-
  missed;
  And from our hearts this cry
    was wrung —
To fill with fond regret and tears
The days of our remaining years —
  "When you and I were young,
    my boy,
  When you and I were young."

UNEXPRESSED

DEEP in my heart that aches with
  the repression,
  And strives with plenitude of
    bitter pain,
There lives a thought that clamors
  for expression,
  And spends its undelivered
    force in vain.

What boots it that some other
  may have thought it?
  The right of thoughts' expres-
    sion is divine;
The price of pain I pay for it has
  bought it,
  I care not who lays claim to it
    —'t is mine!

And yet not mine until it be deliv-
  ered;
  The manner of its birth shall
    prove the test.
Alas, alas, my rock of pride is
  shivered —
  I beat my brow — the thought
    still unexpressed.

SONG OF SUMMER

Dis is gospel weathah sho'—
  Hills is sawt o' hazy.
Meddahs level ez a flo'
  Callin' to de lazy.
Sky all white wif streaks o' blue,
  Sunshine softly gleamin',
D'ain't no wuk hit 's right to do,
  Nothin' 's right but dreamin'.

Dreamin' by de rivah side
  Wif de watahs glist'nin',
Feelin' good an' satisfied
  Ez you lay a-list'nin'
To the little nakid boys
  Splashin' in de watah,
Hollerin' fu' to spress deir joys
  Jes' lak youngsters ought to.

Squir'l a-tippin' on his toes,
  So 's to hide an' view you;
Whole flocks o' camp-meetin'
      crows
  Shoutin' hallelujah.
Peckahwood erpon de tree
  Tappin' lak a hammah;
Jaybird chattin' wif a bee,
  Tryin' to teach him grammah.

Breeze is blowin' wif perfume,
  Jes'.enough to tease you;
Hollyhocks is all in bloom,
  Smellin' fu' to please you.
Go 'way, folks, an' let me 'lone,
  Times is gettin' dearah—
Summah's settin' on de th'one,
  An' I 'm a-layin' neah huh!

SPRING SONG

A BLUE-BELL springs upon the
      ledge,
A lark sits singing in the hedge;
Sweet perfumes scent the balmy
      air,
And life is brimming everywhere.
What lark and breeze and blue-
      bird sing,
      Is Spring, Spring, Spring!

No more the air is sharp and cold;
The planter wends across the wold,
And, glad, beneath the shining
      sky
We wander forth, my love and I.
And ever in our hearts doth ring
      This song of Spring, Spring!

For life is life and love is love,
  'Twixt maid and man or dove and
      dove.
Life may be short, life may be
      long,
But love will come, and to its
      song
Shall this refrain for ever cling
      Of Spring, Spring, Spring!

TO LOUISE

OH, the poets may sing of their
      Lady Irenes,
And may rave in their rhymes
      about wonderful queens;
But I throw my poetical wings to
      the breeze,

PAUL LAURENCE DUNBAR

And soar in a song to my Lady
    Louise.
A sweet little maid, who is dearer,
    I ween,
Than any fair duchess, or even a
    queen.
When speaking of her I can't plod
    in my prose,
For she 's the wee lassie who gave
    me a rose.

Since poets, from seeing a lady's
    lip curled,
Have written fair verse that has
    sweetened the world;
Why, then, should not I give the
    space of an hour
To making a song in return for a
    flower?
I have found in my life — it has
    not been so long —
There are too few of flowers — too
    little of song.
So out of that blossom, this lay of
    mine grows,
For the dear little lady who gave
    me the rose.

I thank God for innocence, dearer
    than Art,
That lights on a by-way which
    leads to the heart,
And led by an impulse no less
    than divine,
Walks into the temple and sits at
    the shrine.
I would rather pluck daisies that
    grow in the wild,

Or take one simple rose from the
    hand of a child,
Then to breathe the rich fragrance
    of flowers that bide
In the gardens of luxury, passion,
    and pride.

I know not, my wee one, how
    came you to know
Which way to my heart was the
    right way to go;
Unless in your purity, soul-clean
    and clear,
God whispers his messages into
    your ear.
You have now had my song, let
    me end with a prayer
That your life may be always
    sweet, happy, and fair;
That your joys may be many, and
    absent your woes,
O dear little lady who gave me
    the rose!

THE RIVALS

'T WAS three an' thirty year ago,
When I was ruther young, you
    know,
I had my last an' only fight
About a gal one summer night.
'T was me an' Zekel Johnson;
    Zeke
'N' me 'd be'n spattin' 'bout a
    week,
Each of us tryin' his best to show
That he was Liza Jones's beau.

[27]

We could n't neither prove the thing,
Fur she was fur too sharp to fling
One over fur the other one
An' by so doin' stop the fun
That we chaps did n't have the sense
To see she got at our expense,
But that 's the way a feller does,
Fur boys is fools an' allus was.
An' when they 's females in the game
I reckon men 's about the same.
Well, Zeke an' me went on that way
An' fussed an' quarrelled day by day;
While Liza, mindin' not the fuss,
Jest kep' a-goin' with both of us,
Tell we pore chaps, that 's Zeke an' me,
Was jest plum mad with jealousy.
Well, fur a time we kep' our places,
An' only showed by frownin' faces
An' looks 'at well our meanin' boded
How full o' fight we both was loaded.
At last it come, the thing broke out,
An' this is how it come about.
One night ('t was fair, you 'll all agree)

I got Eliza's company,
An' leavin' Zekel in the lurch,
Went trottin' off with her to church.
An' jest as we had took our seat
(Eliza lookin' fair an' sweet),
Why, I jest could n't help but grin
When Zekel come a-bouncin' in
As furious as the law allows.
He 'd jest be'n up to Liza's house,
To find her gone, then come to church
To have this end put to his search.
I guess I laffed that meetin' through,
An' not a mortal word I knew
Of what the preacher preached er read
Er what the choir sung er said.
Fur every time I 'd turn my head
I could n't skeercely help but see
'At Zekel had his eye on me.
An' he 'ud sort o' turn an' twist
An' grind his teeth an' shake his fist.
I laughed, fur la! the hull church seen us,
An' knowed that suthin' was between us.
Well, meetin' out, we started hum,
I sorter feelin' what would come.
We 'd jest got out, when up stepped Zeke,
An' said, " Scuse me, I 'd like to speak

To you a minute." "Cert," said
    I —
A-nudgin' Liza on the sly
An' laughin' in my sleeve with
    glee,
I asked her, please, to pardon me.
We walked away a step er two,
Jest to git out o' Liza's view,
An' then Zeke said, "I want to
    know
Ef you think you 're Eliza's beau,
An' 'at I 'm goin' to let her go
Hum with sich a chap as you?"
An' I said bold, "You bet I do."
Then Zekel, sneerin', said 'at he
Did n't want to hender me.
But then he 'lowed the gal was
    his
An' 'at he guessed he knowed his
    biz,
An' was n't feared o' all my kin
With all my friends an' chums
    throwed in.
Some other things he mentioned
    there
That no born man could no ways
    bear
Er think o' ca'mly tryin' to stan'
Ef Zeke had be'n the bigges' man
In town, an' not the leanest runt
'At time an' labor ever stunt.
An' so I let my fist go "bim,"
I thought I 'd mos' nigh finished
    him.
But Zekel did n't take it so.
He jest ducked down an' dodged
    my blow

An' then come back at me so hard,
I guess I must 'a' hurt the yard,
Er spilet the grass plot where I
    fell,
An' sakes alive it hurt me; well,
It would n't be'n so bad, you see,
But he jest kep' a-hittin' me.
An' I hit back an' kicked an'
    pawed,
But 't seemed 't was mostly air I
    clawed,
While Zekel used his science well
A-makin' every motion tell.
He punched an' hit, why, good-
    ness lands,
Seemed like he had a dozen hands.
Well, afterwhile they stopped the
    fuss,
An' some one kindly parted us.
All beat an' cuffed an' clawed an'
    scratched,
An' needin' both our faces
    patched,
Each started hum a different way;
An' what o' Liza, do you say,
Why, Liza — little humbug —
    dern her,
Why, she 'd gone home with
    Hiram Turner.

THE LOVER AND THE MOON

A LOVER whom duty called over
    the wave,
With himself communed:
    "Will my love be true

[29]

If left to herself? Had I better not sue
Some friend to watch over her,
good and grave?
But my friend might fail in my
need," he said,
"And I return to find love
dead.
Since friendships fade like the
flow'rs of June,
I will leave her in charge of the
stable moon."

Then he said to the moon: "O
dear old moon,
Who for years and years from
thy thrown above
Hast nurtured and guarded
young lovers and love,
My heart has but come to its
waiting June,
And the promise time of the
budding vine;
Oh, guard thee well this love
of mine."
And he harked him then while
all was still,
And the pale moon answered
and said, "I will."

And he sailed in his ship o'er
many seas,
And he wandered wide o'er
strange far strands:
In isles of the south and in Ori-
ent lands,
Where pestilence lurks in the
breath of the breeze.

But his star was high, so he
braved the main,
And sailed him blithely home
again;
And with joy he bended his
footsteps soon
To learn of his love from the
matron moon.

She sat as of yore, in her olden
place,
Serene as death, in her silver
chair.
A white rose gleamed in her
whiter hair,
And the tint of a blush was on
her face.
At sight of the youth she sadly
bowed
And hid her face 'neath a gracious cloud.
She faltered faint on the night's
dim marge,
But "How," spoke the youth,
"have you kept your
charge?"

The moon was sad at a trust ill-
kept;
The blush went out in her
blanching cheek,
And her voice was timid and
low and weak,
As she made her plea and sighed
and wept.
"Oh, another prayed and another plead,

[30]

And I could n't resist," she
   answering said;
"But love still grows in the
   hearts of men:
Go forth, dear youth, and love
   again."

But he turned him away from her
   proffered grace.
"Thou art false, O moon, as
   the hearts of men,
I will not, will not love again."
And he turned sheer 'round with
   a soul-sick face
   To the sea, and cried: "Sea,
     curse the moon,
Who makes her vows and for-
   gets so soon."
And the awful sea with anger
   stirred,
And his breast heaved hard as
   he lay and heard.

And ever the moon wept down in
   rain,
   And ever her sighs rose high in
     wind;
   But the earth and sea were deaf
     and blind,
And she wept and sighed her
   griefs in vain.
   And ever at night, when the
     storm is fierce,
   The cries of a wraith through
     the thunder pierce;
   And the waves strain their aw-
     ful hands on high

To tear the false moon from the
   sky.

CONSCIENCE AND RE-MORSE

"GOOD-BYE," I said to my con-
   science —
   "Good-bye for aye and aye,"
And I put her hands off harshly,
   And turned my face away;
And conscience smitten sorely
   Returned not from that day.

But a time came when my spirit
   Grew weary of its pace;
And I cried: "Come back, my
   conscience;
   I long to see thy face."
But conscience cried: "I cannot;
   Remorse sits in my place."

IONE

I

AH, yes, 't is sweet still to remem-
   ber,
   Though 't were less painful to
     forget;
For while my heart glows like an
   ember,
   Mine eyes with sorrow's drops
     are wet,
   And, oh, my heart is aching
     yet.
It is a law of mortal pain

That old wounds, long ac-
counted well,
Beneath the memory's potent
spell,
Will wake to life and bleed again.

So 't is with me; it might be bet-
ter
If I should turn no look be-
hind,—
If I could curb my heart, and fet-
ter
From reminiscent gaze my
mind,
Or let my soul go blind — go
blind!
But would I do it if I could?
Nay! ease at such a price were
spurned;
For, since my love was once re-
turned,
All that I suffer seemeth good.

I know, I know it is the fashion,
When love has left some heart
distressed,
To weight the air with wordful
passion;
But I am glad that in my
breast
I ever held so dear a guest.
Love does not come at every nod,
Or every voice that calleth
"hasten;"
He seeketh out some heart to
chasten,
And whips it, wailing, up to God!

Love is no random road wayfarer
Who where he may must sip his
glass.
Love is the King, the Purple-
Wearer,
Whose guard recks not of tree
or grass
To blaze the way that he may
pass.
What if my heart be in the blast
That heralds his triumphant
way;
Shall I repine, shall I not say:
"Rejoice, my heart, the King has
passed!"

In life, each heart holds some sad
story —
The saddest ones are never told.
I, too, have dreamed of fame and
glory,
And viewed the future bright
with gold;
But that is as a tale long told.
Mine eyes have lost their youthful
flash,
My cunning hand has lost its
art;
I am not old, but in my heart
The ember lies beneath the ash.

I loved! Why not? My heart
was youthful,
My mind was filled with
healthy thought.
He doubts not whose own self is
truthful,

PAUL LAURENCE DUNBAR

Doubt by dishonesty is taught;
So loved I boldly, fearing
naught.
I did not walk this lowly earth;
Mine was a newer, higher
sphere,
Where youth was long and life
was dear,
And all save love was little worth.

Her likeness! Would that I
might limn it,
As Love did, with enduring
art;
Nor dust of days nor death may
dim it,
Where it lies graven on my
heart,
Of this sad fabric of my life a
part.
I would that I might paint her
now
As I beheld her in that day,
Ere her first bloom had passed
away,
And left the lines upon her brow.

A face serene that, beaming
brightly,
Disarmed the hot sun's glances
bold.
A foot that kissed the ground so
lightly,
He frowned in wrath and
deemed her cold,
But loved her still though he
was old.

A form where every maiden grace
Bloomed to perfection's richest
flower,—
The statued pose of conscious
power,
Like lithe-limbed Dian's of the
chase.

Beneath a brow too fair for frowning,
Like moon-lit deeps that glass
the skies
Till all the hosts above seem
drowning,
Looked forth her steadfast hazel eyes,
With gaze serene and purely
wise.
And over all, her tresses rare,
Which, when, with his desire
grown weak,
The Night bent down to kiss
her cheek,
Entrapped and held him captive
there.

This was Ione; a spirit finer
Ne'er burned to ash its house
of clay;
A soul instinct with fire diviner
Ne'er fled athwart the face of
day,
And tempted Time with earthly
stay.
Her loveliness was not alone
Of face and form and tresses'
hue;

For aye a pure, high soul shone
    through
Her every act: this was Ione.

II

'T was in the radiant summer
    weather,
    When God looked, smiling,
      from the sky;
And we went wand'ring much to-
    gether
    By wood and lane, Ione and
      I,
Attracted by the subtle tie
Of common thoughts and com-
    mon tastes,
    Of eyes whose vision saw the
      same,
    And freely granted beauty's
      claim
Where others found but worthless
    wastes.

We paused to hear the far bells
    ringing
    Across the distance, sweet and
      clear.
We listened to the wild bird's
    singing
    The song he meant for his
      mate's ear,
    And deemed our chance to do
      so dear.
We loved to watch the warrior
    Sun,
    With flaming shield and flaunt-
      ing crest,

Go striding down the gory
    West,
When Day's long fight was fought
    and won.

And life became a different
    story;
    Where'er I looked, I saw new
      light.
Earth's self assumed a greater
    glory,
    Mine eyes were cleared to
      fuller sight.
. Then first I saw the need and
    might
Of that fair band, the singing
    throng,
    Who, gifted with the skill di-
      vine,
    Take up the threads of life,
      spun fine,
And weave them into soulful
    song.

They sung for me, whose passion
    pressing
    My soul, found vent in song
      nor line.
They bore the burden of express-
    ing
    All that I felt, with art's de-
      sign,
    And every word of theirs was
      mine.
I read them to Ione, ofttimes,
    By hill and shore, beneath fair
      skies,

And she looked deeply in mine
        eyes,
And knew my love spoke through
        their rhymes.

Her life was like the stream that
        floweth,
    And mine was like the waiting
        sea;
Her love was like the flower that
        bloweth,
    And mine was like the search-
        ing bee —
    I found her sweetness all for
        me.
God plied him in the mint of
        time,
    And coined for us a golden day,
    And rolled it ringing down
        life's way
With love's sweet music in its
        chime.

And God unclasped the Book of
        Ages,
    And laid it open to our sight;
Upon the dimness of its pages,
    So long consigned to rayless
        night,
    He shed the glory of his light.
We read them well, we read them
        long,
    And ever thrilling did we see
    That love ruled all human-
        ity,—
The master passion, pure and
        strong.

III

To-day my skies are bare and
        ashen,
    And bend on me without a
        beam.
Since love is held the master-pas-
        sion,
    Its loss must be the pain su-
        preme —
    And grinning Fate has wrecked
        my dream.
But pardon, dear departed Guest,
    I will not rant, I will not rail;
    For good the grain must feel
        the flail;
There are whom love has never
        blessed.

I had and have a younger brother,
    One whom I loved and love to-
        day
As never fond and doting mother
    Adored the babe who found its
        way
    From heavenly scenes into her
        day. .
Oh, he was full of youth's new
        wine,—
    A man on life's ascending slope,
    Flushed with ambition, full of
        hope;
And every wish of his was mine.

A kingly youth; the way before
        him
    Was thronged with victories to
        be won;

So joyous, too, the heavens o'er
    him
    Were bright with an unchang-
      ing sun,—
    His days with rhyme were over-
      run.
Toil had not taught him Nature's
    prose,
    Tears had not dimmed his bril-
      liant eyes,
    And sorrow had not made him
      wise;
His life was in the budding rose.

I know not how I came to
    waken,
    Some instinct pricked my soul
      to sight;
My heart by some vague thrill
    was shaken,—
    A thrill so true and yet so
      slight,
    I hardly deemed I read aright.
As when a sleeper, ign'rant why,
    Not knowing what mysterious
      hand
    Has called him out of slumber-
      land,
Starts up to find some danger
    nigh.

Love is a guest that comes, un-
    bidden,
    But, having come, asserts his
      right;
He will not be repressed nor hid-
    den.

And so my brother's dawning
    plight
    Became uncovered to my sight.
Some sound-mote in his passing
    tone
    Caught in the meshes of my
      ear;
    Some little glance, a shade too
      dear,
Betrayed the love he bore Ione.

What could I do? He was my
    brother,
    And young, and full of hope
      and trust;
I could not, dared not try to
    smother
    His flame, and turn his heart to
      dust.
    I knew how oft life gives a
      crust
To starving men who cry for
    bread;
    But he was young, so few his
      days,
    He had not learned the great
      world's ways,
Nor Disappointment's volumes
    read.

However fair and rich the booty,
    I could not make his loss my
      gain.
For love is dear, but dearer
    duty,
    And here my way was clear and
      plain.

I saw how I could save him pain.
And so, with all my day grown
    dim,
    That this loved brother's sun
        might shine,
    I joined his suit, gave over
        mine,
And sought Ione, to plead for him.

I found her in an eastern bower,
    Where all day long the am'rous
        sun
Lay by to woo a timid flower.
    This day his course was well-
        nigh run,
    But still with lingering art he
        spun
Gold fancies on the shadowed
    wall.
    The vines waved soft and green
        above,
    And there where one might tell
        his love,
I told my griefs — I told her all!

I told her all, and as she heark-
    ened,
    A tear-drop fell upon her dress.
With grief her flushing brow was
    darkened;
    One sob that she could not re-
        press
    Betrayed the depths of her dis-
        tress.
Upon her grief my sorrow fed,
    And I was bowed with unlived
        years,

My heart swelled with a sea of
    tears,
The tears my manhood could not
    shed.

The world is Rome, and Fate is
    Nero,
    Disporting in the hour of
        doom.
God made us men; times make the
    hero —
    But in that awful space of
        gloom
    I gave no thought but sorrow's
        room.
All — all was dim within that
    bower,
    What time the sun divorced the
        day;
    And all the shadows, glooming
        gray,
Proclaimed the sadness of the
    hour.

She could not speak — no word
    was needed;
    Her look, half strength and half
        despair,
Told me I had not vainly pleaded,
    That she would not ignore my
        prayer.
    And so she turned and left me
        there,
And as she went, so passed my
    bliss;
    She loved me, I could not mis-
        take —

But for her own and my love's
sake,
Her womanhood could rise to
this!

My wounded heart fled swift to
cover,
And life at times seemed very
drear.
My brother proved an ardent
lover —
What had so young a man to
fear?
He wed Ione within the year.
No shadow clouds her tranquil
brow,
Men speak her husband's name
with pride,
While she sits honored at his
side —
She is — she must be happy now!

I doubt the course I took no
longer,
Since those I love seem satisfied.
The bond between them will grow
stronger
As they go forward side by
side;
Then will my pains be jus-
fied.
Their joy is mine, and that is
best —
I am not totally bereft;
For I have still the mem'ry
left —
Love stopped with me — a Royal
Guest!

RELIGION

I AM no priest of crooks nor
creeds,
For human wants and human
needs
Are more to me than prophets'
deeds;
And human tears and human
cares
Affect me more than human
prayers.

Go, cease your wail, lugubrious
saint!
You fret high Heaven with your
plaint.
Is this the "Christian's joy" you
paint?
Is this the Christian's boasted
bliss?
Avails your faith no more than
this?

Take up your arms, come out with
me,
Let Heav'n alone; humanity
Needs more and Heaven less from
thee.
With pity for mankind look
'round;
Help them to rise — and Heaven
is found.

DEACON JONES' GRIEVANCE

I 've been watchin' of 'em, par-
    son,
  An' I 'm sorry fur to say
'At my mind is not contented
  With the loose an' keerless
    way
'At the young folks treat the mu-
    sic;
  'T ain't the proper sort o'
    choir.
Then I don't believe in Chris-
    tuns
, A-singin' hymns for hire.

But I never would 'a' mur-
    mured
  An' the matter might 'a' gone
Ef it was n't fur the antics
  'At I 've seen 'em kerry on;
So I thought it was my dooty
  Fur to come to you an' ask
Ef you would n't sort o' gently
  Take them singin' folks to task.

Fust, the music they 've be'n
    singin'
  Will disgrace us mighty soon;
It 's a cross between a opry
  An' a ol' cotillion tune.
With its dashes an' its quavers
  An' its hifalutin style —
Why, it sets my head to swim-
    min'
  When I 'm comin' down the
    aisle.

Now it might be almost decent
  Ef it was n't fur the way
'At they git up there an' sing it,
  Hey dum diddle, loud and gay.
Why, it shames the name o'
    sacred
  In its brazen wordliness,
An' they 've even got " Ol' Hun-
    dred "
  In a bold, new-fangled dress.

You 'll excuse me, Mr. Parson,
  Ef I seem a little sore;
But I 've sung the songs of Isr'el
  For threescore years an' more,
An' it sort o' hurts my feelin's
  Fur to see 'em put away
Fur these harum-scarum ditties
  'At is capturin' the day.

There 's anuther little happ'nin'
  'At I 'll mention while I 'm
    here,
Jes' to show 'at my objections
  All is offered sound and clear.
It was one day they was singin'
  An' was doin' well enough —
Singin' good as people could sing
  Sich an awful mess o' stuff —

When the choir give a holler,
  An' the organ give a groan,
An' they left one weak-voiced fel-
    ler
  A-singin' there alone!
But he stuck right to the music,
  Tho' 't was tryin' as could
    be;

[39]

An' when I tried to help him,
  Why, the hull church scowled
    at me.

You say that's so-low singin',
  Well, I pray the Lord that I
Growed up when folks was
    willin'
  To sing their hymns so high.
Why, we never had sich doin's
  In the good ol' Bethel days,
When the folks was all con-
    tented
  With the simple songs of
    praise.

Now I may have spoke too open,
  But 't was too hard to keep
    still,
An' I hope you'll tell the singers
  'At I bear 'em no ill-will.
'At they all may git to glory
  Is my wish an' my desire,
But they'll need some extry train-
    in'
  'Fore they jine the heavenly
    choir.

ALICE

KNOW you, winds that blow your
    course
  Down the verdant valleys,
That somewhere you must, per-
    force,
  Kiss the brow of Alice?
When her gentle face you find,
Kiss it softly, naughty wind.

Roses waving fair and sweet
  Thro' the garden alleys,
Grow into a glory meet
  For the eye of Alice;
Let the wind your offering bear
Of sweet perfume, faint and rare,

Lily holding crystal dew
  In your pure white chalice,
Nature kind hath fashioned you
  Like the soul of Alice;
It of purest white is wrought,
Filled with gems of crystal
    thought.

AFTER THE QUARREL

So we, who've supped the self-
    same cup,
  To-night must lay our friend-
    ship by;
Your wrath has burned your
    judgment up,
  Hot breath has blown the ashes
    high.
You say that you are wronged —
    ah, well,
  I count that friendship poor,
    at best
A bauble, a mere bagatelle,
  That cannot stand so slight a
    test.

I fain would still have been your
    friend,
  And talked and laughed and
    loved with you;

But since it must, why, let it end;
  The false but dies, 't is not the
    true.
So we are favored, you and I,
  Who only want the living
    truth.
It was not good to nurse the lie;
  'T is well it died in harmless
    youth.

I go from you to-night to sleep.
  Why, what 's the odds? why
    should I grieve?
I have no fund of tears to weep
  For happenings that undeceive.
The days shall come, the days
    shall go
  Just as they came and went be-
    fore.
The sun shall shine, the streams
    shall flow
Though you and I are friends no
    more.

And in the volume of my years,
  Where all my thoughts and
    acts shall be,
The page whereon your name
    appears
  Shall be forever sealed to me.
Not that I hate you over-much,
  'T is less of hate than love de-
    fied;
Howe'er, our hands no more shall
    touch,
  We 'll go our ways, the world is
    wide.

BEYOND THE YEARS

I

BEYOND the years the answer lies,
Beyond where brood the grieving
    skies
  And Night drops tears.
Where Faith rod-chastened smiles
    to rise
  And doff its fears,
And carping Sorrow pines and
    dies —
  Beyond the years.

II

Beyond the years the prayer for rest
Shall beat no more within the
    breast;
  The darkness clears,
And Morn perched on the moun-
    tain's crest
  Her form uprears —
The day that is to come is best,
  Beyond the years.

III

Beyond the years the soul shall find
That endless peace for which it
    pined,
  For light appears,
And to the eyes that still were blind
  With blood and tears,
Their sight shall come all uncon-
    fined
  Beyond the years.

[41]

AFTER A VISIT

I be'n down in ole Kentucky
　Fur a week er two, an' say,
'T wuz ez hard ez breakin' oxen
　Fur to tear myse'f away.
Allus argerin' 'bout fren'ship
　An' yer hospitality —
Y' ain't no right to talk about it
　Tell you be'n down there to see.

See jest how they give you welcome
　To the best that 's in the land,
Feel the sort o' grip they give you
　When they take you by the hand.
Hear 'em say, "We 're glad to
　have you,
　Better stay a week er two;"
An' the way they treat you makes
　you
　Feel that ev'ry word is true.

Feed you tell you hear the buttons
　Crackin' on yore Sunday vest;
Haul you roun' to see the wonders
　Tell you have to cry for rest.
Drink yer health an' pet an' praise
　you
　Tell you git to feel ez great
Ez the Sheriff o' the county
　Er the Gov'ner o' the State.

Wife, she sez I must be crazy
　'Cause I go on so, an' Nelse
He 'lows, "Goodness gracious!
　daddy,
　Cain't you talk about nuthin'
　else?"

Well, pleg-gone it, I 'm jes' tickled,
　Bein' tickled ain't no sin;
I be'n down in ole Kentucky,
　An' I want o' go ag'in.

CURTAIN

Villain shows his indiscretion,
Villain's partner makes confession.
Juvenile, with golden tresses,
Finds her pa and dons long dresses.
Scapegrace comes home money-
　laden,
Hero comforts tearful maiden,
Soubrette marries loyal chappie,
Villain skips, and all are happy.

THE SPELLIN'-BEE

I never shall furgit that night
　when father hitched up Dob-
　bin,
An' all us youngsters clambered in
　an' down the road went bob-
　bin'
To school where we was kep'
　at work in every kind o'
　weather,
But where that night a spellin'-
　bee was callin' us together.
'Twas one o' Heaven's banner
　nights, the stars was all a
　glitter,
The moon was shinin' like the
　hand o' God had jest then lit
　her.

The ground was white with spotless snow, the blast was sort o' stingin';
But underneath our round-abouts, you bet our hearts was singin'.
That spellin'-bee had be'n the talk o' many a precious moment,
The youngsters all was wild to see jes' what the precious show meant,
An' we whose years was in their teens was little less desirous
O' gittin' to the meetin' so 's our sweethearts could admire us.
So on we went so anxious fur to satisfy our mission
That father had to box our ears, to smother our ambition.
But boxin' ears was too short work to hinder cur arrivin',
He jest turned roun' an' smacked us all, an' kep' right on a-drivin'.
Well, soon the schoolhouse hove in sight, the winders beamin' brightly;
The sound o' talkin' reached our ears, and voices laffin' lightly.
It puffed us up so full an' big 'at I 'll jest bet a dollar,
There wa'n't a feller there but felt the strain upon his collar.
So down we jumped an' in we went ez sprightly ez you make 'em,

But somethin' grabbed us by the knees an' straight began to shake 'em.
Fur once within that lighted room, our feelin's took a canter,
An' scurried to the zero mark ez quick ez Tam O'Shanter.
'Cause there was crowds o' people there, both sexes an' all stations;
It looked like all the town had come an' brought all their relations.
The first I saw was Nettie Gray, I thought that girl was dearer
'N' gold; an' when I got a chance, you bet I sidged up near her.
An' Farmer Dobbs's girl was there, the one 'at Jim was sweet on,
An' Cyrus Jones an' Mandy Smith an' Faith an' Patience Deaton.
Then Parson Brown an' Lawyer Jones were present — all attention,
An' piles on piles of other folks too numerous to mention.
The master rose an' briefly said: "Good friends, dear brother Crawford,
To spur the pupils' minds along, a little prize has offered.
To him who spells the best to-

night — or 't may be ' her '—
no tellin'—
He offers ez a jest reward, this
precious work on spellin'."
A little blue-backed spellin'-book
with fancy scarlet trimmin';
We boys devoured it with our
eyes — so did the girls an'
women.
He held it up where all could see,
then on the table set it,
An' ev'ry speller in the house felt
mortal bound to get it.
At his command we fell in line,
prepared to do our dooty,
Outspell the rest an' set 'em down,
an' carry home the booty.
'T was then the merry times began, the blunders, an' the
laffin',
The nudges an' the nods an' winks
an' stale good-natured chaffin'.
Ole Uncle Hiram Dane was there,
the clostest man a-livin',
Whose only bugbear seemed to be
the dreadful fear o' givin'.
His beard was long, his hair uncut, his clothes all bare an'
dingy;
It was n't 'cause the man was
pore, but jest so mortal
stingy;
An' there he sot by Sally Riggs
a-smilin' an' a-smirkin',
An' all his children lef' to home a
diggin' an' a-workin'.

A widower he was, an' Sal was
thinkin' 'at she 'd wing him;
I reckon he was wond'rin' what
them rings o' hern would
bring him.
An' when the spellin'-test commenced, he up an' took his
station,
A-spellin' with the best o' them
to beat the very nation.
An' when he 'd spell some young-
ster down, he 'd turn to look
at Sally,
An' say: " The teachin' nowadays
can't be o' no great vally."
But true enough the adage says,
" Pride walks in slipp'ry
places,"
Fur soon a thing occurred that
put a smile on all our faces.
The laffter jest kep' ripplin' 'roun'
an' teacher could n't quell it,
Fur when he give out " charity "
ole Hiram could n't spell it.
But laffin' 's ketchin' an' it
throwed some others off their
bases,
An' folks 'u'd miss the very word
that seemed to fit their cases.
Why, fickle little Jessie Lee come
near the house upsettin'
By puttin' in a double " kay " to
spell the word " coquettin'."
An' when it come to Cyrus Jones,
it tickled me all over —
Him settin' up to Mandy Smith
an' got sot down on " lover."

PAUL LAURENCE DUNBAR

But Lawyer Jones of all gone men
  did shorely look the gonest,
When he found out that he 'd fur-
  got to put the " h " in " honest."
An' Parson Brown, whose sermons were too long fur tol-
  eration,
Caused lots o' smiles by missin'
  when they give out " con-
  densation."
So one by one they giv' it up —
  the big words kep' a-landin',
Till me an' Nettie Gray was left,
  the only ones a-standin',
An' then my inward strife began
  — I guess my mind was
  petty —
I did so want that spellin'-book;
  but then to spell down Nettie
Jest sort o' went ag'in my grain —
  I somehow could n't do it,
An' when I git a notion fixed,
  I 'm great on stickin' to it.
So when they giv' the next word
  out — I had n't orter tell
  it,
But then 't was all fur Nettie's
  sake — I missed so 's she
  could spell it.
She spelt the word, then looked at
  me so lovin'-like an' mello',
I tell you 't sent a hunderd pins
  a shootin' through a fello'.

O' course I had to stand the jokes
  an' chaffin' of the fello's,
But when they handed her the
  book I vow I was n't jealous.
We sung a hymn, an' Parson
  Brown dismissed us like he
  orter,
Fur, la! he 'd learned a thing er
  two an' made his blessin'
  shorter.
'T was late an' cold when we got
  out, but Nettie liked cold
  weather,
An' so did I, so we agreed we 'd
  jest walk home together.
We both wuz silent, fur of words
  we nuther had a surplus,
'Till she spoke out quite sudden
  like, " You missed that word
  on purpose."
Well, I declare it frightened me;
  at first I tried denyin',
But Nettie, she jest smiled an'
  smiled, she knowed that I
  was lyin'.
Sez she: " That book is yourn by
  right;" sez I: " It never
  could be —
I — I — you — ah —" an' there
  I stuck, an' well she under-
  stood me.
So we agreed that later on when
  age had giv' us tether,
We 'd jine our lots an' settle down
  to own that book together.

[45]

KEEP A-PLUGGIN' AWAY

I 've a humble little motto
That is homely, though it 's
  true,—
  Keep a-pluggin' away.
It 's a thing when I 've an object
That I always try to do,—
  Keep a-pluggin' away.
When you 've rising storms to
  quell,
When opposing waters swell,
It will never fail to tell,—
  Keep a-pluggin' away.

If the hills are high before
And the paths are hard to climb,
  Keep a-pluggin' away.
And remember that successes
Come to him who bides his
  time,—
  Keep a-pluggin' away.
From the greatest to the least,
None are from the rule released.
Be thou toiler, poet, priest,
  Keep a-pluggin' away.

Delve away beneath the surface,
There is treasure farther down,—
  Keep a-pluggin' away.
Let the rain come down in tor-
  rents,
Let the threat'ning heavens frown,
  Keep a-pluggin' away.
When the clouds have rolled
  away,

There will come a brighter day
All your labor to repay,—
  Keep a-pluggin' away.

There 'll be lots of sneers to swal-
  low,
There 'll be lots of pain to bear,—
  Keep a-pluggin' away.
If you 've got your eye on heaven,
Some bright day you 'll wake up
  there,—
  Keep a-pluggin' away.
Perseverance still is king;
Time its sure reward will bring;
Work and wait unwearying,—
  Keep a-pluggin' away.

NIGHT OF LOVE

THE moon has left the sky, love,
  The stars are hiding now,
And frowning on the world, love,
  Night bares her sable brow.
The snow is on the ground, love,
  And cold and keen the air is.
I 'm singing here to you, love;
  You 're dreaming there in Paris.

But this is Nature's law, love,
  Though just it may not seem,
That men should wake to sing,
  love,
  While maidens sleep and dream.
Them care may not molest, love,
  Nor stir them from their slum-
  bers,

PAUL LAURENCE DUNBAR

Though midnight find the swain,
 love,
 Still halting o'er his numbers.

I watch the rosy dawn, love,
 Come stealing up the east,
While all things round rejoice,
 love,
 That Night her reign has
 ceased.
The lark will soon be heard, love,
 And on his way be winging;
When Nature's poets wake, love,
 Why should a man be singing?

COLUMBIAN ODE

I

Four hundred years ago a tangled
 waste
 Lay sleeping on the west At-
 lantic's side;
Their devious ways the Old
 World's millions traced
 Content, and loved, and la-
 bored, dared and died,
While students still believed the
 charts they conned,
 And revelled in their thriftless
 ignorance,
Nor dreamed of other lands that
 lay beyond
 Old Ocean's dense, indefinite
 expanse.

II

But deep within her heart old Na-
 ture knew
 That she had once arrayed, at
 Earth's behest,
Another offspring, fine and fair
 to view,—
 The chosen suckling of the
 mother's breast.
The child was wrapped in vest-
 ments soft and fine,
 Each fold a work of Nature's
 matchless art;
The mother looked on it with love
 divine,
 And strained the loved one
 closely to her heart.
And there it lay, and with the
 warmth grew strong
 And hearty, by the salt sea
 breezes fanned,
Till Time with mellowing touches
 passed along,
 And changed the infant to a
 mighty land.

III

But men knew naught of this, till
 there arose
 That mighty mariner, the
 Genoese,
Who dared to try, in spite of fears
 and foes,
 The unknown fortunes of un-
 sounded seas.
O noblest of Italia's sons, thy
 bark

[47]

Went not alone into that shroud-
  ing night!
O dauntless darer of the rayless
  dark,
  The world sailed with thee to
    eternal light!
The deer-haunts that with game
  were crowded then
  To-day are tilled and cultivated
    lands;
The schoolhouse tow'rs where
  Bruin had his den,
  And where the wigwam stood
    the chapel stands;
The place that nurtured men of
  savage mien
  Now teems with men of Na-
    ture's noblest types;
Where moved the forest-foliage
  banner green,
  Now flutters in the breeze the.
    stars and stripes!

A BORDER BALLAD

OH, I have n't got long to live, for
  we all
  Die soon, e'en those who live
    longest;
And the poorest and weakest are
  taking their chance
  Along with the richest and
    strongest.
So it 's heigho for a glass and a
  song,
  And a bright eye over the table,

And a dog for the hunt when the
  game is flush,
  And the pick of a gentleman's
    stable.

There is Dimmock o' Dune, he
  was here yester-night,
  But he 's rotting to-day on Glen
    Arragh;
'T was the hand o' MacPherson
  that gave him the blow,
  And the vultures shall feast on
    his marrow.
But it 's heigho for a brave old
  song
  And a glass while we are able;
Here 's a health to death and an-
  other cup
  To the bright eye over the table.

I can show a broad back and a
  jolly deep chest,
  But who argues now on ap-
    pearance?
A blow or a thrust or a stumble
  at best
  May send me to-day to my
    clearance.
Then it 's heigho for the things I
  love,
  My mother 'll be soon wearing
    sable,
But give me my horse and my dog
  and my glass,
  And a bright eye over the table.

PAUL LAURENCE DUNBAR

AN EASY-GOIN' FELLER

Ther' ain't no use in all this
  strife,
An' hurryin', pell-mell, right thro'
  life.
I don't believe in goin' too fast
To see what kind o' road you 've
  passed.
It ain't no mortal kind o' good,
'N' I would n't hurry ef I could.
I like to jest go joggin' 'long,
To limber up my soul with song;
To stop awhile 'n' chat the men,
'N' drink some cider now an'
  then.
Do' want no boss a-standin' by
To see me work; I allus try
To do my dooty right straight up,
An' earn what fills my plate an'
  cup.
An' ez fur boss, I 'll be my own,
I like to jest be let alone,
To plough my strip an' tend my
  bees,
An' do jest like I doggoned please.
My head 's all right, an' my
  heart 's meller,
But I 'm a easy-goin' feller.

A NEGRO LOVE SONG

Seen my lady home las' night,
  Jump back, honey, jump back.
Hel' huh han' an' sque'z it tight,
  Jump back, honey, jump back.
Hyeahd huh sigh a little sigh,

Seen a light gleam f'om huh eye,
An' a smile go flittin' by —
  Jump back, honey, jump back.

Hyeahd de win' blow thoo de
  pine,
  Jump back, honey, jump back.
Mockin'-bird was singin' fine,
  Jump back, honey, jump back.
An' my hea't was beatin' so,
When I reached my lady's do',
Dat I could n't ba' to go —
  Jump back, honey, jump back.

Put my ahm aroun' huh wais',
  Jump back, honey, jump back.
Raised huh lips an' took a tase,
  Jump back, honey, jump back.
Love me, honey, love me true?
Love me well ez I love you?
An' she answe'd, " 'Cose I do "—
  Jump back, honey, jump back.

THE DILETTANTE: A MODERN TYPE

He scribbles some in prose and
  verse,
  And now and then he prints it;
He paints a little,— gathers some
  Of Nature's gold and mints it.

He plays a little, sings a song,
  Acts tragic rôles, or funny;
He does, because his love is strong,
  But not, oh, not for money!

He studies almost everything
From social art to science;
A thirsty mind, a flowing spring,
Demand and swift compliance.

He looms above the sordid
crowd —
At least through friendly lenses;
While his mamma looks pleased
and proud,
And kindly pays expenses.

BY THE STREAM

By the stream I dream in calm
delight, and watch as in a
glass,
How the clouds like crowds of
snowy-hued and white-robed
maidens pass,
And the water into ripples breaks
and sparkles as it spreads,
Like a host of armored knights
with silver helmets on their
heads.
And I deem the stream an emblem
fit of human life may go,
For I find a mind may sparkle
much and yet but shallows
show,
And a soul may glow with myriad
lights and wondrous mys-
teries,
When it only lies a dormant thing
and mirrors what it sees.

THE COLORED SOLDIERS

If the muse were mine to tempt it
And my feeble voice were
strong,
If my tongue were trained to
measures,
I would sing a stirring song.
I would sing a song heroic
Of those noble sons of Ham,
Of the gallant colored soldiers
Who fought for Uncle Sam!

In the early days you scorned
them,
And with many a flip and flout
Said " These battles are the white
man's,
And the whites will fight them
out."
Up the hills you fought and fal-
tered,
In the vales you strove and bled,
While your ears still heard the
thunder
Of the foes' advancing tread.

Then distress fell on the nation,
And the flag was drooping low;
Should the dust pollute your ban-
ner?
No! the nation shouted, No!
So when War, in savage triumph,
Spread abroad his funeral
pall —
Then you called the colored sol-
diers,
And they answered to your call.

PAUL LAURENCE DUNBAR

And like hounds unleashed and
  eager
For the life blood of the prey,
Sprung they forth and bore them
  bravely
In the thickest of the fray.
And where'er the fight was hot-
  test,
Where the bullets fastest fell,
There they pressed unblanched
  and fearless
At the very mouth of hell.

Ah, they rallied to the standard
  To uphold it by their might;
None were stronger in the labors,
  None were braver in the fight.
From the blazing breach of Wag-
  ner
To the plains of Olustee,
They were foremost in the fight
Of the battles of the free.

And at Pillow! God have mercy
  On the deeds committed there,
And the souls of those poor vic-
  tims
  Sent to Thee without a prayer.
Let the fulness of Thy pity
  O'er the hot wrought spirits
  sway
Of the gallant colored soldiers
  Who fell fighting on that day!

Yes, the Blacks enjoy their freedom,
  And they won it dearly, too;

For the life blood of their thou-
  sands
Did the southern fields bedew.
In the darkness of their bondage,
  In the depths of slavery's night,
Their muskets flashed the dawn-
  ing,
  And they fought their way to
  light.

They were comrades then and
  brothers,
  Are they more or less to-day?
They were good to stop a bullet
  And to front the fearful fray.
They were citizens and soldiers,
  When rebellion raised its head;
And the traits that made them
  worthy, —
  Ah! those virtues are not dead.

They have shared your nightly
  vigils,
  They have shared your daily
  toil ;
And their blood with yours com-
  mingling
Has enriched the Southern soil.

They have slept and marched and
  suffered
  'Neath the same dark skies as
  you,
They have met as fierce a foeman,
  And have been as brave and
  true.

And their deeds shall find a record
  In the registry of Fame;
For their blood has cleansed com-
  pletely
  Every blot of Slavery's shame.
So all honor and all glory
  To those noble sons of Ham—
The gallant colored soldiers
  Who fought for Uncle Sam!

NATURE AND ART

TO MY FRIEND CHARLES BOOTH
NETTLETON

I

THE young queen Nature, ever
  sweet and fair,
  Once on a time fell upon evil
  days.
  From hearing oft herself dis-
  cussed with praise,
There grew within her heart the
  longing rare
To see herself; and every passing
  air
  The warm desire fanned into
  lusty blaze.
  Full oft she sought this end by
  devious ways,
But sought in vain, so fell she in
  despair.
For none within her train nor by
  her side
  Could solve the task or give the
  envied boon.
So day and night, beneath the
  sun and moon,

She wandered to and fro unsatis-
  fied,
  Till Art came by, a blithe in-
  ventive elf,
  And made a glass wherein she
  saw herself.

II

Enrapt, the queen gazed on her
  glorious self,
  Then trembling with the thrill
  of sudden thought,
  Commanded that the skilful
  wight be brought
That she might dower him with
  lands and pelf.
Then out upon the silent sea-lapt
  shelf
  And up the hills and on the
  downs they sought
  Him who so well and won-
  drously had wrought;
And with much search found and
  brought home the elf.
  But he put by all gifts with sad
  replies,
And from his lips these words
  flowed forth like wine:
  "O queen, I want no gift but
  thee," he said.
She heard and looked on him with
  love-lit eyes,
Gave him her hand, low murmuring, "I am thine,"
  And at the morrow's dawning
  they were wed.

PAUL LAURENCE DUNBAR

AFTER WHILE
A POEM OF FAITH

I THINK that though the clouds
    be dark,
That though the waves dash o'er
    the bark,
Yet after while the light will
    come,
And in calm waters safe at home
    The bark will anchor.
Weep not, my sad-eyed, gray-
    robed maid,
Because your fairest blossoms
    fade,
That sorrow still o'erruns your
    cup,
And even though you root them
    up,
        The weeds grow ranker.

For after while your tears shall
    cease,
And sorrow shall give way to
    peace;
The flowers shall bloom, the
    weeds shall die,
And in that faith seen, by and by
    Thy woes shall perish.
Smile at old Fortune's adverse
    tide,
Smile when the scoffers sneer and
    chide.
Oh, not for you the gems that
    pale,
And not for you the flowers that
    fail;
        Let this thought cherish:

That after while the clouds will
    part,
And then with joy the waiting
    heart
Shall feel the light come stealing
    in,
That drives away the cloud of sin
    And breaks its power.
And you shall burst your chrysa-
    lis,
And wing away to realms of
    bliss,
Untrammelled,   pure,   divinely
    free,
Above all earth's anxiety
    From that same hour.

THE OL' TUNES

You kin talk about yer anthems
    An' yer arias an' sich,
An' yer modern choir-singin'
    That you think so awful rich;
But you orter heerd us youngsters
    In the times now far away,
A-singin' o' the ol' tunes
    In the ol'-fashioned way.

There was some of us sung treble
    An' a few of us growled bass,
An' the tide o' song flowed
    smoothly
    With its 'comp'niment o' grace;
There was spirit in that music,
    An' a kind o' solemn sway,
A-singin' o' the ol' tunes
    In the ol'-fashioned way.

I remember oft o' standin'
  In my homespun pantaloons —
On my face the bronze an' freckles
  O' the suns o' youthful Junes —
Thinkin' that no mortal minstrel
  Ever chanted sich a lay
As the ol' tunes we was singin'
  In the ol'-fashioned way.

The boys 'ud always lead us,
  An' the girls 'ud all chime in
Till the sweetness o' the singin'
  Robbed the list'nin' soul o' sin;
An' I used to tell the parson
  'T was as good to sing as pray,
When the people sung the ol'
    tunes
  In the ol'-fashioned way.

How I long ag'in to hear 'em
  Pourin' forth from soul to soul,
With the treble high an' meller,
  An' the bass's mighty roll;
But the times is very diff'rent,
  An' the music heerd to-day
Ain't the singin' o' the ol' tunes
  In the ol'-fashioned way.

Little screechin' by a woman,
  Little squawkin' by a man,
Then the organ's twiddle-twaddle,
  Jest the empty space to span, —
An' ef you should even think it,
  'T is n't proper fur to say
That you want to hear the ol'
    tunes
  In the ol'-fashioned way.

But I think that some bright
    mornin',
  When the toils of life air o'er,
An' the sun o' heaven arisin'
  Glads with light the happy
    shore,
I shall hear the angel chorus,
  In the realms of endless day,
A-singin' o' the ol' tunes
  In the ol'-fashioned way.

MELANCHOLIA

Silently without my window,
  Tapping gently at the pane,
  Falls the rain.
Through the trees sighs the breeze
  Like a soul in pain.
Here alone I sit and weep;
Thought hath banished sleep.

Wearily I sit and listen
  To the water's ceaseless drip.
  To my lip
Fate turns up the bitter cup,
  Forcing me to sip;
'T is a bitter, bitter drink,
Thus I sit and think, —

Thinking things unknown and
    awful,
  Thoughts on wild, uncanny
    themes,
  Waking dreams.
Spectres dark, corpses stark,
  Show the gaping seams
Whence the cold and cruel knife
Stole away their life.

PAUL LAURENCE DUNBAR

Bloodshot eyes all strained and
staring,
  Gazing ghastly into mine;
  Blood like wine
On the brow — clotted now—
  Shows death's dreadful sign.
Lonely vigil still I keep;
Would that I might sleep!

Still, oh, still, my brain is whirl-
ing!
  Still runs on my stream of
thought;
  I am caught
In the net fate hath set.
  Mind and soul are brought
To destruction's very brink;
Yet I can but think!

Eyes that look into the future,—
  Peeping forth from out my
mind,
  They will find
Some new weight, soon or late,
  On my soul to bind,
  Crushing all its courage out,—
Heavier than doubt.

Dawn, the Eastern monarch's
daughter,
  Rising from her dewy bed,
  Lays her head
'Gainst the clouds' sombre
shrouds
  Now half fringed with red.
O'er the land she 'gins to peep;
Come, O gentle Sleep!

Hark! the morning cock is crow-
ing;
  Dreams, like ghosts, must hie
away;
  'Tis the day.
Rosy morn now is born;
  Dark thoughts may not stay.
Day my brain from foes will keep;
Now, my soul, I sleep.

THE WOOING

A YOUTH went faring up and
down,
  Alack and well-a-day.
He fared him to the market town,
  Alack and well-a-day.
And there he met a maiden fair,
With hazel eyes and auburn hair;
His heart went from him then and
there,
  Alack and well-a-day.

She posies sold right merrily,
  Alack and well-a-day;
But not a flower was fair as she,
  Alack and well-a-day.
He bought a rose and sighed a
sigh,
"Ah, dearest maiden, would that I
Might dare the seller too to buy!"
  Alack and well-a-day.

She tossed her head, the coy coquette,
  Alack and well-a-day.

[55]

"I'm not, sir, in the market yet,"
    Alack and well-a-day.
"Your love must cool upon a
    shelf;
Tho' much I sell for gold and
    pelf,
I 'm yet too young to sell myself,"
    Alack and well-a-day.

The youth was filled with sorrow
    sore,
    Alack and well-a-day.
And looked he at the maid once
    more,
    Alack and well-a-day.
Then loud he cried, "Fair maid-
    en, if
Too young to sell, now as I live,
You're not too young yourself to
    give,"
    Alack and well-a-day.

The little maid cast down her
    eyes,
    Alack and well-a-day.
And many a flush began to rise,
    Alack and well-a-day.
"Why, since you are so bold," she
    said,
"I doubt not you are highly bred,
So take me!" and the twain were
    wed,
    Alack and well-a-day.

MERRY AUTUMN

IT's all a farce,— these tales they
    tell
    About the breezes sighing,
And moans astir o'er field and
    dell,
    Because the year is dying.

Such principles are most absurd,—
    I care not who first taught
    'em;
There's nothing known to beast
    or bird
    To make a solemn autumn.

In solemn times, when grief holds
    sway
    With countenance distressing,
You'll note the more of black and
    gray
    Will then be used in dressing.

Now purple tints are all around;
    The sky is blue and mellow;
And e'en the grasses turn the
    ground
    From modest green to yellow.

The seed burrs all with laughter
    crack
    On featherweed and jimson;
And leaves that should be dressed
    in black
    Are all decked out in crimson.

A butterfly goes winging by;
    A singing bird comes after;

And Nature, all from earth to
    sky,
  Is bubbling o'er with laughter.

The ripples wimple on the rills,
  Like sparkling little lasses;
The sunlight runs along the hills,
  And laughs among the grasses.

The earth is just so full of fun
  It really can't contain it;
And streams of mirth so freely
    run
  The heavens seem to rain it.

Don't talk to me of solemn days
  In autumn's time of splendor,
Because the sun shows fewer rays,
  And these grow slant and slen-
    der.

Why, it's the climax of the
    year, —
  The highest time of living! —
Till naturally its bursting cheer
  Just melts into thanksgiving.

WHEN DE CO'N PONE'S HOT

Dey is times in life when Nature
  Seems to slip a cog an' go,
Jes' a-rattlin' down creation,
  Lak an ocean's overflow;
When de worl' jes' stahts a-spin-
    nin'
  Lak a picaninny's top,

An' yo' cup o' joy is brimmin'
  'Twell it seems about to slop,
An' you feel jes' lak a racah,
  Dat is trainin' fu' to trot —
When yo' mammy says de blessin'
  An' de co'n pone 's hot.

When you set down at de table,
  Kin' o' weary lak an' sad,
An' you 'se jes' a little tiahed
  An' purhaps a little mad;
How yo' gloom tu'ns into glad-
    ness,
  How yo' joy drives out de
    doubt
When de oven do' is opened,
  An' de smell comes po'in' out;
Why, de 'lectric light o' Heaven
  Seems to settle on de spot,
When yo' mammy says de blessin'
  An' de co'n pone 's hot.

When de cabbage pot is steamin'
  An' de bacon good an' fat,
When de chittlins is a-sputter'n'
  So 's to show you whah dey 's
    at;
Tek away yo' sody biscuit,
  Tek away yo' cake an' pie,
Fu' de glory time is comin',
  An' it 's 'preachin' mighty
    nigh,
An' you want to jump an' hollah,
  Dough you know you 'd bettah
    not,
When yo' mammy says de blessin'
  An' de co'n pone 's hot.

[57]

I have hyeahd o' lots o' sermons,
  An' I 've hyeahd o' lots o'
    prayers, '
An' I 've listened to some singin'
  Dat has tuck me up de stairs
Of de Glory-Lan' an' set me
  Jes' below de Mastah's th'one,
An' have lef' my hea't a-singin'
  In a happy aftah tone;
But dem wu'ds so sweetly mur-
    mured
  Seem to tech de softes' spot,
When my mammy says de blessin',
  An' de co'n pone 's hot.

BALLAD

I KNOW my love is true,
  And oh the day is fair.
The sky is clear and blue,
The flowers are rich of hue,
  The air I breathe is rare,
  I have no grief or care;
For my own love is true,
  And oh the day is fair.

My love is false I find,
  And oh the day is dark.
Blows sadly down the wind,
While sorrow holds my mind;
  I do not hear the lark,
  For quenched is life's dear
    spark,—
My love is false I find,
  And oh the day is dark!

For love doth make the day
  Or dark or doubly bright;
Her beams along the way
Dispel the gloom and gray.
  She lives and all is bright,
  She dies and life is night.
For love doth make the day,
  Or dark or doubly bright.

THE CHANGE HAS COME

THE change has come, and Helen
    sleeps —
Not sleeps; but wakes to greater
    deeps
  Of wisdom, glory, truth, and
    light,
  Than ever blessed her seeking
    sight,
  In this low, long, lethargic
    night,
    Worn out with strife
    Which men call life.

The change has come, and who
    would say
"I would it were not come to-
    day"?
  What were the respite till to-
    morrow?
  Postponement of a certain sor-
    row,
  From which each passing day
    would borrow!
    Let grief be dumb,
    The change has come.

PAUL LAURENCE DUNBAR

COMPARISON

THE sky of brightest gray seems
            dark
    To one whose sky was ever
        white.
To one who never knew a spark,
    Thro' all his life, of love or
        light,
    The grayest cloud seems over-
        bright.

The robin sounds a beggar's note
    Where one the nightingale has
        heard,
But he for whom no silver throat
    Its liquid music ever stirred,
    Deems robin still the sweetest
        bird.

A CORN-SONG

ON the wide veranda white,
    In the purple failing light,
Sits the master while the sun is
        lowly burning;
And his dreamy thoughts are
        drowned
In the softly flowing sound
Of the corn-songs of the field-
        hands slow returning.

        Oh, we hoe de co'n
        Since de ehly mo'n;
        Now de sinkin' sun
        Says de day is done.

O'er the fields with heavy tread,
Light of heart and high of head,

Though the halting steps be la-
        bored, slow, and weary;
Still the spirits brave and strong
Find a comforter in song,
And their corn-song rises ever
        loud and cheery.

        Oh, we hoe de co'n
        Since de ehly mo'n;
        Now de sinkin' sun
        Says de day is done.

To the master in his seat,
Comes the burden, full and sweet,
Of the mellow minor music grow-
        ing clearer,
As the toilers raise the hymn,
Thro' the silence dusk and dim,
To the cabin's restful shelter
        drawing nearer.

        Oh, we hoe de co'n
        Since de ehly mo'n;
        Now de sinkin' sun
        Says de day is done.

And a tear is in the eye
Of the master sitting by,
As he listens to the echoes low-
        replying
To the music's fading calls
As it faints away and falls
Into silence, deep within the cabin
        dying.

        Oh, we hoe de co'n
        Since de ehly mo'n;
        Now de sinkin' sun
        Says de day is done.

[59]

DISCOVERED

SEEN you down at chu'ch las'
        night,
    Nevah min', Miss Lucy.
What I mean? oh, dat 's all right,
    Nevah min', Miss Lucy.
You was sma't ez sma't could be,
But you could n't hide f'om me.
Ain't I got two eyes to see!
    Nevah min', Miss Lucy.

Guess you thought you 's awful
        keen;
    Nevah min', Miss Lucy.
Evahthing you done, I seen;
    Nevah min', Miss Lucy.
Seen him tek yo' ahm jes' so,
When he got outside de do' —
Oh, I know dat man 's yo' beau!
    Nevah min', Miss Lucy.

Say now, honey, wha 'd he say? —
    Nevah min', Miss Lucy!
Keep yo' secrets — dat 's yo'
        way —
    Nevah min', Miss Lucy.
Won't tell me an' I'm yo' pal —
I'm gwine tell his othah gal, —
Know huh, too, huh name is Sal;
    Nevah min', Miss Lucy!

DISAPPOINTED

AN old man planted and dug and
        tended,
    Toiling in joy from dew to
        dew;
The sun was kind, and the rain
        befriended;
    Fine grew his orchard and fair
        to view.
Then he said: "I will quiet my
        thrifty fears,
For here is fruit for my failing
        years."

But even then the storm-clouds
        gathered,
    Swallowing up the azure sky;
The sweeping winds into white
        foam lathered
    The placid breast of the bay,
        hard by;
Then the spirits that raged in the
        darkened air
Swept o'er his orchard and left it
        bare.

The old man stood in the rain, un-
        caring,
    Viewing the place the storm had
        swept;
And then with a cry from his soul
        despairing,
    He bowed him down to the
        earth and wept.
But a voice cried aloud from the
        driving rain;
"Arise, old man, and plant
        again!"

PAUL LAURENCE DUNBAR

INVITATION TO LOVE

COME when the nights are bright
with stars
Or when the moon is mellow;
Come when the sun his golden
bars
Drops on the hay-field yellow.
Come in the twilight soft and
gray,
Come in the night or come in the
day,
Come, O love, whene'er you may,
And you are welcome, welcome.

You are sweet, O Love, dear
Love,
You are soft as the nesting dove.
Come to my heart and bring it rest
As the bird flies home to its wel-
come nest.

Come when my heart is full of
grief
Or when my heart is merry;
Come with the falling of the leaf
Or with the redd'ning cherry.
Come when the year's first blos-
som blows,
Come when the summer gleams
and glows,
Come with the winter's drifting
snows,
And you are welcome, welcome.

HE HAD HIS DREAM

HE had his dream, and all
through life,
Worked up to it through toil and
strife.
Afloat fore'er before his eyes,
It colored for him all his skies:
    The storm-cloud dark
    Above his bark,
The calm and listless vault of blue
Took on its hopeful hue,
It tinctured every passing beam —
    He had his dream.

He labored hard and failed at last,
His sails too weak to bear the
blast,
The raging tempests tore away
And sent his beating bark astray.
    But what cared he
    For wind or sea!
He said, "The tempest will be
short,
My bark will come to port."
He saw through every cloud a
gleam —
    He had his dream.

GOOD-NIGHT

THE lark is silent in his nest,
    The breeze is sighing in its
    flight,
Sleep, Love, and peaceful be thy
    rest.
    Good-night, my love, good-
    night, good-night.

[61]

Sweet dreams attend thee in thy
 sleep,
  To soothe thy rest till morning's light,
And angels round thee vigil keep.
  Good-night, my love, good-
  night, good-night.

Sleep well, my love, on night's
 dark breast,
  And ease thy soul with slumber
  bright;
Be joy but thine and I am blest.
  Good-night, my love, good-
  night, good-night.

A COQUETTE CON-
 QUERED

YES, my ha't 's ez ha'd ez stone —
Go 'way, Sam, an' lemme 'lone.
No; I ain't gwine change my
 min' —
Ain't gwine ma'y you — nuffin' de
 kin'.

Phiny loves you true an' deah?
Go ma'y Phiny; whut I keer?
Oh, you need n't mou'n an' cry —
I don't keer how soon you die.

Got a present! Whut you got?
Somef'n fu' de pan er pot!
Huh! yo' sass do sholy beat —
Think I don't git 'nough to eat?

Whut 's dat un'neaf yo' coat?
Looks des lak a little shoat.

'T ain't no possum! Bless de
 Lamb!
Yes, it is, you rascal, Sam!

Gin it to me; whut you say?
Ain't you sma't now! Oh, go
 'way!
Possum do look mighty nice,
But you ax too big a price.

Tell me, is you talkin' true,
Dat 's de gal's whut ma'ies you?
Come back, Sam; now whah 's
 you gwine?
Co'se you knows dat possum's
 mine!

NORA: A SERENADE

AH, Nora, my Nora, the light
 fades away,
  While Night like a spirit steals
  up o'er the hills;
The thrush from his tree where he
 chanted all day,
  No longer his music in ecstasy
  trills.
Then, Nora, be near me; thy presence doth cheer me,
  Thine eye hath a gleam that is
  truer than gold.

I cannot but love thee; so do not
 reprove me,
  If the strength of my passion
  should make me too bold.

[62]

PAUL LAURENCE DUNBAR

Nora, pride of my heart —
  Rosy cheeks, cherry lips, spar-
    kling with glee,—
Wake from thy slumbers, wher-
    ever thou art;
  Wake from thy slumbers to
    me.

Ah, Nora, my Nora, there's love
    in the air,—
  It stirs in the numbers that
    thrill in my brain;
Oh, sweet, sweet is love with its
    mingling of care,
  Though joy travels only a step
    before pain.
Be roused from thy slumbers and
    list to my numbers;
My heart is poured out in this
    song unto thee.
Oh, be thou not cruel, thou treas-
    ure, thou jewel;
  Turn thine ear to my pleading
    and hearken to me.

OCTOBER

OCTOBER is the treasurer of the
    year,
  And all the months pay bounty
    to her store;
The fields and orchards still their
    tribute bear,
  And fill her brimming coffers
    more and more.
But she, with youthful lavishness,

Spends all her wealth in gaudy
    dress,
  And decks herself in garments
    bold
  Of scarlet, purple, red, and
    gold.

She heedeth not how swift the
    hours fly,
  But smiles and sings her happy
    life along;
She only sees above a shining sky;
  She only hears the breezes' voice
    in song.
Her garments trail the woodlands
    through,
And gather pearls of early dew
  That sparkle, till the roguish
    Sun
  Creeps up and steals them every
    one.

But what cares she that jewels
    should be lost,
  When all of Nature's bounte-
    ous wealth is hers?
Though princely fortunes may
    have been their cost,
  Not one regret her calm de-
    meanor stirs.
Whole-hearted, happy, careless,
    free,
She lives her life out joyously,
  Nor cares when Frost stalks o'er
    her way
  Aud turns her auburn locks to
    gray.

[63]

A SUMMER'S NIGHT

THE night is dewy as a maiden's
        mouth,
    The skies are bright as are a
        maiden's eyes,
    Soft as a maiden's breath the
        wind that flies
Up from the perfumed bosom of
        the South.
Like sentinels, the pines stand in
        the park;
    And hither hastening, like rakes
        that roam,
    With lamps to light their way-
        ward footsteps home,
The fireflies come stagg'ring down
        the dark.

SHIPS THAT PASS IN THE NIGHT

OUT in the sky the great dark
        clouds are massing;
    I look far out into the pregnant
        night,
Where I can hear a solemn boom-
        ing gun
    And catch the gleaming of a
        random light,
That tells me that the ship I seek
        is passing, passing.

My tearful eyes my soul's deep
        hurt are glassing;
    For I would hail and check that
        ship of ships.

I stretch my hands imploring, cry
        aloud,
    My voice falls dead a foot from
        mine own lips,
And but its ghost doth reach that
        vessel, passing, passing.

O Earth, O Sky, O Ocean, both
        surpassing,
    O heart of mine, O soul that
        dreads the dark!
Is there no hope for me?   Is there
        no way
    That I may sight and check that
        speeding bark
Which out of sight and sound is
        passing, passing?

THE DELINQUENT

GOO'-BY, Jinks, I got to hump,
Got to mek dis pony jump;
See dat sun a-goin' down
'N' me a-foolin' hyeah in town!
    Git up, Suke — go long!

Guess Mirandy 'll think I's tight,
Me not home an' comin' on night.
What 's dat stan'in' by de fence?
Pshaw! why don't I lu'n some
        sense?
    Git up, Suke — go long!

Guess I spent down dah at Jinks'
Mos' a dollah fur de drinks.
Bless yo'r soul, you see dat star?
Lawd, but won't Mirandy rar?
    Git up, Suke — go long!

PAUL LAURENCE DUNBAR

Went dis mo'nin', hyeah it 's night,
Dah 's de cabin dah in sight.
Who 's dat stan'in' in de do'?
Dat must be Mirandy, sho',
    Git up, Suke — go long!

Got de close-stick in huh han',
Dat look funny, goodness lan',
Sakes alibe, but she look glum!
Hyeah, Mirandy, hyeah I come!
    Git up, Suke — go long!

    Ef 't had n't a' b'en fur you, you
slow ole fool, I 'd a' be'n home
long fo' now!

DAWN

An angel, robed in spotless white,
Bent down and kissed the sleeping
    Night.
Night woke to blush; the sprite
    was gone.
Men saw the blush and called it
    Dawn.

A DROWSY DAY

The air is dark, the sky is gray,
    The misty shadows come and
    go,
And here within my dusky room
Each chair looks ghostly in the
    gloom.
    Outside the rain falls cold and
    slow —

Half-stinging drops, half-blinding
    spray.

Each slightest sound is magnified,
    For drowsy quiet holds her
    reign;
The burnt stick in the fireplace
    breaks,
The nodding cat with start
    awakes,
    And then to sleep drops off
    again,
Unheeding Towser at her side.

I look far out across the lawn,
    Where huddled stand the silly
    sheep;
My work lies idle at my hands,
My thoughts fly out like scattered
    strands
    Of thread, and on the verge of
    sleep —
Still half awake — I dream and
    yawn.

What spirits rise before my eyes!
    How various of kind and form!
Sweet memories of days long past,
The dreams of youth that could
    not last,
    Each smiling calm, each raging
    storm,
That swept across my early skies.

Half seen, the bare, gaunt-fingered
    boughs
    Before my window sweep and
    sway,
And chafe in tortures of unrest.

My chin sinks down upon my
    breast;
I cannot work on such a day,
But only sit and dream and
    drowse.

DIRGE

PLACE this bunch of mignonette
    In her cold, dead hand;
When the golden sun is set,
    Where the poplars stand,
Bury her from sun and day,
Lay my little love away
    From my sight.

She was like a modest flower
    Blown in sunny June,
Warm as sun at noon's high hour,
    Chaster than the moon.
Ah, her day was brief and bright,
Earth has lost a star of light;
    She is dead.

Softly breathe her name to me,—
    Ah, I loved her so.
Gentle let your tribute be;
    None may better know
Her true worth than I who weep
O'er her as she lies asleep —
    Soft asleep.

Lay these lilies on her breast,
    They are not more white
Than the soul of her, at rest
    'Neath their petals bright.
Chant your aves soft and low,

Solemn be your tread and slow,—
    She is dead.

Lay her here beneath the grass,
    Cool and green and sweet,
Where the gentle brook may pass
    Crooning at her feet.
Nature's bards shall come and
    sing,
And the fairest flowers shall spring
    Where she lies.

Safe above the water's swirl,
    She has crossed the bar;
Earth has lost a precious pearl,
    Heaven has gained a star,
That shall ever sing and shine,
Till it quells this grief of mine
    For my love.

HYMN

WHEN storms arise
And dark'ning skies
    About me threat'ning lower,
To thee, O Lord, I raise mine
    eyes,
To thee my tortured spirit flies
    For solace in that hour.

The mighty arm
Will let no harm
    Come near me nor befall me;
Thy voice shall quiet my alarm,
When life's great battle waxeth
    warm —
    No foeman shall appall me.

Upon thy breast
Secure I rest,
  From sorrow and vexation;
No more by sinful cares oppressed,
But in thy presence ever blest,
  O God of my salvation.

PREPARATION

THE little bird sits in the nest and
    sings
  A shy, soft song to the morning
    light;
And it flutters a little and prunes
    its wings.
  The song is halting and poor
    and brief,
  And the fluttering wings scarce
    stir a leaf;
But the note is a prelude to
    sweeter things,
  And the busy bill and the flutter
    slight
  Are proving the wings for a
    bolder flight!

THE DESERTED PLAN-
TATION

OH, de grubbin'-hoe 's a-rustin' in
    de co'nah,
  An' de plow 's a-tumblin' down
    in de fiel',
While de whippo'will 's a-wailin'
    lak a mou'nah
  When his stubbo'n hea't is try-
    in' ha'd to yiel'.

In de furrers whah de co'n was
    allus wavin',
  Now de weeds is growin' green
    an' rank an' tall;
An' de swallers roun' de whole
    place is a-bravin'
  Lak dey thought deir folks had
    allus owned it all.

An' de big house stan's all quiet
    lak an' solemn,
  Not a blessed soul in pa'lor,
    po'ch, er lawn;
Not a guest, ner not a ca'iage lef'
    to haul 'em,
  Fu' de ones dat tu'ned de latch-
    string out air gone.

An' de banjo's voice is silent in de
    qua'ters,
  D' ain't a hymn ner co'n-song
    ringin' in de air;
But de murmur of a branch's pass-
    in' waters
  Is de only soun' dat breks de
    stillness dere.

Whah 's de da'kies, dem dat used
    to be a-dancin'
  Evry night befo' de ole cabin
    do'?
Whah 's de chillun, dem dat used
    to be a-prancin'
  Er a-rollin' in de san' er on de
    flo'?

Whah 's ole Uncle Mordecai an'
    Uncle Aaron?

Whah 's Aunt Doshy, Sam, an'
    Kit, an' all de res'?
Whah 's ole Tom de da'ky fiddlah,
    how 's he farin'?
Whah 's de gals dat used to sing
    an' dance de bes'?

Gone! not one o' dem is lef' to tell
    de story;
    Dey have lef' de deah ole place
      to fall away.
Could n't one o' dem dat seed it in
    its glory
    Stay to watch it in de hour of
      decay?

Dey have lef' de ole plantation to
    de swallers,
    But it hol's in me a lover till de
      las';
Fu' I fin' hyeah in de memory dat
    follers
    All dat loved me an' dat I loved
      in de pas'.

So I 'll stay an' watch de deah ole
    place an' tend it
    Ez I used to in de happy days
      gone by.
'Twell de othah Mastah thinks
    it 's time to end it,
    An' calls me to my qua'ters in
      de sky.

THE SECRET

WHAT says the wind to the wav-
    ing trees?
    What says the wave to the
      river?
What means the sigh in the passing
    breeze?
    Why do the rushes quiver?
Have you not heard the fainting
    cry
Of the flowers that said " Good-
    bye, good-bye "?

List how the gray dove moans and
    grieves
    Under the woodland cover;
List to the drift of the falling
    leaves,
    List to the wail of the lover.
Have you not caught the message
    heard
Already by wave and breeze and
    bird?

Come, come away to the river's
    bank,
    Come in the early morning;
Come when the grass with dew is
    dank,
    There you will find the warn-
      ing —
A hint in the kiss of the quicken-
    ing air
Of the secret that birds and
    breezes bear.

PAUL LAURENCE DUNBAR

THE WIND AND THE SEA

I stood by the shore at the death
    of day,
  As the sun sank flaming red;
And the face of the waters that
    spread away
  Was as gray as the face of the
    dead.

And I heard the cry of the wan-
    ton sea
  And the moan of the wailing
    wind;
For love's sweet pain in his heart
    had he,
  But the gray old sea had sinned.

The wind was young and the sea
    was old,
  But their cries went up to-
    gether;
The wind was warm and the sea
    was cold,
  For age makes wintry weather.

So they cried aloud and they wept
    amain,
  Till the sky grew dark to hear
    it;
And out of its folds crept the misty
    rain,
  In its shroud, like a troubled
    spirit.

For the wind was wild with a
    hopeless love,
  And the sea was sad at heart

At many a crime that he wot of,
  Wherein he had played his part.

He thought of the gallant ships
    gone down
  By the will of his wicked waves;
And he thought how the church-
    yard in the town
  Held the sea-made widows'
    graves.

The wild wind thought of the love
    he had left
  Afar in an Eastern land,
And he longed, as long the much
    bereft,
  For the touch of her perfumed
    hand.

In his winding wail and his deep-
    heaved sigh
  His aching grief found vent;
While the sea looked up at the
    bending sky
  And murmured: " I repent."

But e'en as he spoke, a ship came
    by,
  That bravely ploughed the
    main,
And a light came into the sea's
    green eye,
  And his heart grew hard again.

Then he spoke to the wind:
    " Friend, seest thou not
  Yon vessel is eastward bound?
Pray speed with it to the happy
    spot

Where thy loved one may be
found."

And the wind rose up in a dear
delight,
And after the good ship sped;
But the crafty sea by his wicked
might
Kept the vessel ever ahead.

Till the wind grew fierce in his
despair,
And white on the brow and lip.
He tore his garments and tore his
hair,
And fell on the flying ship.

And the ship went down, for a
rock was there,
And the sailless sea loomed
black;
While burdened again with dole
and care,
The wind came moaning back.

And still he moans from his bosom
hot
Where his raging grief lies pent,
And ever when the ships come not,
The sea says: " I repent."

RIDING TO TOWN

WHEN labor is light and the
morning is fair,
I find it a pleasure beyond all
compare

To hitch up my nag and go hur-
rying down
And take Katie May for a ride
into town;
For bumpety-bump goes the
wagon,
But tra-la-la-la our lay.
There 's joy in a song as we rattle
along
In the light of the glorious day.

A coach would be fine, but a
spring wagon's good;
My jeans are a match for Kate's
gingham and hood;
The hills take us up and the vales
take us down,
But what matters that? we are
riding to town,
And bumpety-bump goes the
wagon,
But tra-la-la-la sing we.
There 's never a care may live in
the air
That is filled with the breath
of our glee.

And after we 've started, there 's
naught can repress
The thrill of our hearts in their
wild happiness;
The heavens may smile or the
heavens may frown,
And it 's all one to us when we 're
riding to town.
For bumpety-bump goes the
wagon,
But tra-la-la-la we shout,

PAUL LAURENCE DUNBAR

For our hearts they are clear and
    there 's nothing to fear,
And we 've never a pain nor a
    doubt.

The wagon is weak and the road-
    way is rough,
And tho' it is long it is not long
    enough,
For mid all my ecstasies this is the
    crown
To sit beside Katie and ride into
    town,
    When bumpety-bump goes the
        wagon,
        But tra-la-la-la our song;
And if I had my way, I 'd be will-
    ing to pay
    If the road could be made twice
        as long.

WE WEAR THE MASK

WE wear the mask that grins and
    lies,
It hides our cheeks and shades our
    eyes,—
This debt we pay to human guile;
With torn and bleeding hearts we
    smile,
And mouth with myriad subtle-
    ties.

Why should the world be over-
    wise,
In counting all our tears and
    sighs?

Nay, let them only see us, while
    We wear the mask.

We smile, but, O great Christ,
    our cries
To thee from tortured souls arise.
We sing, but oh the clay is vile
Beneath our feet, and long the
    mile;
But let the world dream other-
    wise,
    We wear the mask!

THE MEADOW LARK

THOUGH the winds be dank,
    And the sky be sober,
        And the grieving Day
        In a mantle gray
    Hath let her waiting maiden
        robe her,—
    All the fields along
    I can hear the song
Of the meadow lark,
        As she flits and flutters,
        And laughs at the thunder
            when it mutters.
        O happy bird, of heart most
            gay
        To sing when skies are gray!

When the clouds are full,
    And the tempest master
        Lets the loud winds sweep
        From his bosom deep
    Like heralds of some dire disas-
        ter,

Then the heart alone
To itself makes moan;
And the songs come slow,
    While the tears fall fleeter,
    And silence than song by far
        seems sweeter.
    Oh, few are they along the
        way
    Who sing when skies are
        gray!

ONE LIFE

OH, I am hurt to death, my
    Love;
    The shafts of Fate have pierced
        my striving heart,
And I am sick and weary of
    The endless pain and smart.
My soul is weary of the strife,
And chafes at life, and chafes at
    life.

Time mocks me with fair prom-
    ises;
    A blooming future grows a bar-
        ren past,
Like rain my fair full-blossomed
    trees
    Unburden in the blast.
The harvest fails on grain and
    tree,
Nor comes to me, nor comes to
    me.

The stream that bears my hopes
    abreast

Turns ever from my way its
    pregnant tide.
My laden boat, torn from its rest,
    Drifts to the other side.
So all my hopes are set astray,
And drift away, and drift away.

The lark sings to me at the morn,
    And near me wings her sky-
        ward-soaring flight;
But pleasure dies as soon as born,
    The owl takes up the night,
And night seems long and doubly
    dark;
I miss the lark, I miss the lark.

Let others labor as they may,
    I'll sing and sigh alone, and
        write my line.
Their fate is theirs, or grave or
    gay,
    And mine shall still be mine.
I know the world holds joy and
    glee,
But not for me,—'t is not for me.

CHANGING TIME

THE cloud looked in at the win-
    dow,
    And said to the day, "Be dark!"
And the roguish rain tapped hard
    on the pane,
    To stifle the song of the lark.

The wind sprang up in the tree
    tops

PAUL LAURENCE DUNBAR

And shrieked with a voice of
death,
But the rough-voiced breeze, that
shook the trees,
Was touched with a violet's
breath.

DEAD

A KNOCK is at her door, but she
is weak;
Strange dews have washed the
paint streaks from her
cheek;
She does not rise, but, ah, this
friend is known,
And knows that he will find her
all alone.
So opens he the door, and with
soft tread
Goes straightway to the richly
curtained bed.
His soft hand on her dewy head
he lays.
A strange white light she gives
him for his gaze.
Then, looking on the glory of her
charms,
He crushes her resistless in his
arms.

Stand back! look not upon this
bold embrace,
Nor view the calmness of the
wanton's face;
With joy unspeakable and 'bated
breath,

She keeps her last, long liaison
with death!

A CONFIDENCE

UNCLE JOHN, he makes me tired;
Thinks 'at he's jest so all-fired
Smart, 'at he kin pick up, so,
Ever'thing he wants to know.
Tried to ketch me up last night,
But you bet I would n't bite.
I jest kep' the smoothes' face,
But I led him sich a chase,
Could n't corner me, you bet—
I skipped all the traps he set.
Makin' out he wan'ed to know
Who was this an' that girl's beau;
So 's he 'd find out, don't you see,
Who was goin' 'long with me.
But I answers jest ez sly,
An' I never winks my eye,
Tell he hollers with a whirl,
" Look here, ain't you got a girl? "
Y' ought 'o seen me spread my
eyes,
Like he 'd took me by surprise,
An' I said, " Oh, Uncle John,
Never thought o' havin' one."
An' somehow that seemed to tickle
Him an' he shelled out a nickel.
Then you ought to seen me leave
Jest a-laffin' in my sleeve.
Fool him — well, I guess I did;
He ain't on to this here kid.
Got a girl! well, I guess yes,
Got a dozen more or less,
But I got one reely one,

[73]

Not no foolin' ner no fun;
Fur I 'm sweet on her, you see,
An' I ruther guess 'at she
Must be kinder sweet on me,
So we 're keepin' company.
Honest Injun! this is true,
Ever' word I 'm tellin' you!
But you won't be sich a scab
Ez to run aroun' an' blab.
Mebbe 't ain't the way with you,
But you know some fellers do.
Spoils a girl to let her know
'At you talk about her so.
Don't you know her? her name 's
    Liz,
Nicest girl in town she is.
Purty? ah, git out, you gilly —
Liz 'ud purt 'nigh knock you silly.
Y' ought 'o see her when she 's
    dressed
All up in her Sunday best,
All the fellers nudgin' me,
An' a-whisperin', gemunee!
Betcher life 'at I feel proud
When she passes by the crowd.
'T 's kinder nice to be a-goin'
With a girl 'at makes some show-
    in'—
One you know 'at hain't no snide,
Makes you feel so satisfied.
An' I 'll tell you she 's a trump,
Never even seen her jump
Like some silly girls 'ud do,
When I 'd hide and holler " Boo! "
She 'd jest laff an' say " Git out!
What you hollerin' about? "
When some girls 'ud have a fit

That 'un don't git skeered a bit,
Never makes a bit o' row
When she sees a worm er cow.
Them kind 's few an' far between;
Bravest girl I ever seen.
Tell you 'nuther thing she 'll do,
Mebbe you won't think it 's true,
But if she 's jest got a dime
She 'll go halvers ever' time.
Ah, you goose, you need n't laff;
That 's the kinder girl to have.
If you knowed her like I do,
Guess you 'd kinder like her too.
Tell you somep'n' if you 'll swear
You won't tell it anywhere.
Oh, you got to cross yer heart
Earnest, truly, 'fore I start.
Well, one day I kissed her cheek;
Gee, but I felt cheap an' weak,
'Cause at first she kinder flared,
'N', gracious goodness! I was
    scared.
But I need n't been, fer la!
Why, she never told her ma.
That 's what I call grit, don't
    you?
Sich a girl 's worth stickin' to.

PHYLLIS

Phyllis, ah, Phyllis, my life is a
    gray day,
  Few are my years, but my griefs
    are not few,
Ever to youth should each day be
    a May-day,

PAUL LAURENCE DUNBAR

Warm wind and rose-breath and
   diamonded dew —
Phyllis, ah, Phyllis, my life is a
   gray day.

Oh for the sunlight that shines on
   a May-day!
   Only the cloud hangeth over
     my life.
Love that should bring me youth's
   happiest heyday
   Brings me but seasons of sor-
     row and strife;
Phyllis, ah, Phyllis, my life is a
   gray day.

Sunshine or shadow, or gold day
   or gray day,
   Life must be lived as our des-
     tinies rule;
Leisure or labor or work day or
   play day —
   Feasts for the famous and fun
     for the fool;
Phyllis, ah, Phyllis, my life is a
   gray day.

RIGHT'S SECURITY

WHAT if the wind do howl with-
   out,
And turn the creaking weather-
   vane;
What if the arrows of the rain
Do beat against the window-pane?
Art thou not armored strong and
   fast

Against the sallies of the blast?
Art thou not sheltered safe and
   well
Against the flood's insistent swell?

What boots it, that thou stand'st
   alone,
And laughest in the battle's face
When all the weak have fled the
   place
And let their feet and fears keep
   pace?
Thou wavest still thine ensign,
   high,
And shoutest thy loud battle-cry;
Higher than e'er the tempest
   roared,
It cleaves the silence like a sword.

Right arms and armors, too, that
   man
Who will not compromise with
   wrong;
Though single, he must front the
   throng,
And wage the battle hard and
   long.
Minorities, since time began,
Have shown the better side of
   man;
And often in the lists of Time
One man has made a cause sub-
   lime!

IF

IF life were but a dream, my Love,
   And death the waking time;

If day had not a beam, my Love,
And night had not a rhyme,—
A barren, barren world were
this
Without one saving gleam;
I'd only ask that with a kiss
You'd wake me from the
dream.

If dreaming were the sum of
days,
And loving were the bane;
If battling for a wreath of bays
Could soothe a heart in pain,—
I'd scorn the meed of battle's
might,
All other aims above
I'd choose the human's higher
right,
To suffer and to love!

THE SONG

My soul, lost in the music's mist,
Roamed, rapt, 'neath skies of ame-
thyst.
The cheerless streets grew summer
meads,
The Son of Phœbus spurred his
steeds,
And, wand'ring down the mazy
tune,
December lost its way in June,
While from a verdant vale I
heard
The piping of a love-lorn bird.

A something in the tender strain
Revived an old, long-conquered
pain,
And as in depths of many seas,
My heart was drowned in mem-
ories.
The tears came welling to my
eyes,
Nor could I ask it otherwise;
For, oh! a sweetness seems to
last
Amid the dregs of sorrows past.

It stirred a chord that here of
late
I'd grown to think could not vi-
brate.
It brought me back the trust of
youth,
The world again was joy and
truth.
And Avice, blooming like a
bride,
Once more stood trusting at my
side.
But still, with bosom desolate,
The 'lorn bird sang to find his
mate.

Then there are trees, and lights
and stars,
The silv'ry tinkle of guitars;
And throbs again as throbbed that
waltz,
Before I knew that hearts were
false.
Then like a cold wave on a shore,

PAUL LAURENCE DUNBAR

Comes silence and she sings no
  more.
I wake, I breathe, I think again,
And walk the sordid ways of men.

SIGNS OF THE TIMES

Air a-gittin' cool an' coolah,
  Frost a-comin' in de night,
Hicka' nuts an' wa'nuts fallin',
  Possum keepin' out o' sight.
Tu'key struttin' in de ba'nya'd,
  Nary step so proud ez his;
Keep on struttin', Mistah Tu'key,
  Yo' do' know whut time it is.

Cidah press commence a-squeakin'
  Eatin' apples sto'ed away,
Chillun swa'min' 'roun' lak ho'-
  nets,
  Huntin' aigs ermung de hay.
Mistah Tu'key keep on gobblin'
  At de geese a-flyin' souf,
Oomph! dat bird do' know whut 's
  comin';
  Ef he did he 'd shet his mouf.

Pumpkin gittin' good an' yallah
  Mek me open up my eyes;
Seems lak it 's a-lookin' at me
  Jes' a-la'in' dah sayin' " Pies."
Tu'key gobbler gwine 'roun' blow-
  in',
    Gwine 'roun' gibbin' sass an'
    slack;
Keep on talkin', Mistah Tu'key,
  You ain't seed no almanac.

Fa'mer walkin' th'oo de ba'nya'd
  Seein' how things is comin' on,
Sees ef all de fowls is fatt'nin' —
  Good times comin' sho 's you
    bo'n.
Hyeahs dat tu'key gobbler brag-
  gin',
  Den his face break in a smile —
Nebbah min', you sassy rascal,
  He 's gwine nab you atter while.

Choppin' suet in de kitchen,
  Stonin' raisins in de hall,
Beef a-cookin' fu' de mince meat,
  Spices groun' — I smell 'em all.
Look hyeah, Tu'key, stop dat
  gobblin',
  You ain' luned de sense ob
    feah,
You ol' fool, yo' naik 's in dangah,
  Do' you know Thanksgibbin 's
    hyeah?

WHY FADES A DREAM?

Why fades a dream?
  An iridescent ray
Flecked in between the tryst
  Of night and day.
  Why fades a dream? —
Of consciousness the shade
Wrought out by lack of light and
  made
  Upon life's stream.
  Why fades a dream?

That thought may thrive,
  So fades the fleshless dream;

[77]

Lest men should learn to trust
  The things that seem.
   So fades a dream,
That living thought may grow
And like a waxing star-beam glow
  Upon life's stream —
   So fades a dream.

THE SPARROW

A LITTLE bird, with plumage
    brown,
Beside my window flutters down,
A moment chirps its little strain,
Ten taps upon my window-pane,
And chirps again, and hops along,
To call my notice to its song;
But I work on, nor heed its lay,
Till, in neglect, it flies away. .

So birds of peace and hope and
    love
Come fluttering earthward from
    above,
To settle on life's window-sills,
And ease our load of earthly ills;
But we, in traffic's rush and din
Too deep engaged to let them in,
With deadened heart and sense
    plod on,
Nor know our loss till they are
    gone.

SPEAKIN' O' CHRISTMAS

BREEZES blowin' middlin' brisk,
Snow-flakes thro' the air a-whisk,
Fallin' kind o' soft an' light,

Not enough to make things white,
But jest sorter siftin' down
So 's to cover up the brown
Of the dark world's rugged ways
'N' make things look like holidays.
Not smoothed over, but jest
    specked,
Sorter strainin' fur effect,
An' not quite a-gittin' through
What it started in to do.
Mercy sakes! it does seem queer
Christmas day is 'most nigh here.
Somehow it don't seem to me
Christmas like it used to be,—
Christmas with its ice an' snow,
Christmas of the long ago.
You could feel its stir an' hum
Weeks an' weeks before it come;
Somethin' in the atmosphere
Told you when the day was near,
Did n't need no almanacs;
That was one o' Nature's fac's.
Every cottage decked out gay —
Cedar wreaths an' holly spray —
An' the stores, how they were
    drest,
Tinsel tell you could n't rest;
Every winder fixed up pat,
Candy canes, an' things like that;
Noah's arks, an' guns, an' dolls,
An' all kinds o' fol-de-rols.
Then with frosty bells a-chime,
Slidin' down the hills o' time,
Right amidst the fun an' din
Christmas come a-bustlin' in,
Raised his cheery voice to call
Out a welcome to us all;

Hale and hearty, strong an' bluff,
That was Christmas, sure enough.
Snow knee-deep an' coastin' fine,
Frozen mill-ponds all ashine,
Seemin' jest to lay in wait,
Beggin' you to come an' skate.
An' you 'd git your gal an' go
Stumpin' cheerily thro' the snow,
Feelin' pleased an' skeert an'
    warm
'Cause she had a-holt yore arm.
Why, when Christmas come in, we
Spent the whole glad day in glee,
Havin' fun an' feastin' high
An' some courtin' on the sly.
Bustin' in some neighbor's door
An' then suddenly, before
He could give his voice a lift,
Yellin' at him, " Christmas gift."
Now sich things are never heard,
" Merry Christmas " is the word.
But it 's only change o' name,
An' means givin' jest the same.
There 's too many new-styled ways
Now about the holidays.
I 'd jest like once more to see
Christmas like it used to be!

LONESOME

MOTHER 's gone a-visitin' to spend
    a month er two,
An', oh, the house is lonesome ez a
    nest whose birds has flew
To other trees to build ag'in; the
    rooms seem jest so bare

That the echoes run like sperrits
    from the kitchen to the
    stair.
The shetters flap more lazy-like
    'n what they used to do,
Sence mother 's gone a-visitin' to
    spend a month er two.

We 've killed the fattest chicken
    an' we've cooked her to a
    turn;
We 've made the richest gravy,
    but I jest don't give a durn
Fur nothin' 'at I drink er eat, er
    nothin' 'at I see.
The food ain't got the pleasant
    taste it used to have to me.
They 's somep'n' stickin' in my
    throat ez tight ez hardened
    glue,
Sence mother 's gone a-visitin' to
    spend a month er two.

The hollyhocks air jest ez pink,
    they 're double ones at that,
An' I wuz prouder of 'em than a
    baby of a cat.
But now I don't go near 'em,
    though they nod an' blush at
    me,
Fur they 's somep'n' seems to gall
    me in their keerless sort o'
    glee
An' all their fren'ly noddin' an'
    their blushin' seems to say:
" You 're purty lonesome, John,
    old boy, sence mother 's gone
    away."

The neighbors ain't so fren'ly ez it
  seems they 'd ort to be;
They seem to be a-lookin' kinder
  sideways like at me,
A-kinder feared they 'd tech me
  off ez ef I wuz a match,
An' all because 'at mother 's gone
  an' I 'm a-keepin' batch!
I 'm shore I don't do nothin'
  worse 'n what I used to do
'Fore mother went a-visitin' to
  spend a month er two.

The sparrers ac's more fearsome
  like an' won't hop quite so
  near,
The cricket's chirp is sadder, an'
  the sky ain't ha'f so clear;
When ev'nin' comes, I set an'
  smoke tell my eyes begin to
  swim,
An' things aroun' commence to
  look all blurred an' faint an'
  dim.
Well, I guess I 'll have to own up
  'at I 'm feelin' purty blue
Sence mother 's gone a-visitin' to
  spend a month er two.

GROWIN' GRAY

HELLO, ole man, you 're a-gittin'
  gray,
An' it beats ole Ned to see the
  way
'At the crow's feet 's a-getherin'
  aroun' yore eyes;

Tho' it ought n't to cause me no
  su'prise,
Fur there 's many a sun 'at you 've
  seen rise
An' many a one you 've seen go
  down
Sence yore step was light an' yore
  hair was brown,
An' storms an' snows have had
  their way —
Hello, ole man, you 're a-gittin'
  gray.

Hello, ole man, you 're a-gittin'
  gray,
An' the youthful pranks 'at you
  used to play
Are dreams of a far past long ago
That lie in a heart where the fires
  burn low —
That has lost the flame though it
  kept the glow,
An' spite of drivin' snow an' storm,
Beats bravely on forever warm.
December holds the place of
  May —
Hello, ole man, you 're a-gittin'
  gray.

Hello, ole man, you 're a-gittin'
  gray —
Who cares what the carpin' youngsters say?
For, after all, when the tale is told,
Love proves if a man is young or
  old!
Old age can't make the heart grow
  cold

When it does the will of an honest
  mind;
When it beats with love fur all
  mankind;
Then the night but leads to a fairer
  day —
Hello, ole man, you 're a-gittin'
  gray!

TO THE MEMORY OF
MARY YOUNG

GOD has his plans, and what if we
With our sight be too blind to see
Their full fruition; cannot he,
Who made it, solve the mystery?
One whom we loved has fall'n
  asleep,
Not died; although her calm be
  deep,
Some new, unknown, and strange
  surprise
In Heaven holds enrapt her eyes.

And can you blame her that her
  gaze
Is turned away from earthly ways,
When to her eyes God's light and
  love
Have giv'n the view of things
  above?
A gentle spirit sweetly good,
The pearl of precious womanhood;
Who heard the voice of duty
  clear,
And found her mission soon and
  near.

She loved all nature, flowers fair,
The warmth of sun, the kiss of air,
The birds that filled the sky with
  song,
The stream that laughed its way
  along.
Her home to her was shrine and
  throne,
But one love held her not alone;
She sought out poverty and grief,
Who touched her robe and found
  relief.

So sped she in her Master's
  work,
Too busy and too brave to shirk,
When through the silence, dusk
  and dim,
God called her and she fled to him.
We wonder at the early call,
And tears of sorrow can but fall
For her o'er whom we spread the
  pall;
But faith, sweet faith, is over
  all.

The house is dust, the voice is
  dumb,
But through undying years to
  come,
The spark that glowed within her
  soul
Shall light our footsteps to the
  goal.
She went her way; but oh, she
  trod
The path that led her straight to
  God.

Such lives as this put death to
        scorn;
They lose our day to find God's
        morn.

WHEN MALINDY SINGS

G'WAY an' quit dat noise, Miss
        Lucy —
    Put dat music book away;
What 's de use to keep on tryin'?
    Ef you practise twell you 're
        gray,
You cain't sta't no notes a-flyin'
    Lak de ones dat rants and rings
F'om de kitchen to be big woods
    When Malindy sings.

You ain't got de nachel o'gans
    Fu' to make de soun' come right,
You ain't got de tu'ns an' twistin'
    Fu' to make it sweet an' light.
Tell you one thing now, Miss
        Lucy,
    An' I 'm tellin' you fu' true,
When hit comes to raal right
        singin',
    'T ain't no easy thing to do.

Easy 'nough fu' folks to hollah,
    Lookin' at de lines an' dots,
When dey ain't no one kin sence it,
    An' de chune comes in, in spots;
But fu' real melojous music,
    Dat jes' strikes yo' hea't and
        clings,
Jes' you stan' an' listen wif me
    When Malindy sings.

Ain't you nevah hyeahd Malindy?
    Blessed soul, tek up de cross!
Look hyeah, ain't you jokin',
        honey?
    Well, you don't know whut you
        los'.
Y' ought to hyeah dat gal a-wa'b-
        lin',
    Robins, la'ks, an' all dem things,
Heish dey moufs an' hides dey
        face.
    When Malindy sings.

Fiddlin' man jes' stop his fiddlin',
    Lay his fiddle on de she'f;
Mockin'-bird quit tryin' to whistle,
    'Cause he jes' so shamed hisse'f.
Folks a-playin' on de banjo
    Draps dey fingahs on de
        strings —
Bless yo' soul — fu'gits to move
        em,
    When Malindy sings.

She jes' spreads huh mouf and hol-
        lahs,
    "Come to Jesus," twell you
        hyeah
Sinnahs' tremblin' steps and voices,
    Timid-lak a-drawin' neah;
Den she tu'ns to "Rock of Ages,"
    Simply to de cross she clings,
An' you fin' yo' teahs a-drappin'
    When Malindy sings.

Who dat says dat humble praises
    Wif de Master nevah counts?

Heish yo' mouf, I hyeah dat music,
　　Ez hit rises up an' mounts —
Floatin' by de hills an' valleys,
　　Way above dis buryin' sod,
Ez hit makes its way in glory
　　To de very gates of God!

Oh, hit 's sweetah dan de music
　　Of an edicated band;
An' hit 's 'dearah dan de battle's
　　Song o' triumph in de lan'.
It seems holier dan evenin'
　　When de solemn chu'ch bell
　　　rings,
Ez I sit an' ca'mly listen
　　While Malindy sings.

Towsah, stop dat ba'kin', hyeah
　　me!
　　Mandy, mek dat chile keep still;
Don't you hyeah de echoes callin'
　　F'om de valley to de hill?
Let me listen, I can hyeah it,
　　Th'oo de bresh of angels' wings,
Sof' an' sweet, "Swing Low,
　　Sweet Chariot,"
　　Ez Malindy sings.

THE PARTY

Dey had a gread big pahty
　　down to Tom's de othah
　　night;
Was I dah? You bet! I nevah
　　in my life see sich a sight;
All de folks f'om fou' plantations
　　was invited, an' dey come,
Dey come troopin' thick ez chillun
　　when dey hyeahs a fife an'
　　drum.
Evahbody dressed deir fines'—
　　Heish yo' mouf an' git
　　away,
Ain't seen no sich fancy dressin'
　　sence las' quah'tly meetin'
　　day;
Gals all dressed in silks an' satins,
　　not a wrinkle ner a crease,
Eyes a-battin', teeth a-shinin', haih
　　breshed back, ez slick ez
　　grease;
Sku'ts all tucked an' puffed an'
　　ruffled, evah blessed seam an'
　　stitch;
Ef you 'd seen 'em wif deir mistus,
　　could n't swahed to which
　　was which.
Men all dressed up in Prince Al-
　　berts, swaller-tails 'u'd tek yo'
　　bref!
I cain't tell you nothin' 'bout it,
　　y' ought to seen it fu' yo'se'f.
Who was dah? Now who you
　　askin'? How you 'spect I
　　gwine to know?
You mus' think I stood an'
　　counted evahbody at de do.'
Ole man Babah's house-boy Isaac,
　　brung dat gal, Malindy Jane,
Huh a-hangin' to his elbow, him
　　a-struttin' wif a cane;
My, but Hahvey Jones was jeal-
　　ous! seemed to stick him lak
　　a tho'n;

But he laughed with Viney Cah-
  teh, tryin' ha'd to not let on,
But a pusson would 'a' noticed
  f'om de d'rection of his look,
Dat he was watchin' ev'ry step dat
  Ike an' Lindy took.
Ike he foun' a cheer an' asked huh:
  "Won't you set down?" wif
  a smile,
An' she answe'd up a-bowin',
  "Oh, I reckon 't ain't wuth
  while."
Dat was jes' fu' style, I reckon,
  'cause she sot down jes' de
  same,
An' she stayed dah 'twell he
  fetched huh fu' to jine some
  so't o' game;
Den I hyeahd huh sayin' propah,
  ez she riz to go away,
"Oh, you raly mus' excuse me,
  fu' I hardly keers to play."
But I seen huh in a minute wif de
  othahs on de flo',
An' dah was n't any one o' dem
  a-playin' any mo';
Comin' down de flo' a-bowin' an'
  a-swayin' an' a-swingin',
Puttin' on huh high-toned mannahs all de time dat she was
  singin':
"Oh, swing Johnny up an' down,
  swing him all aroun',
Swing Johnny up an' down, swing
  him all aroun',
Oh, swing Johnny up an' down,
  swing him all aroun'

Fa' you well, my dahlin'.'"
Had to laff at ole man Johnson,
  he 's a caution now, you bet —
Hittin' clost onto a hunderd, but
  he 's spry an' nimble yet;
He 'lowed how a-so't o' gigglin',
  "I ain't ole, I 'll let you see,
D'ain't no use in gittin' feeble, now
  you youngstahs jes' watch
  me,"
An' he grabbed ole Aunt Marier
  — weighs th'ee hunderd mo'
  er less,
An' he spun huh 'roun' de cabin
  swingin' Johnny lak de res'.
Evahbody laffed an' hollahed:
  "Go it! Swing huh, Uncle
  Jim!"
An' he swung huh too, I reckon,
  lak a youngstah, who but
  him.
Dat was bettah 'n young Scott
  Thomas, tryin' to be so awful
  smaht.
You know when dey gits to singin'
  an' dey comes to dat ere paht:
  "In some lady's new brick
  house,
  In some lady's gyahden.
    Ef you don't let me out, I
    will jump out,
  So fa' you well, my dahlin'.'"
Den dey 's got a circle 'roun' you,
  an' you 's got to break de
  line;
Well, dat dahky was so anxious,
  lak to bust hisse'f a-tryin';

Kep' on blund'rin' 'roun' an'
    foolin' 'twell he giv' one
    gread big jump,
Broke de line, an lit head-fo'most
    in de fiah-place right plump;
Hit 'ad fiah in it, mind you; well,
    I thought my soul I 'd bust,
Tried my best to keep f'om laffin',
    but hit seemed like die I
    must!
Y' ought to seen dat man a-scram-
    blin' f'om de ashes an' de
    grime.
Did it bu'n him! Sich a question,
    why he did n't give it time;
Th'ow'd dem ashes and dem cin-
    dahs evah which-a-way I
    guess,
An' you nevah did, I reckon, clap
    yo' eyes on sich a mess;
Fu' he sholy made a picter an' a
    funny one to boot,
Wif his clothes all full o' ashes
    an' his face all full o' soot.
Well, hit laked to stopped de
    pahty, an' I reckon lak ez
    not
Dat it would ef Tom's wife,
    Mandy, had n't happened on
    de spot,
To invite us out to suppah — well,
    we scrambled to de table,
An' I 'd lak to tell you 'bout it —
    what we had — but I ain't
    able,
Mention jes' a few things, dough
    I know I had n't orter,

Fu' I know 't will staht a hank'rin'
    an' yo' mouf 'll 'mence to
    worter.
We had wheat bread white ez cot-
    ton an' a egg pone jes like
    gol',
Hog jole, bilin' hot an' steamin'
    roasted shoat an' ham sliced
    cold —
Look out! What 's de mattah wif
    you? Don't be fallin' on de
    flo';
Ef it 's go'n' to 'fect you dat way,
    I won't tell you nothin'
    mo'.
Dah now — well, we had hot
    chittlin's — now you 's tryin'
    ag'in to fall,
Cain't you stan' to hyeah about it?
    S'pose you'd been an' seed it
    all;
Seed dem gread big sweet pertaters,
    layin' by de possum's side,
Seed dat coon in all his gravy,
    reckon den you 'd up and
    died!
Mandy 'lowed "you all mus'
    'scuse me, d' wa'n't much
    upon my she'ves,
But I 's done my bes' to suit you,
    so set down an' he'p
    yo'se'ves."
Tom, he 'lowed: "I don't b'lieve
    in 'pologisin' an' perfessin',
Let 'em tek it lak dey ketch it.
    Eldah Thompson, ask de
    blessin'."

PAUL LAURENCE DUNBAR

Wish you 'd seed dat colo'ed
preachah cleah his th'oat an'
bow his head;
One eye shet, an' one eye open,—
dis is evah wud he said:
" Lawd, look down in tendah
mussy on sich generous hea'ts
ez dese;
Make us truly thankful, amen.
Pass dat possum, ef you
please!"
Well, we eat and drunk ouah
po'tion, 'twell dah was n't
nothin' lef,
An' we felt jes' like new sausage,
we was mos' nigh stuffed to
def!
Tom, he knowed how we 'd be
feelin', so he had de fiddlah
'roun',
An' he made us cleah de cabin
fu' to dance dat suppah
down.
Jim, de fiddlah, chuned his fiddle,
put some rosum on his
bow,
Set a pine box on de table, mounted
it an' let huh go!
He 's a fiddlah, now I tell you, an'
he made dat fiddle ring,
'Twell de ol'est an' de lamest had
to give deir feet a fling.

Jigs, cotillions, reels an' break-
downs, cordrills an' a waltz
er two;
Bless yo' soul, dat music winged
'em an' dem people lak to
flew.
Cripple Joe, de old rheumatic,
danced dat flo' f'om side to
middle,
Th'owed away his crutch an'
hopped it; what 's rheumatics
'ginst a fiddle?
Eldah Thompson got so tickled
dat he lak to los' his grace,
Had to tek bofe feet an' hol' dem
so 's to keep 'em in deir place.
An' de Christuns an' de sinnahs
got so mixed up on dat flo',
Dat I don't see how dey 'd pahted
ef de trump had chanced to
blow.
Well, we danced dat way an' capahed in de mos' redic'lous
way,
'Twell de roostahs in de bahnyard
cleahed deir th'oats an' crowed
fu' day.
Y' ought to been dah, fu' I tell
you evahthing was rich an'
prime,
An' dey ain't no use in talkin', we
jes had one scrumptious time!

[86]

LOVE'S APOTHEOSIS

Love me. I care not what the
circling years
    To me may do.
If, but in spite of time and tears,
    You prove but true.

Love me — albeit grief shall dim
mine eyes,
    And tears bedew,
I shall not e'en complain, for then
my skies
    Shall still be blue.

Love me, and though the winter
snow shall pile,
    And leave me chill,
Thy passion's warmth shall make
for me, meanwhile,
    A sun-kissed hill.

And when the days have length-
ened into years,
    And I grow old,
Oh, spite of pains and griefs and
cares and fears,
    Grow thou not cold.

Then hand and hand we shall pass
up the hill,
    I say not down;
That twain go up, of love, who 've
loved their fill,—
    To gain love's crown.

Love me, and let my life take up
thine own,
    As sun the dew.
Come, sit, my queen, for in my
heart a throne
    Awaits for you!

THE PARADOX

I am the mother of sorrows,
    I am the ender of grief;
I am the bud and the blossom,
    I am the late-falling leaf.

I am thy priest and thy poet,
    I am thy serf and thy king;
I cure the tears of the heartsick,
    When I come near they shall
sing.

White are my hands as the snow-
drop;
    Swart are my fingers as clay;
Dark is my frown as the midnight,
    Fair is my brow as the day.

Battle and war are my minions,
    Doing my will as divine;
I am the calmer of passions,
    Peace is a nursling of mine.

Speak to me gently or curse me,
    Seek me or fly from my sight;
I am thy fool in the morning,
    Thou art my slave in the night.

Down to the grave will I take
    thee,
    Out from the noise of the
      strife;
Then shalt thou see me and know
    me —
    Death, then, no longer, but life.

Then shalt thou sing at my com-
    ing,
    Kiss me with passionate breath,
Clasp me and smile to have
    thought me
    Aught save the foeman of
      Death.

Come to me, brother, when weary,
    Come when thy lonely heart
      swells;
I 'll guide thy footsteps and lead
    thee
    Down where the Dream Wom-
      an dwells.

OVER THE HILLS

Over the hills and the valleys of
    dreaming
    Slowly I take my way.
Life is the night with its dream-
    visions teeming,
    Death is the waking at day.

Down thro' the dales and the bow-
    ers of loving,
    Singing, I roam afar.

Daytime or night-time, I con-
    stantly roving,—
    Dearest one, thou art my star.

WITH THE LARK

Night is for sorrow and dawn is
    for joy,
Chasing the troubles that fret and
    annoy;
Darkness for sighing and daylight
    for song,—
Cheery and chaste the strain,
    heartfelt and strong.
All the night through, though I
    moan in the dark,
I wake in the morning to sing
    with the lark.

Deep in the midnight the rain
    whips the leaves,
Softly and sadly the wood-spirit
    grieves.
But when the first hue of dawn
    tints the sky,
I shall shake out my wings like
    the birds and be dry;
And though, like the rain-drops, I
    grieved through the dark,
I shall wake in the morning to
    sing with the lark.

On the high hills of heaven, some
    morning to be,
Where the rain shall not grieve
    thro' the leaves of the tree,

PAUL LAURENCE DUNBAR

There my heart will be glad for
   the pain I have known,
For my hand will be clasped in the
   hand of mine own;
And though life has been hard and
   death's pathway been dark,
I shall wake in the morning to
   sing with the lark.

IN SUMMER

OH, summer has clothed the earth
   In a cloak from the loom of
     the sun!
And a mantle, too, of the skies'
   soft blue,
   And a belt where the rivers run.

And now for the kiss of the wind,
   And the touch of the air's soft
     hands,
With the rest from strife and the
   heat of life,
   With the freedom of lakes and
     lands.

I envy the farmer's boy
   Who sings as he follows the
     plow;
While the shining green of the
   young blades lean
   To the breezes that cool his
     brow.

He sings to the dewy morn,
   No thought of another's ear;

But the song he sings is a chant
   for kings
   And the whole wide world to
     hear.

He sings of the joys of life,
   Of the pleasures of work and
     rest,
From an o'erfull heart, without
   aim or art;
   'T is a song of the merriest.

O ye who toil in the town,
   And ye who moil in the mart,
Hear the artless song, and your
   faith made strong
   Shall renew your joy of heart.

Oh, poor were the worth of the
   world
   If never a song were heard,—
If the sting of grief had no re-
   lief,
   And never a heart were stirred.

So, long as the streams run down,
   And as long as the robins trill,
Let us taunt old Care with a
   merry air,
   And sing in the face of ill.

THE MYSTIC SEA

THE smell of the sea in my nos-
   trils,
   The sound of the sea in mine
     ears;

The touch of the spray on my
   burning face,
   Like the mist of reluctant tears.

The blue of the sky above me,
   The green of the waves be-
   neath;
The sun flashing down on a gray-
   white sail
   Like a scimitar from its sheath.

And ever the breaking billows,
   And ever the rocks' disdain;
And ever a thrill in mine inmost
   heart
That my reason cannot explain.

So I say to my heart, "Be silent,
   The mystery of time is here;
Death's way will be plain when
   we fathom the main,
   And the secret of life be clear."

A SAILOR'S SONG

OH for the breath of the briny
   deep,
And the tug of the bellying sail,
With the sea-gull's cry across the
   sky
And a passing boatman's hail.
For, be she fierce or be she gay,
The sea is a famous friend alway.

Ho! for the plains where the
   dolphins play,
And the bend of the mast and
   spars,

And a fight at night with the wild
   sea-sprite
When the foam has drowned the
   stars.
And, pray, what joy can the lands-
   man feel
Like the rise and fall of a sliding
   keel?

Fair is the mead; the lawn is fair
And the birds sing sweet on the
   lea;
But the echo soft of a song aloft
Is the strain that pleases me;
And swish of rope and ring of
   chain
Are music to men who sail the
   main.

Then, if you love me, let me sail
While a vessel dares the deep;
For the ship's my wife, and the
   breath of life
Are the raging gales that sweep;
And when I'm done with calm
   and blast,
A slide o'er the side, and rest at
   last.

THE BOHEMIAN

BRING me the livery of no other
   man.
   I am my own to robe me at my
   pleasure.
   Accepted rules to me disclose no
   treasure:

What is the chief who shall my
garments plan?
No garb conventional but I 'll
attack it.
(Come, why not don my span-
gled jacket?)

ABSENCE

GOOD-NIGHT, my love, for I have
dreamed of thee
In waking dreams, until my soul
is lost —
Is lost in passion's wide and shore-
less sea,
Where, like a ship, unruddered, it
is tost
Hither and thither at the wild
waves' will.
There is no potent Master's voice
to still
This newer, more tempestuous
Galilee!

The stormy petrels of my fancy
fly
In warning course across the
darkening green,
And, like a frightened bird, my
heart doth cry
And seek to find some rock of rest
between
The threatening sky and the re-
lentless wave.
It is not length of life that grief
doth crave,
But only calm and peace in which
to die.

Here let me rest upon this single
hope,
For oh, my wings are weary of the
wind,
And with its stress no more may
strive or cope.
One cry has dulled mine ears,
mine eyes are blind,—
Would that o'er all the interven-
ing space,
I might fly forth and see thee face
to face.
I fly; I search, but, love, in gloom
I grope.

Fly home, far bird, unto thy waiting nest;
Spread thy strong wings above the
wind-swept sea.
Beat the grim breeze with thy un-
ruffled breast
Until thou sittest wing to wing
with me.
Then, let the past bring up its
tales of wrong;
We shall chant low our sweet con-
nubial song,
Till storm and doubt and past no
more shall be!

HER THOUGHT AND HIS

THE gray of the sea, and the gray
of the sky,
A glimpse of the moon like a half-
closed eye.
The gleam on the waves and the
light on the land,

A thrill in my heart,— and — my
sweetheart's hand.

She turned from the sea with a
woman's grace,
And the light fell soft on her
upturned face,
And I thought of the flood-tide of
infinite bliss
That would flow to my heart from
a single kiss.

But my sweetheart was shy, so I
dared not ask
For the boon, so bravely I wore
the mask.
But into her face there came a
flame:—
I wonder could she have been
thinking the same?

THE RIGHT TO DIE

I HAVE no fancy for that ancient
cant
That makes us masters of our des-
tinies,
And not our lives, to hold or give
them up
As will directs; I cannot, will not
think
That men, the subtle worms, who
plot and plan
And scheme and calculate with
such shrewd wit,
Are such great blund'ring fools as
not to know

When they have lived enough.
                    Men court not death
When there are sweets still left in
life to taste.
Nor will a brave man choose to
live when he,
Full deeply drunk of life, has
reached the dregs,
And knows that now but bitter-
ness remains.
He is the coward who, outfaced
in this,
Fears the false goblins of another
life.
I honor him who being much
harassed
Drinks of sweet courage until
drunk of it,—
Then seizing Death, reluctant, by
the hand,
Leaps with him, fearless, to eternal peace!

BEHIND THE ARRAS

As in some dim baronial hall re-
strained,
A prisoner sits, engirt by secret
doors
And waving tapestries that argue
forth
Strange passages into the outer
air;
So in this dimmer room which we
call life,
Thus sits the soul and marks with
eye intent

That mystic curtain o'er the por-
tal death;
Still deeming that behind the
arras lies
The lambent way that leads to
lasting light.
Poor fooled and foolish soul!
Know now that death
Is but a blind, false door that no-
where leads,
And gives no hope of exit final,
free.

WHEN THE OLD MAN SMOKES

In the forenoon's restful quiet,
When the boys are off at school,
When the window lights are
shaded
And the chimney-corner cool,
Then the old man seeks his arm-
chair,
Lights his pipe and settles back;
Falls a-dreaming as he draws it
Till the smoke-wreaths gather
black.

And the tear-drops come a-trick-
ling
Down his cheeks, a silver
flow —
Smoke or memories you wonder,
But you never ask him,— no;
For there's something almost sa-
cred
To the other family folks

In those moods of silent dreaming
When the old man smokes.

Ah, perhaps he sits there dream-
ing
Of the love of other days
And of how he used to lead her
Through the merry dance's
maze;
How he called her "little prin-
cess,"
And, to please her, used to
twine
Tender wreaths to crown her
tresses,
From the "matrimony vine."

Then before his mental vision
Comes, perhaps, a sadder day,
When they left his little princess
Sleeping with her fellow clay.
How his young heart throbbed,
and pained him!
Why, the memory of it chokes!
Is it of these things he's thinking
When the old man smokes?

But some brighter thoughts pos-
sess him,
For the tears are dried the
while.
And the old, worn face is wrin-
kled
In a reminiscent smile,
From the middle of the forehead
To the feebly trembling lip,

[95]

At some ancient prank remembered
Or some long unheard-of quip.

Then the lips relax their tension
And the pipe begins to slide,
Till in little clouds of ashes,
It falls softly at his side;
And his head bends low and lower
Till his chin lies on his breast,
And he sits in peaceful slumber
Like a little child at rest.

Dear old man, there's something
sad'ning,
In these dreamy moods of yours,
Since the present proves so fleet-
ing,
All the past for you endures.
Weeping at forgotten sorrows,
Smiling at forgotten jokes;
Life epitomized in minutes,
When the old man smokes.

THE GARRET

Within a London garret high,
Above the roofs and near the sky,
My ill-rewarding pen I ply
To win me bread.
This little chamber, six by four,
Is castle, study, den, and more,—
Altho' no carpet decks the floor,
Nor down, the bed.

My room is rather bleak and bare;
I only have one broken chair,
But then, there's plenty of fresh
air,—
Some light, beside.
What tho' I cannot ask my friends
To share with me my odds and
ends,
A liberty my aerie lends,
To most denied.

The bore who falters at the stair
No more shall be my curse and
care,
And duns shall fail to find my lair
With beastly bills.
When debts have grown and
funds are short,
I find it rather pleasant sport
To live " above the common sort "
With all their ills.

I write my rhymes and sing away,
And dawn may come or dusk or
day:
Tho' fare be poor, my heart is
gay,
And full of glee.
Though chimney-pots be all my
views;
'T is nearer for the winging
Muse,
So I am sure she'll not refuse
To visit me.

PAUL LAURENCE DUNBAR

TO E. H. K.

ON THE RECEIPT OF A FAMILIAR
POEM

To me, like hauntings of a vagrant breath
  From some far forest which I
  once have known,
The perfume of this flower of
verse is blown.
Tho' seemingly soul-blossoms faint
to death,
Naught that with joy she bears
e'er withereth.
  So, tho' the pregnant years have
  come and flown,
Lives come and gone and altered like mine own,
This poem comes to me a shib-
boleth:
Brings sound of past communings
to my ear,
  Turns round the tide of time
  and bears me back
    Along an old and long un-
    traversed way;
Makes me forget this is a later
year,
  Makes me tread o'er a reminiscent track,
    Half sad, half glad, to one
    forgotten day!

A BRIDAL MEASURE

COME, essay a sprightly measure,
Tuned to some light song of
  pleasure.

Maidens, let your brows be
crowned
As we foot this merry round.

From the ground a voice is sing-
ing,
From the sod a soul is springing.
  Who shall say 't is but a clod
  Quick'ning upward toward its
  God?

Who shall say it? Who may
know it,
That the clod is not a poet
  Waiting but a gleam to waken
  In a spirit music-shaken?

Phyllis, Phyllis, why be waiting?
In the woods the birds are mating.
  From the tree beside the wall,
  Hear the am'rous robin call.

Listen to yon thrush's trilling;
Phyllis, Phyllis, are you willing,
  When love speaks from cave
  and tree,
  Only we should silent be?

When the year, itself renewing,
All the world with flowers is
  strewing,
  Then through Youth's Arcadian
  land,
  Love and song go hand in hand.

Come, unfold your vocal treasure,
Sing with me a nuptial measure,—
  Let this springtime gambol be
  Bridal dance for you and me.

[97]

VENGEANCE IS SWEET

WHEN I was young I longed for
    Love,
And held his glory far above
All other earthly things. I cried:
" Come, Love, dear Love, with me
    abide; "
And with my subtlest art I wooed,
And eagerly the wight pursued.
But Love was gay and Love was
    shy,
He laughed at me and passed me
    by.

Well, I grew old and I grew gray,
When Wealth came wending
    down my way.
I took his golden hand with glee,
And comrades from that day were
    we.
Then Love came back with dole-
    ful face,
And prayed that I would give him
    place.
But, though his eyes with tears
    were dim,
I turned my back and laughed at
    him.

A HYMN

AFTER READING " LEAD, KINDLY
LIGHT."

LEAD gently, Lord, and slow,
    For oh, my steps are weak,
And ever as I go,
    Some soothing sentence speak;

That I may turn my face
    Through doubt's obscurity
Toward thine abiding-place,
    E'en tho' I cannot see.

For lo, the way is dark;
    Through mist and cloud I grope,
Save for that fitful spark,
    The little flame of hope.

Lead gently, Lord, and slow,
    For fear that I may fall;
I know not where to go
    Unless I hear thy call.

My fainting soul doth yearn
    For thy green hills afar;
So let thy mercy burn —
    My greater, guiding star!

JUST WHISTLE A BIT

JUST whistle a bit, if the day be
    dark,
    And the sky be overcast:
If mute be the voice of the piping
    lark,
    Why, pipe your own small blast.

And it's wonderful how o'er the
    gray sky-track
The truant warbler comes steal-
    ing back.
But why need he come? for your
    soul's at rest,
And the song in the heart, — ah,
    that is best.

[98]

PAUL LAURENCE DUNBAR

Just whistle a bit, if the night be
    drear
And the stars refuse to shine:
And a gleam that mocks the star-
    light clear
    Within you glows benign.

Till the dearth of light in the
    glooming skies
Is lost to the sight of your soul-lit
    eyes.
What matters the absence of moon
    or star?
The light within is the best by far.

Just whistle a bit, if there's work
    to do,
    With the mind or in the soil.
And your note will turn out a
    talisman true
    To exorcise grim Toil.

It will lighten your burden and
    make you feel
That there's nothing like work as
    a sauce for a meal.
And with song in your heart and
    the meal in — its place,
There'll be joy in your bosom and
    light in your face.

Just whistle a bit, if your heart
    be sore;
'Tis a wonderful balm for pain.
Just pipe some old melody o'er
    and o'er
    Till it soothes like summer rain.

And perhaps 't would be best in a
    later day,
When Death comes stalking down
    the way,
To knock at your bosom and see
    if you're fit,
Then, as you wait calmly, just
    whistle a bit.

THE BARRIER

THE Midnight wooed the Morn-
    ing-Star,
    And prayed her: "Love come
      nearer;
Your swinging coldly there afar
    To me but makes you dearer!"

The Morning-Star was pale with
    dole
    As said she, low replying:
"Oh, lover mine, soul of my soul,
    For you I too am sighing.

"But One ordained when we
    were born,
    In spite of Love's insistence,
That Night might only view the
    Morn
    Adoring at a distance."

But as she spoke the jealous Sun
Across the heavens panted.
"Oh, whining fools," he cried,
    "have done;
    Your wishes shall be granted!"

He hurled his flaming lances far;
The twain stood unaffrighted —
And Midnight and the Morning-
Star
Lay down in death united!

DREAMS

DREAM on, for dreams are sweet:
Do not awaken!
Dream on, and at thy feet
Pomegranates shall be shaken.

Who likeneth the youth
Of life to morning?
'Tis like the night in truth,
Rose-coloured dreams adorning.

The wind is soft above,
The shadows umber.
(There is a dream called Love.)
Take thou the fullest slumber!

In Lethe's soothing stream,
Thy thirst thou slakest.
Sleep, sleep; 't is sweet to dream.
Oh, weep when thou awakest!

THE DREAMER

TEMPLES he built and palaces of
air,
And, with the artist's parent-
pride aglow,
His fancy saw his vague ideals
grow
Into creations marvellously fair;

He set his foot upon Fame's
nether stair.
But ah, his dream,— it had
entranced him so
He could not move. He could
no farther go;
But paused in joy that he was even
there!

He did not wake until one day
there gleamed
Thro' his dark consciousness a
light that racked
His being till he rose, alert to act.
But lo! what he had dreamed, the
while he dreamed,
Another, wedding action unto
thought,
Into the living, pulsing world
had brought.

WAITING

THE sun has slipped his tether
And galloped down the west.
(Oh, it's weary, weary waiting,
love.)
The little bird is sleeping
In the softness of its nest.
Night follows day, day follows
dawn,
And so the time has come and
gone:
And it's weary, weary waiting,
love.

The cruel wind is rising
With a whistle and a wail.

PAUL LAURENCE DUNBAR

(And it's weary, weary waiting,
   love.)
My eyes are seaward straining
   For the coming of a sail;
But void the sea, and void the
   beach
Far and beyond where gaze can
   reach!
   And it's weary, weary waiting,
      love.

I heard the bell-buoy ringing —
   How long ago it seems!
(Oh, it's weary, weary waiting,
   love.)
And ever still, its knelling
   Crashes in upon my dreams.
The banns were read, my frock
   was sewn;
Since then two seasons' winds
   have blown —
   And it's weary, weary waiting,
      love.

The stretches of the ocean
   Are bare and bleak to-day.
(Oh, it's weary, weary waiting,
   love.)
My eyes are growing dimmer —
   Is it tears, or age, or spray?
But I will stay till you come home.
Strange ships come in across the
   foam!
   But it's weary, weary waiting,
      love.

THE END OF THE CHAPTER

Ah, yes, the chapter ends to-day;
We even lay the book away;
But oh, how sweet the moments
   sped
Before the final page was read!

We tried to read between the lines
The Author's deep-concealed de-
   signs;
But scant reward such search se-
   cures;
You saw my heart and I saw
   yours.

The Master, — He who penned
   the page
And bade us read it, — He is sage:
And what he orders, you and I
Can but obey, nor question why.

We read together and forgot
The world about us. Time was
   not.
Unheeded and unfelt, it fled.
We read and hardly knew we
   read.

Until beneath a sadder sun,
We came to know the book was
   done.
Then, as our minds were but new
   lit,
It dawned upon us what was writ;

And we were startled. In our
   eyes,

Looked forth the light of great
    surprise.
Then as a deep-toned tocsin tolls,
A voice spoke forth: "Behold
    your souls!"

I do, I do. I cannot look
Into your eyes: so close the book.
But brought it grief or brought it
    bliss,
No other page shall read like this!

SYMPATHY

I KNOW what the caged bird feels,
    alas!
  When the sun is bright on the
    upland slopes;
When the wind stirs soft through
    the springing grass,
And the river flows like a stream
    of glass;
  When the first bird sings and
    the first bud opes,
And the faint perfume from its
    chalice steals —
I know what the caged bird feels!

I know why the caged bird beats
    his wing
  Till its blood is red on the cruel
    bars;
For he must fly back to his perch
    and cling
When he fain would be on the
    bough a-swing;
  And a pain still throbs in the
    old, old scars

And they pulse again with a keener
    sting —
I know why he beats his wing!

I know why the caged bird sings,
    ah me,
  When his wing is bruised and
    his bosom sore,—
When he beats his bars and he
    would be free;
It is not a carol of joy or glee,
  But a prayer that he sends from
    his heart's deep core,
But a plea, that upward to Heaven
    he flings —
I know why the caged bird sings!

LOVE AND GRIEF

OUT of my heart, one treach'rous
    winter's day,
I locked young Love and threw
    the key away.
Grief, wandering widely, found
    the key,
And hastened with it, straight-
    way, back to me,
With Love beside him. He un-
    locked the door
And bade Love enter with him
    there and stay.
And so the twain abide for ever-
    more.

LOVE'S CHASTENING

Once Love grew bold and arro-
    gant of air,

PAUL LAURENCE DUNBAR

Proud of the youth that made him
    fresh and fair;
So unto Grief he spake, "What
    right hast thou
To part or parcel of this heart?"
    Grief's brow
Was darkened with the storm of
    inward strife;
Thrice smote he Love as only he
    might dare,
And Love, pride purged, was chas-
    tened all his life.

MORTALITY

Ashes to ashes, dust unto dust,
What of his loving, what of his
    lust?
What of his passion, what of his
    pain?
What of his poverty, what of his
    pride?
Earth, the great mother, has called
    him again:
Deeply he sleeps, the world's ver-
    dict defied.
Shall he be tried again? Shall he
    go free?
Who shall the court convene?
    Where shall it be?
No answer on the land, none from
    the sea.
Only we know that as he did, we
    must:
You with your theories, you with
    your trust,—
Ashes to ashes, dust unto dust!

LOVE

A life was mine full of the close
    concern
  Of many-voiced affairs. The
    world sped fast;
  Behind me, ever rolled a preg-
    nant past.
A present came equipped with lore
    to learn.
Art, science, letters, in their turn,
  Each one allured me with its
    treasures vast;
  And I staked all for wisdom,
    till at last
Thou cam'st and taught my soul
    anew to yearn.
  I had not dreamed that I could
    turn away
From all that men with brush
    and pen had wrought;
  But ever since that memorable
    day
When to my heart the truth of
    love was brought,
  I have been wholly yielded to
    its sway,
And had no room for any other
    thought.

SHE GAVE ME A ROSE

She gave a rose,
  And I kissed it and pressed it.
I love her, she knows,
  And my action confessed it.
She gave me a rose,
  And I kissed it and pressed it.

Ah, how my heart glows,
  Could I ever have guessed it?
It is fair to suppose
  That I might have repressed it:
She gave me a rose,
  And I kissed it and pressed it.

'T was a rhyme in life's prose
  That uplifted and blest it.
Man's nature, who knows
  Until love comes to test it?
She gave me a rose,
  And I kissed it and pressed it.

Be thy far home by mountain,
  vale, or sea.
My yearning heart may never find
  its rest
Until thou liest rapt upon my
  breast.
The wind may bring its perfume
  from the south,
Is it so sweet as breath from my
  love's mouth?
Oh, naught that surely is, and
  naught that seems
May turn me from the lady of my
  dreams.

DREAM SONG I

Long years ago, within a distant
  clime,
Ere Love had touched me with
  his wand sublime,
I dreamed of one to make my life's
  calm May
The panting passion of a summer's day.
And ever since, in almost sad sus-
  pense,
I have been waiting with a soul
  intense
To greet and take unto myself
  the beams,
Of her, my star, the lady of my
  dreams.

O Love, still longed and looked
  for, come to me,

DREAM SONG II

Pray, what can dreams avail
  To make love or to mar?
The child within the cradle rail
  Lies dreaming of the star.
But is the star by this beguiled
To leave its place and seek the
  child?

The poor plucked rose within its
  glass
  Still dreameth of the bee;
But, tho' the lagging moments
  pass,
  Her Love she may not see.
If dream of child and flower fail,
Why should a maiden's dreams
  prevail?

PAUL LAURENCE DUNBAR

CHRISTMAS IN THE HEART

The snow lies deep upon the
      ground,
And winter's brightness all around
Decks bravely out the forest sere,
With jewels of the brave old year.
The coasting crowd upon the hill
With some new spirit seems to
      thrill;
And all the temple bells achime.
Ring out the glee of Christmas
      time.

In happy homes the brown oak-
      bough
Vies with the red-gemmed holly
      now;
And here and there, like pearls,
      there show
The berries of the mistletoe.
A sprig upon the chandelier
Says to the maidens, "Come not
      here!"
Even the pauper of the earth
Some kindly gift has cheered to
      mirth!

Within his chamber, dim and cold,
There sits a grasping miser old.
He has no thought save one of
      gain,—
To grind and gather and grasp
      and drain.
A peal of bells, a merry shout
Assail his ear: he gazes out
Upon a world to him all gray,
And snarls, "Why, this is Christ-
      mas Day!"

No, man of ice,— for shame, for
      shame!
For "Christmas Day" is no mere
      name.
No, not for you this ringing cheer,
This festal season of the year.
And not for you the chime of bells
From holy temple rolls and swells.
In day and deed he has no part —
Who holds not Christmas in his
      heart!

THE KING IS DEAD

Aye, lay him in his grave, the old
      dead year!
His life is lived — fulfilled his
      destiny.
Have you for him no sad, regret-
      ful tear
To drop beside the cold, unfol-
      lowed bier?
Can you not pay the tribute of a
      sigh?

Was he not kind to you, this dead
      old year?
Did he not give enough of earthly
      store?
Enough of love, and laughter, and
      good cheer?
Have not the skies you scanned
      sometimes been clear?

How, then, of him who dies, could
you ask more?

It is not well to hate him for the
pain
He brought you, and the sorrows
manifold.
To pardon him these hurts still I
am fain;
For in the panting period of his
reign,
He brought me new wounds, but
he healed the old.

One little sigh for thee, my poor,
dead friend —
One little sigh while my com-
panions sing.
Thou art so soon forgotten in the
end;
We cry e'en as thy footsteps downward tend:
"The king is dead! long live the
king!"

THEOLOGY

THERE is a heaven, for ever, day
by day,
The upward longing of my soul
doth tell me so.
There is a hell, I'm quite as sure;
for pray,
If there were not, where would
my neighbours go?

RESIGNATION

LONG had I grieved at what I
deemed abuse;
But now I am as grain within
the mill.
If so be thou must crush me for
thy use,
Grind on, O potent God, and
do thy will!

LOVE'S HUMILITY

As some rapt gazer on the lowly
earth,
Looks up to radiant planets,
ranging far,
So I, whose soul doth know thy
wondrous worth
Look longing up to thee as to a
star.

PRECEDENT

THE poor man went to the rich
man's doors,
"I come as Lazarus came," he
said.
The rich man turned with humble
head,—
"I will send my dogs to lick your
sores!"

SHE TOLD HER BEADS

SHE told her beads with down-
cast eyes,
Within the ancient chapel dim;
And ever as her fingers slim

Slipt o'er th' insensate ivories,
My rapt soul followed, spaniel-
wise.
Ah, many were the beads she wore;
But as she told them o'er and
o'er,
They did not number all my sighs.
My heart was filled with unvoiced
cries
And prayers and pleadings un-
expressed;
But while I burned with Love's
unrest,
She told her beads with down-
cast eyes.

LITTLE LUCY LANDMAN

OH, the day has set me dreaming
In a strange, half solemn way
Of the feelings I experienced
On another long past day,—
Of the way my heart made music
When the buds began to blow,
And o' little Lucy Landman
Whom I loved long years ago.

It 's in spring, the poet tells us,
That we turn to thoughts of
love,
And our hearts go out a-wooing
With the lapwing and the dove.
But whene'er the soul goes seeking
Its twin-soul, upon the wing,
I 've a notion, backed by mem'ry,
That it 's love that makes the
spring.

I have heard a robin singing
When the boughs were brown
and bare,
And the chilling hand of winter
Scattered jewels through the air.
And in spite of dates and seasons,
It was always spring, I know,
When I loved Lucy Landman
In the days of long ago.

Ah, my little Lucy Landman,
I remember you as well
As if 't were only yesterday
I strove your thoughts to tell,—
When I tilted back your bonnet,
Looked into your eyes so true,
Just to see if you were loving
Me as I was loving you.

Ah, my little Lucy Landman
It is true it was denied
You should see a fuller summer
And an autumn by my side.
But the glance of love's sweet sun-
light
Which your eyes that morning
gave
Has kept spring within my bosom,
Though you lie within the
grave.

THE GOURD

IN the heavy earth the miner
Toiled and laboured day by day,
Wrenching from the miser moun-
tain
Brilliant treasure where it lay.

And the artist worn and weary
 Wrought with labour manifold
That the king might drink his
    nectar
 From a goblet made of gold.

On the prince's groaning table
 Mid the silver gleaming bright
Mirroring the happy faces
 Giving back the flaming light,
Shine the cups of priceless crystal
 Chased with many a lovely line,
Glowing now with warmer colour,
 Crimsoned by the ruby wine.

In a valley sweet with sunlight,
 Fertile with the dew and rain,
Without miner's daily labour,
 Without artist's nightly pain,
There there grows the cup I drink
    from,
 Summer's sweetness in it stored,
And my lips pronounce a blessing
 As they touch an old brown
    gourd.

Why, the miracle at Cana
 In the land of Galilee,
Tho' it puzzles all the scholars,
 Is no longer strange to me.
For the poorest and the humblest
 Could a priceless wine afford,
If they 'd only dip up water
 With a sunlight-seasoned gourd.

So a health to my old comrade,
 And a song of praise to sing

When he rests inviting kisses
 In his place beside the spring.
Give the king his golden goblets,
 Give the prince his crystal
    hoard;
But for me the sparkling water
 From a brown and brimming
    gourd!

THE KNIGHT

Our good knight, Ted, girds his
    broadsword on
 (And he wields it well, I
    ween);
He 's on his steed, and away has
    gone
 To the fight for king and queen.
What tho' no edge the broadsword
    hath?
What tho' the blade be made of
    lath?
 'T is a valiant hand
 That wields the brand,
So, foeman, clear the path!

He prances off at a goodly pace;
 'T is a noble steed he rides,
That bears as well in the speedy
    race
 As he bears in battle-tides.
What tho' 't is but a rocking-chair
That prances with this stately air?
 'T is a warrior bold
 The reins doth hold,
Who bids all foes beware!

PAUL LAURENCE DUNBAR

THOU ART MY LUTE

Thou art my lute, by thee I
    sing,—
  My being is attuned to thee.
Thou settest all my words a-wing,
And meltest me to melody.

Thou art my life, by thee I live,
    From thee proceed the joys I
      know;
Sweetheart, thy hand has power
    to give
    The meed of love — the cup of
      woe.

Thou art my love, by thee I lead
    My soul the paths of light along,
From vale to vale, from mead to
      mead,
    And home it in the hills of song.

My song, my soul, my life, my all,
    Why need I pray or make my
      plea,
Since my petition cannot fall;
    For I 'm already one with thee!

THE PHANTOM KISS

One night in my room, still and
    beamless,
    With will and with thought in
      eclipse,
I rested in sleep that was dream-
    less;
    When softly there fell on my
      lips

A touch, as of lips that were press-
    ing
    Mine own with the message of
      bliss —
A sudden, soft, fleeting caressing,
    A breath like a maiden's first
      kiss.

I woke — and the scoffer may
    doubt me —
    I peered in surprise through the
      gloom;
But nothing and none were about
    me,
    And I was alone in my room.

Perhaps 't was the wind that
    caressed me
    And touched me with dew-laden
      breath;
Or, maybe, close-sweeping, there
    passed me
    The low-winging Angel of
      Death.

Some sceptic may choose to dis-
    dain it,
    Or one feign to read it aright;
Or wisdom may seek to explain
    it —
    This mystical kiss in the night.

But rather let fancy thus clear it:
    That, thinking of me here alone,
The miles were made naught, and,
    in spirit,
    Thy lips, love, were laid on
      mine own.

COMMUNION

In the silence of my heart,
  I will spend an hour with thee,
When my love shall rend apart
  All the veil of mystery:

All that dim and misty veil
  That shut in between our souls
When Death cried, " Ho, maiden,
    hail ! "
  And your barque sped on the
    shoals.

On the shoals? Nay, wrongly
    said.
  On the breeze of Death that
    sweeps
Far from life, thy soul has sped
  Out into unsounded deeps.

I shall take an hour.and come
  Sailing, darling, to thy side.
Wind nor sea may keep me from
  Soft communings with my bride.

I shall rest my head on thee
  As I did long days of yore,
When a calm, untroubled sea
  Rocked thy vessel at the shore.

I shall take thy hand in mine,
  And live o'er the olden days
When thy smile to me was wine,—
  Golden wine thy word of praise,

For the carols I had wrought
  In my soul's simplicity;

For the petty beads of thought
  Which thine eyes alone could
    see.

Ah, those eyes, love-blind, but keen
  For my welfare and my weal!
Tho' the grave-door shut between,
  Still their love-lights o'er me
    steal.

I can see thee thro' my tears,
  As thro' rain we see the sun.
What tho' cold and cooling years
  Shall their bitter courses run,—

I shall see thee still and be
  Thy true lover evermore,
And thy face shall be to me
  Dear and helpful as before.

Death may vaunt and Death may
    boast,
  But we laugh his pow'r to
    scorn ;
He is but a slave at most,—
  Night that heralds coming morn.

I shall spend an hour with thee
  Day by day, my little bride.
True love laughs at mystery,
  Crying, " Doors of Death, fly
    wide."

MARE RUBRUM

In Life's Red Sea with faith I
    plant my feet,
  And wait the sound of that sus-
    taining word

Which long ago the men of
Israel heard,
When Pharaoh's host behind them,
fierce and fleet,
Raged on, consuming with re-
vengeful heat.
Why are the barrier waters
still unstirred? —
That struggling faith may die
of hope deferred?
Is God not sitting in His ancient
seat?

The billows swirl above my trembling limbs,
And almost chill my anxious
heart to doubt
And disbelief, long conquered
and defied.
But tho' the music of my hopeful
hymns
Is drowned by curses of the raging rout,
No voice yet bids th' opposing
waves divide!

IN AN ENGLISH GARDEN

IN this old garden, fair, I walk
to-day
Heart-charmed with all the
beauty of the scene:
The rich, luxuriant grasses'
cooling green,
The wall's environ, ivy-decked and
gray,

The waving branches with the
wind at play,
The slight and tremulous
blooms that show between,
Sweet all: and yet my yearning
heart doth lean
Toward Love's Egyptian flesh-
pots far away.

Beside the wall, the slim Labur-
num grows
And flings its golden flow'rs to
every breeze.
But e'en among such soothing
sights as these,
I pant and nurse my soul-devour-
ing woes.
Of all the longings that our
hearts wot of,
There is no hunger like the want
of love!

THE CRISIS

A MAN of low degree was sore oppressed,
Fate held him under iron-handed
sway,
And ever, those who saw him
thus distressed
Would bid him bend his stub-
born will and pray.
But he, strong in himself and obdurate,
Waged, prayerless, on his losing
fight with Fate.

Friends gave his proffered hand
    their coldest clasp,
  Or took it not at all; and Pov-
    erty,
That bruised his body with relent-
    less grasp,
  Grinned, taunting, when he
    struggled to be free. ·
But though with helpless hands he
    beat the air,
His need extreme yet found no
    voice in prayer.

Then he prevailed; and forthwith
    snobbish Fate,
  Like some whipped cur, came
    fawning at his feet;
Those who had scorned forgave
    and called him great —
  His friends found out that
    friendship still was sweet.
But he, once obdurate, now bowed
    his head
In prayer, and trembling with its
    import, said:

" Mere human strength may stand
    ill-fortune's frown;
  So I prevailed, for human
    strength was mine;
But from the killing pow'r of
    great renown,
  Naught may protect me save a
    strength divine.
Help me, O Lord, in this my
    trembling cause;
I scorn men's curses, but I dread
    applause! "

THE CONQUERORS

THE BLACK TROOPS IN CUBA

ROUND the wide earth, from the
    red field your valour has won,
Blown with the breath of the far-
    speaking gun,
      Goes the word.
Bravely you spoke through the bat-
    tle cloud heavy and dun.
Tossed though the speech toward
    the mist-hidden sun,
      The world heard.

Hell would have shrunk from you
    seeking it fresh from the fray,
Grim with the dust of the battle,
    and gray
      From the fight.
Heaven would have crowned you,
    with crowns not of gold but
    of bay,
Owning you fit for the light of
    her day,
      Men of night.

Far through the cycle of years and
    of lives that shall come,
There shall speak voices long muf-
    fled and dumb,
      Out of fear.
And through the noises of trade
    and the turbulent hum,
Truth shall rise over the militant
    drum,
      Loud and clear.

Then on the cheek of the honester
    nation that grows,

PAUL LAURENCE DUNBAR

All for their love of you, not for
　　your woes,
　　　　There shall lie
Tears that shall be to your souls as
　　the dew to the rose;
Afterward thanks, that the pres-
　　ent yet knows
　　　　Not to ply!.

ALEXANDER CRUMMELL
— DEAD

BACK to the breast of thy mother,
Child of the earth!
E'en her caress can not smother
What thou hast done.
Follow the trail of the westering
　　sun
Over the earth.
Thy light and his were as one —
Sun, in thy worth.
Unto a nation whose sky was as
　　night,
Camest thou, holily, bearing thy
　　light:
And the dawn came,
In it thy fame
Flashed up in a flame.

Back to the breast of thy mother —
To rest.
Long hast thou striven;
Dared where the hills by the light-
　　ning of heaven were riven;
Go now, pure shriven.
Who shall come after thee, out of
　　the clay —

Learned one and leader to show
　　us the way?
Who shall rise up when the world
　　gives the test?
Think thou no more of this —
Rest!

WHEN ALL IS DONE

WHEN all is done, and my last
　　word is said,
And ye who loved me murmur,
　　" He is dead,"
Let no one weep, for fear that I
　　should know,
And sorrow too that ye should
　　sorrow so.

When all is done and in the ooz-
　　ing clay,
Ye lay this cast-off hull of mine
　　away,
Pray not for me, for, after long
　　despair,
The quiet of the grave will be a
　　prayer.

For I have suffered loss and
　　grievous pain,
The hurts of hatred and the
　　world's disdain,
And wounds so deep that love,
　　well-tried and pure,
Had not the pow'r to ease them
　　or to cure.

When all is done, say not my day
　　is o'er,

And that thro' night I seek a dim-
    mer shore:
Say rather that my morn has just
    begun,—
I greet the dawn and not a setting
    sun,
        When all is done.

THE POET AND THE BABY

How's a man to write a sonnet,
    can you tell,—
How 's he going to weave the dim,
    poetic spell,—
    When a-toddling on the floor
    Is the muse he must adore,
And this muse he loves, not
    wisely, but too well?

Now, to write a sonnet, every one
    allows,
One must always be as quiet as a
    mouse;
    But to write one seems to me
    Quite superfluous to be,
When you 've got a little sonnet
    in the house.

Just a dainty little poem, true and
    fine,
That is full of love and life in
    every line,
    Earnest, delicate, and sweet,
    Altogether so complete

That I wonder what 's the use of
    writing mine.

DISTINCTION

" I AM but clay," the sinner plead,
    Who fed each vain desire.
" Not only clay," another said,
    " But worse, for thou art mire."

THE SUM

A LITTLE dreaming by the way,
A little toiling day by day;
A little pain, a little strife,
A little joy,— and that is life.

A little short-lived summer's
    morn,
When joy seems all so newly born,
When one day's sky is blue above,
And one bird sings,— and that is
    love.

A little sickening of the years,
The tribute of a few hot tears
Two folded hands, the failing
    breath,
And peace at last,— and that is
    death.

Just dreaming, loving, dying so,
The actors in the drama go —
A flitting picture on a wall,
Love, Death, the themes; but is
    that all?

PAUL LAURENCE DUNBAR

SONNET

ON AN OLD BOOK WITH UNCUT
LEAVES

EMBLEM of blasted hope and lost
    desire,
    No finger ever traced thy yel-
        low page
    Save Time's. Thou hast not
        wrought to noble rage
The hearts thou wouldst have
    stirred. Not any fire
Save sad flames set to light a fu-
    neral pyre
    Dost thou suggest. Nay,— im-
        potent in age,
    Unsought, thou holdst a corner
        of the stage
And ceasest even dumbly to aspire.

How different was the thought of
    him that writ.
    What promised he to love of
        ease and wealth,
When men should read and kin-
    dle at his wit.
    But here decay eats up the book
        by stealth,
While it, like some old maiden,
    solemnly,
Hugs its incongruous virginity!

ON THE SEA WALL

I SIT upon the old sea wall,
    And watch the shimmering sea,
.Where soft and white the moon-
        beams fall,

Till, in a fantasy,
Some pure white maiden's funeral
        pall
    The strange light seems to me.

The waters break upon the shore
    And shiver at my feet,
While I dream old dreams o'er
    · and o'er,
    And dim old scenes repeat;
Tho' all have dreamed the same
        before,
    They still seem new and sweet.

The waves still sing the same old
        song
    That knew an elder time;
The breakers' beat is not more
        strong,
    Their music more sublime;
And poets thro' the ages long
    Have set these notes to rhyme.

But this shall not deter my lyre,
    Nor check my simple strain;
If I have not the old-time fire,
    I know the ancient pain:
The hurt of unfulfilled desire,—
    The ember quenched by rain.

I know the softly shining sea
    That rolls this gentle swell
Has snarled and licked its tongues
        at me
    And bared its fangs as well;
That 'neath its smile so heavenly,
    There lurks the scowl of hell!

[115]

But what of that? I strike my
    string
  (For songs in youth are sweet);
I 'll wait and hear the waters
    bring
  Their loud resounding beat;
Then, in her own bold numbers
    sing
  The Ocean's dear deceit!

TO A LADY PLAYING THE HARP

THY tones are silver melted into
    sound,
  And as I dream
I see no walls around,
  But seem to hear
  A gondolier
Sing sweetly down some slow Ve-
    netian stream.

Italian skies — that I have never
    seen —
  I see above.
(Ah, play again, my queen;
  Thy fingers white
  Fly swift and light
And weave for me the golden
    mesh of love.)

Oh, thou dusk sorceress of the
    dusky eyes
  And soft dark hair,
'T is thou that mak'st my skies
  So swift to change
  To far and strange;

But far and strange, thou still
    dost make them fair.

Now thou dost sing, and I am lost
    in thee
  As one who drowns
In floods of melody.
  Still in thy art
  Give me this part,
Till perfect love, the love of lov-
    ing crowns.

CONFESSIONAL

SEARCH thou my heart;
  If there be guile,
It shall depart
  Before thy smile.

Search thou my soul;
  Be there deceit,
'T will vanish whole
  Before thee, sweet.

Upon my mind
  Turn thy pure lens;
Naught shalt thou find
  Thou canst not cleanse.

If I should pray,
  I scarcely know
In just what way
  My prayers would go.

So strong in me
  I feel love's leaven,
I 'd bow to thee
  As soon as Heaven!

PAUL LAURENCE DUNBAR

MISAPPREHENSION

Out of my heart, one day, I
    wrote a song,
With my heart's blood imbued,
Instinct with passion, tremulously
    strong,
    With grief subdued;
    Breathing a fortitude
    Pain-bought.
And one who claimed much love
    for what I wrought,
    Read and considered it,
    And spoke:
" Ay, brother,—'t is well writ,
    But where 's the joke? "

PROMETHEUS

Prometheus stole from Heaven
    the sacred fire
    And swept to earth with it o'er
    land and sea.
He lit the vestal flames of poesy,
Content, for this, to brave celes-
    tial ire.

Wroth were the gods, and with
    eternal hate
    Pursued the fearless one who
    ravished Heaven
    That earth might hold in fee
    the perfect leaven
To lift men's souls above their
    low estate.

But judge you now, when poets
    wield the pen,

Think you not well the wrong
    has been repaired?
'T was all in vain that ill Pro-
    metheus fared:
The fire has been returned to
    Heaven again!

We have no singers like the ones
    whose note
    Gave challenge to the noblest
    warbler's song.
    We have no voice so mellow,
    sweet, and strong
As that which broke from Shelley's
    golden throat.

The measure of our songs is our
    desires:
    We tinkle where old poets used
    to storm.
    We lack their substance tho' we
    keep their form:
We strum our banjo-strings and
    call them lyres.

LOVE'S PHASES

Love hath the wings of the but-
    terfly,
    Oh, clasp him but gently,
Pausing and dipping and flutter-
    ing by
    Inconsequently.
Stir not his poise with the breath
    of a sigh;
Love hath the wings of the but-
    terfly.

Love hath the wings of the eagle
bold,
  Cling to him strongly —
What if the look of the world be
cold,
  And life go wrongly?
Rest on his pinions, for broad is
their fold;
Love hath the wings of the eagle
bold.

Love hath the voice of the nightin-
gale,
  Hearken his trilling —
List to his song when the moon-
light is pale,—
  Passionate, thrilling.
Cherish the lay, ere the lilt of it
fail;
Love hath the voice of the nightin-
gale.

Love hath the voice of the storm
at night,
  Wildly defiant.
Hear him and yield up your soul
to his might,
  Tenderly pliant.
None shall regret him who heed
him aright;
Love hath the voice of the storm
at night.

FOR THE MAN WHO FAILS

THE world is a snob, and the man
who wins

Is the chap for its money's
worth:
And the lust for success causes
half of the sins
  That are cursing this brave old
earth.
For it's fine to go up, and the
world's applause
  Is sweet to the mortal ear;
But the man who fails in a noble
cause
  Is a hero that's no less dear.

'T is true enough that the laurel
crown
  Twines but for the victor's
brow;
For many a hero has lain him
down
  With naught but the cypress
bough.
There are gallant men in the los-
ing fight,
  And as gallant deeds are done
As ever graced the captured
height
  Or the battle grandly won.

We sit at life's board with our
nerves highstrung,
  And we play for the stake of
Fame,
And our odes are sung and our
banners hung
  For the man who wins the
game.
But I have a song of another kind

Than breathes in these fame-
wrought gales,—
An ode to the noble heart and
mind
Of the gallant man who fails!

The man who is strong to fight his
fight,
And whose will no front can
daunt,
If the truth be truth and the right
be right,
Is the man that the ages want.
Tho' he fail and die in grim de-
feat,
Yet he has not fled the strife,
And the house of Earth will seem
more sweet
For the perfume of his life.

HARRIET BEECHER STOWE

She told the story, and the whole
world wept
At wrongs and cruelties it had
not known
But for this fearless woman's
voice alone.
She spoke to consciences that
long had slept:
Her message, Freedom's clear
reveille, swept
From heedless hovel to compla-
cent throne.
Command and prophecy were
in the tone

And from its sheath the sword
of justice leapt.
Around two peoples swelled a
fiery wave,
But both came forth transfig-
ured from the flame.
Blest be the hand that dared be
strong to save,
And blest be she who in our
weakness came —
Prophet and priestess! At one
stroke she gave
A race to freedom and herself
to fame.

VAGRANTS

Long time ago, we two set out,
My soul and I.
I know not why,
For all our way was dim with
doubt.
I know not where
We two may fare:
Though still with every changing
weather,
We wander, groping on together.

We do not love, we are not
friends,
My soul and I.
He lives a lie;
Untruth lines every way he wends.
A scoffer he
Who jeers at me:

And so, my comrade and my
    brother,
We wander on and hate each
    other.

Ay, there be taverns and to spare,
    Beside the road;
      But some strange goad
Lets me not stop to taste their
    fare.
      Knew I the goal
      Toward which my soul
And I made way, hope made life
    fragrant:
But no. We wander, aimless, va-
    grant!

A WINTER'S DAY

Across the hills and down the
    narrow ways,
    And up the valley where the
      free winds sweep,
      The earth is folded in an er-
      mined sleep
That mocks the melting mirth of
    myriad Mays.
Departed her disheartening duns
    and grays,
    And all her crusty black is cov-
      ered deep.
    Dark streams are locked in
      Winter's donjon-keep,
And made to shine with keen, un-
    wonted rays.

O icy mantle, and deceitful snow!
    What world-old liars in your
      hearts ye are!
    Are there not still the darkened
      seam and scar
Beneath the brightness that you
    fain would show?
Come from the cover with thy
    blot and blur,
O reeking Earth, thou whited
    sepulchre!

MY LITTLE MARCH
GIRL

Come to the pane, draw the cur-
    tain apart,
There she is passing, the girl of
    my heart;
See where she walks like a queen
    in the street,
Weather-defying, calm, placid and
    sweet.
Tripping along with impetuous
    grace,
Joy of her life beaming out of her
    face,
Tresses all truant-like, curl upon
    curl,
Wind-blown and rosy, my little
    March girl.

Hint of the violet's delicate
    bloom,
Hint of the rose's pervading per-
    fume!

PAUL LAURENCE DUNBAR

How can the wind help from kiss-
    ing her face,—
Wrapping her round in his stormy
    embrace?
But still serenely she laughs at his
    rout,
She is the victor who wins in the
    bout.
So may life's passions about her
    soul swirl,
Leaving it placid,— my little
    March girl.

What self-possession looks out of
    her eyes!
What are the wild winds, and
    what are the skies,
Frowning and glooming when,
    brimming with life,
Cometh the little maid ripe for the
    strife?
Ah! Wind, and bah! Wind, what
    might have you now?
What can you do with that inno-
    cent brow?
Blow, Wind, and grow, Wind,
    and eddy and swirl,
But bring her to me, Wind,— my
    little March girl.

REMEMBERED

SHE sang, and I listened the
    whole song thro'.
  (It was sweet, so sweet, the
    singing.)

The stars were out and the moon
    it grew
From a wee soft glimmer way out
    in the blue
  To a bird thro' the heavens
    winging.

She sang, and the song trembled
    down to my breast,—
  (It was sweet, so sweet the
    singing.)
As a dove just out of its fledgling
    nest,
And, putting its wings to the first
    sweet test,
  Flutters homeward so wearily
    winging.

She sang and I said to my heart
    "That song,
  That was sweet, so sweet i' the
    singing,
Shall live with us and inspire us
    long,
And thou, my heart, shalt be brave
    and strong
  For the sake of those words
    a-winging.

The woman died and the song
    was still.
  (It was sweet, so sweet, the
    singing.)
But ever I hear the same low
    trill,
Of the song that shakes my heart
    with a thrill,
  And goes forever winging.

[121]

LOVE DESPOILED

As lone I sat one summer's day,
  With mien dejected, Love
    came by;
His face distraught, his locks
    astray,
  So slow his gait, so sad his eye,
  I hailed him with a pitying cry:

"Pray, Love, what has disturbed
    thee so?"
  Said I, amazed. "Thou seem'st
    bereft;
And see thy quiver hanging
    low,—
  What, not a single arrow left?
  Pray, who is guilty of this
    theft?"

Poor Love looked in my face and
    cried:
  "No thief were ever yet so bold
To rob my quiver at my side.
  But Time, who rules, gave ear
    to Gold,
  And all my goodly shafts are
    sold."

THE LAPSE

This poem must be done to-day;
  Then, I'll e'en to it.
I must not dream my time away,—
  I'm sure to rue it.
The day is rather bright, I know
  The Muse will pardon

My half-defection, if I go
  Into the garden.
It must be better working
    there,—
  I'm sure it's sweeter:
And something in the balmy air
  May clear my metre.

[*In the Garden.*]

Ah this is noble, what a sky!
  What breezes blowing!
The very clouds, I know not why,
  Call one to rowing.
The stream will be a parad'se
  To-day, I'll warrant.
I know the tide that's on the rise
  Will seem a torrent;
I know just how the leafy boughs
  Are all a-quiver;
I know how many skiffs and scows
  Are on the river.
I think I'll just go out awhile
  Before I write it;
When Nature shows us such a
    smile,
  We shouldn't slight it.
For Nature always makes desire
  By giving pleasure;
And so 't will help me put more
    fire
  Into my measure.

[*On the River.*]

The river's fine, I'm glad I came,
  That poem's teasing;
But health is better far than fame,
  Though cheques are pleasing.

[122]

PAUL LAURENCE DUNBAR

I don't know what I did it for,—
This air's a poppy.
I'm sorry for my editor,—
He'll get no copy!

THE WARRIOR'S PRAYER

LONG since, in sore distress, I
heard one pray,
"Lord, who prevailest with resistless might,
Ever from war and strife keep me
away,
My battles fight!"

I know not if I play the Pharisee,
And if my brother after all be
right;
But mine shall be the warrior's
plea to thee —
Strength for the fight.

I do not ask that thou shalt front
the fray,
And drive the warring foeman
from my sight;
I only ask, O Lord, by night, by
day,
Strength for the fight!

When foes upon me press, let me
not quail
Nor think to turn me into
coward flight.
I only ask, to make mine arms
prevail,
Strength for the fight!

Still let mine eyes look ever on the
foe,
Still let mine armor case me
strong and bright;
And grant me, as I deal each right-
eous blow,
Strength for the fight!

And when, at eventide, the fray
is done,
My soul to Death's bedchamber
do thou light,
And give me, be the field or lost
or won,
Rest from the fight!

FAREWELL TO ARCADY

WITH sombre mien, the Evening
gray
Comes nagging at the heels of
Day,
And driven faster and still faster
Before the dusky-mantled Master,
The light fades from her fearful
eyes,
She hastens, stumbles, falls, and
dies.

Beside me Amaryllis weeps;
The swelling tears obscure the
deeps
Of her dark eyes, as, mistily,
The rushing rain conceals the sea.
Here, lay my tuneless reed away,—
I have no heart to tempt a lay.

[123]

I scent the perfume of the rose
Which by my crystal fountain
    grows.
In this sad time, are roses blow-
    ing?
And thou, my fountain, art thou
    flowing,

While I who watched thy waters
    spring
Am all too sad to smile or sing?
Nay, give me back my pipe again,
It yet shall breathe this single
    strain:
    Farewell to Arcady!

THE VOICE OF THE BANJO

In a small and lonely cabin out
    of noisy traffic's way,
Sat an old man, bent and feeble,
    dusk of face, and hair of gray,
And beside him on the table, bat-
    tered, old, and worn as he,
Lay a banjo, droning forth this
    reminiscent melody:

"Night is closing in upon us,
    friend of mine, but don't be
    sad;
Let us think of all the pleasures
    and the joys that we have had.
Let us keep a merry visage, and be
    happy till the last,
Let the future still be sweetened
    with the honey of the past.

"For I speak to you of summer
    nights upon the yellow sand,
When the Southern moon was
    sailing high and silvering all
    the land;
And if love tales were not sacred,
    there's a tale that I could
    tell
Of your many nightly wanderings
    with a dusk and lovely belle.

"And I speak to you of care-free
    songs when labour's hour was
    o'er,
And a woman waiting for your
    step outside the cabin door,
And of something roly-poly that
    you took upon your lap,
While you listened for the stum-
    bling, hesitating words, 'Pap,
    pap.'

"I could tell you of a 'possum
    hunt across the wooded
    grounds,
I could call to mind the sweetness
    of the baying of the hounds,
You could lift me up and smelling
    of the timber that's in me,
Build again a whole green forest
    with the mem'ry of a tree.

"So the future cannot hurt us
    while we keep the past in
    mind,
What care I for trembling fingers,
    — what care you that you are
    blind?

[124]

Time may leave us poor and
stranded, circumstance may
make us bend;
But they 'll only find us mellower,
won't they, comrade? — in
the end."

THE STIRRUP CUP

COME, drink a stirrup cup with me,
Before we close our rouse.
You 're all aglow with wine, I
know:
The master of the house,
Unmindful of our revelry,
Has drowned the carking devil
care,
And slumbers in his chair.

Come, drink a cup before we start;
We 've far to ride to-night.
And Death may take the race we
make,
And check our gallant flight:
But even he must play his part,
And tho' the look he wears be
grim,
We 'll drink a toast to him!

For Death,— a swift old chap is
he,
And swift the steed He rides.
He needs no chart o'er main or
mart,
For no direction bides.
So, come, a final cup with me,
And let the soldiers' chorus
swell,—
To hell with care, to hell!

A CHOICE

THEY please me not — these
solemn songs
That hint of sermons covered up.
'T is true the world should heed
its wrongs,
But in a poem let me sup,
Not simples brewed to cure or
ease
Humanity's confessed disease,
But the spirit-wine of a singing
line,
Or a dew-drop in a honey cup!

THEN AND NOW

THEN

HE loved her, and through many
    years,
Had paid his fair devoted court,
Until she wearied, and with sneers
Turned all his ardent love to sport.

That night within his chamber
    lone,
He long sat writing by his bed
A note in which his heart made
    moan
For love; the morning found him
    dead.

NOW

Like him, a man of later day
Was jilted by the maid he sought,
And from her presence turned
    away,
Consumed by burning, bitter
    thought.

He sought his room to write — a
    curse
Like him before and die, I ween.
Ah no, he put his woes in verse,
And sold them to a magazine.

AT CHESHIRE CHEESE

WHEN first of wise old Johnson
    taught,
My youthful mind its homage
    brought,

And made the pond'rous crusty
    sage
The object of a noble rage.

Nor did I think (How dense we
    are!)
That any day, however far,
Would find me holding, unre-
    pelled,
The place that Doctor Johnson
    held!

But change has come and time has
    moved,
And now, applauded, unreproved,
I hold, with pardonable pride,
The place that Johnson occupied.

Conceit! Presumption! What is
    this?
You surely read my words amiss;
Like Johnson I,— a man of mind!
How could you ever be so blind?

No. At the ancient "Cheshire
    Cheese,"
Blown hither by some vagrant
    breeze,
To dignify my shallow wit,
In Doctor Johnson's seat I sit!

MY CORN-COB PIPE

Men may sing of their Havanas,
    elevating to the stars
The real or fancied virtues of their
    foreign-made cigars;

But I worship Nicotina at a dif-
    ferent sort of shrine,
And she sits enthroned in glory in
    this corn-cob pipe of mine.

It's as fragrant as the meadows
    when the clover is in bloom;
It's as dainty as the essence of the
    daintiest perfume;
It's as sweet as are the orchards
    when the fruit is hanging ripe,
With the sun's warm kiss upon
    them — is this corn-cob pipe.

Thro' the smoke about it clinging,
    I delight its form to trace,
Like an oriental beauty with a veil
    upon her face;
And my room is dim with vapour
    as a church when censers
    sway,
As I clasp it to my bosom — in a
    figurative way.

It consoles me in misfortune and
    it cheers me in distress,
And it proves a warm partaker of
    my pleasures in success;
So I hail it as a symbol, friendship's
    true and worthy type,
And I press my lips devoutly to
    my corn-cob pipe.

IN AUGUST

WHEN August days are hot an'
    dry,
When burning copper is the sky,

I'd rather fish than feast or fly
In airy realms serene and high.

I'd take a suit not made for looks,
Some easily digested books,
Some flies, some lines, some bait,
    some hooks,
Then would I seek the bays and
    brooks.

I would eschew mine every task,
In Nature's smiles my soul should
    bask,
And I methinks no more could
    ask,
Except — perhaps — one   little
    flask.

In case of accident, you know,
Or should the wind come on to
    blow,
Or I be chilled or capsized, so,
A flask would be the only go.

Then could I spend a happy
    time,—
A bit of sport, a bit of rhyme
(A bit of lemon, or of lime,
To make my bottle's contents
    prime).

When August days are hot an'
    dry,
I won't sit by an' sigh or die,
I'll get my bottle (on the sly)
And go ahead, and fish, and lie!

PAUL LAURENCE DUNBAR

THE DISTURBER

OH, what shall I do? I am wholly
    upset;
I am sure I 'll be jailed for a
    lunatic yet.
I 'll be out of a job — it 's the
    thing to expect
When I 'm letting my duty go by
    with neglect.
You may judge the extent and de-
    gree of my plight
When I 'm thinking all day and
    a-dreaming all night,
And a-trying my hand at a rhyme
    on the sly,
All on account of a sparkling eye.

There are those who say men
    should be strong, well-a-day!
But what constitutes strength in
    a man? Who shall say?
I am strong as the most when it
    comes to the arm.
I have aye held my own on the
    playground or farm.
And when I 've been tempted, I
    have n't been weak;
But now — why, I tremble to
    hear a maid speak.
I used to be bold, but now I 've
    grown shy,
And all on account of a sparkling
    eye.

There once was a time when my
    heart was devout,
But now my religion is open to
    doubt.
When parson is earnestly preach-
    ing of grace,
My fancy is busy with drawing
    a face,
Thro' the back of a bonnet most
    piously plain;
'I draw it, redraw it, and draw
    it again.'
While the songs and the sermon
    unheeded go by,—
All on account of a sparkling eye.

Oh, dear little conjurer, give o'er
    your wiles,
It is easy for you, you 're all
    blushes and smiles:
But, love of my heart, I am sorely
    perplexed;
I am smiling one minute and sigh-
    ing the next;
And if it goes on, I 'll drop hackle
    and flail,
And go to the parson and tell him
    my tale.
I warrant he 'll find me a cure
    for the sigh
That you 're aye bringing forth
    with the glance of your eye.

EXPECTATION

YOU 'LL be wonderin' whut 's de
    reason
    I 's a grinnin' all de time,
An' I guess you t'ink my sperits
    Mus' be feelin' mighty prime.

Well, I 'fess up, I is tickled
   As a puppy at his paws.
But you need n't think I 's crazy,
   I ain' laffin' 'dout a cause.

You 's a wonderin' too, I reckon,
   Why I does n't seem to eat,
An' I notice you a lookin'
   Lak you felt completely beat
When I 'fuse to tek de bacon,
   An' don' settle on de ham.
Don' you feel no feah erbout me,
   Jes' keep eatin', an' be ca'm.

Fu' I 's waitin' an' I 's watchin'
   'Bout a little t'ing I see —
D' othah night I 's out a walkin'
   An' I passed a 'simmon tree.
Now I 's whettin' up my hongry,
   An' I 's laffin' fit to kill,
Fu' de fros' done turned de 'sim-
     mons,
   An' de possum 's eat his fill.

He done go'ged hisse'f owdacious,
   An' he stayin' by de tree!
Don' you know, ol' Mistah Pos-
     sum
   Dat you gittin' fat fu' me?
'T ain't no use to try to 'spute it,
   'Case I knows you 's gittin'
     sweet
Wif dat 'simmon flavoh thoo you,
   So I 's waitin' fu' yo' meat.

An' some ebenin' me an Towsah
   Gwine to come an' mek a call,

We jes' drap in onexpected
   Fu' to shek yo' han', dat 's all.
Oh, I knows dat you 'll be tickled,
   Seems lak I kin see you smile,
So pu'haps I mought pu'suade you
   Fu' to visit us a while.

LOVER'S LANE

SUMMAH night an' sighin' breeze,
   'Long de lovah's lane;
Frien'ly, shadder-mekin' trees,
   'Long de lovah's lane.
White folks' wo'k all done up
     gran'—
Me an' 'Mandy han'-in-han'
Struttin' lak we owned de lan',
   'Long de lovah's lane.

Owl a-settin' 'side de road,
   'Long de lovah's lane,
Lookin' at us lak he knowed
   Dis uz lovah's lane.
Go on, hoot yo' mou'nful tune,
You ain' nevah loved in June,
An' come hidin' f'om de moon
   Down in lovah's lane.

Bush it ben' an' nod an' sway,
   Down in lovah's lane,
Try'n' to hyeah me whut I say
   'Long de lovah's lane.
But I whispahs low lak dis,
An' my 'Mandy smile huh bliss —
Mistah Bush he shek his fis',
   Down in lovah's lane.

Whut I keer ef day is long,
  Down in lovah's lane.
I kin allus sing a song
  'Long de lovah's lane.
An' de wo'ds I hyeah an' say
Meks up fu' de weary day
W'en I 's strollin' by de way,
  Down in lovah's lane.

An' dis t'ought will allus rise
  Down in lovah's lane;
Wondah whethah in de skies
  Dey 's a lovah's lane.
Ef dey ain't, I tell you true,
'Ligion do look mighty blue,
'Cause I do' know whut I 'd do
  'Dout a lovah's lane.

PROTEST

Who say mẏ hea't ain't true to
  you?
  Dey bettah heish dey mouf.
I knows I loves you thoo an' thoo
  In watah time er drouf.
I wush dese people 'd stop dey
  talkin',
Don't mean no mo' dan chicken's
  squawkin':
I guess I knows which way I 's
  walkin',
  I knows de norf f'om souf.

I does not love Elizy Brown,
  I guess I knows my min'.
You allus try to tek me down
  Wid evaht'ing you fin'.

Ef dese hyeah folks will keep on
  fillin'
Yo' haid wid nonsense, an' you 's
  willin'
I bet some day dey 'll be a killin'
  Somewhaih along de line.

O' cose I buys de gal ice-cream,
  Whut else I gwine to do?
I knows jes' how de t'ing 'u'd
  seem
  Ef I 'd be sho't wid you.,
On Sunday, you 's at chu'ch
  a-shoutin',
Den all de week you go 'roun'
  poutin'—
I 's mighty tiahed o' all dis
  doubtin',
  I tell you cause I 's true.

HYMN

O li'l' lamb out in de col',
De Mastah call you to de fol',
  O li'l' lamb!
He hyeah you bleatin' on de hill;
Come hyeah an' keep yo' mou'nin'
  still,
    O li'l' lamb!

De Mastah sen' de Shepud fo'f;
He wandah souf, he wandah no'f,
  O li'l' lamb!
He wandah eas', he wandah
  wes';
De win' a-wrenchin' at his breas',
  O li'l' lamb!

Oh, tell de Shepud whaih you hide;
He want you walkin' by his side,
　　O li'l' lamb!
He know you weak, he know you
　　so';
But come, don' stay away no mo',
　　O li'l' lamb!

An' af'ah while de lamb he hyeah
De Shepud's voice a-callin' cleah —
　　Sweet li'l' lamb!
He answah f'om de brambles thick,
" O Shepud, I 's a-comin' quick "—
　　O li'l' lamb!

LITTLE BROWN BABY

LITTLE brown baby wif spa'klin'
　　eyes,
　　Come to yo' pappy an' set on his
　　knee.
What you been doin', suh — mak-
　　in' san' pies?
　　Look at dat bib — you 's ez
　　du'ty ez me.
Look at dat mouf — dat 's mer-
　　lasses, I bet;
　　Come hyeah, Maria, an' wipe
　　off his han's.
Bees gwine to ketch you an' eat
　　you up yit,
　　Bein' so sticky an sweet — good-
　　ness lan's!

Little brown baby wif spa'klin'
　　eyes,
　　Who 's pappy's darlin' an'
　　who 's pappy's chile?

Who is it all de day nevah once
　　tries
　　Fu' to be cross, er once loses dat
　　smile?
Whah did you git dem teef? My,
　　you 's a scamp!
　　Whah did dat dimple come f'om
　　in yo' chin?
Pappy do' know you — I b'lieves
　　you 's a tramp;
　　Mammy, dis hyeah 's some ol'
　　straggler got in!

Let 's th'ow him outen de do' in
　　de san',
　　We do' want stragglers a-layin'
　　'roun' hyeah;
Let's gin him 'way to de big
　　buggah-man;
　　I know he 's hidin' erroun'
　　hyeah right neah.
Buggah-man, buggah-man, come
　　in de do',
　　Hyeah 's a bad boy you kin have
　　fu' to eat.
Mammy an' pappy do' want him
　　no mo',
　　Swaller him down f'om his haid
　　to his feet!

Dah, now, I t'ought dat you 'd
　　hug me up close.
　　Go back, ol' buggah, you sha'n't
　　have dis boy.
He ain't no tramp, ner no strag-
　　gler, of co'se;
　　He 's pappy's pa'dner an' play-
　　mate an' joy.

Come to you' pallet now — go to
    yo' res';
  Wisht you could allus know
    ease an' cleah skies;
Wisht you could stay jes' a chile
    on my breas'—
  Little brown baby wif spa'klin'
    eyes!

TIME TO TINKER 'ROUN'!

SUMMAH 's nice, wif sun a-shinin',
  Spring is good wif greens and
    grass,
An' dey 's some t'ings nice 'bout
    wintah,
  Dough hit brings de freezin'
    blas;
But de time dat is de fines',
  Whethah fiel's is green er brown,
Is w'en de rain 's a-po'in'
  An' dey 's time to tinker 'roun.

Den you men's de mule's ol'
    ha'ness,
  An' you men's de broken chair.
Hummin' all de time you 's wo'kin'
  Some ol' common kind o' air.
Evah now an' then you looks out,
  Tryin' mighty ha'd to frown,
But you cain't, you 's glad hit 's
    rainin',
  An' dey 's time to tinker 'roun'.

Oh, you 'ten's lak you so anxious
  Evah time it so't o' stops.

W'en hit goes on, den you reckon
  Dat de wet 'll he'p de crops.
But hit ain't de crops you 's aftah;
  You knows w'en de rain comes
    down
Dat 's hit 's too wet out fu'
    wo'kin',
  An' dey 's time to tinker roun'.

Oh, dey 's fun inside de co'n-crib,
  An' dey 's laffin' at de ba'n;
An' dey 's allus some one jokin',
  Er some one to tell a ya'n.
Dah 's a quiet in yo' cabin,
  Only fu' de rain's sof' soun';
So you 's mighty blessed happy
  W'en dey 's time to tinker
    'roun'!

THE REAL QUESTION

FOLKS is talkin' 'bout de money,
    'bout de silvah an' de gold;
All de time de season 's changin'
    an' de days is gittin' cold.
An' dey 's wond'rin' 'bout de
    metals, whethah we'll have
    one er two.
While de price o' coal is risin' an'
    dey 's two months' rent
    dat 's due.

Some folks says dat gold 's de only
    money dat is wuff de name,
Den de othahs rise an' tell 'em
    dat dey ought to be ashame,

[135]

An' dat silvah is de only thing to
    save us f'om de powah
Of de gold-bug ragin' 'roun' an'
    seekin' who he may de-
    vowah.

Well, you folks kin keep on
    shoutin' wif yo' gold er
    silvah cry,
But I tell you people hams is
    sceerce an' fowls is roostin'
    high.'
An' hit ain't de so't o' money dat
    is pesterin' my min',
But de question I want answehed 's
    how to get at any kin'!

JILTED

Lucy done gone back on me,
    Dat 's de way wif life.
Evaht'ing was movin' free,
    T'ought I had my wife.
Den some dahky comes along,
Sings my gal a little song,
Since den, evaht'ing 's gone wrong,
    Evah day dey 's strife.

Did n't answeh me to-day,
    W'en I called huh name,
Would you t'ink she 'd ac' dat way
    W'en I ain't to blame?
Dat 's de way dese women do,
W'en dey fin's a fellow true,
Den dey 'buse him thoo an' thoo;
    Well, hit 's all de same.

Somep'n's wrong erbout my lung,
    An' I 's glad hit 's so.
Doctah says 'at I 'll die young,
    Well, I wants to go!
Whut 's de use o' livin' hyeah,
W'en de gal you loves so deah,
Goes back on you clean an' cleah —
    I sh'd like to know?

THE NEWS

Whut dat you whisperin' keepin'
    f'om me?
Don't shut me out 'cause I 's ol'
    an' can't see.
Somep'n's gone wrong dat 's
    a-causin' you dread,—
Don't be afeared to tell — Whut!
    mastah dead?

Somebody brung de news early
    to-day,—
One of de sojers he led, do you
    say?
Did n't he foller whah ol' mastah
    lead?
How kin he live w'en his leadah
    is dead?

Let me lay down awhile, dah by
    his bed;
I wants to t'ink,— hit ain't cleah
    in my head: —
Killed while a-leadin' his men into
    fight,—
Dat 's whut you said, ain't it, did
    I hyeah right?

Mastah, my mastah, dead dah in
   de fiel'?
Lif' me up some,— dah, jes' so I
   kin kneel.
I was too weak to go wid him, dey
   said,
Well, now I 'll — fin' him — so —
   mastah is dead.

Yes, suh, I 's comin' ez fas' ez I
   kin,—
'T was kin' o' da'k, but hit 's
   lightah agin:
P'omised yo' pappy I 'd allus tek
   keer
Of you,— yes, mastah,— I 's follerin',— hyeah!

CHRISMUS ON THE PLAN-
TATION

It was Chrismus Eve, I mind hit
   fu' a mighty gloomy day —
Bofe de weathah an' de people —
   not a one of us was gay;
Cose you 'll t'ink dat 's mighty
   funny 'twell I try to mek hit
   cleah,
Fu' a da'ky 's allus happy when de
   holidays is neah.

But we was n't, fu' dat mo'nin'
   Mastah 'd tol' us we mus' go,
He 'd been payin' us sence freedom, but he could n't pay no
   mo';

He wa'n't nevah used to plannin'
   'fo' he got so po' an' ol',
So he gwine to give up tryin', an'
   de homestead mus' be sol'.

I kin see him stan'in' now erpon
   de step ez cleah ez day,
Wid de win' a-kind o' fondlin'
   thoo his haih all thin an'
   gray;
An' I 'membah how he trimbled
   when he said, " It 's ha'd fu'
   me,
Not to mek yo' Chrismus brightah,
   but I 'low it wa'n't to be."

All de women was a-cryin', an' de
   men, too, on de sly,
An' I noticed somep'n shinin' even
   in ol' Mastah's eye.
But we all stood still to listen ez
   ol' Ben come f'om de crowd
An' spoke up, a-try'n' to steady
   down his voice and mek it
   loud: —

"Look hyeah, Mastah, I 's been
   servin' you' fu' lo! dese many
   yeahs,
An' now, sence we 's got freedom
   an' you 's kind o' po', hit
   'pears
Dat you want us all to leave you
   'cause you don't t'ink you can
   pay.
Ef my membry has n't fooled me,
   seem dat whut I hyead you
   say.

"Er in othah wo'ds, you wants us
   to fu'git dat you 's been kin',
An' ez soon ez you is he'pless, we 's
   to leave you hyeah behin'.
Well, ef dat 's de way dis freedom
   ac's on people, white er black,
You kin jes' tell Mistah Lincum
   fu' to tek his freedom back.

"We gwine wo'k dis ol' plantation fu' whatevah we kin git,
Fu' I know hit did suppo't us, an'
   de place kin do it yit.
Now de land is yo's, de hands is
   ouahs, an' I reckon we 'll be
   brave,
An' we 'll bah ez much ez you do
   w'en we has to scrape an'
   save."

Ol' Mastah stood dah trimblin',
   but a-smilin' thoo his teahs,
An' den hit seemed jes' nachul-
   like, de place fah rung wid
   cheahs,
An' soon ez dey was quiet, some
   one sta'ted sof' an' low:
"Praise God," an' den we all
   jined in, "from whom all
   blessin's flow!"

Well, dey wasn't no use tryin',
   ouah min's was sot to stay,
An' po' ol' Mastah couldn't plead
   ner baig, ner drive us 'way,
An' all at once, hit seemed to us,
   de day was bright agin,
So evahone was gay dat night, an'
   watched de Chrismus in.

ANGELINA

WHEN de fiddle gits to singin' out
   a ol' Vahginny reel,
An' you 'mence to feel a ticklin' in
   yo' toe an' in yo' heel;
Ef you t'ink you got 'uligion an'
   you wants to keep it, too,
You jes' bettah tek a hint an' git
   yo'self clean out o' view.
Case de time is mighty temptin'
   when de chune is in de
   swing,
Fu' a darky, saint or sinner man,
   to cut de pigeon-wing.
An' you couldn't he'p f'om dancin' ef yo' feet was boun' wif
   twine,
When Angelina Johnson comes
   a-swingin' down de line.

Don't you know Miss Angelina?
   She 's de da'lin' of de place.
W'y, dey ain't no high-toned lady
   wif sich mannahs an' sich
   grace.
She kin move across de cabin, wif
   its planks all rough an' wo';
Jes' de same 's ef she was dancin'
   on ol' mistus' ball-room flo'.
Fact is, you do' see no cabin —
   evaht'ing you see look grand,
An' dat one ol' squeaky fiddle
   soun' to you jes' lak a ban';
Cotton britches look lak broadclof
   an' a linsey dress look fine,
When Angelina Johnson comes
   a-swingin' down de line.

[138]

Some folks say dat dancin 's sin-
    ful, an' de blessed Lawd, dey
    say,
Gwine to punish us fu' steppin'
    w'en we hyeah de music play.
But I tell you I don' b'lieve it, fu'
    de Lawd is wise and good,
An' he made de banjo's metal an'
    he made de fiddle's wood,
An' he made de music in dem, so
    I don' quite t'ink he 'll keer
Ef our feet keeps time a little to
    de melodies we hyeah.
W'y, dey 's somep'n' downright
    holy in de way our faces
    shine,
When Angelina Johnson comes
    a-swingin' down de line.

Angelina steps so gentle, Angelina
    bows so low,
An' she lif' huh sku't so dainty dat
    huh shoetop skacely show:
An' dem teef o' huh'n a-shinin', ez
    she tek you by de han'—
Go 'way, people, d' ain't anothah
    sich a lady in de lan'!
When she 's movin' thoo de figgers
    er a-dancin' by huhse'f,
Folks jes' stan' stock-still a-sta'-
    in', an' dey mos' nigh hol's
    dey bref;
An' de young mens, dey 's a-sayin',
    "I 's gwine mek dat damsel
    mine,"
When Angelina Johnson comes
    a-swingin' down de line.

FOOLIN' WID DE SEASONS

Seems lak folks is mighty curus
    In de way dey t'inks an' ac's.
Dey jes' spen's dey days a-mixin'
    Up de t'ings in almanacs.
Now, I min' my nex' do' neigh-
    bour,—
He 's a mighty likely man,
But he nevah t'inks o' nuffin
    'Ceptin' jes' to plot an' plan.

All de wintah he was plannin'
    How he 'd gethah sassafras
Jes' ez soon ez evah Springtime
    Put some greenness in de grass.
An' he 'lowed a little soonah
    He could stan' a coolah breeze
So 's to mek a little money
    F'om de sugah-watah trees.

In de summah, he 'd be waihin'
    Out de linin' of his soul,
Try 'n' ca'ci'late an' fashion
    How he 'd git his wintah coal;
An' I b'lieve he got his jedgement
    Jes' so tuckahed out an' thinned
Dat he t'ought a robin's whistle
    Was de whistle of de wind.

Why won't folks gin up dey plan-
    nin',
An' jes' be content to know
Dat dey 's gittin' all dat 's fu' dem
    In de days dat come an' go?
Why won't folks quit movin' for-
    rard?
    Ain't hit bettah jes' to stan'

An' be satisfied wid livin'
   In de season dat 's at han'?

Hit 's enough fu' me to listen
   W'en de birds is singin' 'roun',
'Dout a-guessin' whut 'll happen
   W'en de snow is on de groun'.
In de Springtime an' de summah,
   I lays sorrer on de she'f;
An' I knows ol' Mistah Wintah
   Gwine to hustle fu' hisse'f.

We been put hyeah fu' a pu'pose,
   But de questun dat has riz
An' made lots o' people diffah
   Is jes' whut dat pu'pose is.
Now, accordin' to my reas'nin',
   Hyeah 's de p'int whaih I 's
      arriv,
Sence de Lawd put life into us,
   We was put hyeah fu' to live!

MY SORT O' MAN

I DON'T believe in 'ristercrats
   An' never did, you see;
The plain ol' homelike sorter folks
   Is good enough fur me.
O' course, I don't desire a man
   To be too tarnal rough,
But then, I think all folks should
      know
   When they air nice enough.

Now there is folks in this here
      world,
   From peasant up to king,
Who want to be so awful nice
   They overdo the thing.
That 's jest the thing that makes
      me sick,
   An' quicker 'n a wink
I set it down that them same
      folks
   Ain't half so good 's you
      think.

I like to see a man dress nice,
   In clothes becomin' too;
I like to see a woman fix
   As women orter to do;
An' boys an' gals I like to see
   Look fresh an' young an'
      spry,—
We all must have our vanity
   An' pride before we die.

But I jedge no man by his
      clothes,—
   Nor gentleman nor tramp;
The man that wears the finest suit
   May be the biggest scamp,
An' he whose limbs air clad in rags
   That make a mournful sight,
In life's great battle may have
      proved
   A hero in the fight.

I don't believe in 'ristercrats;
   I like the honest tan
That lies upon the healthful cheek
   An' speaks the honest man;
I like to grasp the brawny hand
   That labor's lips have kissed,

For he who has not labored here
　　Life's greatest pride has
　　　　missed:

The pride to feel that yore own
　　　　strength
　　Has cleaved fur you the way
To heights to which you were not
　　　　born,
　　But struggled day by day.
What though the thousands sneer
　　　　an' scoff,
　　An' scorn yore humble birth?
Kings are but puppets; you are
　　　　king
　　By right o' royal worth.

The man who simply sits an' waits
　　Fur good to come along,
Ain't worth the breath that one
　　　　would take
　　To tell him he is wrong.
Fur good ain't flowin'·round this
　　　　world
　　Fur every fool to sup;
You 've got to put yore see-ers on,
　　An' go an' hunt it up.

Good goes with honesty, I say,
　　To honour an' to bless;
To rich an' poor alike it brings
　　A wealth o' happiness.
The 'ristercrats ain't got it all,
　Fur much to their su'prise,
That 's one of earth's most blessed
　　　　things
　　They can't monopolize.

POSSUM

Ef dey 's anyt'ing dat riles me
　　An' jes' gits me out o' hitch,
Twell I want to tek my coat off,
　　So 's to r'ar an' t'ar an' pitch,
Hit 's to see some ign'ant white
　　　　man
　　'Mittin' dat owdacious sin —
W'en he want to cook a possum
　　Tekin' off de possum's skin.

W'y dey ain't no use in talkin',
　　Hit jes' hu'ts me to de hea't
Fu' to see dem foolish people
　　Th'owin' 'way de fines' pa't.
W'y, dat skin is jes' ez tendah
An' ez juicy ez kin be;
I knows all erbout de critter —
　　Hide an' haih — don't talk to
　　　　me!

Possum skin is jes lak shoat skin;
　　Jes' you swinge an' scrope it
　　　　down,
Tek a good sha'p knife an' sco' it,
　　Den you bake it good an' brown.
Huh-uh! honey, you 's so happy
Dat yo' thoughts is 'mos' a sin
When you 's settin' dah a-chawin'
　　On dat possum's cracklin' skin.

White folks t'ink dey know 'bout
　　　　eatin',
　　An' I reckon dat dey do
Sometimes git a little idee
　　Of a middlin' dish er two;

[141]

But dey ain't a t'ing dey knows of
Dat I reckon cain't be beat
W'en we set down at de table
    To a unskun possum's meat!

ON THE ROAD

I 's boun' to see my gal to-night —
    Oh, lone de way, my dearie!
De moon ain't out, de stars ain't
        bright —
    Oh, lone de way, my dearie!
Dis hoss o' mine is pow'ful slow,
But when I does git to yo' do'
Yo' kiss 'll pay me back, an' mo',
    Dough lone de way, my dearie.

De night is skeery-lak an' still —
    Oh, lone de way, my dearie!
'Cept fu' dat mou'nful whippo'-
        will —
    Oh, lone de way, my dearie!
De way so long wif dis slow pace,
'T 'u'd seem to me lak savin' grace
Ef you was on a nearer place,
    Fu' lone de way, my dearie.

I hyeah de hootin' of de owl —
    Oh, lone de way, my dearie!
I wish dat watch-dog would n't
        howl —
    Oh, lone de way, my dearie!
An' evaht'ing, bofe right an' lef',
Seem p'int'ly lak hit put itse'f
In shape to skeer me half to def —
    Oh, lone de way, my dearie!

I whistles so 's I won't be feared —
    Oh lone de way, my dearie!
But anyhow I 's kin' o' skeered,
    Fu' lone de way, my dearie.
De sky been lookin' mighty glum,
But you kin mek hit lighten some,
Ef you 'll jes' say you 's glad I
        come,
    Dough lone de way, my dearie.

A DEATH SONG

LAY me down beneaf de willers in
        de grass,
Whah de branch 'll go a-singin' as
        it pass.
    An' w'en I 's a-layin' low,
    I kin hyeah it as it go
Singin', " Sleep, my honey, tek yo'
        res' at las'."

Lay me nigh to whah hit meks a
        little pool,
An' de watah stan's so quiet lak
        an' cool,
    Whah de little birds in spring,
    Ust to come an' drink an' sing,
An' de chillen waded on dey way
        to school.

Let me settle w'en my shouldahs
        draps dey load
Nigh enough to hyeah de noises in
        de road;
    Fu' I t'ink de las' long res'
    Gwine to soothe my sperrit bes'
Ef I 's layin' 'mong de t'ings I 's
        allus knowed.

[142]

PAUL LAURENCE DUNBAR

A BACK-LOG SONG

De axes has been ringin' in de
   woods de blessid day,
  An' de chips has been a-fallin'
    fa' an' thick;
Dey has cut de bigges' hick'ry dat
   de mules kin tote away,
  An' dey 's laid hit down and
    soaked it in de crik.
Den dey tuk hit to de big house an'
   dey piled de wood erroun'
  In de fiah-place f'om ash-flo' to
    de flue,
While ol' Ezry sta'ts de hymn dat
   evah yeah has got to soun'
  When de back-log fus' com-
    mence a-bu'nin' thoo.

Ol' Mastah is a-smilin' on de
   da'kies f'om de hall,
Ol' Mistus is a-stannin' in de do',
An' de young folks, males an'
   misses, is a-tryin', one an'
   all,
  Fu' to mek us feel hit 's Chris-
    mus time fu' sho'.
An' ouah hea'ts are full of pleasure,
   fu' we know de time is
   ouahs
  Fu' to dance er do jes' whut we
    wants to do.
An' dey ain't no ovahseer an' no
   othah kind o' powahs
  Dat kin stop us while dat log
    is bu'nin thoo.

Dey 's a-wokin' in de qua'tahs a-
   preparin' fu' de feas',
  So de little pigs is feelin' kind o'
    shy.
De chickens ain't so trus'ful ez
   dey was, to say de leas',
  An' de wise ol' hens is roostin'
    mighty high.
You could n't git a gobblah fu' to
   look you in de face —
  I ain't sayin' whut de tu'ky
    'spects is true;
But hit 's mighty dange'ous trav'-
   lin' fu' de critters on de
   place
  F'om de time dat log commence a
    bu'nin' thoo.

Some one 's tunin' up his fiddle
   dah, I hyeah a banjo's ring,
  An', bless me, dat 's de tootin' of
    a ho'n!
Now dey 'll evah one be runnin'
   dat has got a foot to fling,
  An' dey 'll dance an' frolic on
    f'om now 'twell mo'n.
Plunk de banjo, scrap de fiddle,
   blow dat ho'n yo' level bes',
  Keep yo' min' erpon de chune
    an' step it true.
Oh, dey ain't no time fu' stoppin'
   an' dey ain't no time fu'
   res',
  Fu' hit 's Chrismus an' de back-
    log 's bu'nin' thoo!

LULLABY

BEDTIME 's come fu' little boys.
  Po' little lamb.
Too tiahed out to make a noise,
  Po' little lamb.
You gwine t' have to-morrer sho'?
Yes, you tole me dat befo',
Don't you fool me, chile, no mo',
  Po' little lamb.

You been bad de livelong day,
  Po' little lamb.
Th'owin' stones an' runnin' 'way,
  Po' little lamb.
My, but you 's a-runnin' wil',
Look jes' lak some po' folks chile;
Mam' gwine whup you atter while,
  Po' little lamb.

Come hyeah! you mos' tiahed to
      def,
  Po' little lamb.
Played yo'se'f clean out o' bref,
  Po' little lamb.
See dem han's now — sich a sight!
Would you evah b'lieve dey's
      white?
Stan' still twell I wash 'em right,
  Po' little lamb.

Jes' cain't hol' yo' haid up straight,
  Po' little lamb.
Had n't oughter played so late,
  Po' little lamb.
Mammy do' know whut she 'd do,
Ef de chillun's all lak you;
  You 's a caution now fu' true,
  Po' little lamb.

Lay yo' haid down in my lap,
  Po' little lamb.
Y' ought to have a right good slap,
  Po' little lamb.
You been runnin' roun' a heap.
Shet dem eyes an' don't you peep,
Dah now, dah now, go to sleep,
  Po' little lamb.

THE PHOTOGRAPH

SEE dis pictyah in my han'?
  Dat 's my gal;
Ain't she purty? goodness lan'!
  Huh name Sal.
Dat 's de very way she be —
Kin' o' tickles me to see
Huh a-smilin' back at me.

She sont me dis photygraph
  Jes' las' week;
An' aldough hit made me laugh —
  My black cheek
Felt somethin' a-runnin' queer;
Bless yo' soul, it was a tear
Jes' f'om wishin' she was here.

Often when I 's all alone
  Layin' here,
I git t'inkin' 'bout my own
  Sallie dear;
How she say dat I 's huh beau,
An' hit tickles me to know
Dat de gal do love me so.

Some bright day I 's goin' back,
  Fo' de la!

PAUL LAURENCE DUNBAR

An' ez sho' 's my face is black,
  Ax huh pa
Fu' de blessed little miss
Who 's a-smilin' out o dis
Pictyah, lak she wan'ed a kiss!

JEALOUS

Hyeah come Cæsar Higgins,
Don't he think he 's fine?
Look at dem new riggin's
Ain't he tryin' to shine?
Got a standin' collar
An' a stove-pipe hat,
I 'll jes' bet a dollar
Some one gin him dat.

Don't one o' you mention,
Nothin' 'bout his cloes,
Don't pay no attention,
Er let on you knows
Dat he 's got 'em on him,
Why, 't 'll mek him sick,
Jes go on an' sco'n him,
My, ain't dis a trick!

Look hyeah, whut 's he doin'
Lookin' t' othah way?
Dat ere move 's a new one,
Some one call him, " Say! "
Can't you see no pusson —
Puttin' on you' airs,
Sakes alive, you 's wuss'n
Dese hyeah millionaires.

Need n't git so flighty,
Case you got dat suit.
Dem cloes ain't so mighty,—

Second hand to boot,
I 's a-tryin' to spite you!
Full of jealousy!
Look hyeah, man, I 'll fight
  you,
Don't you fool wid me!

PARTED

De breeze is blowin' 'cross de bay.
  My lady, my lady;
De ship hit teks me far away,
  My lady, my lady;
Ole Mas' done sol' me down de
    stream;
Dey tell me 't ain't so bad 's hit
    seem,
  My lady, my lady.

O' co'se I knows dat you 'll be
    true,
  My lady, my lady;
But den I do' know whut to do,
  My lady, my lady;
I knowed some day we 'd have to
    pa't,
But den hit put' nigh breaks my
    hea't,
  My lady, my lady.

De day is long, de night is black,
  My lady, my lady;
I know you 'll wait twell I come
    back,
  My lady, my lady;
I 'll stan' de ship, I 'll stan' de
    chain,

[145]

But I 'll come back, my darlin'
    Jane,
    My lady, my lady.

Jes' wait, jes' b'lieve in whut I
    say,
    My lady, my lady;
D' ain't nothin' dat kin keep me
    'way,
    My lady, my lady;
A man 's a man, an' love is love;
God knows ouah hea'ts, my little
    dove;
He 'll he'p us f'om his th'one
    above,
    My lady, my lady.

TEMPTATION

I DONE got 'uligion, honey, an' I 's
    happy ez a king;
Evahthing I see erbout me 's jes'
    lak sunshine in de spring;
An' it seems lak I do' want to do
    anothah blessid thing
But jes' run an' tell de neighbours,
    an' to shout an' pray an'
    sing.

I done shuk my fis' at Satan, an'
    I 's gin de worl' my back;
I do' want no hendrin' causes now
    a-both'rin' in my track;
Fu' I 's on my way to glory, an' I
    feels too sho' to miss.
W'y, dey ain't no use in sinnin'
    when 'uligion 's sweet ez dis.

Talk erbout a man backslidin' w'en
    he 's on de gospel way;
No, suh, I done beat de debbil, an'
    Temptation 's los' de day.
Gwine to keep my eyes right
    straight up, gwine to shet my
    eahs, an' see
Whut ole projick Mistah Satan 's
    gwine to try to wuk on me.

Listen, whut dat soun' I hyeah
    dah? 'tain't no one commence
    to sing;
It 's a fiddle; git erway dah! don'
    you hyeah dat blessid
    thing?
W'y, dat 's sweet ez drippin' honey,
    'cause, you knows, I draws de
    bow,
An' when music 's sho' 'nough
    music, I 's de one dat 's sho'
    to know.

W'y, I 's done de double shuffle,
    twell a body could n't res',
Jes' a-hyeahin' Sam de fiddlah play
    dat chune his level bes';
I could cut a mighty caper, I could
    gin a mighty fling
Jes' right now, I 's mo' dan suttain
    I could cut de pigeon wing.

Look hyeah, whut 's dis I 's been
    sayin'? whut on urf 's tuk
    holt o' me?
Dat ole music come nigh runnin'
    my 'uligion up a tree!

PAUL LAURENCE DUNBAR

Cleah out wif dat dah ole fiddle,
  don' you try dat trick agin;
Did n't think I could be tempted,
  but you lak to made me sin!

POSSUM TROT

I 've journeyed 'roun' consid'able,
  a-seein' men an' things,
An' I 've learned a little of the
  sense that meetin' people
  brings;
But in spite of all my travellin',
  an' of all I think I know,
I 've got one notion in my head,
  that I can't git to go;
An' it is that the folks I meet in
  any other spot
Ain't half so good as them I
  knowed back home in Possum
  Trot.

I know you 've never heerd the
  name, it ain't a famous
  place,
An' I reckon ef you 'd search the
  map you could n't find a trace
Of any sich locality as this I 've
  named to you;
But never mind, I know the place,
  an' I love it dearly too.
It don't make no pretensions to
  bein' great or fine,
The circuses don't come that way,
  they ain't no railroad line.
It ain't no great big city, where
  the schemers plan an' plot,

But jest a little settlement, this
  place called Possum Trot.

But don't you think the folks that
  lived in that outlandish place
Were ignorant of all the things
  that go for sense or grace.
Why, there was Hannah Dyer, you
  may search this teemin' earth
An' never find a sweeter girl, er
  one o' greater worth;
An' Uncle Abner Williams, a-
  leanin' on his staff,
It seems like I kin hear him talk,
  an' hear his hearty laugh.
His heart was big an' cheery as a
  sunny acre lot,
Why, that 's the kind o' folks we
  had down there at Possum
  Trot.

Good times? Well, now, to suit
  my taste,— an' I 'm some hard
  to suit,—
There ain't been no sich pleasure
  sence, an' won't be none to
  boot,
With huskin' bees in Harvest time,
  an' dances later on,
An' singin' school, an taffy pulls,
  an' fun from night till
  dawn.
Revivals come in winter time, bap-
  tizin's in the spring,
You 'd ought to seen those people
  shout, an' heerd 'em pray an'
  sing;

[147]

You 'd ought to 've heard ole Parson Brown a-throwin' gospel
shot
Among the saints an' sinners in
the days of Possum Trot.

We live up in the city now, my
wife was bound to come;
I hear aroun' me day by day the
endless stir an' hum.
I reckon that it done me good, an'
yet it done me harm,
That oil was found so plentiful
down there on my ole farm.
We 've got a new-styled preacher,
our church is new-styled too,
An' I 've come down from what I
knowed to rent a cushioned
pew.
But often when I 'm settin' there,
it 's foolish, like as not,
To think of them ol' benches in
the church at Possum Trot.

I know that I 'm ungrateful, an'
sich thoughts must be a sin,
But I find myself a wishin' that
the times was back agin.
With the huskin's an' the frolics,
an' the joys I used to know,
When I lived at the settlement, a
dozen years ago.
I don't feel this way often, I 'm
scarcely ever glum,
For life has taught me how to take
her chances as they come.
But now an' then my mind goes
back to that ol' buryin' plot,

That holds the dust of some I
loved, down there at Possum
Trot.

DELY

Jes' lak toddy wahms you thoo'
  Sets yo' haid a reelin',
Meks you ovah good and new,
  Dat 's de way I 's feelin'.
Seems to me hit's summah time,
  Dough hit 's wintah reely,
I 's a feelin' jes' dat prime —
  An' huh name is Dely.

Dis hyeah love 's a cu'rus thing,
  Changes 'roun' de season,
Meks you sad or meks you sing,
  'Dout no urfly reason.
Sometimes I go mopin' 'roun',
  Den agin I 's leapin';
Sperits allus up an' down
  Even when I 's sleepin'.

Fu' de dreams comes to me den,
  An' dey keeps me pitchin',
Lak de apple dumplin's w'en
  Bilin' in de kitchen.
Some one sot to do me hahm,
  Tryin' to ovahcome me,
Ketchin' Dely by de ahm
  So 's to tek huh f'om me.

Mon, you bettah b'lieve I fights
  (Dough hit 's on'y seemin');
I 's a hittin' fu' my rights
  Even w'en I 's dreamin'.

[148]

But I 'd let you have 'em all,
  Give 'em to you freely,
Good an' bad ones, great an' small,
  So 's·you leave me Dely.

Dely got dem meltin' eyes,
  Big an' black an' tendah.
Dely jes' a lady-size,
  Delikit an' slendah.
Dely brown ez brown kin be
  An' huh haih is curly;
Oh, she look so sweet to me,—
  Bless de precious girlie!

Dely brown ez brown kin be,
  She ain' no mullatter;
She pure cullud,— don' you see
  Dat 's jes' whut 's de mattah?
Dat 's de why I love huh so,
  D' ain't no mix about huh,
Soon 's you see huh face you know
  D' ain't no chanst to doubt huh.

Folks dey go to chu'ch an' pray
  So 's to git a blessin'.
Oomph, dey bettah come my way,
  Dey could lu'n a lesson.
Sabbaf day I don' go fu',
  Jes' to see my pigeon;
I jes' sets an' looks at huh,
  Dat 's enuff 'uligion.

BREAKING THE CHARM

CAUGHT Susanner whistlin'; well,
It 's most nigh too good to tell.
'Twould 'a' b'en too good to see
Ef it had n't b'en fur me,

Comin' up so soft an' sly
That she didn' hear me nigh.
I was pokin' 'round that day,
An' ez I come down the way,
First her whistle strikes my ears,—
Then her gingham dress appears;
So with soft step up I slips.
Oh, them dewy, rosy lips!
Ripe ez cherries, red an' round,
Puckered up to make the sound.
She was lookin' in the spring,
Whistlin' to beat anything,—
"Kitty Dale" er "In the Sweet."
I was jest so mortal beat
That I can't quite ricoleck
What the toon was, but I 'speck
'T was some hymn er other, fur
Hymny things is jest like her.
Well she went on fur awhile
With her face all in a smile,
An' I never moved, but stood
Stiller 'n a piece o' wood —
Would n't wink ner would n't stir,
But a-gazin' right at her,
Tell she turns an' sees me — my!
Thought at first she 'd try to fly.
But she blushed an' stood her
  ground.
Then, a-slyly lookin' round,
She says: "Did you hear me,
  Ben?"
"Whistlin' woman, crowin' hen,"
Says I, lookin' awful stern.·
Then the red commenced to burn
In them cheeks o' hern. Why, la!
Reddest red you ever saw —
Pineys wa'n't a circumstance.

You'd 'a' noticed in a glance
She was pow'rful shamed an'
    skeart;
But she looked so sweet an' peart,
That a idee struck my head;
So I up an' slowly said:
"Woman whistlin' brings shore
    harm,
Jest one thing 'll break the charm."
"And what's that?" "Oh,
    my!" says I, ·
"I don't like to tell you."
    "Why?"
Says Susanner. "Well, you see
It would kinder fall on me."
Course I knowed that she'd in-
    sist,—
So I says: "You must be kissed
By the man that heard you whistle;
Everybody says that this 'll
Break the charm and set you free
From the threat'nin' penalty."
She was blushin' fit to kill,
But she answered, kinder still:
"I don't want to have no harm,
Please come, Ben, an' break the
    charm."
Did I break that charm?—oh,
    well,
There's some things I must n't
    tell.
I remember, afterwhile,
Her a-sayin' with a smile:
"Oh, you quit,— you sassy dunce,
You jest caught me whistlin' *once*."
Ev'ry sence that when I hear
Some one whistlin' kinder clear,

I most break my neck to see
Ef it's Susy; but, dear me,
I jest find I've b'en to chase
Some blamed boy about the place.
Dad's b'en noticin' my way,
An' last night I heerd him say:
"We must send fur Dr. Glenn,
Mother; somethin's wrong with
    Ben!"

HUNTING SONG

Tek a cool night, good an'
    cleah,
  Skiff o' snow upon de groun';
Jes' 'bout fall-time o' de yeah
  W'en de leaves is dry an
    brown;
Tek a dog an' tek a axe,
  Tek a lantu'n in yo' han',
Step light whah de switches
    cracks,
  Fu' dey's huntin' in de lan'.
Down thoo de valleys an' ovah de
    hills,
  Into de woods whah de 'simmon-
    tree grows,
Wakin' an' skeerin' de po' whip-
    po'wills,
  Huntin' fu' coon an' fu' 'possum
    we goes.

Blow dat ho'n dah loud an'
    strong,
  Call de dogs an' da'kies neah;
Mek its music cleah an' long,
  So de folks at home kin hyeah.

Blow it twell de hills an' trees
   Sen's de echoes tumblin' back;
Blow it twell de back'ard breeze
   Tells de folks we 's on de
      track.
Coons is a-ramblin' an' 'possums
   is out;
   Look at dat dog; you could set
      on his tail!
Watch him now — steady,— min'
      — what you 's about,
   Bless me, dat animal 's got on
      de trail!

Listen to him ba'kin now!
   Dat means bus'ness, sho 's you
      bo'n;
Ef he 's struck de scent I 'low
   Dat ere 'possum 's sholy gone.
Knowed dat dog fu' fo'teen
   yeahs,
   An' I nevah seed him fail
W'en he sot dem flappin' eahs
   An' went off upon a trail.
Run, Mistah 'Possum, an' run,
   Mistah Coon,
   No place is safe fu' yo' ramblin'
      to-night;
Mas' gin' de lantu'n an' God gin
   de moon,
   An' a long hunt gins a good ap-
      petite.

Look hyeah, folks, you hyeah
   dat change?
   Dat ba'k is sha'per dan de res'.
Dat ere soun' ain't nothin'
   strange,—

Dat dog 's talked his level
   bes'.
Somep'n' 's treed, I know de
   soun'.
   Dah now,— wha 'd I tell
      you? see!
Dat ere dog done run him
   down;
   Come hyeah, he'p cut down
      dis tree.
Ah, Mistah 'Possum, we got you
   at las'—
   Need n't play daid, laying dah
      on de groun';
Fros' an' de 'simmons has made
   you grow fas',—
   Won't he be fine when he 's
      roasted up brown!

A LETTER

Dear Miss Lucy: I been t'inkin'
   dat I 'd write you long fo' dis,
But dis writin' 's mighty tejous, an'
   you know jes' how it is.
But I 's got a little lesure, so I teks
   my pen in han'
Fu' to let you know my feelin's
   since I retched dis furrin' lan'.
I 's right well, I 's glad to tell you
   (dough dis climate ain't to
   blame),
An' I hopes w'en dese lines reach
   you, dat dey 'll fin' yo' se'f de
   same.
Cose I 'se feelin kin' o' homesick
   — dat 's ez nachul ez kin be,

W'en a feller's mo'n th'ee thou-
    sand miles across dat awful
    sea.
·(Don't you let nobidy fool you
    'bout de ocean bein' gran';
If you want to see de billers, you
    jes' view dem f'om de lan'.)
'Bout de people? We been t'inkin'
    dat all white folks was alak;
But dese Englishmen is diffunt,
    an' dey's curus fu' a fac'.
Fust, dey's heavier an' redder in
    dey make-up an' dey looks,
An' dey don't put salt nor pepper
    in a blessed t'ing dey cooks!
W'en dey gin you good ol' tu'nips,
    ca'ots, pa'snips, beets, an'
    sich,
Ef dey ain't some one to tell you,
    you cain't 'stinguish which is
    which.
W'en I t'ought I's eatin' chicken
    — you may b'lieve dis hyeah's
    a lie —
But de waiter beat me down dat I
    was eatin' rabbit pie.
An' dey'd t'ink dat you was crazy
    — jes' a reg'lar ravin' loon,
Ef you'd speak erbout a 'possum
    or a piece o' good ol' coon.
O, hit's mighty nice, dis trav'lin',
    an' I's kin o' glad I come.
But, I reckon, now I's willin' fu'
    to tek my way back home.
I done see de Crystal Palace, an'
    I's hyeahd dey string-band
    play,

But I has n't seen no banjos layin'
    nowhahs roun' dis way.
Jes' gin ol' Jim Bowles a banjo,
    an' he'd not go very fu',
'Fo' he'd outplayed all dese fid-
    dlers, wif dey flourish and
    dey stir. ·
Evahbiddy dat I's met wif has
    been ·monst'ous kin an' good;
But I t'ink I'd lak it better to be
    down in Jones's wood,
Where we ust to have sich frolics,
    Lucy, you an' me an' Nelse,
Dough my appetite 'ud call me, ef
    dey was n't nuffin else.
I'd jes' lak to have some sweet-
    pertaters roasted in de skin;
I's a-longin' fu' my chittlin's an'
    my mustard greens ergin;
I's a-wishin' fu' some buttermilk,
    an' co'n braid, good an'
    brown,
An' a drap o' good ol' bourbon fu'
    to wash my feelin's down!
An' I's comin' back to see you jes'
    as ehly as I kin,
So you better not go spa'kin' wif
    dat wuffless scoun'el Quin!
Well, I reckon, I mus' close now;
    write ez soon's dis reaches
    you;
Gi' my love to Sister Mandy an'
    to Uncle Isham, too.
Tell de folks I sen' 'em howdy;
    gin a kiss to pap an' mam;
Closin' I is, deah Miss Lucy,
    Still Yo' Own True-Lovin' SAM.

P. S. Ef you cain't mek out dis
   letter, lay it by erpon de she'f,
An' when I git home, I 'll read
   it, darlin', to you my own se'f.

CHRISMUS IS A-COMIN'

BONES a-gittin' achy,
Back a-feelin' col',
Han's a-growin' shaky,
Jes' lak I was ol'.
Fros' erpon de meddah
Lookin' mighty white;
Snowdraps lak a feddah
Slippin' down at night.
Jes' keep t'ings a-hummin'
Spite o' fros' an' showahs,
Chrismus is a-comin'
An' all de week is ouahs.

Little mas' a-axin',
" Who is Santy Claus? "
Meks it kin' o' taxin'
Not to brek de laws.
Chillun 's pow'ful tryin'
To a pusson's grace
W'en dey go a pryin'
Right on th'oo you' face
Down ermong yo' feelin's;
Jes' 'pears lak dat you
Got to change you' dealin's
So 's to tell 'em true.

An' my pickaninny —
Dreamin' in his sleep!
Come hyeah, Mammy Jinny,
Come an' tek a peep.

Ol' Mas' Bob an' Missis
In dey house up daih
Got no chile lak dis is,
D' ain't none anywhaih.
Sleep, my little lammy,
Sleep, you little limb,
He do' know whut mammy
Done saved up fu' him.

Dey 'll be banjo pickin',
Dancin' all night thoo.
Dey 'll be lots o' chicken,
Plenty tukky, too.
Drams to wet yo' whistles
So 's to drive out chills.
Whut I keer fu' drizzles
Fallin' on de hills?
Jes' keep t'ings a-hummin'
Spite o' col' an' showahs,
Chrismus day 's a-comin',
An' all de week is ouah•

A CABIN TALE

THE YOUNG MASTER ASKS FOR A STORY

WHUT you say, dah? huh, uh!
   chile,
You 's enough to dribe me wile.
Want a sto'y; jes' hyeah dat!
Whah' 'll I git a sto'y at?
Di'n' I tell you th'ee las' night?
Go 'way, honey, you ain't right.
I got somep'n' else to do,
'Cides jes' tellin' tales to you.
Tell you jes' one? Lem me see
Whut dat one 's a-gwine to be.

[153]

When you 's ole, yo membry fails;
Seems lak I do' know no tales.
Well, set down dah in dat cheer,
Keep still ef you wants to hyeah.
Tek dat chin up off yo' han's,
Set up nice now. Goodness lan's!
Hol' yo'se'f up lak yo' pa.
Bet nobidy evah saw
Him scrunched down lak you was
   den —
High-tone boys meks high-tone
   men.

   Once dey was a ole black bah,
Used to live 'roun' hyeah some-
   whah
In a cave. He was so big
He could ca'y off a pig
Lak you picks a chicken up,
Er yo' leetles' bit o' pup.
An' he had two gread big eyes,
Jes' erbout a saucer's size.
Why, dey looked lak balls o' fiah
Jumpin' 'roun' erpon a wiah
W'en dat bah was mad; an' laws!
But you ought to seen his paws!
Did I see 'em? How you 'spec
I 's a-gwine to ricollec'
Dis hyeah ya'n I 's try'n' to spin
Ef you keeps on puttin' in?
You keep still an' don't you cheep
Less I 'll sen' you off to sleep.
Dis hyeah bah 'd go trompin'
   'roun'
Eatin' evahthing he foun';
No one could n't have a fa'm
But dat bah 'u'd do' em ha'm;

And dey could n't ketch de scamp.
Anywhah he wan'ed to tramp.
Dah de scoun'el 'd mek his track,
Do his du't an' come on back.
He was sich a sly ole limb,
Traps was jes' lak fun to him.

   Now, down neah whah Mistah
     Bah
Lived, dey was a weasel dah;
But dey was n't fren's a-tall
Case de weasel was so small.
An' de bah 'u'd, jes' fu' sass,
Tu'n his nose up w'en he 'd pass.
Weasels 's small o' cose, but my!
Dem air animiles is sly.
So dis hyeah one says, says he,
" I 'll jes' fix dat bah, you see."
So he fixes up his plan
An' hunts up de fa'merman.
When de fa'mer see him come,
He 'mence lookin' mighty glum,
An' he ketches up a stick;
But de weasel speak up quick:
" Hol' on, Mistah Fa'mer man,
I wan' 'splain a little plan.
Ef you waits, I 'll tell you whah
An' jes' how to ketch ol' Bah.
But I tell yow now you mus'
Gin me one fat chicken fus'."
Den de man he scratch his haid,
Las' he say, " I 'll mek de trade."
So de weasel et his hen,
Smacked his mouf and says,
   " Well, den,
Set yo' trap an' bait ternight,
An' I 'll ketch de bah all right."

Den he ups an' goes to see
Mistah Bah, an' says, says he:
"Well, fren' Bah, we *ain't* been
    fren's,
But ternight ha'd feelin' 'en's.
Ef you ain't too proud to steal,
We kin git a splendid meal.
Cose I would n't come to you,
But it mus' be done by two;
Hit 's a trap, but we kin beat
All dey tricks an' git de meat."
"Cose I 's wif you," says de bah,
"Come on, weasel, show me
    whah."
Well, dey trots erlong ontwell
Dat air meat beginned to smell
In de trap. Den weasel say:
"Now you put yo' paw dis way
While I hol' de spring back so,
Den you grab de meat an' go."
Well, de bah he had to grin
Ez he put his big paw in,
Den he juked up; but — kerbing!
Weasel done let go de spring.
"Dah now," says de weasel, "dah,
I done cotched you, Mistah Bah!"
O, dat bah did sno't and spout,
Try'n' his bestes' to git out,
But de weasel say, "Goo'-bye!
Weasel small, but weasel sly."
Den he tu'ned his back an' run
Tol' de fa'mer whut he done.
So de fa'mer come down dah,
Wif a axe and killed de bah.

    Dah now, ain't dat sto'y fine?
Run erlong now, nevah min'.

Want some mo', you rascal, you?
No, suh! no, suh! dat 'll do.

———

AT CANDLE-LIGHTIN'
TIME

WHEN I come in f'om de co'n-fiel'
    aftah wo'kin' ha'd all day,
It 's amazin' nice to fin' my sup-
    pah all erpon de way;
An' it 's nice to smell de coffee
    bubblin' ovah in de pot,
An' it 's fine to see de meat a-
    sizzlin' teasin'-lak an' hot.

But when suppah-time is ovah, an'
    de t'ings is cleahed away;
Den de happy hours dat foller are
    de sweetes' of de day.
When my co'ncob pipe is sta'ted,
    an' de smoke is drawin'
    prime,
My ole 'ooman says, "I reckon,
    Ike, it 's candle-lightin' time."

Den de chillun snuggle up to me,
    an' all commence to call,
"Oh, say, daddy, now it 's time
    to mek de shadders on de
    wall."
So I puts my han's togethah —
    evah daddy knows de way, —
An' de chillun snuggle closer roun'
    ez I begin to say: —

"Fus' thing, hyeah come Mistah
    Rabbit; don' you see him wo'k
    his eahs?

Huh, uh! dis mus' be a donkey,—
    look, how innercent he 'pears!
Dah 's de ole black swan a-swim-
    min'— ain't she got a' awful
    neck?
Who 's dis feller dat 's a-comin'?
    Why, dat 's ole dog Tray, I
    'spec'!"

Dat 's de way I run on, tryin' fu'
    to please 'em all I can;
Den I hollahs, "Now be keerful
    — dis hyeah las' 's de buga-
    man!"
An' dey runs an' hides dey faces;
    dey ain't skeered — dey 's let-
    tin' on:
But de play ain't raaly ovah twell
    dat buga-man is gone.

So I jes' teks up my banjo, an' I
    plays a little chune,
An' you see dem haids come peepin'
    out to listen mighty soon.
Den my wife says, "Sich a pappy
    fu' to give you sich a fright!
Jes, you go to baid, an' leave him:
    say yo' prayers an' say good-
    night."

WHISTLING SAM

I HAS hyeahd o' people dancin' an'
    I 's hyeahd o' people singin'.
An' I 's been 'roun' lots of othahs
    dat could keep de banjo
    ringin';

But of all de whistlin' da'kies dat
    have lived an' died since Ham,
De whistlin'est I evah seed was
    ol' Ike Bates's Sam.
In de kitchen er de stable, in de
    fiel' er mowin' hay,
You could hyeah dat boy a-whis-
    tlin' pu'ty nigh a mile er-
    way,—
Puck'rin' up his ugly features
    'twell you could n't see his
    eyes,
Den you 'd hyeah a soun' lak dis
    un f'om dat awful puckah
    rise:

When dey had revival meetin' an'
    de Lawd's good grace was
    flowin'
On de groun' dat needed wat'rin'
    whaih de seeds of good was
    growin',
While de othahs was a-singin' an'
    a-shoutin' right an' lef',
You could hyeah dat boy a-whis-
    tlin' kin' o' sof' beneaf his
    bref:

PAUL LAURENCE DUNBAR

At de call fu' colo'ed soldiers,
Sam enlisted 'mong de res'
Wid de blue o' Gawd's great ahmy
wropped about his swellin'
breas',
An' he laffed an' whistled loudah
in his youfful joy an' glee
Dat de govament would let him
he'p to mek his people free.
Daih was lots o' ties to bin' him,
pappy, mammy, an' his
Dinah,—
Dinah, min' you, was his sweet-
hea't, an' dey was n't nary
finah;
But he lef' 'em all, I tell you, lak
a king he ma'ched away,
Try'n' his level bes' to whistle,
happy, solemn, choky, gay:

To de front he went an' bravely
fought de foe an' kep' his
sperrit,
An' his comerds said his whistle
made 'em strong when dey
could hyeah it.
When a saber er a bullet cut some
frien' o' his'n down,
An' de time 'u'd come to trench
him an' de boys 'u'd gethah
'roun',

An' dey could n't sta't a hymn-
tune, mebbe none o' dem
'u'd keer,
Sam 'u'd whistle "Sleep in Jesus,"
an' he knowed de Mastah 'd
hyeah.
In de camp, all sad discouraged,
he would cheer de hea'ts of
all,
When above de soun' of labour
dey could hyeah his whistle
call:

When de cruel wah was ovah an'
de boys come ma'chin' back,
Dey was shouts an' cries an'
blessin's all erlong dey happy
track,
An' de da'kies all was happy; souls
an' bodies bofe was freed.
Why, hit seemed lak de Redeemah
mus' 'a' been on earf indeed.
Dey was gethahed all one evenin'
jes' befo' de cabin do',
When dey hyeahd somebody
whistlin' kin' o' sof' an' sweet
an' low.
Dey could n't see de whistlah, but
de hymn was cleah and
ca'm,
An' dey all stood daih a-listenin'
ontwell Dinah shouted,
"Sam!"

An' dey seed a little da'ky way off
   yandah thoo de trees
Wid his face all in a puckah mekin'
   jes' sich soun's ez dese:

HOW LUCY BACKSLID

De times is mighty stirrin' 'mong
   de people up ouah way,
Dey 'sputin' an' dey argyin' an'
   fussin' night an' day;
An' all dis monst'ous trouble dat
   hit meks me tiahed to tell
Is 'bout dat Lucy Jackson dat was
   sich a mighty belle.

She was de preachah's favoured,
   an' he tol' de chu'ch one
   night
Dat she travelled thoo de cloud o'
   sin a-bearin' of a light;
But, now, I 'low he t'inkin' dat she
   mus' 'a' los' huh lamp,
Case Lucy done backslided an' dey
   trouble in de camp.

Huh daddy wants to beat huh, but
   huh mammy daihs him to,
Fu' she lookin' at de question f'om
   a ooman's pint o' view;
An' she say dat now she would n't
   have it diff'ent ef she could;
Dat huh darter only acted jes' lak
   any othah would.

Cose you know w'en women argy,
   dey is mighty easy led
By dey hea'ts an' don't go foolin'
   'bout de reasons of de haid.
So huh mammy laid de law down
   (she ain' reckernizin' wrong),
But you got to mek erlowance fu'
   de cause dat go along.

Now de cause dat made Miss Lucy
   fu' to th'ow huh grace away·
I 's afeard won't baih no 'spection
   w'en hit come to jedgement
   day;
Do' de same t'ing been a-wo'kin'
   evah sence de worl' began,—
De ooman disobeyin' fu' to 'tice
   along a man.

Ef you 'tended de revivals which
   we held de wintah pas',
You kin rickolec' dat convuts was
   a-comin' thick an' fas';
But dey ain't no use in talkin', dey
   was all lef' in de lu'ch
W'en ol' Mis' Jackson's dartah
   foun' huh peace an' tuk de
   chu'ch.

W'y, she shouted ovah evah inch
   of Ebenezah's flo';·
Up into de preachah's pulpit an'
   f'om dah down to de do';
Den she hugged an' squeezed huh
   mammy, an' she hugged an'
   kissed huh dad,
An' she struck out at huh sistah,
   people said, lak she was mad.

I has 'tended some revivals dat
  was lively in my day,
An' I 's seed folks git 'uligion in
  mos' evah kin' o' way;
But I tell you, an' you b'lieve me
  dat I 's speakin' true indeed,
Dat gal tuk huh 'ligion ha'dah dan
  de ha'dest yit I 's seed.

Well, f'om dat, 't was " Sistah
  Jackson, won't you please do
  dis er dat? "
She mus' allus sta't de singin'
  w'en dey 'd pass erroun' de
  hat,
An' hit seemed dey was n't nuffin'
  in dat chu'ch dat could go by
'Dout sistah Lucy Jackson had a
  finger in de pie.

But de sayin' mighty trufeful dat
  hit easiah to sail
W'en de sea is ca'm an' gentle dan
  to weathah out a gale.
Dat 's whut made dis ooman's
  trouble; ef de sto'm had kep'
  away,
She 'd 'a' had enough 'uligion fu'
  to lasted out huh day.

Lucy went wid 'Lishy Davis, but
  w'en she jined chu'ch, you
  know
Dah was lots o' little places dat, of
  cose, she could n't go;
An' she had to gin up dancin' an'
  huh singin' an' huh play.—

Now hit 's nachul dat sich goin's-
  on 'u'd drive a man away.

So, w'en Lucy got so solemn, Ike
  he sta'ted fu' to go
Wid a gal who was a sinnah an'
  could mek a bettah show.
Lucy jes' went on to meetin' lak
  she did n't keer a rap,
But my 'sperunce kep' me t'inkin'
  dah was somep'n' gwine to
  drap.

Fu' a gal won't let 'uligion er no
  othah so't o' t'ing
Stop huh w'en she teks a notion
  dat she wants a weddin' ring.
You kin p'omise huh de blessin's
  of a happy aftah life
(An' hit 's nice to be a angel), but
  she 'd ravah be a wife.

So w'en Chrismus come an' mastah gin a frolic on de lawn,
Did n't 'sprise me not de littlest
  seein' Lucy lookin' on.
An' I seed a wa'nin' lightnin' go
  a-flashin' f'om huh eye
Jest ez 'Lishy an' his new gal went
  a-gallivantin' by.

An' dat Tildy, umph! she giggled,
  an' she gin huh dress a flirt
Lak de people she was passin' was
  ez common ez de dirt;
An' de minit she was dancin', w'y
  dat gal put on mo' aihs
Dan a cat a-tekin' kittens up a
  paih o' windin' staihs.

PAUL LAURENCE DUNBAR

She could 'fo'd to show huh
  sma'tness, fu' she could n't
he'p but know
Dat wid jes' de present dancahs
  she was ownah of de flo';
But I t'ink she 'd kin' o' cooled
  down ef she happened on de
  sly
Fu' to noticed dat 'ere lightnin'
  dat I seed in Lucy's eye.

An' she would n't been so 'ston-
  ished w'en de people gin a
  shout,
An' Lucy th'owed huh mantle
  back an' come a-glidin' out.
Some ahms was dah to tek huh an'
  she fluttahed down de flo'
Lak a feddah f'om a bedtick w'en
  de win' commence to blow.

Soon ez Tildy see de trouble, she
  jes' tu'n an' toss huh haid,
But seem lak she los' huh sperrit,
  all huh darin'ness was daid.
Did n't cut anothah capah nary
  time de blessid night;
But de othah one, hit looked lak
  could n't git enough delight.

W'en you keeps a colt a-stan'nin'
  in de stable all along,
W'en he do git out hit 's nachul
  he 'll be pullin' mighty strong.
Ef you will tie up yo' feelin's,
  hyeah 's de bes' advice to tek,
Look out fu' an awful loosin' w'en
  de string dat hol's 'em brek.

Lucy's mammy groaned to see huh,
  an' huh pappy sto'med an' to',
But she kep' right on a-hol'in' to
  de centah of de flo'.
So dey went an' ast de pastoh ef he
  could n't mek huh quit,
But de tellin' of de sto'y th'owed
  de preachah in a fit.

Tildy Taylor chewed huh hank'-
  cher twell she 'd chewed it in
  a hole,—
All de sinnahs was rejoicin' 'cause
  a lamb had lef' de fol',
An' de las' I seed o' Lucy, she an'
  'Lish was side an' side:
I don't blame de gal fu' dancin',
  an' I could n't ef I tried.

Fu' de men dat wants to ma'y
  ain't a-growin' 'roun' on
  trees,
An' de gal dat wants to git one
  sholy has to try to please.
Hit 's a ha'd t'ing fu' a ooman fu'
  to pray an' jes' set down,
An' to sacafice a husban' so 's to
  try to gain a crown.

Now, I don' say she was justified
  in follerin' huh plan;
But aldough she los' huh 'ligion,
  yit she sholy got de man.
Latah on, w'en she is suttain dat
  de preachah 's made 'em fas'
She kin jes' go back to chu'ch an'
  ax fu'giveness fu' de pas'!

TWO LITTLE BOOTS

Two little boots all rough an' wo',
    Two little boots!
Law, I's kissed 'em times befo',
    Dese little boots!
Seems de toes a-peepin' thoo
Dis hyeah hole an' sayin' " Boo! "
Evah time dey looks at you —
    Dese little boots.

Membah de time he put 'em on,
    Dese little boots;
Riz an' called fu' 'em by dawn,
    Dese little boots;
Den he tromped de livelong day,
Laffin' in his happy way,
Evaht'ing he had to say,
    " My little boots! "

Kickin' de san' de whole day long,
    Dem little boots;
Good de cobblah made 'em strong,
    Dem little boots!
Rocks was fu' dat baby's use,
I'on had to stan' abuse
W'en you tu'ned dese champeens
        loose,
    Dese little boots!

Ust to make de ol' cat cry,
    Dese little boots;
Den you walked it mighty high,
    Proud little boots!
Ahms akimbo, stan'in' wide,

Eyes a-sayin' " Dis is pride! "
Den de manny-baby stride!
    You little boots.

Somehow, you don' seem so gay,
    Po' little boots,
Sence yo' ownah went erway,
    Po' little boots!
Yo' bright tops don' look so red,
Dese brass tips is dull an' dead;
" Goo'-by," whut de baby said;
    Deah little boots!

Ain't you kin' o' sad yo'se'f,
    You little boots?
Dis is all his mammy's lef',
    Two little boots.
Sence huh baby gone an' died.
Heav'n itse'f hit seem to hide
Des a little bit inside
    Two little boots.

TO THE ROAD

Cool is the wind, for the summer
        is waning,
    Who's for the road?
Sun-flecked and soft, where the
        dead leaves are raining,
    Who's for the road?
Knapsack and alpenstock press
        hand and shoulder,
Prick of the brier and roll of the
        boulder;

THE COMPLETE POEMS OF

This be your lot till the season
	grow older;
	Who's for the road?

Up and away in the hush of the
	morning,
	Who's for the road?
Vagabond he, all conventions a-
	scorning,
	Who's for the road?
Music of warblers so merrily sing-
	ing,
Draughts from the rill from the
	roadside up-springing,
Nectar of grapes from the vines
	lowly swinging,
	These on the road.

Now every house is a hut or a
	hovel,
	Come to the road:
Mankind and moles in the dark
	love to grovel,
	But to the road.
Throw off the loads that are bend-
	ing you double;
Love is for life, only labor is
	trouble;
Truce to the town, whose best gift
	is a bubble:
	Come to the road!

A SPRING WOOING

Come on walkin' wid me, Lucy;
	't ain't no time to mope
	erroun'

W'en de sunshine's shoutin'
	glory in de sky,
An' de little Johnny-Jump-Ups's
	jes' a-springin' f'om de
	groun',
	Den a-lookin' roun' to ax each
	othah w'y.
Don' you hyeah dem cows a-
	mooin'? Dat's dey howdy
	to de spring;
	Ain' dey lookin' most oncom-
	mon satisfied?
Hit's enough to mek a body want
	to spread dey mouf an'
	sing
	Jes' to see de critters all so
	spa'klin'-eyed.

W'y dat squir'l dat jes' run past
	us, ef I did n' know his
	tricks,
	I could swaih he'd got 'uligion
	jes' to-day;
An' dem liza'ds slippin' back an'
	fofe ermong de stones an'
	sticks
	Is a-wigglin' 'cause dey feel so
	awful gay.
Oh, I see yo' eyes a-shinin' dough
	you try to mek me b'lieve
	Dat you ain' so monst'ous happy
	'cause you come;
But I tell you dis hyeah weathah
	meks it moughty ha'd to
	'ceive
	Ef a body's soul ain' blin' an'
	deef an' dumb.

Robin whistlin' ovah yandah ez he
    buil' his little nes';
  Whut you reckon dat he sayin'
    to his mate?
He 's a-sayin' dat he love huh in de
    wo'ds she know de bes',
  An' she lookin' moughty pleased
    at whut he state.
Now, Miss Lucy, dat ah robin
    sholy got his sheer o' sense,
  An' de hen-bird got huh
    mothah-wit fu' true;
So I t'ink ef you 'll ixcuse me, fu'
    I do' mean no erfence,
  Dey 's a lesson in dem birds fu'
    me an' you.

I 's a-buil'in' o' my cabin, an' I 's
    vines erbove de do'
  Fu' to kin' o' gin it sheltah f'om
    de sun;
Gwine to have a little kitchen wid
    a reg'lar wooden flo',
  An' dey 'll be a back verandy
    w'en hit 's done.
I 's a-waitin' fu' you, Lucy, tek de·
    'zample o' de birds,
  Dat 's a-lovin' an' a-matin' evah-
    whaih.
I cain' tell you dat I loves you in
    de robin's music wo'ds,
  But my cabin 's talkin' fu' me
    ovah thaih!

JOGGIN' ERLONG

DE da'kest hour, dey allus say,
Is des' befo' de dawn,

But it 's moughty ha'd a-waitin'
W'ere de night goes frownin'
   ' on;
An' it 's moughty ha'd a-hopin'
W'en de clouds is big an' black,
An' all de t'ings you 's waited fu'
Has failed, er gone to wrack —
But des' keep on a-joggin' wid a
    little bit o' song,
De mo'n is allus brightah w'en de
    night 's been long.

Dey 's lots o' knocks you 's got to
   tek
Befo' yo' journey 's done,
An' dey 's times w'en you 'll be
   wishin'
Dat de weary race was run;
W'en you want to give up tryin'
An' des' float erpon de wave,
W'en you don't feel no mo' sorrer
Ez you t'ink erbout de grave —
Den, des' keep on a-joggin' wid a
    little bit o' song,
De mo'n is allus brightah w'en de
    night 's been long.

De whup-lash sting a good deal
   mo'
De back hit 's knowed befo',
An' de burden 's allus heavies'
Whaih hits weight has made a
   so';
Dey is times w'en tribulation
Seems to git de uppah han'
An' to whip de weary trav'lah
'Twell he ain't got stren'th to
   stan'—

[165]

But des' keep on a-joggin' wid a
    little bit o' song,
De mo'n is allus brightah w'en de
    night 's been long.

IN MAY

OH to have you in May,
    To talk with you under the
        trees,
Dreaming throughout the day,
    Drinking the wine-like breeze,

Oh it were sweet to think
    That May should be ours again,
Hoping it not, I shrink,
    Out of the sight of men.

May brings the flowers to bloom,
    It brings the green leaves to the
        tree,
And the fatally sweet perfume,
    Of what you once were to me.

DREAMS

WHAT dreams we have and how
    they fly .
Like rosy clouds across the sky;
    Of wealth, of fame, of sure suc-
        cess,
    Of love that comes to cheer
        and bless;
And how they wither, how they
    fade,
The waning wealth, the jilting
    jade —

The fame that for a moment
    gleams,
Then flies forever,— dreams, ah
    — dreams!

O burning doubt and long regret,
O tears with which our eyes are
    wet,
    Heart-throbs, heart-aches, the
        glut of pain,
    The somber cloud, the bitter
        rain,
You were not of those dreams —
    ah! well,
Your full fruition who can tell?
    Wealth, fame, and love, ah!
        love that beams
    Upon our souls, all dreams —
        ah! dreams.

THE TRYST

DE night creep down erlong de
    lan',
    De shadders rise an' shake,
De frog is sta'tin' up his ban',
    De cricket is awake;
My wo'k is mos' nigh done, Celes',
    To-night I won't be late,
I 's hu'yin' thoo my level bes',
    Wait fu' me by de gate.

De mockin'-bird 'll sen' his glee
    A-thrillin' thoo and thoo,
I know dat ol' magnolia-tree
    Is smellin' des' fu' you;
De jessamine erside de road
    Is bloomin' rich an' white,

[166]

PAUL LAURENCE DUNBAR

My hea't's a-th'obbin' 'cause it
    knowed
  You'd wait fu' me to-night.

Hit's lonesome, ain't it, stan'in'
    thaih
  Wid no one nigh to talk?
But ain't dey whispahs in de aih
  Erlong de gyahden walk?
Don't somep'n kin' o' call my
    name,
  An' say " he love you bes' "?
Hit's true, I wants to say de
    same,
  So wait fu' me, Celes'.

Sing somep'n fu' to pass de time,
  Outsing de mockin'-bird,
You got de music an' de rhyme,
  You beat him wid de word.
I's comin' now, my wo'k is done,
  De hour has come fu' res',
I wants to fly, but only run —
  Wait fu' me, deah Celes'.

A PLEA

Treat me nice, Miss Mandy
    Jane,
  Treat me nice.
Dough my love has tu'ned my
    brain,
  Treat me nice.
I ain't done a t'ing to shame,
Lovahs all ac's jes' de same:
Don't you know we ain't to blame?
  Treat me nice!

Cose I know I's talkin' wild;
  Treat me nice;
I cain't talk no bettah, child,
  Treat me nice;
Whut a pusson gwine to do,
W'en he come a-cou'tin' you
All a-trimblin' thoo and thoo?
  Please be nice.

Reckon I mus' go de paf
  Othahs do:
Lovahs lingah, ladies laff;
  Mebbe you
Do' mean all the things you say,
An' pu'haps some latah day
W'en I baig you ha'd, you may
  Treat me nice!

THE DOVE

Out of the sunshine and out of
  the heat,
Out of the dust of the grimy
  street,
A song fluttered down in the form
  of a dove,
And it bore me a message, the one
  word — Love!

Ah, I was toiling, and oh, I was
  sad:
I had forgotten the way to be glad.
Now, smiles for my sadness and
  for my toil, rest
Since the dove fluttered down to
  its home in my breast!

A WARM DAY IN WINTER

" Sunshine on de medders,
  Greenness on de way;
Dat's de blessed reason
  I sing all de day."
Look hyeah! Whut you axin'?
  Whut meks me so merry?
'Spect to see me sighin'
  W'en hit 's wa'm in Febawary?

'Long de stake an' rider
  Seen a robin set;
W'y, hit 'mence a-thawin',
  Groun' is monst'ous wet.
Den you stan' dah wond'rin',
  Lookin' skeert an' stary;
I 's a right to caper
  .W'en hit 's wa'm in Febawary.

Missis gone a-drivin',
  Mastah gone to shoot;
Ev'ry da'ky lazin'
  In de sun to boot.
Qua'tah 's moughty pleasant,
  Hangin' 'roun' my Mary;
Cou'tin' boun' to prospah
  W'en hit 's wa'm in Febawary.

Cidah look so pu'ty
  Po'in' f'om de jug —
Don' you see it 's happy?
  Hyeah it laffin'— glug?
Now 's de time fu' people
  Fu' to try an' bury
All dey grief an' sorrer,
  W'en hit 's wa'm in Febawary.

SNOWIN'

Dey is snow upon de meddahs,
  dey is snow upon de hill,
An' de little branch's watahs is
  all glistenin' an' still;
De win' goes roun' de cabin lak a
  sperrit wan'erin' 'roun'.
An' de chillen shakes an' shivahs
  as dey listen to de soun'.
Dey is hick'ry in de fiahplace,
  whah de blaze is risin' high,
But de heat it meks ain't wa'min'
  up de gray clouds in de sky.
Now an' den I des peep outside,
  . den I hurries to de do',
Lawd a mussy on my body, how I
  wish it would n't snow!

I kin stan' de hottes' summah, I
  kin stan' de wettes' fall,
I kin stan' de chilly springtime in
  de ploughland, but dat 's
  all;
Fu' de ve'y hottes' fiah nevah tells
  my skin a t'ing,
W'en de snow commence a-flyin',
  an' de win' begin to sing.
Dey is plenty wood erroun' us, an'
  I chop an' tote it in,
But de t'oughts dat I 's a t'inkin'
  while I 's wo'kin' is a sin.
I kin keep f'om downright swahin'
  all de time I 's on de go,
But my hea't is full o' cuss-wo'ds
  w'en I 's trampin' thoo de
  snow.

What you say, you Lishy Davis,
  dat you see a possum's tracks?
Look hyeah, boy, you stop yo'
  foolin', bring ol' Spot, an'
  bring de ax.
Is I col'? Go way, now, Mandy,
  what you t'ink I's made of?
  — sho,
W'y dis win' is des ez gentle, an'
  dis ain't no kin' o' snow.
Dis hyeah weathah 's des ez healthy
  ez de wa'mest summah days.
All you chillen step up lively, pile
  on wood an' keep a blaze.
What's de use o' gittin' skeery
  case dey 's snow upon de
  groun'?
Huh-uh, I 's a reg'lar snowbird ef
  dey 's any possum 'roun'.

Go on, Spot, don' be so foolish;
  don' you see de signs o' feet.
What you howlin' fu? Keep still,
  suh, cose de col' is putty
  sweet;
But we goin' out on bus'ness, an'
  hit 's bus'ness o' de kin'
Dat mus' put a dog an' dahky in
  a happy frame o' min'.
Yes, you 's col'; I know it, Spotty,
  but you des stay close to me,
An' I 'll mek you hot ez cotton
  w'en we strikes de happy tree.
No, I don' lak wintah weathah,
  an' I 'd wush 't uz allus
  June,
Ef it was n't fu' de trackin' o' de
  possum an' de coon.

KEEP A SONG UP ON DE WAY

OH, de clouds is mighty heavy
An' de rain is mighty thick;
  Keep a song up on de way.
An' de waters is a rumblin'
On de boulders in de crick,
  Keep a song up on de way.
Fu' a bird ercross de road
Is a-singin' lak he knowed
Dat we people did n't daih
Fu' to try de rainy aih
  Wid a song up on de way.

What 's de use o' gittin' mopy,
Case de weather ain' de bes'!
  Keep a song up on de way.
W'en de rain is fallin' ha'des',
Dey 's de longes' times to res'
  Keep a song up on de way.
Dough de plough 's a-stan'in' still
Dey 'll be watah fu' de mill,
Rain mus' come ez well ez sun
'Fo' de weathah's wo'k is done,
  Keep a song up on de way. ·

W'y hit 's nice to hyeah de showahs
Fallin' down ermong de trees:
  Keep a song up on de way.
Ef de birds don' bothah 'bout it,
But go singin' lak dey please,
  Keep a song up on de way.
You don' s'pose I 's gwine to see
Dem ah fowls do mo' dan me?
No, suh, I 'll des chase dis frown,
An' aldough de rain fall down,
  Keep a song up on de way.

THE TURNING OF THE BABIES IN THE BED

Woman's sho' a cur'ous critter,
    an' dey ain't no doubtin' dat.
She's a mess o' funny capahs f'om
    huh slippahs to huh hat.
Ef you tries to un'erstan' huh, an'
    you fails, des' up an' say:
"D' ain't a bit o' use to try to
    un'erstan' a woman's way."

I don' mean to be complainin', but
    I 's jes' a-settin' down
Some o' my own obserwations,
    w'en I cas' my eye eroun'.
Ef you ax me fu' to prove it, I
    ken do it mighty fine,
Fu' dey ain't no bettah 'zample
    den dis ve'y wife o' mine.

In de ve'y hea't o' midnight, w'en
    I 's sleepin' good an' soun',
I kin hyeah a so't o' rustlin' an'
    somebody movin' 'roun'. ·
An' I say, " Lize, whut you do-
    in'? " But she frown an' shek
    huh haid,
" Heish yo' mouf, I 's only tu'nin'
    of de chillun in de bed.

" Don' you know a chile gits rest-
    less, layin' all de night one
    way?
An' you' got to kind o' 'range him
    sev'al times befo' de day?
So de little necks won't worry, an'
    de little backs won't break;

Don' you t'ink case chillun 's chil-
    lun dey hain't got no pain an'
    ache."

So she shakes 'em, an' she twists
    'em, an' she tu'ns 'em 'roun'
    erbout,
'Twell I don' see how de chillun
    evah keeps f'om hollahin' out.
Den she lif's 'em up head down-
    'ards, so 's dey won't git livah-
    grown,
But dey snoozes des' ez peaceful
    ez a liza'd on a stone.

W'en hit 's mos' nigh time fu'
    wakin' on de dawn o' jedg-
    ment day,
Seems lak I kin hyeah ol' Gab'iel
    lay his trumpet down an' say,
" Who dat walkin' 'roun' so easy,
    down on earf ermong de
    dead? "—
'T will be Lizy up a-tu'nin' of de
    chillun in de bed.

THE DANCE

Heel and toe, heel and toe,
    That is the song we sing;
Turn to your partner and curtsey
    low,
    Balance and forward and swing.
Corners are draughty and meadows
    are white,
This is the game for a winter's
    night.

[170]

PAUL LAURENCE DUNBAR

Hands around, hands around,
  Trip it, and not too slow;
Clear is the fiddle and sweet its
    sound,
  Keep the girls' cheeks aglow.
Still let your movements be dainty
    and light,
This is the game for a winter's
    night.

Back to back, back to back,
  Turn to your place again;
Never let lightness nor nimble-
    ness lack,
  Either in maidens or men.
Time hasteth ever, beware of its
    flight,
Oh, what a game for a winter's
    night!

Slower now, slower now,
  Softer the music sighs;
Look, there are beads on your
    partner's brow
  Though there be light in her
    eyes.
Lead her away and her grace re-
    quite,
So goes the game on a winter's
    night.

SOLILOQUY OF A TURKEY

Day 's a so't o' threatenin' feelin'
    in de blowin' of de breeze,
  An' I 's feelin' kin' o' squeamish
    in de night;

I 's a-walkin' 'roun' a-lookin' at
    de diffunt style o' trees,
  An' a-measurin' dey thickness
    an' dey height.
Fu' dey 's somep'n mighty 'spicious
    in de looks de da'kies give,
  Ez dey pass me an' my fambly
    on de groun','
So it 'curs to me dat lakly, ef I
    caihs to try an' live,
  It concehns me fu' to 'mence to
    look erroun'.

Dey 's a cu'ious kin' o' shivah
    runnin' up an' down my back,
  An' I feel my feddahs rufflin'
    all de day,
An' my laigs commence to trimble
    evah blessid step I mek;
  W'en I sees a ax, I tu'ns my
    head away.
Folks is go'gin' me wid goodies,
    an' dey 's treatin' me wid caih,
  An' I 's fat in spite of all dat I
    kin do.
I 's mistrus'ful of de kin'ness dat 's
    erroun' me evahwhaih,
  Fu' it 's jes' too good, an' fre-
    quent, to be true.

Snow 's a-fallin' on de medders, all
    erroun' me now is white,
  But I 's still kep' on a-roostin'
    on de fence;
Isham comes an' feels, my breas'-
    bone, an' he hefted me las'
    night,

[171]

An' he 's gone erroun' a-grinnin'
  evah sence.
'T ain't de snow dat meks me
  shivah; 't ain't de col' dat
  meks me shake;
'T ain't de wintah-time itse'f
  dat 's 'fectin' me;
But I t'ink de time is comin',
  an' I 'd bettah mek a break,
Fu' to set wid Mistah Possum
  in his tree.

W'en you hyeah de da'kies singin',
  an' de quahtahs all is gay,
'T ain't de time fu' birds lak me
  to be 'erroun';
W'en de hick'ry chips is flyin', an'
  de log 's been ca'ied erway,
Den hit 's dang'ous to be roostin'
  nigh he groun'.

Grin on, Isham! Sing on, da'k-
  ies! But I flop my wings an'
  go
  Fu' de sheltah of de ve'y highest tree,
Fu' dey 's too much close ertention
  — an' dey's too much fallin'
  snow —
  An' it 's too nigh Chris'mus
  mo'nin' now fu' me.

FISHING

W'en I git up in de mo'nin' an'
  de clouds is big an' black,
Dey 's a kin' o' wa'nin' shivah goes
  a-scootin' down my back;

Den I says to my ol' ooman ez I
  watches down de lane,
" Don't you so't o' reckon, Lizy,
  dat we gwine to have some
  rain? "

" Go on, man," my Lizy answah,
  " you cain't fool me, not a
  bit,
I don't see no rain a-comin', ef
  you 's wishin' fu' it, quit;
Case de mo' you t'ink erbout it, an
  de mo' you pray an' wish,
W'y de rain stay 'way de longah,
  spechul ef you wants to fish."

But I see huh pat de skillet, an' I
  see huh cas' huh eye
Wid a kin' o' anxious motion to'ds
  de da'kness in de sky;
An' I knows whut she 's a-t'inkin',
  dough she tries so ha'd to
  hide.
She 's a-sayin', " Would n't catfish
  now tas'e monst'ous bully,
  fried? "

Den de clouds git black an' black-
  ah, an' de thundah 'mence to
  roll,
An' de rain, it 'mence a-fallin'.
  Oh, I 's happy, bless my
  soul!
Ez I look at dat ol' skillet, an' I
  'magine I kin see
Jes' a slew o' new-ketched catfish
  sizzlin' daih fu' huh an' me.

'T ain't no use to go a-ploughin',
    fu' de groun' 'll be too
    wet,
So I puts out fu' de big house at
    a moughty pace, you bet,
An' ol' mastah say, " Well, Lishy,
    ef you t'ink hit 's gwine to
    rain,
Go on fishin', hit's de weathah,
    an' I 'low we cain't com-
    plain."

Talk erbout a dahky walkin' wid
    his haid up in de aih!
Have to feel mine evah minute to
    be sho' I got it daih;
En' de win' is cuttin' capahs an'
    a-lashin' thoo de trees,
But de rain keeps on a-singin'
    blessed songs, lak " Tek yo'
    ease."

Wid my pole erpon my shouldah
    an' my wo'm can in my
    han',
I kin feel de fish a-waitin' w'en I
    strikes de rivah's san';
Nevah min', you ho'ny scoun'els,
    need n' swim erroun' an'
    grin,
I 'll be grinnin' in a minute w'en I
    'mence to haul you in.

W'en de fish begin to nibble, an'
    de co'k begin to jump,
I 's erfeahed dat dey 'll quit bitin',
    case dey hyeah my hea't go
    " thump,"

'Twell de co'k go way down
    undah, an' I raise a awful
    shout,
Ez a big ol' yallah belly comes a
    gallivantin' out.

Need n't wriggle, Mistah Catfish,
    case I got you jes' de same,
You been eatin', I 'll be eatin', an'
    we needah ain't to blame.
But you need n't feel so lonesome
    fu' I 's th'owin' out to see
Ef dey ain't some of yo' comrades
    fu' to keep you company.

Spo't, dis fishin'! now you talkin',
    w'y dey ain't no kin' to beat;
I don' keer ef I is soakin', laigs,
    an' back, an' naik, an' feet,
It 's de spo't I 's lookin' aftah.
    Hit 's de pleasure an' de fun,
Dough I knows dat Lizy 's waitin'
    wid de skillet w'en I 's done.

A PLANTATION
PORTRAIT

HAIN'T you see my Mandy Lou,
    Is it true?
Whaih you been f'om day to day,
    Whaih, I say?
Dat you say you nevah seen
    Dis hyeah queen
Walkin' roun' f'om fiel' to street
    Smilin' sweet?

Slendah ez a saplin' tree;
    Seems to me

[173]

W'en de win' blow f'om de bay
  She jes' sway
Lak de reg'lar saplin' do
  Ef hit 's grew
Straight an' graceful, 'dout a limb,
  Sweet an' slim. .

Browner den de frush's wing,
  An' she sing
Lak he mek his wa'ble ring
  In de spring;
But she sholy beat de frush,
  Hyeah me, hush:
W'en she sing, huh teef kin show
  White ez snow.

Eyes ez big an' roun' an' bright
  Ez de light
Whut de moon gives in de prime
  Harvest time.
An' huh haih a woolly skein,
  Black an' plain.
Hol's you wid a natchul twis'
  Close to bliss. .

Tendah han's dat mek yo' own
  Feel lak stone;
Easy steppin', blessid feet,
  Small an' sweet.
Hain't you seen my Mandy Lou,
  Is it true?
Look at huh befo' she 's gone,
  Den pass on!

A LITTLE CHRISTMAS BASKET

De win' is hollahin' "Daih you"
  to de shuttahs an' de fiah,

De snow 's a-sayin' "Got you" to
  de groun',
Fu' de wintah weathah 's come
    widout a-askin' ouah de-
    siah,
  An' he 's laughin' in his sleeve
    at whut he foun';
Fu' dey ain't nobody ready wid
    dey fuel er dey food,
  An' de money bag look timid
    lak, fu' sho',
So we want ouah Chrismus
    sermon, but we 'd lak it ef
    you could
  Leave a little Chrismus basket
    at de do'.

Wha 's de use o' tellin' chillen
    'bout a Santy er a Nick,
  An' de sto'ies dat a body allus
    tol'?
When de harf is gray wid ashes
    an' you has n't got a stick
  Fu' to warm dem when dey
    little toes is col'?
Wha 's de use o' preachin' 'ligion
    to a man dat 's sta'ved to
    def,
  An' a-tellin' him de Mastah
    will pu'vide?
Ef you want to tech his feelin's,
    save yo' sermons an' yo'
    bref,
  Tek a little Chrismus basket by
    yo' side.

'T ain't de time to open Bibles an'
    to lock yo' cellah do',

'T ain't de time to talk o' bein'
　good to men;
Ef you want to preach a sermon
　　ez you nevah preached
　　befo',
　Preach dat sermon wid a shoat
　　er wid er hen;
Bein' good is heap sight bettah den
　　a-dallyin' wid sin,
　An' dey ain't nobody roun' dat
　　knows it mo',
But I t'ink dat 'ligion 's sweeter
　　w'en it kind o' mixes in
　Wid a little Chrismus basket at
　　de do'.

THE VALSE

WHEN to sweet music my lady
　is dancing
　My heart to mild frenzy her
　　beauty inspires.
Into my face are her brown eyes
　a-glancing,
　And swift my whole frame
　　thrills with tremulous fires.
Dance, lady, dance, for the mo-
　ments are fleeting,
　Pause not to place yon refractory
　　curl;
Life is for love and the night is
　for sweeting;
　Dreamily, joyously, circle and
　　whirl.

Oh, how those viols are throbbing
　and pleading;

A prayer is scarce needed in
　sound of their strain.
Surely and lightly as round you
　are speeding,
　You turn to confusion my heart
　　and my brain.
Dance, lady, dance to the viol's
　soft calling,
　Skip it and trip it as light as the
　　air;
Dance, for the moments like rose
　leaves are falling,
　Strikes, now, the clock from its
　　place on the stair.

Now sinks the melody lower and
　lower,
　The weary musicians scarce
　　seeming to play.
Ah, love, your steps now are
　slower and slower,
　The smile on your face is more
　　sad and less gay.
Dance, lady, dance to the brink of
　our parting,
　My heart and your step must not
　　fail to be light.
Dance! Just a turn — tho' the
　tear-drop be starting.
　Ah — now it is done — so —
　　my lady, good-night!

REPONSE

WHEN Phyllis sighs and from her
　eyes
The light dies out; my soul re-
　plies

With misery of deep-drawn breath,
E'en as it were at war with
death.

When Phyllis smiles, her glance
beguiles
My heart through love-lit woodland aisles,
And through the silence high and
clear,
A wooing warbler's song I hear.

But if she frown, despair comes
down,
I put me on my sack-cloth gown;
So frown not, Phyllis, lest I die,
But look on me with smile or
sigh.

MY SWEET BROWN GAL

W'en de clouds is hangin' heavy
in de sky,
An' de win's's a-taihin' moughty
vig'rous by,
I don' go a-sighin' all erlong de
way;
I des' wo'k a-waitin' fu' de close
o' day.

Case I knows w'en evenin' draps
huh shadders down,
I won' care a smidgeon fu' de
weathah's frown;
Let de rain go splashin', let de
thundah raih,
Dey's a happy sheltah, an' I's
goin' daih.

Down in my ol' cabin wa'm ez
mammy's toas',
'Taters in de fiah layin' daih to
roas';
No one daih to cross me, got no
talkin' pal,
But I's got de comp'ny o' my
sweet brown gal.

So I spen's my evenin' listenin' to
huh sing,
Lak a blessid angel; how huh
voice do ring!
Sweetah den a bluebird flutterin'
erroun',
W'en he sees de steamin' o' de
new ploughed groun'.

Den I hugs huh closah, closah to
my breas'.
Need n't sing, my da'lin', tek you'
hones' res'.
Does I mean Malindy, Mandy,
Lize er Sal?
No, I means my fiddle — dat's
my sweet brown gal!

SPRING FEVER

GRASS commence a-comin'
Thoo de thawin' groun',
Evah bird dat whistles
Keepin' noise erroun';
Cain't sleep in de mo'nin',
Case befo' it's light
Bluebird an' de robin,
Done begun to fight.

Bluebird sass de robin,
  Robin sass him back,
Den de bluebird scol' him
  'Twell his face is black.
Would n' min' de quoilin'
  All de mo'nin' long,
'Cept it wakes me early,
  Case hit 's done in song.

Anybody wo'kin'
  Wants to sleep ez late
Ez de folks 'll 'low him,
  An' I wish to state
(Co'se dis ain't to scattah,
  But 'twix' me an' you),
I could stan' de bedclothes,
  Kin' o' latah, too.

'T ain't my natchul feelin',
  Dis hyeah mopin' spell.
I stan's early risin'
  Mos'ly moughty well;
But de ve'y minute,
  I feel Ap'il's heat,
Bless yo' soul, de bedclothes
  Nevah seemed so sweet.

Mastah, he 's a-scol'in',
  Case de han's is slow,
All de hosses balkin',
  Jes' cain't mek 'em go.
Don' know whut 's de mattah,
  Hit 's a funny t'ing,
Less'n hit 's de fevah
  Dat you gits in spring.

THE VISITOR

Little lady at de do',
  W'y you stan' dey knockin'?
Nevah seen you ac' befo'
  In er way so shockin'.
    Don' you know de sin it is
    Fu' to git my temper riz
    W'en I 's got de rheumatiz
  An' my jints is lockin'?

No, ol' Miss ain't sont you down,
  Don' you tell no story;
I been seed you hangin' 'roun'
  Dis hyeah te'itory.
    You des come fu' me to tell
    You a tale, an' I ain'—
      well —
    Look hyeah, what is dat I
      smell?
  Steamin' victuals? Glory!

Come in, Missy, how you do?
  Come up by de fiah,
I was jokin', chile, wid you;
  Bring dat basket nighah.
    Huh uh, ain't dat lak ol'
      Miss,
    Sen'in' me a feas' lak dis?
    Rheumatiz cain't stop my
      bliss,
  Case I 's feelin' spryah.

Chicken meat an' gravy, too,
  Hot an' still a-heatin';
Good ol' sweet pertater stew;
  Missy b'lieves in treatin'.
    Des set down, you blessed
      chile,

Daddy got to t'ink a while,
Den a story mek you smile
W'en he git thoo eatin'.

SONG

WINTAH, summah, snow er
    shine,
Hit 's all de same to me,
Ef only I kin call you mine,
    An' keep you by my knee.

Ha'dship, frolic, grief er caih,
    Content by night an' day,
Ef only I kin see you whaih
    You wait beside de way.

Livin', dyin', smiles er teahs,
    My soul will still be free,
Ef only thoo de comin' yeahs
    You walk de worl' wid me.

Bird-song, breeze-wail, chune er
    moan,
    What puny t'ings dey 'll be,
Ef w'en I 's seemin' all erlone,
    I knows yo' hea't 's wid me.

THE COLORED BAND

W'EN de colo'ed ban' comes
    ma'chin' down de street,
Don't you people stan' daih
    starin'; lif' yo' feet!
    Ain't dey playin'? Hip, hoo-
    ray!

Stir yo' stumps an' cleah de
    way,
Fu' de music dat dey mekin' can't
    be beat.

Oh, de major man 's a-swingin'
    of his stick,
An' de pickaninnies crowdin'
    roun' him thick;
    In his go'geous uniform,
    He 's de lightnin' of de sto'm,
An' de little clouds erroun' look
    mighty slick.

You kin hyeah a fine perfo'mance
    w'en de white ban's sere-
    nade,
    An' dey play dey high-toned
    music mighty sweet,
But hit 's Sousa played in rag-
    time, an' hit 's Rastus on
    Parade,
    W'en de colo'ed ban' comes
    ma'chin' down de street.

W'en de colo'ed ban' comes ma'ch-
    in' down de street
You kin hyeah de ladies all erroun'
    repeat:
    " Ain't dey handsome? Ain't
    dey gran'?
    Ain't dey splendid? Goodness,
    lan'!
W'y dey 's pu'fect f'om dey fo'-
    heads to dey feet! "
An' sich steppin' to de music down
    de line,

'T ain't de music by itself dat meks
    it fine,
  Hit 's de walkin', step by step,
An' de keepin' time wid " Hep,"
Dat it mek a common ditty soun'
    divine.

Oh, de white ban' play hits music,
    an' hit 's mighty good to
    hyeah,
An' it sometimes leaves a ticklin'
    in yo' feet;
But de hea't goes into bus'ness fu'
    to he'p erlong de eah,
  W'en de colo'ed ban' goes ma'ch-
    in' down de street.

Or does some brighter spirit, un-
    forlorn,
  Send you, my little sister of the
    wood,
To say to some one on a cloudful
    morn,
  " Life lives through death, my
    brother, all is good ? "

With meditative hearts the others
    go
  The memory of their dead to
    dress anew.
But, sister mine, bide here that I
    may know,
  Life grows, through death, as
    beautiful as you.

TO A VIOLET FOUND ON
ALL SAINTS' DAY

BELATED wanderer of the ways of
    spring,
  Lost in the chill of grim No-
    vember rain,
Would I could read the message
    that you bring
  And find in it the antidote for
    pain.

Does some sad spirit out beyond
    the day,
  Far looking to the hours forever
    dead,
Send you a tender offering to lay
  Upon the grave of us, the liv-
    ing dead?

INSPIRATION

AT the golden gate of song
Stood I, knocking all day long,
But the Angel, calm and cold,
Still refused and bade me, " Hold."

Then a breath of soft perfume,
Then a light within the gloom;
Thou, Love, camest to my side,
And the gates flew open wide.

Long I dwelt in this domain,
Knew no sorrow, grief, or pain;
Now you bid me forth and free,
Will you shut these gates on me?

[179]

MY LADY OF CASTLE GRAND

GRAY is the palace where she
    dwells,
    Grimly the poplars stand
There by the window where she
    sits,
    My Lady of Castle Grand.

There does she bide the livelong
    day,
    Grim as the poplars are,
Ever her gaze goes reaching out,
    Steady, but vague and far.

Bright burn the fires in the castle
    hall,
    Brightly the fire-dogs stand;
But cold is the body and cold the
    heart
    Of my Lady of Castle Grand.

Blue are the veins in her lily-white
    hands,
    Blue are the veins in her brow;
Thin is the line of her blue drawn
    lips,
    Who would be haughty now?

Pale is the face at the window-
    pane,
    Pale as the pearl on her breast,
" Roderick, love, wilt come again?
    Fares he to east or west? "

The shepherd pipes to the shep-
    herdess,
The bird to his mate in the
    tree,
And ever she sighs as she hears
    their song,
    " Nobody sings for me."

The scullery maids have swains
    enow
    Who lead them the way of love,
But lonely and loveless their mis-
    tress sits
    At her window up above.

Loveless and lonely she waits and
    waits,
    The saddest in all the land;
Ah, cruel and lasting is love-blind
    pride,
    My Lady of Castle Grand.

DRIZZLE

HIT's been drizzlin' an' been
    sprinklin',
    Kin' o' techy all day long.
I ain't wet enough fu' toddy,
    I 's too damp to raise a song,
An' de case have set me t'inkin',
    Dat dey 's folk des lak de rain,
Dat goes drizzlin' w'en dey 's
    talkin',
    An' won't speak out flat an'
    plain.

Ain't you nevah set an' listened
    At a body 'splain his min'?

[180]

W'en de t'oughts dey keep on
   drappin'
   Was n't big enough to fin'?
Dem 's whut I call drizzlin'
   people,
   Othahs call 'em mealy mouf,
But de fust name hits me bettah,
   Case dey nevah tech a drouf.

Dey kin talk from hyeah to yandah,
   An' f'om yandah hyeah ergain,
An' dey don' mek no mo' 'pression,
   Den dis powd'ry kin' o' rain.
En yo' min' is dry ez cindahs,
   Er a piece o' kindlin' wood,
'T ain't no use a-talkin' to 'em,
   Fu' dey drizzle ain't no good.

Gimme folks dat speak out nachul,
   Whut 'll say des whut dey mean,
Whut don't set dey wo'ds so
   skimpy
   Dat you got to guess between.
I want talk des' lak de showahs
   Whut kin wash de dust erway,
Not dat sprinklin' convusation,
   Dat des drizzle all de day.

DE CRITTERS' DANCE

AIN'T nobody nevah tol' you not a
   wo'd a-tall,
'Bout de 'time dat all de critters
   gin dey fancy ball?
Some folks tell it in a sto'y, some
   folks sing de rhyme,
'Peahs to me you ought to hyeahed
   it, case hit 's ol' ez time.

Well, de critters all was p'osp'ous,
   now would be de chance
Fu' to tease ol' Pa'son Hedgehog,
   givin' of a dance;
Case, you know, de critters'
   preachah was de stric'est kin',
An' he nevah made no 'lowance fu'
   de frisky min'.

So dey sont dey inbitations, Raccoon writ 'em all,
" Dis hyeah note is to inbite you
   to de Fancy Ball;
Come erlong an' bring yo' ladies,
   bring yo' chillun too,
Put on all yo' bibs an' tuckahs,
   show whut you kin do."

W'en de night come, dey all
   gathahed in a place dey
   knowed,
Fu' enough erway f'om people,
   nigh enough de road,
All de critters had ersponded, Hop-
   Toad up to Baih,
An' I 's hyeah to tell you, Pa'son
   Hedgehog too, was daih.

Well, dey talked an' made dey
   'bejunce, des lak critters
   do,
An' dey walked an' p'omenaded
   'roun' an' thoo an' thoo;
Jealous ol' Mis'. Fox, she whispah,
   " See Mis' Wildcat daih,
Ain't hit scan'lous, huh a-comin'
   wid huh shouldahs baih?"

[181]

Ol' man T'utle was n't honin' fu'
   no dancin' tricks,
So he stayed by ol' Mis' Tu'tle,
   talkin' politics;
Den de ban' hit 'mence a-playin'
   critters all to place,
Fou' ercross an' fou' stan' sideways, smilin' face to face.

'Fessah Frog, he play de co'net,
   Cricket play de fife,
Slews o' Grasshoppahs a-fiddlin'
   lak to save dey life;
Mistah Crow, 'he call de figgers,
   settin' in a tree,
Huh, uh! how dose critters sas-
   shayed was a sight to see.

Mistah Possom swing Mis' Rabbit up an' down de flo',
Ol' man Baih, he ain't so nimble,
   an' it mek him blow;
Raccoon dancin' wid Mis' Squ'il
   squeeze huh little han',
She say, " Oh, now ain't you awful, quit it, goodness lan'! "

Pa'son Hedgehog groanin' awful at
   his converts' shines,
'Dough he peepin' thoo his fingahs
   at dem movin' lines,
'Twell he cain't set still no longah
   w'en de fiddles sing,
Up he jump, an' bless you, honey,
   cut de pigeon-wing.

Well, de critters lak to fainted jes'
   wid dey su'prise,

Sistah Fox, she vowed she was n't
   gwine to b'lieve huh eyes;
But dey could n't be no 'sputin'
   'bout it any mo':
Pa'son Hedgehog was a-cape'in' all
   erroun' de flo.'

Den dey all jes' capahed scan'lous
   case dey did n't doubt,
Dat dey still could go to meetin';
   who could tu'n 'em out?
So wid dancin' an' uligion, dey
   was in de fol',
Fu' a-dancin' wid de Pa'son could-
   n't hu't de soul.

WHEN DEY 'LISTED COL-
ORED SOLDIERS

Dey was talkin' in de cabin, dey
   was talkin' in de hall;
But I listened kin' o' keerless, not
   a-t'inkin' 'bout it all;
An' on Sunday, too, I noticed, dey
   was whisp'rin' mighty much,
Stan'in' all erroun' de roadside
   w'en dey let us out o'
   chu'ch.
But I did n't t'ink erbout it 'twell
   de middle of de week,
An' my 'Lias come to see me, an'
   somehow he could n't speak.
Den I seed all in a minute whut
   he 'd come to see me
   for;—
Dey had 'listed colo'ed sojers an'
   my 'Lias gwine to wah.

Oh, I hugged him, an' I kissed
    him, an' I baiged him not to
    go;
But he tol' me dat his conscience,
    hit was callin' to him so,
An' he could n't baih to lingah
    w'en he had a chanst to
    fight
For de freedom dey had gin him
    an' de glory of de right.
So he kissed me, an' he lef' me,
    w'en I 'd p'omised to be true;
An' dey put a knapsack on him,
    an' a coat all colo'ed blue.
So I gin him pap's ol' Bible f'om
    de bottom of de draw',—
W'en dey 'listed colo'ed sojers an'
    my 'Lias went to wah.

But I t'ought of all de weary miles
    dat he would have to tramp,
An' I could n't be contented w'en
    dey tuk him to de camp.
W'y my hea't nigh broke wid
    grievin' 'twell I seed him on
    de street;
Den I felt lak I could go an' th'ow
    my body at his feet.
For his buttons was a-shinin', an'
    his face was shinin', too,
An' he looked so strong an' mighty
    in his coat o' sojer blue,
Dat I hollahed, " Step up, man-
    ny," dough my th'oat was so'
    an' raw,—
W'en dey 'listed colo'ed sojers an'
    my 'Lias went to wah.

Ol' Mis' cried w'en mastah lef'
    huh, young Miss mou'ned huh
    brothah Ned,
An' I did n't know dey feelin's is
    de ve'y wo'ds dey said
W'en I tol' 'em I was so'y. Dey
    had done gin up dey all;
But dey only seemed mo' proudah
    dat dey men had hyeahed de
    call.
Bofe my mastahs went in gray
    suits, an' I loved de Yankee
    blue,
But I t'ought dat I could sorrer
    for de losin' of 'em too;
But I could n't, for I did n't know
    de ha'f o' whut I saw,
'Twell dey 'listed colo'ed sojers an'
    my 'Lias went to wah.

Mastah Jack come home all sickly;
    he was broke for life, dey
    said;
An' dey lef' my po' young mastah
    some'r's on de roadside,—
    dead.
W'en de women cried an' mou'ned
    'em, I could feel it thoo an'
    thoo,
For I had a loved un fightin' in de
    way o' dangah, too.
Den dey tol' me dey had laid him
    some'r's way down souf to
    res',
Wid de flag dat he had fit for
    shinin' daih acrost his
    breas'.

Well, I cried, but den I reckon
  dat's whut Gawd had called
  him for,
W'en dey 'listed colo'ed sojers an'
  my 'Lias went to wah.

LINCOLN

Hurt was the nation with a
  mighty wound,
And all her ways were filled with
  clam'rous sound.
Wailed loud the South with unremitting grief,
And wept the North that could
  not find relief.
Then madness joined its harshest
  tone to strife:
A minor note swelled in the song
  of life.
'Till, stirring with the love that
  filled his breast,
But still, unflinching at the right's
  behest,
Grave Lincoln came, strong
  handed, from afar,
The mighty Homer of the lyre of
  war.
'T was he who bade the raging
  tempest cease,
Wrenched from his harp the har-
  mony of peace,
Muted the strings, that made the
  discord,—Wrong,
And gave his spirit up in thun-
  d'rous song.

Oh mighty Master of the mighty
  lyre,
Earth heard and trembled at thy
  strains of fire:
Earth learned of thee what Heav'n
  already knew,
And wrote thee down among her
  treasured few.

ENCOURAGEMENT

Who dat knockin' at de do'?
Why, Ike Johnson,—yes, fu' sho!
Come in, Ike. I's mighty glad
You come down. I t'ought you's
  mad
At me 'bout de othah night,
An' was stayin' 'way fu' spite.
Say, now, was you mad fu' true
W'en I kin' o' laughed at you?
  Speak up, Ike, an' 'spress yo'se'f.

'T ain't no use a-lookin' sad,
An' a-mekin' out you's mad;
Ef you's gwine to be so glum,
Wondah why you evah come.
I don't lak nobidy 'roun'
Dat jes' shet dey mouf an'
  frown,—
Oh, now, man, don't act a dunce!
Cain't you talk? I tol' you once,
  Speak up, Ike, an' 'spress yo'se'f.

Wha'd you come hyeah fu' to-
  night?
Body'd t'ink yo' haid ain't right.
I's done all dat I kin do,—

[184]

PAUL LAURENCE DUNBAR

Dressed perticler, jes' fu' you;
Reckon I 'd 'a' bettah wo'
My ol' ragged calico.
Aftah all de pains I 's took,
Cain't you tell me how I look?
　Speak up, Ike, an' 'spress yo'se'f.

Bless my soul! I 'mos' fu'got
Tellin' you 'bout Tildy Scott.
Don't you know, come Thu'sday
　night,
She gwine ma'y Lucius White?
Miss Lize say I allus wuh
Heap sight laklier 'n huh;
An' she 'll git me somep'n new,
Ef I wants to ma'y too.
　Speak up, Ike, an' 'spress yo'se'f.

I could ma'y in a week,
Ef de man I wants 'ud speak.
Tildy's presents 'll be fine,
But dey would n't ekal mine.
Him whut gits me fu' a wife
'Ll be proud, you bet yo' life.
I 's had offers; some ain't quit;
But I has n't ma'ied yit!
　Speak up, Ike, an' 'spress yo'se'f.

Ike, I loves you,— yes, I does;
You 's my choice, and allus was.
Laffin' at you ain't no harm.—
Go 'way, dahky, whah 's yo' arm?
Hug　me　closer — dah,　dat 's
　right!
Was n't you a awful sight,
Havin' me to baig you so?
Now　ax　whut　you　want　to
　· know,—
　Speak up, Ike, an' 'spress yo'se'f!

THE BOOGAH MAN

W'EN de evenin' shadders
　Come a-glidin' down,
Fallin' black an' heavy
　Ovah hill an' town,
Ef you listen keerful,
　Keerful ez you kin,
So 's you boun' to notice
　Des a drappin' pin;
Den you 'll hyeah a funny
　Soun' ercross de lan';
Lay low; dat 's de callin'
　Of de Boogah Man!

Woo-oo, woo-oo!
　Hyeah him ez he go erlong de
　　way;
Woo-oo, woo-oo!
　Don' you wish de night 'ud tu'n
　　to day? ·
Woo-oo, woo-oo!
　Hide yo' little peepers 'hind yo'
　　han';
Woo-oo, woo-oo!
　Callin' of de Boogah Man.

W'en de win 's a-shiverin'
　Thoo de gloomy lane,
An' dey comes de patterin'
　Of de evenin' rain,
W'en de owl 's a-hootin',
　Out daih in de wood,
Don' you wish, my honey,
　Dat you had been good?
'T ain't no use to try to
　Snuggle up to Dan;
Bless you, dat 's de callin'
　Of de Boogah Man!

[185]

Ef you loves yo' mammy,
  An' you min's yo' pap,
Ef you nevah wriggles
  Outen Sukey's lap;
Ef you says yo' "Lay me"
  Evah single night
'Fo' dey tucks de kivers
  An' puts out de light,
Den de rain kin pattah
  Win' blow lak a fan,
But you need n' bothah
  'Bout de Boogah Man!

THE WRAITH

Ah me, it is cold and chill
  And the fire sobs low in the
    grate,
While the wind rides by on the
    hill,
  And the logs crack sharp with
    hate.

And she, she is cold and sad
  As ever the sinful are,
But deep in my heart I am glad
  For my wound and the coming
    scar.

Oh, ever the wind rides by
  And ever the raindrops grieve;
But a voice like a woman's sigh
  Says, "Do you believe, be-
    lieve?"

Ah, you were warm and sweet,
Sweet as the May days be;

Down did I fall at your feet,
  Why did you hearken to me?

Oh, the logs they crack and whine,
  And the water drops from the
    eaves;
But it is not rain but brine
  Where my dead darling grieves.

And a wraith sits by my side,
  A spectre grim and dark;
Are you gazing here open-eyed
  Out to the lifeless dark?

But ever the wind rides on,
  And we sit close within;
Out of the face of the dawn,
  I and my darling,— sin.

SILENCE

'Tis better to sit here beside the
    sea,
  Here on the spray-kissed beach,
In silence, that between such
    friends as we
  Is full of deepest speech.

WHIP-POOR-WILL AND KATY-DID

Slow de night's a-fallin',
An' I hyeah de callin,
  Out erpon de lonesome hill;
Soun' is moughty dreary,
Solemn-lak an' skeery,
  Sayin' fu' to "whip po' Will."

Now hit's moughty tryin',
Fu' to hyeah dis cryin',
  'Deed hit's mo' den I kin stan';
Sho' wid all our slippin',
Dey's enough of whippin'
  'Dout a bird a'visin' any man.

In de noons o' summah
Dey's anothah hummah
  Sings anothah song instid;
An' his th'oat's a-swellin'
Wid de joy o' tellin',
  But he says dat "Katy did."

Now I feels onsuhtain;
Won't you raise de cu'tain
  Ovah all de ti'ngs dat's hid?
W'y dat feathahed p'isen
Goes erbout a-visin'
  Whippin' Will w'en Katy
    did?

'LONG TO'DS NIGHT

Daih's a moughty soothin'
    feelin'
  Hits a dahky man,
    'Long to'ds night.
W'en de row is mos' nigh ended,
  Den he stops to fan,
    'Long to'ds night.
De blue smoke f'om his cabin
    is a-callin' to him
    "Come;"
He smell de bacon cookin', an' he
    hyeah de fiah hum;

An' he 'mence to sing, 'dough
    wo'kin' putty nigh
    done made him dumb,
  'Long to'ds night.

Wid his hoe erpon his shouldah
  Den he goes erlong,
    'Long to'ds night.
An' he keepin' time a-steppin'
  Wid a little song,
    'Long to'ds night.
De restin'-time's a-comin', an' de
    time to drink an' eat;
A baby's toddlin' to'ds him on hits
    little dusty feet;
An' a-goin' to'ds his cabin, an'
    his suppah's moughty
    sweet,
  'Long to'ds night.

Daih his Ca'line min' de kettle,
  Rufus min' de chile,
    'Long to'ds night;
An' de sweat roll down his
    forred,
  Mixin' wid his smile,
    'Long to'ds night.
He toss his piccaninny, an' he hum
    a little chune;
De wokin' all is ovah, an' de sup-
    pah comin' soon;
De wo'kin' time's Decembah, but
    de restin' time is
    June,
  'Long to'ds night.

Dey's a kin' o' doleful feelin',
Hits a tendah place,
    'Long to'ds night;

Dey's a moughty glory in him
  Shinin' thoo his face,
    Long to'ds night.
De cabin's lak de big house, an'
      de fiah's lak de sun;
His wife look moughty lakly, an'
    de chile de puttiest
    one;
W'y, hit's blessid, jes' a-livin'
    w'en a body's wo'k is
    done.
    'Long to'ds night.

A GRIEVANCE

W'EN de snow's a-fallin'
  An' de win' is col'.
Mammy 'mence a-callin',
  Den she 'mence to scol',
"Lucius Lishy Brackett,
  Don't you go out do's,
Button up yo' jacket,
  Les'n you'll git froze."

I sit at de windah
  Lookin' at de groun',
Nuffin nigh to hindah,
  Mammy ain' erroun';
Wish't she would n' mek me
  Set down in dis chaih;
Pshaw, it would n't tek me
  Long to git some aih.

So I jump down nimble
  Ez a boy kin be,
Dough I's all a-trimble
  Feahed some one'll see;
Bet in a half a minute
  I fly out de do'

An' I's knee-deep in it,
  Dat dah blessed snow.

Den I hyeah a pattah
  Come acrost de flo'.
Den dey comes a clattah
  At de cabin do';
An' my mammy holler
  Spoilin' all my joy,
"Come in f'om dat waller,
  Don't I see you, boy?"

W'en de snow's a-sievin'
  Down ez sof' ez meal,
Whut's de use o' livin'
  'Cept you got de feel
Of de stuff dat's fallin'
  'Roun' an' white an' damp,
'Dout some one a-callin',
  "Come in hyeah, you scamp!

DINAH KNEADING
DOUGH

I HAVE seen full many a sight
Born of day or drawn by night:
Sunlight on a silver stream,
Golden lilies all a-dream,
Lofty mountains, bold and proud,
Veiled beneath the lacelike cloud;
But no lovely sight I know
Equals Dinah kneading dough.

Brown arms buried elbow-deep
Their domestic rhythm keep,
As with steady sweep they go
Through the gently yielding
    dough.

PAUL LAURENCE DUNBAR

Maids may vaunt their finer
    charms—
Naught to me like Dinah's arms;
Girls may draw, or paint, or
    sew —
I love Dinah kneading dough.

Eyes of jet and teeth of pearl,
Hair, some say, too tight a-curl;
But the dainty maid I deem
Very near perfection's dream.
Swift she works, and only flings
Me a glance — the least of things.
And I wonder, does she know
That my heart is in the dough?

TO A CAPTIOUS CRITIC

DEAR critic, who my lightness so
    deplores,
Would I might study to be prince
    of bores,
Right wisely would I rule that
    dull estate —
But, sir, I may not, till you
    abdicate.

DAT OL' MARE O' MINE

WANT to trade me, do you, mis-
    tah? Oh, well, now, I
    reckon not,
W'y you could n't buy my Sukey
    fu' a thousan' on de spot.
        Dat ol' mare o' mine?

Yes, huh coat ah long an' shaggy,
    an' she ain't no shakes to
    see;
Dat 's a ring-bone, yes, you right,
    suh, an' she got a on'ry
    knee,
But dey ain't no use in talkin',
    she de only hoss fu' me,
        Dat ol' mare o' mine.

Co'se, I knows dat Suke 's con-
    tra'y, an' she moughty ap'
    to vex;
But you got to mek erlowance fu'
    de nature of huh sex;
        Dat ol' mare o' mine.
Ef you pull her on de lef' han';
    she plum 'termined to go
    right,
A cannon could n't skeer huh, but
    she boun' to tek a fright
At a piece o' common paper, or
    anyt'ing whut's white,
        Dat ol' mare o' mine.

W'en my eyes commence to fail
    me, dough, I trus'es to
    huh sight,
An' she 'll tote me safe an' hones'
    on de ve'y da'kes' night,
        Dat ol' mare o' mine.
Ef I whup huh, she jes' switch
    huh tail, an' settle to a
    walk,
Ef I whup huh mo', she shek huh
    haid, an' lak ez not, she
    balk.

[189]

But huh sense ain't no ways
    lackin', she do evah t'ing
    but talk,
    Dat ol' mare o' mine.

But she gentle ez a lady w'en she
    know huh beau kin see.
An' she sholy got mo' gumption
    any day den you or me,
    Dat ol' mare o' mine.
She 's a leetle slow a-goin,' an' she
    moughty ha'd to sta't,
But we 's gittin' ol' togathah, an'
    she 's closah to my hea't,
An' I does n't reckon, mistah, dat
    she 'd sca'cely keer to pa't;
    Dat ol' mare o' mine.

W'y I knows de time dat cidah 's
    kin' o' muddled up my haid,
Ef it had n't been fu' Sukey
    hyeah, I reckon I 'd been
    daid;
    Dat ol' mare o' mine.
But she got me in de middle o'
    de road an' tuk me
    home,
An' she would n't let me wandah,
    ner she would n't let me
    roam,
Dat 's de kin' o' hoss to tie to
    w'en you 's seed de cidah's
    foam,
    Dat ol' mare o' mine.

You kin talk erbout yo' heaven,
    you kin talk erbout yo' hell,

Dey is people, dey is hosses, den
    dey's cattle, den dey 's—
    well —
    Dat ol' mare o' mine;
She de beatenes' t'ing dat evah
    struck de medders o' de
    town,
An' aldough huh haid ain't fittin'
    fu' to waih no golden
    crown.
D' ain't a blessed way fu' Petah
    fu' to tu'n my Sukey down,
    Dat ol' mare o' mine.

IN THE MORNING

'Lias! 'Lias! Bless de Lawd!
Don' you know de day 's
    erbroad?
Ef you don' git up, you scamp,
Dey 'll be trouble in dis camp.
T'ink I gwine to let you sleep
W'ile I meks yo' boa'd an' keep?
Dat 's a putty howdy-do —
Don' you hyeah me, 'Lias — you?

Bet ef I come crost dis flo'
You won' fin' no time to sno'.
Daylight all a-shinin' in
W'ile you sleep — w'y hit 's a sin!
Ain't de can'le-light enough
To bu'n out widout a snuff,
But you go de mo'nin' thoo
Bu'nin' up de daylight too?

'Lias, don' you hyeah me call?
No use tu'nin' to'ds de wall;

PAUL LAURENCE DUNBAR

I kin hyeah dat mattuss squeak;
Don' you hyeah me w'en I speak?
Dis hyeah clock done struck off
    six —
Ca'line, bring me dem ah sticks!
Oh, you down, suh; huh, you
    down —
Look hyeah, don' you daih to
    frown.

Ma'ch yo'se'f an' wash yo' face,
Don' you splattah all de place;
I got somep'n else to do,
'Sides jes' cleanin' aftah you.
Tek dat comb an' fix yo' haid —
Looks jes' lak a feddah baid.
Look hyeah, boy, I let you see
You sha' n't roll yo' eyes at me.

Come hyeah; bring me dat ah
    strap!
Boy, I 'll whup you 'twell you
    drap;
You done felt yo'se'f too stròng,
An' you sholy got me wrong.
Set down at dat table thaih;
Jes' you whimpah ef you daih!
Evah mo'nin' on dis place,
Seem lak I mus' lose my grace.

Fol' yo' han's an' bow yo' haid —
Wait ontwell de blessin' 's said;
"Lawd, have mussy on ouah
    souls —"
(Don' you daih to tech dem
    rolls —)
"Bless de food we gwine to
    eat —"

(You set still — I *see* yo' feet;
You jes' try dat trick agin!)
"Gin us peace an' joy. Amen!"

THE POET

He sang of life, serenely sweet,
    With, now and then, a deeper
    note.
    From some high peak, nigh yet
    remote,
He voiced the world's absorbing
    beat.

He sang of love when earth was
    young,
    And Love, itself, was in his
    lays.
    But ah, the world, it turned to
    praise
A jingle in a broken tongue.

A FLORIDA NIGHT

Win' a-blowin' gentle so de san'
    lay low,
    San' a little heavy f'om de rain,
All de pa'ms a-wavin' an' a-weav-
    in' slow,
    Sighin' lak a sinnah-soul in
    pain.
Alligator grinnin' by de ol'
    lagoon,
Mockin'-bird a-singin' to be big
    full moon,

'Skeeter go a-skimmin' to his
    fightin' chune
  (Lizy Ann 's a-waitin' in de
    lane!).

Moccasin a-sleepin' in de cyprus
    swamp;
  Need n't wake de gent'man, not
    fu' me.
Mule, you need n't wake him
    w'en you switch an' stomp,
Fightin' off a 'skeeter er a flea.
Florida is lovely, she 's de fines'
    lan'
Evah seed de sunlight f'om de
    Mastah's han',
'Ceptin' fu' de varmints an' huh
    fleas an' san'
  An' de nights w'en Lizy Ann
    ain' free.

Moon 's a-kinder shaddered on de
    melon patch;
  No one ain't a-watchin' ez I
    go.
Climbin' of de fence so 's not to
    click de latch
  Meks my gittin' in a little
    slow.
Watermelon smilin' as it say,
    " I 's free; "
Alligator boomin', but I let him
    be,
Florida, oh, Florida 's de lan' fu'
    me —
  (Lizy Ann a-singin' sweet an'
    low).

DIFFERENCES

My neighbor lives on the hill,
  And I in the valley dwell,
My neighbor must look down on
    me,
  Must I look up? — ah, well,
My neighbor lives on the hill,
  And I in the valley dwell.

My neighbor reads, and prays,
  And I — I laugh, God wot,
And sing like a bird when the
    grass is green
  In my small garden plot;
But ah, he reads and prays,
  And I — I laugh, God wot.

His face is a book of woe,
  And mine is a song of glee;
A slave he is to the great " They
    say,"
  But I — I am bold and free;
No wonder he smacks of woe,
  And I have the tang of glee.

My neighbor thinks me a fool,
  " The same to yourself," say I;
" Why take your books and take
    your prayers,
  Give me the open sky; "
My neighbor thinks me a fool,
  " The same to yourself," say I.

LONG AGO

De ol' time 's gone, de new
    time 's hyeah
  Wid all hits fuss an' feddahs;

I done fu'got de joy an' cheah
  We knowed all kin's o' wed-
    dahs,
I done fu'got each ol'-time hymn
  We ust to sing in meetin';
I 's leahned de prah's, so neat an'
    trim,
  De preachah keeps us 'peatin'.

Hang a vine by de chimney side,
  An' one by de cabin do';
An' sing a song fu' de day dat
    died,
  De day of long ergo.

My youf, hit 's gone, yes, long
    ergo,
  An' yit I ain't a-moanin';
Hit 's fu' somet'ings I ust to
    know
  I set to-night a-honin'.
De pallet on de ol' plank flo',
  De rain bar'l und' de eaves,
De live oak 'fo' de cabin do',
  Whaih de night dove comes an'
    grieves.

Hang a vine by de chimney side,
  An' one by de cabin do';
An' sing a song fu' de day dat
    died,
  De day of long ergo.

I 'd lak a few ol' frien's to-night
  To come an' set wid me;
An' let me feel dat ol' delight
  I ust to in dey glee.
But hyeah we is, my pipe an' me,
  Wid no one else erbout;

We bofe is choked ez choked kin
    be,
  An' bofe 'll soon go out.

Hang a vine by de chimney side,
  An' one by de cabin do';
An' sing a song fu' de day dat
    died,
  De day of long ergo.

A PLANTATION MELODY

De trees is bendin' in de sto'm,
De rain done hid de mountain's
    fo'm,
  I 's 'lone an' in distress.
But listen, dah 's a voice I hyeah,
A-sayin' to me, loud an' cleah,
  "Lay low in de wildaness."

De lightnin' flash, de bough sway
    low,
My po' sick hea't is trimblin' so,
  It hu'ts my very breas'.
But him dat give de lightnin'
    powah
Jes' bids me in de tryin' howah
  "Lay low in de wildaness."

O brothah, w'en de tempes' beat,
An' w'en yo' weary head an' feet
  Can't fin' no place to res',
Jes' 'membah dat de Mastah 's
    nigh,
An' putty soon you 'll hyeah de
    cry,
  "Lay low in de wildaness."

O sistah, w'en de rain come down,
An' all yo' hopes is 'bout to
    drown,
  Don't ttus' de Mastah less.
He smilin' w'en you t'ink he
    frown,
He ain' gwine let yo' soul sink
    down —
  Lay low in de wildaness.

A SPIRITUAL

De 'cession 's stahted on de gospel
    way,
  De Capting is a-drawin' nigh:
Bettah stop a-foolin' an' a-try to
    pray;
  Lif' up yo' haid w'en de King
    go by!

Oh, sinnah mou'nin' in de dusty
    road,
  Hyeah 's de minute fu' to dry
    yo' eye:
Dey 's a moughty One a-comin'
    fu' to baih yo' load;
  Lif' up yo' haid w'en de King
    go by!

Oh, widder weepin' by yo' hus-
    ban's grave,
  Hit 's bettah fu' to sing den
    sigh:
Hyeah come de Mastah wid de
    powah to save;
  Lif' up yo' haid w'en de King
    go by!

Oh, orphans a-weepin' lak de wid-
    der do,
  An' I wish you 'd tell me why:
De Mastah is a mammy an' a
    pappy too;
  Lif' up yo' haid w'en de King
    go by!

Oh, Moses sot de sarpint in de
    wildahness
  W'en de chillun had com-
    menced to die:
Some 'efused to look, but hit
    cuohed de res';
  Lif' up yo' haid w'en de King
    go by!

Bow down, bow 'way down,
  Bow down,
But lif' up yo' haid w'en de King
    go by!

THE MEMORY OF MARTHA

Out in de night a sad bird moans,
  An', oh, but hit 's moughty
    lonely;
Times I kin sing, but mos' I
    groans,
  Fu' oh, but hit 's moughty
    lonely!
Is you sleepin' well dis evenin',
    Marfy, deah?
W'en I calls you f'om de cabin,
    kin you hyeah?
'T ain't de same ol' place to me,
Nuffin' 's lak hit used to be,

PAUL LAURENCE DUNBAR

W'en I knowed dat you was allus
    some'ers near.

Down by de road de shadders
        grows,
    An', oh, but hit 's moughty
        lonely;
Seem lak de ve'y moonlight
        knows,
    An', oh, but hit 's moughty
        lonely!
Does you know, I 's cryin' fu' you,
        oh, my wife?
Does you know dey ain't no joy
        no mo' in life?
    An' my only t'ought is dis,
    Dat I 's honin' fu' de bliss
Fu' to quit dis groun' o' worri-
        ment an' strife.

Dah on de baid my banjo lays,
    An', oh, but hit 's moughty
        lonely;
Can't even sta't a chune o' praise,
    An', oh, but hit 's moughty
        lonely!
Oh, hit's moughty slow a-waitin'
        hyeah below.
Is you watchin' fu' me, Marfy,
        at de do'?
    Ef you is, in spite o' sin,
    Dey 'll be sho' to let me in,
W'en dey sees yo' face a-shinin',
        den dey 'll know.

W'EN I GITS HOME

It's moughty tiahsome layin'
        'roun'
Dis sorrer-laden earfly groun',
An' oftentimes I thinks, thinks
        I,
'T would be a sweet t'ing des to
        die,
    An' go 'long home.

Home whaih de frien's I loved 'll
        say,
"We 've waited fu' you many a
        day,
Come hyeah an' res' yo'se'f, an'
        know
You 's done wid sorrer an' wid
        woe,
    Now you 's at home."

W'en I gits home some blessid
        day,
I 'lows to th'ow my caihs erway,
An' up an' down de shinin' street,
Go singin' sof' an' low an' sweet,
    W'en I gits home.

I wish de day was neah at han',
I 's tiahed of dis grievin' lan',
I 's tiahed of de lonely yeahs,
·I want to des dry up my teahs,
    An' go 'long home.

Oh, Mastah, won't you sen' de
        call?
My frien's is daih, my hope, my
        all.

[195]

I 's waitin' whaih de road is rough,
I want to hyeah you say,
    " Enough,
    Ol' man, come home! "

" HOWDY, HONEY, HOWDY! "

Do' a-stan'in' on a jar, fiah
    a-shinin' thoo,
Ol' folks drowsin' 'roun' de place,
    wide awake is Lou,
W'en I tap, she answeh, an' I see
    huh 'mence to grin,
" Howdy, honey, howdy, won't
    you step right in? "

Den I step erpon de log layin' at
    de do',
Bless de Lawd, huh mammy an'
    huh pap 's done 'menced to
    sno',
Now 's de time, ef evah, ef I 's
    gwine to try an' win,
" Howdy, honey, howdy, won't
    you step right in? "

No use playin' on de aidge,
    trimblin' on de brink,
W'en a body love a gal, tell huh
    whut he t'ink;
W'en huh hea't is open fu' de love
    you gwine to gin,
Pull yo'se'f togethah, suh, an' step
    right in.

Sweetes' imbitation dat a body
    evah hyeahed,
Sweetah den de music of a love-
    sick mockin'-bird,
Comin' f'om de gal you loves bet-
    tah den yo' kin,
" Howdy, honey, howdy, won't
    you step right in? "

At de gate o' heaven w'en de
    storm o' life is pas',
'Spec' I 'll be a-stan'in', 'twell de
    Mastah say at las',
" Hyeah he stan' all weary, but
    he winned his fight wid sin.
Howdy, honey, howdy, won't you
    step right in? "

THE UNSUNG HEROES

A song for the unsung heroes
    who rose in the country's
    need,
When the life of the land was
    threatened by the slaver's
    cruel greed,
For the men who came from the
    cornfield, who came from the
    plough and the flail,
Who rallied round when they
    heard the sound of the
    mighty man of the rail.

They laid them down in the val-
    leys, they laid them down in
    the wood,
And the world looked on at the
    work they did, and whis-
    pered, " It is good."

They fought their way on the
    hillside, they fought their
    way in the glen,
And God looked down on their
    sinews brown, and said, " I
    have made them men."

They went to the blue lines gladly,
    and the blue lines took them
    in,
And the men who saw their
    muskets' fire thought not of
    their dusky skin.
The gray lines rose and melted
    beneath their scathing show-
    ers,
And they said, " 'T is true, they
    have force to do, these old
    slave boys of ours."

Ah, Wagner saw their glory, and
    Pillow knew their blood,
That poured on a nation's altar,
    a sacrificial flood.
Port Hudson heard their war-cry
    that smote its smoke-filled
    air,
And the old free fires of their
    savage sires again were
    kindled there.

They laid them down where the
    rivers the greening valleys
    gem.
And the song of the thund'rous
    cannon was their sole re-
    quiem,

And the great smoke wreath that
    mingled its hue with the
    dusky cloud,
Was the flag that furled o'er a
    saddened world, and the
    sheet that made their shroud.

Oh, Mighty God of the Battles
    Who held them in Thy
    hand,
Who gave them strength through
    the whole day's length, to
    fight for their native land,
They are lying dead on the hill-
    sides, they are lying dead on
    the plain,
And we have not fire to smite the
    lyre and sing them one brief
    strain.

Give, Thou, some seer the power
    to sing them in their might,
The men who feared the master's
    whip, but did not fear the
    fight;
That he may tell of their virtues
    as minstrels did of old,
Till the pride of face and the hate
    of race grow obsolete and
    cold.

A song for the unsung heroes who
    stood the awful test,
When the humblest host that the
    land could boast went forth
    to meet the best;
A song for the unsung heroes who
    fell on the bloody sod,

Who fought their way from night
to day and struggled up to
God.

THE POOL

By the pool that I see in my
dreams, dear love,
I have sat with you time and
again;
And listened beneath the dank
leaves, dear love,
To the sibilant sound of the
rain.

And the pool, it is silvery bright,
dear love,
And as pure as the heart of a
maid,
As sparkling and dimpling, it
darkles and shines
In the depths of the heart of
the glade.

But, oh, I 've a wish in my soul,
dear love,
(The wish of a dreamer, it
seems,)
That I might wash free of my
sins, dear love,
In the pool that I see in my
dreams.

POSSESSION

Whose little lady is you, chile,
Whose little gal is you?

What 's de use o' kiver'n up yo'
face?
Chile, dat ain't de way to do.
Lemme see yo' little eyes,
Tek yo' little han's down nice,
Lawd, you wuff a million bills,
Huh uh, chile, dat ain't yo'
price.

Honey, de money ain't been made
Dat dey could pay fu' you;
'T ain't no use a-biddin'; you too
high
Fu' de riches' Jap er Jew.
Lemme see you smilin' now,
How dem teef o' yo'n do
shine,
An' de t'ing dat meks me laff
Is dat all o' you is mine.

How 's I gwine to tell you how I
feel,
How 's I gwine to weigh yo'
wuff?
Oh, you sholy is de sweetes' t'ing
Walkin' on dis blessed earf.
Possum is de sweetes' meat,
Cidah is the nices' drink,
But my little lady-bird
Is de bes' of all, I t'ink.

Talk erbout 'uligion he'pin' folks
All thoo. de way o' life,
Gin de res' 'uligion, des' gin me
You, my little lady-wife.
Den de days kin come all ha'd,
Den de nights kin come all
black,

Des' you tek me by de han',
  An' I 'll stumble on de track.

Stumble on de way to Gawd, my
    chile,
  Stumble on, an' mebbe fall;
But I 'll keep a-trottin', while you
    lead on,
  Pickin' an' a-trottin', dat 's all.
Hol' me mighty tight, dough,
    chile,
  Fu' hit 's rough an' rocky lan',
Heaben 's at de en', I know,
  So I 's leanin' on yo' han'.

THE OLD FRONT GATE

W'EN daih 's chillun in de house,
  Dey keep on a-gittin' tall;
But de folks don' seem to see
  Dat dey 's growin' up at all,
'Twell dey fin' out some fine day
  Dat de gals has 'menced to
      grow,
'W'en dey notice as dey pass
  Dat de front gate 's saggin' low.

W'en de hinges creak an' cry,
  An' de bahs go slantin' down,
You kin reckon dat hit 's time
  Fu' to cas' yo' eye erroun',
'Cause daih ain't no 'sputin' dis,
  Hit 's de trues' sign to show
Dat daih 's cou'tin' goin' on
  W'en de ol' front gate sags low.

Oh, you grumble an' complain,
  An' you prop dat gate up right;
But you notice right nex' day
  Dat hit 's in de same ol' plight.
So you fin' dat hit 's a rule,
  An' daih ain' no use to blow,
'W'en de gals is growin' up,
  Dat de front gate will sag low.

Den you t'ink o' yo' young days,
  W'en you cou'ted Sally Jane,
An' you so't o' feel ashamed
  Fu' to grumble an' complain,
'Cause yo' ricerlection says,
  An' you know hits wo'ds is so,
Dat huh pappy had a time
  Wid his front gate saggin' low.

So you jes' looks on an' smiles
  At 'em leanin' on de gate,
Tryin' to t'ink whut he kin say
  Fu' to keep him daih so late,
But you lets dat gate erlone,
  Fu' yo' 'sperunce goes to show,
'Twell de gals is ma'ied off,
  It gwine keep on saggin' low.

DIRGE FOR A SOLDIER

IN the east the morning comes,
Hear the rollin' of the drums
      On the hill.
But the heart that beat as they
    beat
In the battle's raging day heat
      Lieth still.
Unto him the night has come,
Though they roll the morning
    drum.

What is in the bugle's blast?
It is: "Victory at last!
    Now for rest."
But, my comrades, come behold
    him,
Where our colors now enfold him,
    And his breast
Bares no more to meet the blade,
But lies covered in the shade.

What a stir there is to-day!
They are laying him away
    Where he fell.
There the flag goes draped before
    him;
Now they pile the grave sod o'er
    him
    With a knell.
And he answers to his name
In the higher ranks of fame.

There's a woman left to mourn
For the child that she has borne
    In travail.
But her heart beats high and
    higher,
With the patriot mother's fire,
    At the tale.
She has borne and lost a son,
But her work and his are done.

Fling the flag out, let it wave;
They're returning from the
    grave —
    "Double quick!"
And the cymbals now are crash-
    ing,

Bright his comrades' eyes are flash-
    ing
    From the thick
Battle-ranks which knew him
    brave,
No tears for a hero's grave.

In the east the morning comes,
Hear the rattle of the drums
    Far away.
Now no time for grief's pursuing,
Other work is for the doing,
    Here to-day.
He is sleeping, let him rest
With the flag across his breast.

A FROLIC

SWING yo' lady roun' an' roun',
    Do de bes' you know;
Mek yo' bow an' p'omenade
    Up an' down de flo';
Mek dat banjo hump huhse'f,
    Listen at huh talk:
Mastah gone to town to-night;
    'T ain't no time to walk.

Lif' yo' feet an' flutter thoo,
    Run, Miss Lucy, run;
Reckon you'll be cotched an'
    kissed
    'Fo' de night is done.
You don't need to be so proud —
    I 's a-watchin' you,
An' I 's layin' lots o' plans
    Fu' to git you, too.

PAUL LAURENCE DUNBAR

Moonlight on de cotton-fiel'
  Shinin' sof' an' white,
Whippo'will a-tellin' tales
  Out thaih ir de night;
An' yo' cabin 's 'crost de lot:
  Run, Miss Lucy, run;
Reckon you 'll be cotched an'
    kissed
  'Fo' de night is done.

NODDIN' BY DE FIRE

Some folks t'inks hit 's right an'
    p'opah,
  Soon ez bedtime come erroun',
Fu' to scramble to de kiver,
  Lak dey 'd hyeahed de trumpet
    soun'.
But dese people dey all misses
  Whut I mos'ly does desiah;
Dat 's de settin' roun' an' dozin',
  An' a-noddin' by de fiah.

When you 's tiahed out a-hoein',
  Er a-followin' de plough,
Whut 's de use of des a-fallin'
  On yo' pallet lak a cow?
'W'y, de fun is all in waitin'
  In de face of all de tiah,
An' a-dozin' and a-drowsin'
  By a good ol' hick'ry fiah.

Oh, you grunts an' groans an'
    mumbles
  Case yo' bones is full o' col',

Dough you feels de joy a-tricklin'
  Roun' de co'nahs of yo' soul.
An' you 'low anothah minute
  'S sho to git you wa'm an'
    dryah,
W'en you set up pas' yo' bedtime,
  Case you hates to leave de fiah.

Whut 's de use o' downright
    sleepin'?
  You can't feel it while it las',
An' you git up feelin' sorry
  W'en de time fu' it is pas'.
Seem to me dat time too precious,
  An' de houahs too short entiah,
Fu' to sleep, w'en you could spen'
    'em
  Des a-noddin' by de fiah.

LOVE'S CASTLE

Key and bar, key and bar,
  Iron bolt and chain!
And what will you do when the
    King comes
  To enter his domain?

Turn key and lift bar,
  Loose, oh, bolt and chain!
Open the door and let him in,
  And then lock up again.

But, oh, heart, and woe, heart,
  Why do you ache so sore?
Never a moment's peace have you
  Since Love hath passed the door.

Turn key and lift bar,
 And loose bolt and chain;
But Love took in his esquire, Grief,
 And there they both remain.

MORNING SONG OF
LOVE

DARLING, my darling, my heart is
 on the wing,
 It flies to thee this morning like
 a bird,
Like happy birds in springtime my
 spirits soar and sing,
 The same sweet song thine ears
 have often heard.

The sun is in my window, the
 shadow on the lea,
 The wind is moving in the
 branches green,
And all my life, my darling, is
 turning unto thee,
 And kneeling at thy feet, my
 own, my queen.

The golden bells are ringing across
 the distant hill,
 Their merry peals come to me
 soft and clear,
But in my heart's deep chapel all
 incense-filled and still
 A sweeter bell is sounding for
 thee, dear.

The bell of love invites thee to
 come and seek the shrine

Whose altar is erected unto
 thee,
The offerings, the sacrifice, the
 prayers, the chants are
 thine,
 And I, my love, thy humble
 priest will be.

ON A CLEAN BOOK
TO F. N.

LIKE sea-washed sand upon the
 shore,
 So fine and clean the tale,
So clear and bright I almost see,
 The flashing of a sail.

The tang of salt is in its veins,
 The freshness of the spray
God give you love and lore and
 strength,
 To give us such alway.

TO THE EASTERN
SHORE

I 's feelin' kin' o' lonesome in my
 little room to-night,
 An' my min 's done los' de minutes an' de miles,
W'ile it teks me back a-flyin' to
 de country of delight,
 Whaih de Chesapeake goes
 grumblin' er wid smiles.
 Oh, de ol' plantation 's callin'
 to me, Come, come back,

PAUL LAURENCE DUNBAR

Hyeah 's de place fu' you to la-
bouh an' to res',
'Fu my sandy roads is gleamin' w'ile de city ways is
black;
Come back, honey, case yo'
country home is bes'.

I know de moon is shinin' down
erpon de Eastern sho',
An' de bay 's a-sayin' " Howdy " to de lan';
An' de folks is all a-settin' out
erroun' de cabin do',
Wid dey feet a-restin' in de silvah san';
An' de ol' plantation 's callin'
to me, Come, oh, come,
F'om de life dat 's des' a-waih-
in' you erway,
F'om de trouble an' de bustle,
an' de agernizin' hum
Dat de city keeps ergoin' all de
day.

I 's tiahed of de city, tek me back
to Sandy Side,
Whaih de po'est ones kin live
an' play an' eat;
Whaih we draws a simple livin'
f'om de fo'est an' de tide,
An' de days ah faih, an' evah
night is sweet.
Fu' de ol' plantation 's callin'
to me, Come, oh, come.
An' de Chesapeake 's a-sayin'
" Dat 's de t'ing,"

W'ile my little cabin beckons,
dough his mouf is closed
an' dumb,
I 's a-comin, an' my hea't begins to sing.

RELUCTANCE

WILL I have some mo' dat pie?
No, ma'am, thank-ee, dat is —
I —
Bettah quit daihin' me.
Dat ah pie look sutny good:
How 'd you feel now ef I would?
I don' reckon dat I should;
Bettah quit daihin' me.

Look hyeah, I gwine tell de truf,
Mine is sholy one sweet toof:
Bettah quit daihin' me.
Yass'm, yass'm, dat 's all right,
I 's done tried to be perlite:
But dat pie 's a lakly sight,
Wha 's de use o' daihin' me?

My, yo' lips is full an' red,
Don't I wish you 'd tu'n yo' haid?
Bettah quit daihin' me.
Dat ain't faih, now, honey chile,
I 's gwine lose my sense erwhile
Ef you des set daih an' smile,
Bettah quit daihin' me.

Nuffin' don' look ha'f so fine
Ez dem teef, deah, w'en dey shine:
Bettah quit daihin' me.
Now look hyeah, I tells you dis;

[203]

I 'll give up all othah bliss
Des to have one little kiss,
 Bettah quit daihin' me.

Laws, I teks yo' little han',
Ain't it tendah? bless de lan'—
 Bettah quit daihin' me.
I 's so lonesome by myse'f,
'D ain't no fun in livin' lef';
Dis hyeah life 's ez dull ez def:
 Bettah quit daihin' me.

Why n't you tek yo' han' erway?
Yass, I 'll hol' it: but I say
 Bettah quit daihin' me.
Holin' han's is sholy fine.
Seems lak dat 's de weddin' sign.
Wish you 'd say dat you 'd be
 mine;—
 Dah you been daihin' me.

BALLADE

By Mystic's banks I held my
 dream.
 (I held my fishing rod as well,)
The vision was of dace and bream,
 A fruitless vision, sooth to tell.
 But round about the sylvan dell
Were other sweet Arcadian
 shrines,
 Gone now, is all the rural spell,
Arcadia has trolley lines.

Oh, once loved, sluggish, darkling
 stream,

For me no more, thy waters
 swell,
Thy music now the engines'
 scream,
 Thy fragrance now the factory's
 smell;
 Too near for me the clanging
 bell;
A false light in the water shines
 While Solitude lists to her
 knell,—
Arcadia has trolley lines.

Thy wooded lanes with shade and
 gleam
 Where bloomed the fragrant as-
 phodel,
Now bleak commercially teem
 With signs "To Let," "To
 Buy," "To Sell."
 And Commerce holds them
 fierce and fell;
With vulgar sport she now com-
 bines
 Sweet Nature's piping voice to
 quell.
Arcadia has trolley lines.

L'ENVOI.

Oh, awful Power whose works
 repel
 The marvel of the earth's de-
 signs,—
I 'll hie me otherwhere to dwell,
 Arcadia has trolley lines.

PAUL LAURENCE DUNBAR

SPEAKIN' AT DE COU'T-HOUSE

DEY been speakin' at de cou't-
      house,
   An' laws-a-massy me,
'T was de beatness kin' o' doin's
   Dat evah I did see.
Óf cose I had to be dah
   In de middle o' de crowd,
An' I hallohed wid de othahs,
   W'en de speakah riz and bowed.

I was kind o' disapp'inted
   At de smallness of de man,
Case I 'd allus pictered great folks
   On a mo' expansive plan;
But I t'ought I could respect him
   An' tek in de wo'ds he said,
Fu' dey sho was somp'n knowin'
   In de bald spot on his haid.

But hit did seem so't o' funny
   Aftah waitin' fu' a week
Dat de people kep' on shoutin'
   So de man des could n't speak;
De ho'ns dey blared a little,
   Den dey let loose on de
      drums,—
Some one tol' me dey was playin'
   " See de conkerin' hero comes."

" Well," says I, " you all is white
      folks,
   But you 's sutny actin' queer,
What 's de use of heroes comin'
   Ef dey cain't talk w'en dey 's
      here? "

Aftah while dey let him open,
   An' dat man he waded in,
An' he fit de wahs all ovah
   Winnin' victeries lak sin.

W'en he come down to de present,
   Den he made de feathahs fly.
He des waded in on money,
   An' he played de ta'iff high.
An' he said de colah question,
   Hit was ovah, solved, an' done,
Dat de dahky was his brothah,
   Evah blessed mothah's son.

Well he settled all de trouble
   Dat 's been pesterin' de lan',
Den he set down mid de cheerin'
   An' de playin' of de ban'.
I was feelin' moughty happy
   'Twell I hyeahed somebody
      speak,
" Well, dat 's his side of de bus'-
      ness,
   But you wait for Jones nex'
      week."

BLACK SAMSON OF BRANDYWINE

" In the fight at Brandywine, Black
Samson, a giant negro armed with a
scythe, sweeps his way through the
red ranks. . . ." C. M. SKINNER'S
" *Myths and Legends of Our Own
Land.*"

GRAY are the pages of record,
   Dim are the volumes of eld;
Else had old Delaware told us
   More that her history held.

Told us with pride in the story,
  Honest and noble and fine,
More of the tale of my hero,
  Black Samson of Brandywine.

Sing of your chiefs and your no-
    bles,
  Saxon and Celt and Gaul,
Breath of mine ever shall join you,
  Highly I honor them all.
Give to them all of their glory,
  But for this noble of mine,
Lend him a tithe of your tribute,
  Black Samson of Brandywine.

There in the heat of the battle,
  There in the stir of the fight,
Loomed he, an ebony giant,
  Black as the pinions of night.
Swinging his scythe like a mower
  Over a field of grain,
Needless the care of the gleaners,
  Where he had passed amain.

Straight through the human har-
    vest,
  Cutting a bloody swath,
Woe to you, soldier of Briton!
  Death is abroad in his path.
Flee from the scythe of the reaper,
  Flee while the moment is thine,
None may with safety withstand
    him,
  Black Samson of Brandywine.

Was he a freeman or bondman?
  Was he a man or a thing?

What does it matter? His brav-
    'ry
  Renders him royal — a king.
If he was only a chattel,
  Honor the ransom may pay
Of the royal, the loyal black giant
  Who fought for his country
    that day.

Noble and bright is the story,
  Worthy the touch of the lyre,
Sculptor or poet should find it
  Full of the stuff to inspire.
Beat it in brass and in copper,
  Tell it in storied line,
So that the world may remember
  Black Samson of Brandywine.

THE LOOKING-GLASS

Dinah stan' befo' de glass,
  Lookin' moughty neat,
An' huh purty shadder sass
  At huh haid an' feet.
While she sasshay 'roun' an' bow,
Smilin' den an' poutin' now,
An' de lookin'-glass, I 'low
  Say: " Now, ain't she sweet? "

All she do, de glass it see,
  Hit des see, no mo',
Seems to me, hit ought to be
  Drappin' on de flo'.
She go w'en huh time git slack,
Kissin' han's an' smilin' back,
Lawsy, how my lips go smack,
  Watchin' at de do'.

[206]

Wisht I was huh lookin'-glass,
  W'en she kissed huh han';
Does you t'ink I 'd let it pass,
  Settin' on de stan'?
No; I'd des' fall down an' break,
Kin'.o' glad 't uz fu' huh sake;
But de diffunce, dat whut make
  Lookin'-glass an' man.

A MISTY DAY

HEART of my heart, the day is
  chill,
The mist hangs low o'er the
  wooded hill,
The soft white mist and the heavy
  cloud
The sun and the face of heaven
  shroud.
The birds are thick in the dripping
  trees,
That drop their pearls to the beggar breeze;
No songs are rife where songs are
  wont,
Each singer crouches in his haunt.

Heart of my heart, the day is chill,
Whene'er thy loving voice is still,
The cloud and mist hide the sky
  ' from me,
Whene'er thy face I cannot see.
My thoughts fly. back from the
  chill without,
My mind in the storm drops
  doubt on doubt,

No songs arise. Without thee,
  love,
My soul sinks down like a frightened dove.

LI'L' GAL

OH, de weathah it is balmy an' de
  breeze is sighin' low.
    Li'l' gal,
An' de mockin' bird is singin' in
  de locus' by de do',
    Li'l' gal;
Dere 's a hummin' an' a bummin'
  in de lan' f'om eas' to wes',
I 's a-sighin' fu' you, honey, an' I
  nevah know no res'.
Fu' dey 's lots o' trouble brewin'
  an' a-stewin' in my breas',
    Li'l' gal.

Whut 's de mattah wid de weathah,
  whut 's de mattah wid de
  breeze,
    Li'l' gal?
Whut 's de mattah wid de locus'
  dat 's a-singin' in de trees,
    Li'l' gal?
W'y dey knows dey ladies love 'em,
  an' dey knows dey love 'em
  true,
An' dey love 'em back, I reckon,
  des' lak I 's a-lovin' you;
Dat 's de reason dey 's a-weavin'
  an' a-sighin', thoo an' thoo,
    Li'l' gal.

Don't you let no da'ky fool you
  'cause de clo'es he waihs is
  fine,
        Li'l' gal.
Dey's a hones' hea't a-beatin' unnerneaf dese rags o' mine,
        Li'l' gal.
C'ose dey ain' no use in mockin'
  whut de birds an' weathah do,
But I 's say I cain't 'spress it w'en
  I knows I loves you true,
Dat 's de reason I 's a-sighin' an'
  a-singin now fu' you,
        Li'l' gal.

DOUGLASS

Ah, Douglass, we have fall'n on
  evil days,
  Such days as thou, not even thou
    didst know,
    When thee, the eyes of that
      harsh long ago
Saw, salient, at the cross of devious
  ways,
And all the country heard thee
  with amaze.
  Not ended then, the passionate
    ebb and flow,
    The awful tide that battled to
      and fro;
We ride amid a tempest of dis-
  praise.

Now, when the waves of swift dis-
  sension swarm,

And Honor, the strong pilot,
  lieth stark,
Oh, for thy voice high-sounding
  o'er the storm,
  For thy strong arm to guide the
    shivering bark,
The blast-defying power of thy
  form,
  To give us comfort through the
    lonely dark.

WHEN SAM'L SINGS

Hyeah dat singin' in de medders
  Whaih de folks is mekin' hay?
Wo'k is pretty middlin' heavy
  Fu' a man to be so gay.
You kin tell dey 's somep'n special
  . F'om de canter o' de song;
Somep'n sholy pleasin' Sam'l,
  W'en he singin' all day long.

Hyeahd him wa'blin' 'way dis
      mo'nin'
  'Fo' 't was light enough to see.
Seem lak music in de evenin'
  Allus good enough fu' me.
But dat man commenced to hollah
  'Fo' he 'd even washed his face;
Would you b'lieve, de scan'lous
    rascal
  Woke de birds erroun' de place?

Sam'l took a trip a-Sad'day;
  Dressed hisse'f in all he had,
Tuk a cane an' went a-strollin',
  Lookin' mighty pleased an' glad.

PAUL LAURENCE DUNBAR

Some folks don' know whut de
    mattah,
  But I do, you bet yo' life;
Sam'l smilin' an' a-singin'
  'Case he been to see his wife.

She live on de fu' plantation,
  Twenty miles erway er so;
But huh man is mighty happy
  W'en he git de chanst to go.
Walkin' allus ain' de nices'—
  Mo'nin' fin's him on de way—
But he allus comes back smilin',
  Lak his pleasure was his pay.

Den he do a heap o' talkin',
  Do' he mos'ly kin' o' still,
But de wo'ds, dey gits to runnin'
  Lak de watah fu' a mill.
" Whut 's de use o' havin' trouble,
  Whut 's de use o' havin' strife? "
Dat 's de way dis Sam'l preaches
  W'en he been to see his wife.

An' I reckon I git jealous,
  Fu' I laff an' joke an' sco'n,
An' I say, " Oh, go on, Sam'l,
  Des go on, an' blow yo' ho'n."
But I know dis comin' Sad'day,
  Dey 'll be brighter days in life;
An' I 'll be ez glad ez Sam'l
  W'en I go to see my wife.

BOOKER T. WASHINGTON

THE word is writ that he who
  runs may read.

What is the passing breath of
  earthly fame?
But to snatch glory from the hands
  of blame—
That is to be, to live, to strive in-
  deed.
A poor Virginia cabin gave the
  seed,
And from its dark and lowly door
  there came
A peer of princes in the world's
  acclaim,
A master spirit for the nation's
  need.
Strong, silent, purposeful beyond
  his kind,
  The mark of rugged force on
    brow and lip,
Straight on he goes, nor turns to
  look behind
  Where hot the hounds come
    baying at his hip;
With one idea foremost in his
  mind,
  Like the keen prow of some on-
    forging ship.

THE MONK'S WALK

IN this sombre garden close
What has come and passed, who
  knows?
What red passion, what white
  pain
Haunted this dim walk in vain?

Underneath the ivied wall,
Where the silent shadows fall,

Lies the pathway chill and damp
Where the world-quit dreamers
    tramp.

Just across, where sunlight burns,
Smiling at the mourning ferns,
Stand the roses, side by side,   ·
Nodding in their useless pride.

Ferns and roses, who shall say
What you witness day by day?
Covert smile or dropping eye,
As the monks go pacing by.

Has the novice come to-day
Here beneath the wall to pray?
Has the young monk, lately chid-
    den,
Sung his lyric, sweet, forbidden?

Tell me, roses, did you note
That pale father's throbbing
    throat?
Did you hear him murmur,
    " Love! "
As he kissed a faded glove?

Mourning ferns, pray tell me why
Shook you with that passing sigh?
Is it that you chanced to spy
Something in the Abbot's eye?

Here no dream, nor thought of sin,
Where no worlding enters in;
Here no longing, no desire,
Heat nor flame of earthly fire.

Branches waving green above,
Whisper naught of life nor love;

Softened winds that seem a breath,
Perfumed, bring no fear of death.

Is it living thus to live?
Has life nothing more to give?
Ah, no more of smile or sigh —
Life, the world, and love, good-
    bye.

Gray, and passionless, and dim,
Echoing of the solemn hymn,
Lies the walk, 'twixt fern and rose,
Here within the garden close.

LOVE-SONG

If Death should claim me for her
    own to-day,
    And softly I should falter from
    your side,
Oh, tell me, loved one, would my
    memory stay,
    And would my image in your
    heart abide?
Or should I be as some forgotten
    dream,
    That lives its little space, then
    fades entire?
Should Time send o'er you its
    relentless stream,
    To cool your heart, and quench
    for aye love's fire?

I would not for the world, love,
    give you pain,
    Or ever compass what would
    cause you grief;

And, oh, how well I know that
  tears are vain!
  But love is sweet, my dear, and
    life is brief;
So if some day before you I should
  go
  Beyond the sound and sight of
    song and sea,
'T would give my spirit stronger
  wings to know
  That you remembered still and
    wept for me.

SLOW THROUGH THE DARK

Slow moves the pageant of a
  climbing race;
  Their footsteps drag far, far be-
    low the height,
  And, unprevailing by their ut-
    most might,
Seem faltering downward from
  each hard won place.
No strange, swift-sprung excep-
  tion we; we trace
  A devious way thro' dim, uncer-
    tain light,—
  Our hope, through the long
    vistaed years, a sight
Of that our Captain's soul sees
  face to face.
  Who, faithless, faltering that
    the road is steep,
Now raiseth up his drear insistent
  cry?

Who stoppeth here to spend a
  while in sleep
Or curseth that the storm obscures
  the sky?
  Heed not the darkness round
    you, dull and deep;
The clouds grow thickest when
  the summit's nigh.

THE MURDERED LOVER

Say a mass for my soul's repose,
  my brother,
  Say a mass for my soul's repose,
    I need it,
Lovingly lived we, the sons of one
  mother,
  Mine was the sin, but I pray
    you not heed it.

Dark were her eyes as the sloe and
  they called me,
  Called me with voice indepen-
    dent of breath.
God! how my heart beat; her
  beauty appalled me,
  Dazed me, and drew to the sea-
    brink of death.

Lithe was her form like a willow.
  She beckoned,
  What could I do save to follow
    and follow,
Nothing of right or result could be
  reckoned;
  Life without her was unworthy
    and hollow.

[211]

Ay, but I wronged. thee, my
brother, my brother;
Ah, but I loved her, thy beauti-
ful wife.
Shade of our father, and soul of
our mother,
Have I not paid for my love
with my life?

Dark was the night when, re-
vengeful, I met you,
Deep in the heart of a desolate
land.
Warm was the life-blood which
angrily wet you
Sharp was the knife that I felt
from your hand.

Wept you, oh, wept you, alone by
the river,
When my stark carcass you
secretly sank.
Ha, now I see that you tremble
and shiver;
'T was but my spirit that passed
when you shrank!

Weep not, oh, weep not, 't is over,
't is over;
Stir the dark weeds with the
turn of the tide;
Go, thou hast sent me forth, ever
a rover,
Rest and the sweet realm of
heaven denied.

Say a mass for my soul's repose,
my brother,

Say a mass for my soul, I need
it.
Sin of mine was it, and sin of no
other,
Mine was it all, but I pray you
not heed it.

PHILOSOPHY

I BEEN t'inkin' 'bout de preachah;
whut he said de othah
night,
'Bout hit bein' people's dooty,
fu' to keep dey faces bright;
How one ought to live so pleasant
dat ouah tempah never riles,
Meetin' evahbody roun' us wid
ouah very nicest smiles.

Dat 's all right, I ain't a-sputin'
not a t'ing dat soun's lak
fac',
But you don't ketch folks a-grinnin' wid a misery in de
back;
An' you don't fin' dem a-smilin'
w'en dey 's hongry ez kin
be,
Leastways, dat 's how human
natur' allus seems to 'pear
to me.

We is mos' all putty likely fu' to
· have our little cares,
An' I think we 'se doin' fus' rate
w'en we jes' go long and
bears,

Widout breakin' up ouah faces in
  a sickly so't o' grin,
W'en we knows dat in ouah in-
  nards we is p'intly mad ez
  sin.

Oh dey's times fu' bein' pleasant
  an' fu' goin' smilin' roun',
'Cause I don't believe in people
  allus totin' roun' a frown,
But it's easy 'nough to titter w'en
  de stew is smokin' hot,
But hit's mighty ha'd to giggle
  w'en dey's nuffin' in de
  pot.

A PREFERENCE

MASTAH drink his ol' Made'a,
  Missy drink huh sherry wine,
Ovahseah lak his whiskey,
  But dat othah drink is mine,
    Des' 'lasses an' watah, 'lasses
    an' watah.

W'en you git a steamin' hoe-cake
  On de table, go way, man!
'D ain but one t'ing to go wid it,
  'Sides de gravy in de pan,
    Dat's 'lasses an' watah, 'lasses
    an' watah.

W'en hit's 'possum dat you eatin',
  'Simmon beer is moughty sweet;
But fu' evahday consumin'

'D ain't no mo'tal way to beat
  Des' 'lasses an' watah, 'lasses
    an' watah.

W'y de bees is allus busy,
  An' ain' got no time to was'?
Hit's beca'se dey knows de honey
  Dey's a makin', gwine to tas'
    Lak 'lasses an' watah, 'lasses
    an' watah.

Oh, hit's moughty mil' an'
    soothin',
An' hit don' go to yo' haid;
Dat's de reason I's a-backin'
  Up de othah wo'ds I said,
    "Des 'lasses an' watah, 'lasses
    an' watah."

THE DEBT

THIS is the debt I pay
Just for one riotous day,
Years of regret and grief,
Sorrow without relief.

Pay it I will to the end —
Until the grave, my friend,
Gives me a true release —
Gives me the clasp of peace.

Slight was the thing I bought,
Small was the debt I thought,
Poor was the loan at best —
God! but the interest!

ON THE DEDICATION OF DOROTHY HALL

TUSKEGEE, ALA., APRIL 22, 1901.

Not to the midnight of the gloomy
    past,
  Do we revert to-day; we look
    upon
The golden present and the future
    vast
  Whose vistas show us visions of
    the dawn.

Nor shall the sorrows of departed
    years
  The sweetness of our tranquil
    souls annoy,
The sunshine of our hopes dispels
    the tears,
  And clears our eyes to see this
    later joy.

Not ever in the years that God
    hath given
  Have we gone friendless down
    the thorny way,
Always the clouds of pregnant
    black were riven
  By flashes from His own eternal
    day.

The women of a race should be its
    pride;
  We glory in the strength our
    mothers had,
We glory that this strength was
    not denied

To labor bravely, nobly, and be
    glad.

God give to these within this tem-
    ple here,
  Clear vision of the dignity of
    toil,
That virtue in them may its blos-
    soms rear
  Unspotted, fragrant, from the
    lowly soil.

God bless the givers for their noble
    deed,
  Shine on them with the mercy
    of Thy face,
Who come with open hearts to
    help and speed
  The striving women of a strug-
    gling race.

A ROADWAY

Let those who will stride on their
    barren roads
And prick themselves to haste with
    self-made goads,
Unheeding, as they struggle day
    by day,
If flowers be sweet or skies be blue
    or gray:
For me, the lone, cool way by purl-
    ing brooks,
The solemn quiet of the woodland
    nooks,
A song-bird somewhere trilling
    sadly gay,

PAUL LAURENCE DUNBAR

A pause to pick a flower beside the
way.   .

BY RUGGED WAYS

By rugged ways and thro' the
night
We struggle blindly toward the
light;
And groping, stumbling, ever pray
For sight of long delaying day.
The cruel thorns beside the road
Stretch eager points our steps to
goad,
And from the thickets all about
Detaining hands reach threatening
out.

"Deliver us, oh, Lord," we cry,
Our hands uplifted to the sky.
No answer save the thunder's peal,
And onward, onward, still we reel.
"Oh, give us now thy guiding
light;"
Our sole reply, the lightning's
blight.
"Vain, vain," cries one, "in vain
we call;"
But faith serene is over all.

Beside our way the streams are
dried,
And famine mates us side by side.
Discouraged and reproachful eyes
Seek once again the frowning skies.
Yet shall there come, spite storm
and shock,
A Moses who shall smite the rock,

Call manna from the Giver's hand,
And lead us to the promised land!

The way is dark and cold and
steep,
And shapes of horror murder sleep,
And hard the unrelenting years;
But 'twixt our sighs and moans
and tears,
We still can smile, we still can
sing,
Despite the arduous journeying.
For faith and hope their courage
lend,   .
And rest and light are at the end.

LOVE'S SEASONS

When the bees are humming in
the honeysuckle vine
And the summer days are in
their bloom,
Then my love is deepest, oh,
dearest heart of mine,
When the bees are humming in the
honeysuckle vine.

When the winds are moaning o'er
the meadows chill and gray,
And the land is dim with winter
gloom,
Then for thee, my darling, love
will have its way,
When the winds are moaning o'er
the meadows chill and gray.

In the vernal dawning with the
starting of the leaf,

In the merry-chanting time of
spring,
Love steals all my senses, oh, the
happy-hearted thief!
In the vernal morning with the
starting of the leaf.

Always, ever always, even in the
autumn drear,
  When the days are sighing out
  their grief,
Thou art still my darling, dearest of the dear,
Always, ever always, even in the
autumn drear.

TO A DEAD FRIEND

IT is as if a silver chord
  Were suddenly grown mute,
And life's song with its rhythm
  warred
  Against a silver lute.

It is as if a silence fell
  Where bides the garnered sheaf,
And voices murmuring, " It is
  well,"
  Are stifled by our grief.

It is as if the gloom of night
  Had hid a summer's day,
And willows, sighing at their
  plight,
  Bent low beside the way.

For he was part of all the best
  That Nature loves and gives,

And ever more on Memory's breast
He lies and laughs and lives.

TO THE SOUTH

ON ITS NEW SLAVERY

HEART of the Southland, heed me
  pleading now,
Who bearest, unashamed, upon
  my brow
The long kiss of the loving tropic
  sun,
And yet, whose veins with thy red
  current run.

Borne on the bitter winds from
  every hand,
Strange tales are flying over all the
  land,
And Condemnation, with his pinions foul,
Glooms in the place where broods
  the midnight owl.

What art thou, that the world
  should point at thee,
And vaunt and chide the weakness
  that they see?
There was a time they were not
  wont to chide;
Where is thy old, uncompromis-
  ing pride?

Blood-washed, thou shouldst lift
  up thine honored head,
White with the sorrow for thy
  loyal dead

[216]

Who lie on every plain, on every
hill,
And whose high spirit walks the
Southland still:

Whose infancy our mother's hands
have nursed.
Thy manhood, gone to battle un-
accursed,
Our fathers left to till th' reluctant field,
To rape the soil for what she
would not yield;

Wooing for aye, the cold unam'-
rous sod,
Whose growth for them still
meant a master's rod;
Tearing her bosom for the wealth
that gave
The strength that made the toiler
still a slave.

Too long we hear the deep im-
passioned cry
That echoes vainly to the heedless
sky;
Too long, too long, the Mace-
donian call
Falls fainting far beyond the out-
ward wall,

Within whose sweep, beneath the
shadowing trees,
A slumbering nation takes its
dangerous ease;
Too long the rumors of thy hatred
go

For those who loved thee and thy
children so.

Thou must arise forthwith, and
strong, thou must
Throw off the smirching of this
baser dust,
Lay by the practice of this later
creed,
And be thine honest self again
indeed.

There was a time when even slavery's chain
Held in some joys to alternate
with pain,
Some little light to give the night
relief,
Some little smiles to take the place
of grief.

There was a time when, jocund
as the day,
The toiler hoed his row and sung
his lay,
Found something gleeful in the
very air,
And solace for his toiling everywhere.

Now all is changed, within the
rude stockade,
A bondsman whom the greed of
men has made
Almost too brutish to deplore his
plight,
Toils hopeless on from joyless
morn till night.

For him no more the cabin's quiet
rest,
The homely joys that gave to labor
zest;
No more for him the merry banjo's
sound,
Nor trip of lightsome dances footing round.

For him no more the lamp shall
glow at eve,
Nor chubby children pluck him by
the sleeve;
No more for him the master's eyes
be bright,—
He has nor freedom's nor a slave's
delight.

What, was it all for naught, those
awful years
That drenched a groaning land
with blood and tears?
Was it to leave this sly convenient
hell,
That brother fighting his own
brother fell?

When that great struggle held the
world in awe,
And all the nations blanched at
what they saw,
Did Sanctioned Slavery bow its
conquered head
That this unsanctioned crime
might rise instead?

Is it for this we all have felt the
flame,—
This newer bondage and this
deeper shame?
Nay, not for this, a nation's heroes
bled,
And North and South with tears
beheld their dead.

Oh, Mother South, hast thou forgot thy ways,
Forgot the glory of thine ancient
days,
Forgot the honor that once made
thee great,
And stooped to this unhallowèd
estate?

It cannot last, thou wilt come
forth in might,
A warrior queen full armored for
the fight;
And thou wilt take, e'en with thy
spear in rest,
Thy dusky children to thy saving
breast.

Till then, no more, no more the
gladsome song,
Strike only deeper chords, the
notes of wrong;
Till then, the sigh, the tear, the
oath, the moan,
Till thou, oh, South, and thine,
come to thine own.

PAUL LAURENCE DUNBAR

THE HAUNTED OAK

PRAY why are you so bare, so bare,
  Oh, bough of the old oak-tree;
And why, when I go through the
    shade you throw,
  Runs a shudder over me?

My leaves were green as the best,
    I trow,
  And sap ran free in my veins,
But I saw in the moonlight dim
    and weird
  A guiltless victim's pains.

I bent me down to hear his sigh;
  I shook with his gurgling moan,
And I trembled sore when they
    rode away,
  And left him here alone.

They 'd charged him with the old,
    old crime,
  And set him fast in jail:
Oh, why does the dog howl all
    night long,
  And why does the night wind
    wail?

He prayed his prayer and he swore
    his oath,
  And he raised his hand to the
    sky;
But the beat of hoofs smote on his
    ear,
  And the steady tread drew nigh.

Who is it rides by night, by night,
  Over the moonlit road?

And what is the spur that keeps
    the pace,
  What is the galling goad?

And now they beat at the prison
    door,
  "Ho, keeper, do not stay!
We are friends of him whom you
    hold within,
  And we fain would take him
    away

" From those who ride fast on our
    heels
  With mind to do him wrong;
They have no care for his inno-
    cence,
  And the rope they bear is
    long."

They have fooled the jailer with
    lying words,
  They have fooled the man with
    lies;
The bolts unbar, the locks are
    drawn,
  And the great door open flies.

Now they have taken him from
    the jail,
  And hard and fast they ride,
And the leader laughs low down
    in his throat,
  As they halt my trunk beside.

Oh, the judge, he wore a mask of
    black,
  And the doctor one of white,

[219]

And the minister, with his oldest
    son,
  Was curiously bedight.

Oh, foolish man, why weep you
    now?
  'T is but a little space,
And the time will come when these
    shall dread
  The mem'ry of your face.

I feel the rope against my bark,
  And the weight of him in my
    grain,
I feel in the throe of his final woe
  The touch of my own last pain.

And never more shall leaves come
    forth
  On a bough that bears the ban;
I am burned with dread, I am
    dried and dead,
  From the curse of a guiltless
    man.

And ever the judge rides by, rides
    by,
  And goes to hunt the deer,
And ever another rides his soul
  In the guise of a mortal fear.

And ever the man he rides me
    hard,
  And never a night stays he;
For I feel his curse as a haunted
    bough,
  On the trunk of a haunted tree.

WELTSCHMERTZ

You ask why I am sad to-day,
I have no cares, no griefs, you say?
Ah, yes, 't is true, I have no
  grief —
But — is there not the falling
  leaf?

The bare tree there is mourning
  left
With all of autumn's gray bereft;
It is not what has happened me,
Think of the bare, dismantled tree.

The birds go South along the sky,
I hear their lingering, long good-
  bye.
Who goes reluctant from my
  breast?
And yet — the lone and wind-
  swept nest.

The mourning, pale-flowered
  hearse goes by,
Why does a tear come to my eye?
Is it the March rain blowing
  wild?
I have no dead, I know no child.

I am no widow by the bier
Of him I held supremely dear.
I have not seen the choicest one
Sink down as sinks the westering
  sun.

Faith unto faith have I beheld,
For me, few solemn notes have
  swelled;

PAUL LAURENCE DUNBAR

Love bekoned me out to the dawn,
And happily I followed on.

And yet my heart goes out to
  them
Whose sorrow is their diadem;
The falling leaf, the crying bird,
The voice to be, all lost, un-
  heard —

Not mine, not mine, and yet too
  much
The thrilling power of human
  touch,
While all the world looks on and
  scorns
I wear another's crown of thorns.

Count me a priest who under-
  stands
The glorious pain of nail-pierced
  hands;
Count me a comrade of the thief
Hot driven into late belief.

Oh, mother's tear, oh, father's sigh,
Oh, mourning sweetheart's last
  good-bye,
I yet have known no mourning
  save
Beside some brother's brother's
  grave.

ROBERT GOULD SHAW

Why was it that the thunder
  voice of Fate
Should call thee, studious, from
  the classic groves,
Where calm-eyed Pallas with
  still footstep roves,
And charge thee seek the turmoil
  of the state?
What bade thee hear the voice and
  rise elate,
Leave home and kindred and
  thy spicy loaves,
To lead th' unlettered and despised droves
To manhood's home and thunder
  at the gate?

Far better the slow blaze of Learn-
  ing's light,
The cool and quiet of her dearer
  fane,
Than this hot terror of a hopeless
  fight,
This cold endurance of the final
  pain,—
Since thou and those who with
  thee died for right
Have died, the Present teaches,
  but in vain!

ROSES

Oh, wind of the spring-time, oh,
  free wind of May,
When blossoms and bird-song
  are rife;
Oh, joy for the season, and joy for
  the day,
That gave me the roses of life,
  of life,
That gave me the roses of life.

Oh, wind of the summer, sing
    loud in the night,
  When flutters my heart like a
    dove;
One came from thy kingdom, thy
    realm of delight,
  And gave me the roses of love,
    of love,
  And gave me the roses of love.

Oh, wind of the winter, sigh low
    in thy grief,
  I hear thy compassionate breath;
I wither, I fall, like the autumn-
    kissed leaf,
  He gave me the roses of death,
    of death,
  He gave me the roses of death.

A LOVE SONG

AH, love, my love is like a cry in
    the night,
A long, loud cry to the empty sky,
The cry of a man alone in the
    desert,
With hands uplifted, with parch-
    ing lips,

Oh, rescue me, rescue me,
Thy form to mine arms,
The dew of thy lips to my mouth,
Dost thou hear me?— my call
    thro' the night?

Darling, I hear thee and answer,
Thy fountain am I,

All of the love of my soul will I
    bring to thee,
All of the pains of my being shall
    wring to thee,
Deep and forever the song of my
    loving shall sing to thee,
Ever and ever thro' day and thro'
    night shall I cling to thee.
Hearest thou the answer?
Darling, I come, I come.

ITCHING HEELS

Fu' de peace o' my eachin' heels,
    set down;
  Don' fiddle dat chune no mo'.
Don' you see how dat melody stuhs
    me up
  An' baigs me to tek to de flo'?
You knows I's a Christian, good
    an' strong;
  I wusship f'om June to June;
My pra'ahs dey ah loud an' my
    hymns ah long:
  I baig you don' fiddle dat chune.

I's a crick in my back an' a mis-
    ery hyeah
  Whaih de j'ints's gittin' ol' an'
    stiff,
But hit seems lak you brings me
    de bref o' my youf;
  W'y, I's suttain I noticed a
    w'iff.
Don' fiddle dat chune no mo', my
    chile,
  Don' fiddle dat chune no mo';

PAUL LAURENCE DUNBAR

I 'll git up an' taih up dis groun'
  fu' a mile,
  An' den I 'll be chu'ched fu' it,
    sho'.

Oh, fiddle dat chune some mo', I
  say,
  An' fiddle it loud an' fas':
I 's a youngstah ergin in de mi'st
  o' my sin;
  De p'esent 's gone back to de
    pas'.
I 'll dance to dat chune, so des fid-
  dle erway;
  I knows how de backslidah
    feels;
So fiddle it on 'twell de break o'
  de day
  Fu' de sake o' my eachin' heels.

TO AN INGRATE

THIS is to-day, a golden summer's
  day
  And yet — and yet
  My vengeful soul will not for-
    get
The past, forever now forgot, you
  say.

From that half height where I had
  sadly climbed,
  I stretched my hand,
  I lone in all that land,
Down there, where, helpless, you
  were limed.

Our fingers clasped, and dragging
  me a pace,
  You struggled up.
  It is a bitter Cup,
That now for naught, you turn
  away your face.

I shall remember this for aye and
  aye.
  Whate'er may come,
  Although my lips are dumb,
My spirit holds you to that yester-
  day.

IN THE TENTS OF AKBAR

IN the tents of Akbar
  Are dole and grief to-day,
For the flower of all the Indies
  Has gone the silent way.

In the tents of Akbar
  Are emptiness and gloom,
And where the dancers gather,
  The silence of the tomb.

Across the yellow desert,
  Across the burning sands,
Old Akbar wanders madly,
  And wrings his fevered hands.

And ever makes his moaning
  To the unanswering sky,
For Sutna, lovely Sutna,
  Who was so fair to die.

For Sutna danced at morning,
  And Sutna danced at eve;

Her dusky eyes half hidden
  Behind her silken sleeve.

Her pearly teeth out-glancing
  Between her coral lips,
The tremulous rhythm of passion
  Marked by her quivering hips.

As lovely as a jewel
  Of fire and dewdrop blent,
So danced the maiden Sutna
  In gallant Akbar's tent.

And one who saw her dancing,
  Saw her bosom's fall and rise
Put all his body's yearning
  Into his lovelit eyes.

Then Akbar came and drove
    him —
A jackal — from his door,
And bade him wander far and look
  On Sutna's face no more.

Some day the sea disgorges,
  The wilderness gives back,
Those half-dead who have wan-
    dered,
  Aimless, across its track.

And he returned — the 'lover,
  Haggard of brow and spent;
He found fair Sutna standing
  Before her master's tent.

"Not mine, nor Akbar's, Sutna!"
  He cried and closely pressed,
And drove his craven dagger
  Straight to the maiden's breast.

Oh, weep, oh, weep, for Sutna,
  So young, so dear, so fair,
Her face is gray and silent
  Beneath her dusky hair.

And wail, oh, wail, for Akbar,
  Who walks the desert sands,
Crying aloud for Sutna,
  . Wringing his fevered hands.

In the tents of Akbar
  The tears of sorrow run,
But the corpse of Sutna's slayer,
  Lies rotting in the sun.

THE FOUNT OF TEARS

ALL hot and grimy from the road,
  Dust gray from arduous years,
I sat me down and eased my load
  Beside the Fount of Tears.

The waters sparkled to my eye,
  Calm, crystal-like, and cool,
And breathing there a restful sigh,
  I bent me to the pool.

When, lo! a voice cried: " Pilgrim,
    rise,
  Harsh tho' the sentence be,
And on to other lands and skies —
  This fount is not for thee.

"Pass on, but calm thy needless
    fears,
  Some may not love or sin,
An angel guards the Fount of
    Tears;
  All may not bathe therein."

[224]

Then with my burden on my back
  I turned to gaze awhile,
First at the uninviting track,
  Then at the water's smile.

And so I go upon my way,
  Thro'out the sultry years,
But pause no more, by night, by
    day,
  Beside the Fount of Tears.

LIFE'S TRAGEDY

IT may be misery not to sing at all
  And to go silent through the
    brimming day.
It may be sorrow never to be
    loved,
  But deeper griefs than these
    beset the way.

To have come near to sing the
    perfect song
  And only by a half-tone lost
    the key,
There is the potent sorrow, there
    the grief,
  The pale, sad staring of life's
    tragedy.

To have just missed the perfect
    love,
  Not the hot passion of untem-
    pered youth,
But that which lays aside its vanity
  And gives thee, for thy trusting
    worship, truth —

This, this it is to be accursed in-
    deed;
  For if we mortals love, or if we
    sing,
We count our joys not by the
    things we have,
  But by what kept us from the
    perfect thing.

DE WAY T'INGS COME

DE way t'ings come, hit seems to
    me,
Is des' one monst'ous mystery;
De way hit seem to strike a man,
Dey ain't no sense, dey ain't no
    plan;
Ef trouble sta'ts a pilin' down,
It ain't no use to rage er frown,
It ain't no use to strive er pray,
Hit 's mortal boun' to come dat
    way.

Now, ef you 's hongry, an' yo' plate
Des' keep on sayin' to you,
  " Wait,"
Don't mek no diffunce how you
    feel,
'T won't do no good to hunt a
    meal,
Fu' dat ah meal des' boun' to hide
Ontwell de devil 's satisfied,
An' 'twell dey 's some'p'n by to
    cyave
You 's got to ease yo'se'f an' sta've.

But ef dey 's co'n meal on de she'f
You need n't bothah 'roun' yo'se'f,

[225]

Somebody 's boun' to amble in
An' 'vite you to dey co'n meal bin;
An' ef you 's stuffed up to be froat
Wid co'n er middlin', fowl er
    shoat,
Des' look out an' you 'll see fu'
    sho
A 'possum faint befo' yo' do'.

De way t'ings happen, huhuh,
    chile,
Dis worl' 's done puzzled me one
    w'ile;
I 's mighty skeered I 'll fall in
    doubt,
I des' won't try to reason out
De reason why folks strive an'
    plan
A dinnah fu' a full-fed man,
An' shet de do' an' cross de street
F'om one dat raaly needs to eat.

NOON

Shadder in de valley
Sunlight on de hill,
Sut'ny wish dat locus'
Knowed how to be still.
Don't de heat already
Mek a body hum,
'Dout dat insec' sayin'
Hottah days to come?

Fiel' 's a shinin' yaller
Wid de bendin' grain,
Guinea hen a callin',
Now 's de time fu' rain;

Shet yo' mouf, you rascal,
Wha' 's de use to cry?
You do' see no rain clouds
Up dah in de sky.

Dis hyeah sweat 's been po'in'
Down my face sence dawn;
Ain't hit time we 's hyeahin'
Dat ah dinnah ho'n?
Go on, Ben an' Jaspah,
Lif' yo' feet an' fly,
Hit out fu' de shadder
Fo' I drap an' die.

Hongry, lawd a' mussy,
Hongry as a baih,
Seems lak I hyeah dinnah
Callin' evahwhaih;
Daih 's de ho'n a blowin'!
Let dat cradle swing,
One mo' sweep, den da'kies,
Beat me to de spring!

AT THE TAVERN

A lilt and a swing,
And a ditty to sing,
Or ever the night grow old;
The wine is within,
And I 'm sure 't were a sin
For a soldier to choose to be cold,
    my dear,
For a soldier to choose to be cold.

We 're right for a spell,
But the fever is — well,
No thing to be braved, at least;

[226]

PAUL LAURENCE DUNBAR

So bring me the wine;
No low fever in mine,
For a drink is more kind than a
priest, my dear,
For a drink is more kind than a
priest.

DEATH

STORM and strife and stress,
Lost in a wilderness,
Groping to find a way,
Forth to the haunts of day

Sudden a vista peeps,
Out of the tangled deeps,
Only a point — the ray
But at the end is day.

Dark is the dawn and chill,
Daylight is on the hill,
Night is the flitting breath,
Day rides the hills of death.

NIGHT, DIM NIGHT

Night, dim night, and it rains, my
love, it rains,
(Art thou dreaming of me, I
wonder)
The trees are sad, and the wind
complains,
Outside the rolling of the thunder,
And the beat against the panes.

Heart, my heart, thou art mournful in the rain,
(Are thy redolent lips a-
quiver?)
My soul seeks thine, doth it seek
in vain?
My love goes surging like a
river,
Shall its tide bear naught save
pain?

I

Love is the light of the world, my
 dear,
 Heigho, but the world is
 gloomy;
The light has failed and the lamp
 down hurled,
 Leaves only darkness to me.

Love is the light of the world, my
 dear,
 Ah me, but the world is dreary;
The night is down, and my curtain
 furled
 But I cannot sleep, though
 weary.

Love is the light of the world, my
 dear,
 Alas for a hopeless hoping,
When the flame went out in the
 breeze that swirled,
 And a soul went blindly groping.

II

The light was on the golden
 sands,
 A glimmer on the sea;
My soul spoke clearly to thy soul,
 Thy spirit answered me.

Since then the light that gilds the
 sands,
 And glimmers on the sea,

But vainly struggles to reflect
 The radiant soul of thee.

III

The sea speaks to me of you
 All the day long;
Still as I sit by its side
 You are its song.

The sea sings to me of you
 Loud on the reef;
Always it moans as it sings,
 Voicing my grief.

IV

My dear love died last night;
 Shall I clothe her in white?
My passionate love is dead,
 Shall I robe her in red?
But nay, she was all untrue,
 She shall not go drest in blue;
Still my desolate love was brave,
 Unrobed let her go to her grave.

V

There are brilliant heights of
 sorrow
 That only the few may know;
And the lesser woes of the world,
 like waves,
 Break noiselessly, far below.
I hold for my own possessing,
 A mount that is lone and still —
The great high place of a hopeless
 grief,

PAUL LAURENCE DUNBAR

And I call it my "Heart-break
   Hill."
And once on a winter's midnight
   I found its highest crown,
And there in the gloom, my soul
   and I,
   Weeping, we sat us down.

But now when I seek that summit
   We are two ghosts that go;
Only two shades of a thing that
   died,
   Once in the long ago.
So I sit me down in the silence,
   And say to my soul, "Be still,"
So the world may not know we
   died that night,
   From weeping on "Heart-break
   Hill."

A BOY'S SUMMER SONG

'Tis fine to play
In the fragrant hay,
And romp on the golden load;
To ride old Jack
To the barn and back,
Or tramp by a shady road.
To pause and drink,
At a mossy brink;
Ah, that is the best of joy,
And so I say
On a summer's day,
What's so fine as being a boy?
Ha, Ha!

With line and hook
By a babbling brook,
The fisherman's sport we ply;
And list the song
Of the feathered throng
That flit in the branches nigh.
At last we strip
For a quiet dip;
Ah, that is the best of joy.
For this I say
On a summer's day,
What's so fine as being a boy?
Ha, Ha!

THE SAND-MAN

I KNOW a man
With face of tan,
But who is ever kind;
Whom girls and boys
Leaves games and toys
Each eventide to find.

When day grows dim,
They watch for him,
He comes to place his claim;
He wears the crown
Of Dreaming-town;
The sand-man is his name.

When sparkling eyes
Troop sleepywise
And busy lips grow dumb;
When little heads
Nod toward the beds,
We know the sand-man's come.

JOHNNY SPEAKS

THE sand-man he's a jolly old
    fellow,
His face is kind and his voice is
    mellow,
But he makes your eyelids as heavy
    as lead,
And then you got to go off to bed;
 I don't think I like the sand-
    man.

But I've been playing this live-
    long day;
It does make a fellow so tired to
    play!
Oh, my, I'm a-yawning right here
    before ma,

[235]

I'm the sleepiest fellow that ever
you saw.
I think I do like the sand-man.

WINTER-SONG

OH, who would be sad tho' the
sky be a-graying,
And meadow and woodlands are
empty and bare;
For softly and merrily now there
come playing,
The little white birds thro' the
winter-kissed air.

The squirrel's enjoying the rest
of the thrifty,
He munches his store in the old
hollow tree;
Tho' cold is the blast and the
snow-flakes are drifty
He fears the white flock not a
whit more than we.

Chorus:

Then heigho for the flying snow!
Over the whitened roads we go,
With pulses that tingle,
And sleigh-bells a-jingle
For winter's white birds here's a
cheery heigho!

A CHRISTMAS FOLKSONG

DE win' is blowin' wahmah,
An hit's blowin' f'om de bay;
Dey's a so't o' mist a-risin'
All erlong de meddah way;

Dey ain't a hint o' frostin'
On de groun' ner in de sky,
An' dey ain't no use in hopin'
Dat de snow'll 'mence to fly.
It's goin' to be a green Christ-
mas,
An' sad de day fu' me.
I wish dis was de las' one
Dat evah I should see.

Dey's dancin' in de cabin,
Dey's spahkin' by de tree;
But dancin' times an' spahkin'
Are all done pas' fur me.
Dey's feastin' in de big house,
Wid all de windahs wide —
Is dat de way fu' people
To meet de Christmas-tide?
It's goin' to be a green Christ-
mas,
No mattah what you say.
Dey's us dat will remembah
An' grieve de comin' day.

Dey's des a bref o' dampness
A-clingin' to my cheek;
De aih's been dahk an' heavy
An' threatenin' fu' a week,
But not wid signs o' wintah,
Dough wintah'd seem so deah —
De wintah's out o' season,
An' Christmas eve is heah.
It's goin' to be a green Christ-
mas,
An' oh, how sad de day!
Go ax de hongry chu'chya'd,
An' see what hit will say.

Dey's Allen on de hillside,
  An' Marfy in de plain;
Fu' Christmas was like springtime,
  An' come wid sun an' rain.
Dey's Ca'line, John; an' Susie,
  Wid only dis one lef':
An' now de curse is comin'
  Wid murder in hits bref.
    It's goin' to be a green Christ-
        mas —
      Des hyeah my words an'
        see:
    Befo' de summah beckons
      Dey's many 'll weep wid
        me.

THE FOREST GREETING

Good hunting! — aye, good hunt-
    ing,
  Wherever the forests call;
But ever a heart beats hot with
    fear,
  And what of the birds that fall?

Good hunting! — aye, good hunt-
    ing,
    Wherever the north winds
        blow;
But what of the stag that calls for
    his mate?
  And what of the wounded doe?

Good hunting! — aye, good hunt-
    ing;
  And ah! we are bold and strong;

But our triumph call through the
    forest hall
  Is a brother's funeral song.

For we are brothers ever,
  Panther and bird and bear;
Man and the weakest that fear his
    face,
  Born to the nest or lair.

Yes, brothers, and who shall judge
    us?
  Hunters and game are we;
But who gave the right for me to
    smite?
  Who boasts when he smiteth me?

Good hunting! — aye, good hunt-
    ing,
  And dim is the forest track;
But the sportsman Death comes
    striding on:
  Brothers, the way is black.

THE LILY OF THE VALLEY

Sweetest of the flowers a-bloom-
    ing
  In the fragrant vernal days
Is the Lily of the Valley
  With its soft, retiring ways.

Well, you chose this humble blos-
    som
  As the nurse's emblem flower,
Who grows more like her ideal
  Every day and every hour.

Like the Lily of the Valley
In her honesty and worth,
Ah, she blooms in truth and virtue
In the quiet nooks of earth.

Tho' she stands erect in honor
When the heart of mankind
bleeds,
Still she hides her own deserving
In the beauty of her deeds.

In the silence of the darkness
Where no eye may see and know,
There her footsteps shod with
mercy,
And fleet kindness come and go.

Not amid the sounds of plaudits,
Nor before the garish day,
Does she shed her soul's sweet per-
fume,
Does she take her gentle way.

But alike her ideal flower,
With its honey-laden breath,
Still her heart blooms forth its
beauty
In the valley shades of death.

ENCOURAGED

BECAUSE you love me I have
much achieved,
Had you despised me then I must
have failed,
But since I knew you trusted
and believed,

I could not disappoint you and so
prevailed.

TO J. Q.

WHAT are the things that make
life bright?
A star gleam in the night.
What hearts us for the coming
fray?
The dawn tints of the day.
What helps to speed the weary
mile?
A brother's friendly smile.
What turns o' gold the evening
gray?
A flower beside the way.

DIPLOMACY

TELL your love where the roses
blow,
And the hearts of the lilies
quiver,
Not in the city's gleam and glow,
But down by a half-sunned river.
Not in the crowded ball-room's
glare,
That would be fatal, Marie,
Marie,
How can she answer you then and
there?
So come then and stroll with me,
my dear,
Down where the birds call,
Marie, Marie.

PAUL LAURENCE DUNBAR

SCAMP

AIN'T it nice to have a mammy
　W'en you kin' o' tiahed out
Wid a-playin' in de meddah,
　An' a-runnin' roun' about
Till hit's made you mighty hongry,
　An' yo' nose hit gits to know
What de smell means dat's a-
　　comin'
　　F'om de open cabin do'?
　　She wash yo' face,
　　An' mek yo' place,
　You's hongry as a tramp;
Den hit's eat you suppah right
　　away,
　You sta'vin' little scamp.

W'en you's full o' braid an' bacon,
　An' dey ain't no mo' to eat,
An' de lasses dat's a-stickin'
　On yo' face ta'se kin' o' sweet,
Don' you t'ink hit's kin' o' pleasin'
　Fu' to have som'body neah
Dat'll wipe yo' han's an' kiss you
　Fo' dey lif' you f'om you' cheah?
　　To smile so sweet,
　　An' wash yo' feet,
　An' leave 'em co'l an' damp;
Den hit's come let me undress
　　you, now
　You lazy little scamp.

Don' yo' eyes git awful heavy,
　An' yo' lip git awful slack,
Ain't dey som'p'n' kin' o' weak-
　　nin'
　In de backbone of yo' back?

Don' yo' knees feel kin' o' trimbly,
　An' yo' head go bobbin' roun',
W'en you says yo' "Now I lay
　　me,"
　An' is sno'in on de "down"?
　　She kiss yo' nose,
　　She kiss yo' toes,
　An' den tu'n out de lamp,
Den hit's creep into yo' trunnel
　　baid,
　You sleepy little scamp.

WADIN' IN DE CRICK

DAYS git wa'm an' wa'mah,
　School gits mighty dull,
Seems lak dese hyeah teachahs
　Mus' feel mussiful.
Hookey's wrong, I know it
　Ain't no gent'man's trick;
But de aih's a-callin',
　"Come on to de crick."

Dah de watah's gu'glin'
　Ovah shiny stones,
Des hit's ve'y singin'
　Seems to soothe yo' bones.
W'at's de use o' waitin'
　Go on good an' quick:
Dain't no fun lak dis hyeah
　Wadin' in de crick.

W'at dat jay-b'ud sayin'?
　Bettah shet yo' haid,
Fus' t'ing dat you fin' out,
　You'll be layin' daid.

[239]

Jay-bu'ds sich a tattlah,
  Des seem lak his trick
Fu' to tell on folkes
  Wadin' in de crick.

Willer boughs a-bendin'
  Hidin' of de sky,
Wavin' kin' o' frien'ly
  Ez de win' go by,
Elum trees a-shinin',
  Dahk an' green an' thick,
Seem to say, " I see yo'
  Wadin' in de crick."

But de trees don' chattah,
  Dey des look an' sigh
Lak hit's kin' o' peaceful
  Des a-bein' nigh,.
An' yo' t'ank yo' Mastah
  Dat dey trunks is thick
W'en yo' mammy fin's you
  Wadin' in de crick.

Den yo' run behin' dem
  Lak yo' scaihed to def,
Mammy come a-flyin',
  Mos' nigh out o' bref;
But she set down gentle
  An' she drap huh stick,—
An' fus' t'ing, dey's mammy
  Wadin' in de crick.

THE QUILTING

DOLLY sits a-quilting by her
  mother, stich by stitch,
Gracious, how my pulses throb,
  how my fingers itch,

While I note her dainty waist and
  her slender hand,
As she matches this and that, she
  stitches strand by strand.
And I long to tell her Life's a
  quilt and I'm a patch;
Love will do the stitching if she'll
  only be my match.

PARTED

SHE wrapped her soul in a lace of
  lies,
  With a prime deceit to pin it;
And I thought I was gaining a
  fearsome prize,
  So I staked my soul to win it.

We wed and parted on her com-
  plaint,
  And both were a bit of barter,
Tho' I'll confess that I'm no saint,
  I'll swear that she's no martyr.

FOREVER

I HAD not known before
  Forever was so long a word.
The slow stroke of the clock of
  time
  I had not heard.

'Tis hard to learn so late;
  It seems no sad heart really
  learns,
But hopes and trusts and doubts
  and fears,
  And bleeds and burns.

[240]

PAUL LAURENCE DUNBAR

The night is not all dark,
  Nor is the day all it seems,
But each may bring me this re-
      lief —
  My dreams and dreams.

I had not known before
  That Never was so sad a word, ·
So wrap me in forgetfulness —
  I have not heard.

THE PLANTATION
CHILD'S LULLABY

WINTAH time hit comin'
  Stealin' thoo de night;
Wake up in the mo'nin'
  Evah t'ing is white;
Cabin lookin' lonesome
  Stannin' in de snow,
Meks you kin' o' nervous,
  W'en de win' hit blow.

Trompin' back from feedin',
  Col' an' wet an' blue,
Homespun jacket ragged,
  Win' a-blowin' thoo.
Cabin lookin' cheerful,
  Unnerneaf de do',
Yet you kin' o' keerful
W'en de win' hit blow.

Hickory log a-blazin'
  Light a-lookin' red,
Faith o' eyes o' peepin'
  'Rom a trun'le bed,
Little feet a-patterin'
  Cleak across de flo';

Bettah had be keerful
  W'en de win' hit blow.

Suppah done an' ovah,
  Evah t'ing is still;
Listen to de snowman
  Slippin' down de hill.
Ashes on de fiah,
  Keep it wa'm but low.
What's de use o' keerin'
  Ef de win' do blow?

Smoke house full o' bacon,
  Brown an' sweet an' good;
Taters in de cellah,
  'Possum. roam de wood;
Little baby snoozin'
  Des ez ef he know.
What 's de use o' keerin'
  Ef de win' do blow?

TWILIGHT

'TWIXT a smile and a tear,
  'Twixt a song and a sigh,
'Twixt the day and the dark,
  When the night draweth nigh.

Ah, sunshine may fade
  From the heavens above,
No twilight have we
  To the day of our love.

CURIOSITY

MAMMY's in de kitchen, an' de
      do' is shet;
All de pickaninnies climb an' tug
      an' sweat,

Gittin' to de winder, stickin' dah
   . lak flies,
Evah one ermong us des all nose
   an' eyes.

"Whut's she cookin', Isaac?"
   "Whut's she cookin', Jake?"
"Is it sweet pertaters? Is hit pie
   er cake?"
But we couldn't mek out even
   whah we stood
Whut was mammy cookin' dat
   could smell so good.

Mammy spread de winder, an'
   she frown an' frown,
How de pickaninnies come a-tumblin' down!
Den she say: "Ef you-all keeps
   a-peepin' in,
How I'se gwine to whup you, my!
   't 'ill be a sin!
Need n' come a-sniffin' an' a-nosin'
   hyeah,
'Ca'se I knows my business, nevah
   feah."
Won't somebody tell us — how I
   wish dey would! —
Whut is mammy cookin' dat it
   smells so good?

We know she means business, an'
   we dassent stay,
Dough it's mighty tryin' fuh to
   go erway;
But we goes a-troopin' down de
   ol' wood-track

'Twell dat steamin' kitchen brings
   us stealin' back,
Climbin' an' a-peepin' so's to see
   inside.
Whut on earf kin mammy be so
   sha'p to hide?
I'd des up an' tell folks w'en I
   knowed I could,
Ef I was a-cookin' t'ings dat smelt
   so good.

Mammy in de oven, an' I see huh
   smile;
Moufs mus' be a-wat'rin' roun'
   hyeah fuh a mile;
Den we almos' hollah ez we hu'ies
   down,
'Ca'se hit's apple dumplin's, big an'
   fat an' brown!
W'en de do' is opened, solemn lak
   an' slow,
Wisht you see us settin' all dah
   in a row
Innercent an' p'opah, des lak chillun should
W'en dey mammy's cookin' t'ings
   dat smell so good.

OPPORTUNITY

GRANNY'S gone a-visitin',
   Seen huh git huh shawl
W'en I was a-hidin' down
   Hime de gyahden wall.
Seen huh put her bonnet on,
   Seen huh tie de strings,
An' I'se gone to dreamin' now
   'Bout dem cakes an' t'ings.

PAUL LAURENCE DUNBAR

On de she'f behime de do'—
  Mussy, what a feas'!
Soon ez she gits out o' sight,
  I kin eat in peace.
I bin watchin' fu' a week
  Des fu' dis hyeah chance.
Mussy, w'en I gits in daih,
  I'll des sholy dance.

Lemon pie an' gingah-cake,
  Let me set an' t'ink —
Vinegah an' sugah, too,
  Dat'll mek a drink;
Ef dey's one t'ing dat I loves
  Mos' pu'ticlahly,
It is eatin' sweet t'ings an'
  A-drinkin' Sangaree.

Lawdy, won' po' granny raih
  W'en she see de she'f;
W'en I t'ink erbout huh face,
  I's mos' 'shamed myse'f.
Well, she gone, an' 'hyeah I is,
  Back behime de do'—
Look hyeah! gran' 's done 'spected
    me,
  Dain't no sweets no mo'.

Evah sweet is hid erway,
  Job des done up brown;
Pusson t'ink dat someun t'ought
  Dey was t'eves erroun';
Dat des breaks my heart in two,
  Oh how bad I feel!
Des to t'ink my own gramma
  B'lieved dat I 'u'd steal!

PUTTIN' THE BABY
AWAY

EIGHT of 'em hyeah all tol' an' yet
Dese eyes o' mine is wringin' wet;
My haht's a-achin' ha'd an' so',
De way hit nevah ached befo';
My soul's a-pleadin', " Lawd, give
    back
Dis little lonesome baby black,
Dis one, dis las' po' he'pless one
Whose little race was too soon
    run."

Po' Little Jim, des fo' yeahs ol'
A-layin' down so still an' col'.
Somehow hit don' seem ha'dly
    faih,
To have my baby lyin' daih
Wi'dout a smile upon his face,
Wi'dout a look erbout de place;
He ust to be so full o' fun
Hit don' seem right dat all's done,
    done.

Des eight in all but I don' caih,
Dey wa'nt a single one to spaih;
De worl' was big, so was my haht,
An' dis hyeah baby owned hit's
    paht;
De house was po', dey clothes was
    rough,
But daih was meat an' meal
    enough;
An' daih was room fu' little Jim;
Oh! Lawd, what made you call fu'
    him?

It do seem monst'ous ha'd to-day,
To lay dis baby boy away;
I'd learned to love his teasin'
    smile,
He mought o' des been lef' er-
    while;
You wouldn't t'ought wid all de
    folks,
Dat's roun' hyeah mixin' teahs an'
    jokes,
De Lawd u'd had de time to see
Dis chile an' tek him 'way f'om
    me.

But let it go, I reckon Jim,
'Ll des go right straight up to
    Him
Dat took him f'om his mammy's
    nest
An' lef' dis achin' in my breas',
An' lookin' in dat fathah's face
An' 'memberin' dis lone sorrerin'
    place,
He'll say, " Good Lawd, you ought
    to had
Do sumpin' fu' to comfo't dad!"

THE FISHER CHILD'S LUL-
LABY

THE wind is out in its rage to-
    night,
  And your father is far at sea.
The rime on the window is hard
    and white
  But dear, you are near to me.

Heave ho, weave low,
  Waves of the briny deep;
Seethe low and breathe low,
  But sleep you, my little one,
    sleep, sleep.

The little boat rocks in the cove no
    more,
  But the flying sea-gulls wail;
I peer through the darkness that
    wraps the shore,
  For sight of a home set sail.
  Heave ho, weave low,
    Waves of the briny deep;
  Seethe low and breathe low,
    But sleep you, my little one,
    sleep, sleep.

Ay, lad of mine, thy father may
    die
  In the gale that rides the sea,
But we'll not believe it, not you
    and I,
  Who mind us of Galilee.
  Heave ho, weave low,
    Waves of the briny deep;
  Seethe low and breathe low,
    But sleep you, my little one,
    sleep, sleep.

FAITH

I's a-gittin' weary of de way dat
    people do,
De folks dat's got dey 'ligion in
    dey fish-place an' flue;
Dey's allus somep'n comin' so de
    spit'll have to turn,

PAUL LAURENCE DUNBAR

An' hit tain't no p'oposition fu' to
    mek de hickory bu'n.
Ef de sweet pertater fails us an' de
    go'geous yallah yam,
We kin tek a bit o' comfo't f'om
    ouah sto' o' summah jam.
W'en de snow hit git to flyin',
    dat's de Mastah's own desiah,
De Lawd'll run de wintah an' yo'
    mammy'll run de fiah.

I ain' skeered because de win' hit
    staht to raih and blow,
I ain't bothahed w'en he come er
    rattlin' at de do',
Let him taih hisse'f an' shout, let
    him blow an' bawl,

Dat's de time de branches shek an'
    bresh-wood 'mence to fall.
W'en de sto'm er railin' an' de
    shettahs blowin' 'bout,
Dat de time de fiah-place crack
    hits welcome out.
Tain' my livin' business fu' to
    trouble ner enquiah,
De Lawd'll min' de wintah an' my
    mammy'll min' de fiah.

Ash-cake allus gits ez brown w'en
    February's hyeah
Ez it does in bakin' any othah time
    o' yeah.
De bacon smell ez callin'-like, de
    kittle rock an' sing,
De same way in de wintah dat dey
    do it in de spring;

Dey ain't no use in mopin' 'round
    an' lookin' mad an' glum
Erbout de wintah season, fu' hit's
    des plumb boun' to come;

An' ef it comes to runnin' t'ings
    I's willin' to retiah,
De Lawd'll min' de wintah an'
    my mammy'll min' de fiah.

THE FARM CHILD'S LULLABY

OH, the little bird is rocking in
    the cradle of the wind,
  And it's bye, my little wee one,
    bye;
The harvest all is gathered and
    the pippins all are binned;
  Bye, my little wee one, bye;
The little rabbit's hiding in the
    golden shock of corn,
The thrifty squirrel's laughing
    bunny's idleness to scorn;
You are smiling with the angels
    in your slumber, smile till
    morn;
  So it's bye, my little wee one,
    bye.

There'll be plenty in the cellar,
    there'll be plenty on the
    shelf;
  Bye, my little wee one, bye;
There'll be goodly store of sweet-
    ings for a dainty little elf;
  Bye, my little wee one, bye.

The snow may be a-flying o'er the
    meadow and the hill,
The ice has checked the chatter of
    the little laughing rill,
But in your cosey cradle you are
    warm and happy still;
    So bye, my little wee one, bye.

Why, the Bob White thinks the
    snowflake is a brother to his
    song;
    Bye, my little wee one, bye;
And the chimney sings the sweeter
    when the wind is blowing
    strong;
    Bye, my little wee one, bye;
The granary's overflowing, full is
    cellar, crib, and bin,
The wood has paid its tribute and
    the ax has ceased its din;
The winter may not harm you
    when you're sheltered safe
    within;
    So bye, my little wee one, bye.

THE PLACE WHERE THE RAINBOW ENDS

THERE's a fabulous story
Full of splendor and glory,
    That Arabian legends trans-
    cends;
Of the wealth without measure,
The coffers of treasure,
    At the place where the rainbow
    ends.

Oh, many have sought it,
And all would have bought it,
    With the blood we so recklessly
    spend;
But none has uncovered,
The gold, nor discovered
    The spot at the rainbow's end.

They have sought it in battle,
And e'en where the rattle
    Of dice with man's blasphemy
    blends;
But howe'er persuasive,
It still proves evasive,
    This place where the rainbow
    ends.

I own for my pleasure,
I yearn not for treasure,
    Though gold has a power it
    lends;
And I have a notion,
To find without motion,
    The place where the rainbow
    ends.

The pot may hold pottage,
The place be a cottage,
    That a humble contentment de-
    fends,
Only joy fills its coffer,
But spite of the scoffer,
    There's the place where the rain-
    bow ends.

Where care shall be quiet,
And love shall run riot,

PAUL LAURENCE DUNBAR

And I shall find wealth in my
    friends;
Then truce to the story,
Of riches and glory;
    There's the place where the rain-
        bow ends.

HOPE

De dog go howlin' 'long de road,
    De night come shiverin' down;
My back is tiahed of its load,
    I cain't be fu' f'om town.
No mattah ef de way is long,
My haht is swellin' wid a song,
    No mattah 'bout de frownin'
        skies,
    I'll soon be home to see my Lize.

My shadder staggah on de way,
    It's monstous col' to-night;
But I kin hyeah my honey say
    "W'y bless me if de sight
O' you ain't good fu' my so'
        eyes."
(Dat talk's dis lak my lady Lize)
    I's so'y case de way was long
    But Lawd you bring me love
        an' song.

No mattah ef de way is long,
    An' ef I trimbles so'
I knows de fiah's burnin' strong,
    Behime my Lizy's do'.
An' daih my res' an' joy shell be,
Whaih my ol' wife's awaitin'
        me —

Why what I keer fu' stingin'
        blas',
I see huh windah light at las'.

APPRECIATION

My muvver's ist the nicest one
    'At ever lived wiz folks;
She lets you have ze mostes' fun,
    An' laffs at all your jokes.

I got a ol' maid auntie, too,
    The worst you ever saw;
Her eyes ist bore you through and
        through,—
    She ain't a bit like ma.

She's ist as slim as slim can be,
    An' when you want to slide
Down on ze balusters, w'y she
    Says 'at she's harrified.

She ain't as nice as Uncle Ben,
    What says 'at little boys
Won't never grow to be big men
    Unless they're fond of noise.

But muvver's nicer zan 'em all,
    She calls you, " precious lamb,"
An' let's you roll your ten-pin ball,
    An' spreads your bread wiz jam.

An' when you're bad, she ist looks
        sad,
    You fink she's goin' to cry;
An' when she don't you're awful
        glad,
    An' den you're good, Oh, my!

At night, she takes ze softest
    hand,
  An' lays it on your head,
An' says " Be off to Sleepy-Land
  By way o' trundle-bed."

So when you fink what muvver
    knows
  An' aunts an' uncle tan't,
It skeers a feller; ist suppose
  His muvver 'd been a aunt.

A SONG

On a summer's day as I sat by a
    stream,
  A dainty maid came by,
And she blessed my sight like a
    rosy dream,
    And left me there to sigh, to
      sigh,
    And left me there to sigh, to
      sigh.

On another day as I sat by the
    stream,
  This maiden paused a while,
Then I made me bold as I told
    my dream,
    She heard it with a smile, a
      smile,
    She heard it with a smile, a
      smile.

Oh, the months have fled and the
    autumn's red,
  The maid no more goes by;

For my dream came true and the
    maid I wed,
    And now no more I sigh, I
      sigh,
    And now no more I sigh.

DAY

The gray dawn on the mountain
    top
  Is slow to pass away.
Still lays him by in sluggish
    dreams,
  The golden God of day.

And then a light along the hills,
  Your laughter silvery gay;
The Sun God wakes, a bluebird
    trills,
  You come and it is day.

TO DAN

Step me now a bridal measure,
Work give way to love and leisure,
Hearts be free and hearts be gay —
Doctor Dan doth wed to-day.

Diagnosis, cease your squalling —
Check that scalpel's senseless bawl-
    ing,
Put that ugly knife away —
Doctor Dan doth wed to-day.

'Tis no time for things unsightly,
Life's the day and life goes lightly;
Science lays aside her sway —
Love rules Dr. Dan to-day.

Gather, gentlemen and ladies,
For the nuptial feast now made
    is,
Swing your garlands, chant your
    lay
For the pair who wed to-day.

Wish them happy days and many,
Troubles few and griefs not any,
Lift your brimming cups and say
God bless them who wed to-day.

Then a cup to Cupid daring,
Who for conquest ever faring,
With his arrows dares assail
E'en a doctor's coat of mail.

So with blithe and happy hymning
And with harmless goblets brim-
    ming,
Dance a step — musicians play —
Doctor Dan doth wed to-day.

WHAT'S THE USE

WHAT's the use o' folks a-frownin'
    When the way's a little rough?
Frowns lay out the road fur smil-
    in'
    You'll be wrinkled soon enough.
        What's the use?

What's the use o' folks a-sighin'?
    It's an awful waste o' breath,
An' a body can't stand wastin'
    What he needs so bad in death.
        What's the use?

What's the use o' even weepin'?
    Might as well go long an' smile.
Life, our longest, strongest arrow,
    Only lasts a little while.
        What's the use?

A LAZY DAY

THE trees bend down along the
        stream,
    Where anchored swings my tiny
        boat.
The day is one to drowse and
        dream
    And list the thrush's throttling
        note.
When music from his bosom bleeds
Among the river's rustling reeds.

No ripple stirs the placid pool,
    When my adventurous line is
        cast,
A truce to sport, while clear and
        cool,
    The mirrored clouds slide softly
        past.
The sky gives back a blue divine,
And all the world's wide wealth
        is mine.

A pickerel leaps, a bow of light,
The minnows shine from side to
        side.
The first faint breeze comes up
        the tide —
I pause with half uplifted oar,
While night drifts down to claim
        the shore.

ADVICE

W'EN you full o' worry
  'Bout yo' wo'k an' sich,
W'en you kind o' bothered
  Case you can't get rich,
An' yo' neighboh p'ospah
  Past his jest desu'ts,
An' de sneer of comerds
  Stuhes yo' heaht an' hu'ts,
Des don' pet yo' worries,
  Lay 'em on de she'f,
Tek a little trouble
  Brothah, wid yo'se'f.

Ef a frien' comes mou'nin'
  'Bout his awful case,
You know you don' grieve him
  Wid a gloomy face,
But you wrassle wid him,
  Try to tek him in;
Dough hit cracks yo' features,
  Law, you smile lak sin,
Ain't you good ez he is?
  Don' you pine to def;
Tek a little trouble
  Brothah, wid yo'se'f.

Ef de chillun pestahs,
  An' de baby's bad,
Ef yo' wife gits narvous,
  An' you're gettin' mad,
Des you grab yo' boot-strops,
  Hol' yo' body down,
Stop a-tinkin' cuss-w'rds,
  Chase away de frown,
Knock de haid o' worry,
  Twell dey ain' none lef';

Tek a little trouble,
  Brothah, wid yo'se'f.

LIMITATIONS

EF you's only got de powah fe' to
    blow a little whistle,
  Keep ermong de people wid de
    whistles.
Ef you don't, you'll fin' out sho'tly
    dat you's th'owed yo' fines'
    feelin'
  In a place dat's all a bed o' this-
    tles.
'Tain't no use a-goin' now, ez
    sho's you bo'n,
A-squeakin' of yo' whistle 'g'inst
    a gread big ho'n.

Ef you ain't got but a teenchy bit
    o' victuals on de table,
  Whut' de use a-claimin' hit's a
    feas'?
Fe' de folks is mighty 'spicious,
    an' dey's ap' to come a-
    peerin',
  Lookin' fe' de scraps you lef'
    at leas'.
W'en de meal's a-hidin' f'om de
    meal-bin's top,
You needn't talk to hide it; ef you
    sta'ts, des stop.

Ef yo' min' kin only carry half a
    pint o' common idees,
  Don' go roun' a-sayin' hit's a
    bar'l;

[250]

PAUL LAURENCE DUNBAR

'Ca'se de people gwine to test you,
    an' dey'll fin' out you's
    a-lyin',
  Den dey'll twis' yo' sayin's in a
    snarl.
Wuss t'ing in de country dat I
    evah hyahed —
A crow dot sat a-squawkin', " I's
    a mockin'-bird."

A GOLDEN DAY

I FOUND you and I lost you,
  All on a gleaming day.
The day was filled with sunshine,
  And the land was full of May.

A golden bird was singing
  Its melody divine,
I found you and I loved you,
  And all the world was mine.

I found you and I lost you,
  All on a golden day,
But when I dream of you, dear,
  It is always brimming May.

THE UNLUCKY APPLE

'TWAS the apple that in Eden
  Caused our father's primal fall;
And the Trojan War, remem-
    ber —
  'Twas an apple caused it all.
So for weeks I've hesitated,
  You can guess the reason why,
For I want to tell my darling
  She's the apple of my eye.

THE DISCOVERY

THESE are the days of elfs and
  fays :
Who says that with the dreams of
  myth,
These imps and elves disport them-
  selves?
Ah no, along the paths of song
Do all the tiny folk belong.

Round all our homes,
Kobolds and gnomes do daily cling,
Then nightly fling their lanterns
  out.
And shout on shout, they join the
  rout,
And sing, and sing, within the
  sweet enchanted ring.

Where gleamed the guile of moonlight's smile,
Once paused I, listening for a
  while,
And heard the lay, unknown by
  day,—
The fairies' dancing roundelay.

Queen Mab was there, her shim-
  mering hair
Each fairy prince's heart's despair.
She smiled to see their sparkling
  glee,
And once I ween, she smiled at me.

Since when, you may by night or
  day,
Dispute the sway of elf-folk gay;
But, hear me, stay!

[251]

I've learned the way to find Queen
    Mab and elf and fay.

Where e'er by streams, the moon-
    light gleams,
Or on a meadow softly beams,
There, footing round on dew-lit
    ground,
The fairy folk may all be found.

MORNING

THE mist has left the greening
    plain,
The dew-drops shine like fairy
    rain,
The coquette rose awakes again
    Her lovely self adorning.
The Wind is hiding in the trees,
A sighing, soothing, laughing
    tease,
Until the rose says "Kiss me,
    please,"
    'Tis morning, 'tis morning.

With staff in hand and careless-
    free,
The wanderer fares right jauntily,
For towns and houses are, thinks
    he,
    For scorning, for scorning.
My soul is swift upon the wing,
And in its deeps a song I bring;
Come, Love, and we together sing,
    " 'Tis morning, 'tis morning."

THE AWAKENING

I DID not know that life could be
    so sweet,
I did not know the hours could
    speed so fleet,
Till I knew you, and life was sweet
    again.
The days grew brief with love
    and lack of pain —

I was a slave a few short days
    ago,
The powers of Kings and Princes
    now I know;
I would not be again in bondage,
    save
I had your smile, the liberty I
    crave.

LOVE'S DRAFT

THE draft of love was cool and
    sweet
    You gave me in the cup,
But, ah, love's fire is keen and
    fleet,
    And I am burning up.

Unless the tears I shed for you
    Shall quench this burning flame,
It will consume me through and
    through,
    And leave but ash—a name.

[252]

PAUL LAURENCE DUNBAR

A MUSICAL

OUTSIDE the rain upon the street,
  The sky all grim of hue,
Inside, the music-painful sweet,
  And yet I heard but you.

As is a thrilling violin,
  So is your voice to me,
And still above the other strains,
  It sang in ecstasy.

TWELL DE NIGHT IS PAS'

ALL de night long twell de moon
    goes down,
  Lovin' I set at huh feet,
Den fu' de long jou'ney back
    f'om de town,
  Ha'd, but de dreams mek it
    sweet.

All de night long twell de break of
    de day,
  Dreamin' agin in my sleep,
Mandy comes drivin' my sorrers
    away,
    Axin' me, "Wha' fu' you
    weep?"

All de day long twell de sun goes
    down,
  Smilin', I ben' to my hoe,
Fu' dough de weddah git nasty an'
    frown,
  One place I know I kin go.

All my life long twell de night has
    pas'
  Let de wo'k come ez it will,
So dat I fin' you, my honey, at las',
  Somewhaih des ovah de hill.

BLUE

STANDIN' at de winder,
  Feelin' kind o' glum,
Listenin' to de raindrops
  Play de kettle drum,
Lookin' crost de medders
  Swimmin' lak a sea;
Lawd 'a' mussy on us,
  What's de good o' me?

Can't go out a-hoein',
  Wouldn't ef I could;
Groun' too wet fu' huntin',
  Fishin' ain't no good.
Too much noise fo' sleepin',
  No one hyeah to chat;
Des mus' stan' an' listen
  To dat pit-a-pat.

Hills is gittin' misty,
  Valley's gittin' dahk;
Watch-dog's 'mence a-howlin',
  Rathah have 'em ba'k
Dan a-moanin' solemn
  Somewhaih out o' sight;
Rain-crow des a-chucklin'—
  Dis is his delight.

Mandy, bring my banjo,
  Bring de chillen in,

[253]

Come in f'om de kitchen,
  I feel sick ez sin.
Call in Uncle Isaac,
  Call Aunt Hannah, too,
Tain't no use in talkin',
  Chile, I's sholy blue.

DREAMIN' TOWN

COME away to dreamin' town,
  Mandy Lou, Mandy Lou,
Whaih de skies don' nevah frown,
  Mandy Lou;
Whaih he streets is paved with
  gol',
Whaih de days is nevah col',
An' no sheep strays f'om de fol',
  Mandy Lou.

Ain't you tiahed of every day,
  Mandy Lou, Mandy Lou,
Tek my han' an' come away,
  Mandy Lou,
To the place whaih dreams is
  King,
Whaih my heart hol's everything,
An' my soul can allus sing,
  Mandy Lou.

Come away to dream wid me,
  Mandy Lou, Mandy Lou,
Whaih our hands an' hea'ts are
  free,
    Mandy Lou;
Whaih de sands is shinin' white,
Whaih de rivahs glistens bright,
  Mandy Lou.

Come away to dreamland town,
  Mandy Lou, Mandy Lou,
Whaih de fruit is bendin' down,
  Des fu' you.
Smooth your brow of lovin' brown,
An' my love will be its crown;
Come away to dreamin' town,
  Mandy Lou.

AT NIGHT

WHUT time 'd dat clock strike?
    Nine? No — eight;
  I didn't think hit was so late.
Aer chew! I must 'a' got a cough,
  I raally b'lieve I did doze off —
Hit's mighty soothin' to de tiah,
  A-dozin' dis way by de fiah;
Oo oom — hit feels so good to
    stretch
  I sutny is one weary wretch!

Look hyeah, dat boy done gone to
    sleep!
  He des ain't wo'th his boa'd an'
    keep;
I des don't b'lieve he'd bat his
    eyes
    If Gab'el called him fo'm de
    skies!
But sleepin's good dey ain't no
    doubt —
    Dis pipe o' mine is done gone
    out.
Don't bu'n a minute, bless my soul,
  Des please to han' me dat ah
    coal.

[254]

You 'Lias git up now, my son,
  Seems lak my nap is des begun;
You sutny mus' ma'k down de day
  W'en I treats comp'ny dis away!
W'y, Brother Jones, dat drowse
    come on,
  An' laws! I dremp dat you was
    gone!
You 'Lias, whaih yo' mannahs,
    suh,
  To hyeah me call an' nevah
    stuh!

To-morrer mo'nin' w'en I call
  Dat boy'll be sleepin' to beat all,
Don't mek no diffunce how I roah,
  He'll des lay up an' sno' and
    sno'.
Now boy, you done hyeahed whut
    I said,
  You bettah tek yo'se'f yo baid,
Case ef you gits me good an'
    wrong ·
  I'll mek dat sno' a diffunt song.

Dis wood fiah is invitin' dho',
  Hit seems to wa'm de ve'y flo'—
An' nuffin' ain't a whit ez sweet,
  Ez settin' toastin' of yo' feet.
Hit mek you drowsy, too, but La!
  Hyeah, 'Lias, don't you hyeah
    yo' ma?
Ef I gits sta'ted f'om dis cheah
  I' lay, you scamp, I'll mek you
    beah!

To-morrer mo'nin' I kin bawl
  Twell all de neighbohs hyeah
    me call;

An' you'll be snoozin' des ez deep
  Ez if de day was made fu' sleep;
Hit's funny when you got a cough
  Somehow yo' voice seems too fu'
    off—
Can't wake dat boy fu' all I say,
  I reckon he'll sleep daih twell
    day!

KIDNAPED

I HELD my heart so far from harm,
  I let it wander far and free
In mead and mart, without alarm,
  Assured it must come back to
    me.

And all went well till on a day,
  Learned Dr. Cupid wandered
    by
A search along our sylvan way
  For some peculiar butterfly.

A flash of wings, a hurried dive,
  A flutter and a short-lived flit;
This Scientist, as I am alive
  Had seen my heart and captured
    it.

Right tightly now 'tis held among
  The specimens that he has
    trapped,
And sings (Oh, love is ever
    young),
  'Tis passing sweet to be kid-
    naped.

[255]

COMPENSATION

BECAUSE I had loved so deeply,
    Because I had loved so long,
God in His great compassion
    Gave me the gift of song.

Because I have loved so vainly,
    And sung with such faltering
        breath,
The Master in infinite mercy
    Offers the boon of Death.

WINTER'S APPROACH

DE sun hit shine an' de win' hit
        blow,
Ol' Brer Rabbit be a-layin' low,
    He know dat de wintah time
        a-comin',
De huntah man he walk an' wait,
He walk right by Brer Rabbit's
        gate —
    He know —

De dog he lick his sliverin' chop,
An' he tongue 'gin' his mouf go
        flop, flop —
    He —
He rub his nose fu' to clah his
        scent
So's to tell w'ich way dat cotton-
        tail went,
    He —

De huntah's wife she set an' spin
A good wahm coat fu' to wrop him
        in
    She —

She look at de skillet an' she smile,
        oh my!
An' ol' Brer Rabbit got to sholy
        fly.
    Dey know.

ANCHORED

IF thro' the sea of night which
        here surrounds me,
    I could swim out beyond the
        farthest star,
Break every barrier of circumstance
        that bounds me,
    And greet the Sun of sweeter
        life afar,

Tho' near you there is passion,
        grief, and sorrow,
    And out there rest and joy and
        peace and all,
I should renounce that beckoning
        for to-morrow,
    I could not choose to go beyond
        your call.

THE VETERAN

UNDERNEATH the autumn sky,
Haltingly, the lines go by.
Ah, would steps were blithe and
        gay,
As when first they marched away,
Smile on lip and curl on brow, —
Only white-faced gray-beards now,
Standing on life's outer verge,
E'en the marches sound a dirge.

PAUL LAURENCE DUNBAR

Blow, you bugles, play, you fife,
Rattle, drums, for dearest life.
Let the flags wave freely so,
As the marching legions go,
Shout, hurrah and laugh and jest,
This is memory at its best.
(Did you notice at your quip,
That old comrade's quivering lip?)

Ah, I see them as they come,
Stumbling with the rumbling
    drum;
But a sight more sad to me
E'en than these ranks could be
Was that one with cane upraised
Who stood by and gazed and
    gazed,
Trembling, solemn, lips com-
    pressed,
Longing to be with the rest.

Did he dream of old alarms,
As he stood, "presented arms"?
Did he think of field and camp
And the unremitting tramp
Mile on mile — the lonely guard
When he kept his midnight ward?
Did he dream of wounds and scars
In that bitter war of wars?

What of that? He stood and
    stands
In my memory — trembling hands,
Whitened beard and cane and all
As if waiting for the call
Once again: "To arms, my sons,"

And his ears hear far-off guns,
Roll of cannon and the tread
Of the legions of the Dead!

YESTERDAY AND TO-MORROW

YESTERDAY I held your hand,
Reverently I pressed it,
And its gentle yieldingness
From my soul I blessed it.

But to-day I sit alone,
Sad and sore repining;
Must our gold forever know
Flames for the refining?

Yesterday I walked with you,
Could a day be sweeter?
Life was all a lyric song
Set to tricksy meter.

Ah, to-day is like a dirge,—
Place my arms around you,
Let me feel the same dear joy
As when first I found you.

Let me once retrace my steps,
From these roads unpleasant,
Let my heart and mind and soul
All ignore the present.

Yesterday the iron seared
And to-day means sorrow.
Pause, my soul, arise, arise,
Look where gleams the morrow.

THE CHANGE

Love used to carry a bow, you
  know,
  But now he carries a taper;
It is either a length of wax aglow,
  Or a twist of lighted paper.

I pondered a little about the scamp,
  And then I decided to follow
His wandering journey to field and
  camp,
  Up hill, down dale or hollow.

I dogged the rollicking, gay, young
  blade
  In every species of weather;
Till, leading me straight to the
  home of a maid
  He left us there together.

And then I saw it, oh, sweet surprise,
  The taper it set a-burning
The love-light brimming my lady's
  eyes,
  And my heart with the fire of
  yearning.

THE CHASE

The wind told the little leaves to
  hurry,
  And chased them down the way,
While the mother tree laughed
  loud in glee,
  For she thought her babes at
  play.

The cruel wind and the rain
  laughed loudly,
  We'll bury them deep, they said,
And the old tree grieves, and the
  little leaves
  Lie low, all chilled and dead.

SUPPOSE

If 'twere fair to suppose
  That your heart were not taken,
That the dew from the rose
  Petals still were not shaken,
I should pluck you,
  Howe'er you should thorn me
  and scorn me,
And wear you for life as the green
  of the bower.

If 'twere fair to suppose
  That that road was for va-
  grants,
That the wind and the rose,
  Counted all in their fragrance;
Oh, my dear one,
  By love, I should take you and
  make you,
The green of my life from the
  scintillant hour.

THE DEATH OF THE
FIRST BORN

Cover him over with daisies white
  And eke with the poppies red,
Sit with me here by his couch to-
  night,

[258]

PAUL LAURENCE DUNBAR

For the First-Born, Love, is
dead.

Poor little fellow, he seemed so
 fair
As he lay in my jealous arms;
Silent and cold he is lying there
 Stripped of his darling charms.

Lusty and strong he had grown
 forsooth,
Sweet with an infinite grace,
Proud in the force of his conquer-
 ing youth,
 Laughter alight in his face.

Oh, but the blast, it was cruel and
 keen,
 And ah, but the chill it was rare;
The look of the winter-kissed
 flow'r you've seen
 When meadows and fields wer-
 bare.

Can you not wake from this white,
 cold sleep
 And speak to me once again?
True that your slumber is deep,
 so deep,
 But deeper by far is my pain.

Cover him over with daisies white,
 And eke with the poppies red,
Sit with me here by his couch to-
 night,
 For the First-Born, Love, is
 dead.

BEIN' BACK HOME

HOME agin, an' home to stay —
Yes, it's nice to be away.
Plenty things to do an' see,
But the old place seems to me
Jest about the proper thing.
Mebbe 'ts 'cause the mem'ries
 cling
Closer 'round yore place o' birth
'N ary other spot on earth.

W'y it's nice jest settin' here,
Lookin' out an' seein' clear,
'Thout no smoke, ner dust, ner
 haze
In these sweet October days.
What's as good as that there lane,
Kind o' browned from last night's
 rain?
'Pears like home has got the start
When the goal's a feller's heart.

What's as good as that there jay
Screechin' up'ards towards the
 gray
Skies? An' tell me, what's as fine
As that full-leafed pumpkin vine?
Tow'rin' buildin's — yes, they're
 good;
But in sight o' field and wood,
Then a feller understan's
'Bout the house not made with
 han's.

Let the others rant an' roam
When they git away from home;
Jest gi' me my old settee

[259]

An' my pipe beneath a tree;
Sight o' medders green an' still,
Now and then a gentle hill,
Apple orchards, full o' fruit,
Nigh a cider press to boot —

That's the thing jest done up
    brown;
D'want to be too nigh to town;
Want to have the smells an' sights,
An' the dreams o' long still nights,
With the friends you used to know
In the keerless long ago —
Same old cronies, same old folks,
Same old cider, same old jokes.

Say, it's nice a-gittin' back,
When yore pulse is growin' slack,
An' yore breath begins to wheeze
Like a fair-set valley breeze;
Kind o' nice to set aroun'
On the old familiar groun',
Knowin' that when Death does
    come,
That he'll find you right at home.

THE OLD CABIN

In de dead of night I sometimes,
    Git to t'inkin' of de pas'
An' de days w'en slavery helt me
    In my mis'ry — ha'd an' fas'.
Dough de time was mighty tryin',
    In dese houahs somehow hit
        seem
Dat a brightah light come slippin'
    Thoo de kivahs of my dream.

An' my min' fu'gits de whuppins
    Draps de feah o' block an' lash
An' flies straight to somep'n' joy-
        ful   -
    In a secon's lightnin' flash.
Den hit seems I see a vision
    Of a dearah long ago
Of de childern tumblin' roun' me
    By my rough ol' cabin do'.

Talk about yo' go'geous mansions
    An' yo' big house great an'
        gran',
Des bring up de fines' palace
    Dat you know in all de lan'.
But dey's somep'n' dearah to me,
    Somep'n' faihah to my eyes
In dat cabin, less you bring me
    To yo' mansion in de skies.

I kin see de light a-shinin'
    Thoo de chinks atween de logs,
I kin hyeah de way-off bayin'
    Of my mastah's huntin' dogs,
An' de neighin' of de hosses
    Stampin' on de ol' bahn flo',
But above dese soun's de laughin'
    At my deah ol' cabin do'.

We would gethah daih at evenin',
    All my frien's 'ud come erroun'
An' hit wan't no time, twell, bless
        you,
    You could hyeah de banjo's
        soun'.
You could see de dahkies dancin'
    Pigeon wing an' heel an' toe —

Joyous times I tell you people
  Roun' dat same ol' cabin do'.

But at times my t'oughts gits sad-
    dah,
  Ez I riccolec' de folks,
An' dey frolickin' an' talkin'
  Wid dey laughin' an dey jokes.
An' hit hu'ts me w'en I membahs
  Dat I 'll nevah see no mo'
Dem ah faces gethered smilin'
  Roun' dat po' ol' cabin do'.

DESPAIR

LET me close the eyes of my soul
  That I may not see
What stands between thee and me.

Let me shut the ears of my heart
  That I may not hear
A voice that drowns yours, my
    dear.

Let me cut the cords of my life,
  Of my desolate being,
Since cursed is my hearing and see-
    ing.

CIRCUMSTANCES ALTER CASES

TIM Murphy's gon' walkin' wid
    Maggie O'Neill,
      O chone!
If I was her muther, I 'd frown
    on sich foolin',
      O chone!

I'm sure it's unmutherlike, darin'
    an' wrong
To let a gyrul hear tell the sass an'
    the song
Of every young felly that happens
    along,
      O chone!

'An' Murphy, the things that's
    be'n sed of his doin',
      O chone!
'Tis a cud that no dacent folks
    wants to be chewin',
      O chone!
If he came to my door wid his
    cane on a twirl,
Fur to thry to make love to you,
    Biddy, my girl,
Ah, wouldn't I send him away
    wid a whirl,
      O chone!

They say the gossoon is indecent
    and dirty,
      O chone!
In spite of his dressin' so.
      O chone!
Let him dress up ez foine ez a
    king or a queen,
Let him put on more wrinkles
    than ever was seen,
You'll be sure he's no match for
    my little colleen,
      O chone!

Faith the two is comin' back an'
    their walk is all over,
      O chone!

[261]

'Twas a pretty short walk fur to
    take wid a lover,
      O chone!
Why, I believe that Tim Mur-
    phy's a kumin' this way,
Ah, Biddy jest look at him steppin'
    so gay,
I'd niver belave what the gos-
    sipers say,
      O chone!

He's turned in the gate an' he's
    coming a-caperin',
      O chone!
Go, Biddy, go quick an' put on a
    clane apern,
      O chone!
Be quick as ye kin fur he's right at
    the dure;
Come in, master Tim, fur ye're
    welcome I'm shure.
We were talkin' o' ye jest a minute
    before.
      O chone!

TILL THE WIND GETS RIGHT

OH the breeze is blowin' balmy
    An the sun is in a haze;
There's a cloud jest givin' coolness
    To the laziest of days.
There are crowds upon the lake-
    side,
    But the fish refuse to bite,
So I'll wait and go a-fishin'
    When the wind gets right.

Now my boat tugs at her anchor,
    Eager now to kiss the spray,
While the little waves are callin'
    Drowsy sailor come away,
There's a harbor for the happy,
    And its sheen is just in sight,
But I won't set sail to get there,
    Till the wind gets right.

That's my trouble, too, I reckon,
    I've been waitin' all too long,
Tho' the days were always
    Still the wind is always wrong.
An' when Gabriel blows his trum-
    pet,
    In the day o' in the night,
I will still be found waitin',
    Till the wind gets right.

A SUMMER NIGHT

SUMMAH is de lovin' time —
    Do' keer what you say.
Night is allus peart an' prime,
    Bettah dan de day.
Do de day is sweet an' good,
    Birds a-singin' fine,
Pines a-smellin' in de wood,—
    But de night is mine.

Rivah whisperin' "howdy do,"
    Ez it pass you by —
Moon a-lookin' down at you,
    Winkin' on de sly.
Frogs a-croakin' f'om de pon',
    Singin' bass dey fill,
An' you listen way beyon'
    Ol' man whippo'will.

PAUL LAURENCE DUNBAR

Hush up, honey, tek my han',
  Mek yo' footsteps light;
Somep'n' kin' o' hol's de lan'
  On a summah night.
Somep'n' dat you nevah sees
  An' you nevah hyeahs,
But you feels it in de breeze,
  Somep'n' nigh to teahs.

Somep'n' nigh to teahs? dat's so;
  But hit's nigh to smiles.
An' you feels it ez you go
  Down de shinin' miles.
Tek my han', my little dove;
  Hush an' come erway —
Summah is de time fu' love,
  Night-time beats de day!

AT SUNSET TIME

Adown the west a golden glow
  Sinks burning in the sea,
And all the dreams of long ago
  Come flooding back to me.
The past has writ a story strange
  Upon my aching heart,
But time has wrought a subtle
    change,
  My wounds have ceased to
    smart.

No more the quick delight of
    youth,
  No more the sudden pain,
I look no more for trust or truth
  Where greed may compass gain.

What, was it I who bared my
    heart
  Through unrelenting years,
And knew the sting of misery's
    dart,
  The tang of sorrow's tears?

'Tis better now, I do not weep,
  I do not laugh nor care;
My soul and spirit half asleep
  Drift aimless everywhere.
We float upon a sluggish stream,
  We ride no rapids mad,
While life is all a tempered dream
  And every joy half sad.

NIGHT

Silence, and whirling worlds afar
  Through all encircling skies.
What floods come o'er the spirit's
    bar,
  What wondrous thoughts arise.

The earth, a mantle falls away,
  And, winged, we leave the sod;
Where shines in its eternal sway
  The majesty of God.

AT LOAFING-HOLT

Since I left the city's heat
For this sylvan, cool retreat,
High upon the hill-side here
Where the air is clean and clear,
I have lost the urban ways.

[263]

Mine are calm and tranquil days,
Sloping lawns of green are mine,
Clustered treasures of the vine;
Long forgotten plants I know,
Where the best wild berries grow,
Where the greens and grasses
    sprout,
When the elders blossom out.
Now I am grown weather-wise
With the lore of winds and skies.
Mine the song whose soft refrain
Is the sigh of summer rain.
Seek you where the woods are cool,
Would you know the shady pool
Where, throughout the lazy day,
Speckled beauties drowse or play?
Would you find in rest or peace
Sorrow's permanent release?—
Leave the city, grim and gray,
Come with me, ah, come away.
Do you fear the winter chill,
Deeps of snow upon the hill?
'Tis a mantle, kind and warm,
Shielding tender shoots from harm.
Do you dread the ice-clad
    streams,—
They are mirrors for your dreams.
Here's a rouse, when summer's
    past
To the raging winter's blast.
Let him roar and let him rout,
We are armored for the bout.
How the logs are glowing, see!
Who sings louder, they or he?
Could the city be more gay?
Burn your bridges! Come away!

WHEN A FELLER'S ITCHIN' TO BE SPANKED

W'EN us fellers stomp around,
    makin' lots o' noise,
Gramma says, "There's certain
    times come to little boys
W'en they need a shingle or the
    soft side of a plank;"
She says "we're a-itchin' for a
    right good spank."
    An' she says, "Now thes you
        wait,
    It's a-comin'— soon or late,
    W'en a feller's itchin' fer a spank."

W'en a feller's out o' school, you
    know how he feels,
Gramma says we wriggle 'roun'
    like a lot o' eels.
W'y it's like a man that's thes
    home from out o' jail.
What's the use o' scoldin' if we
    pull Tray's tail?
    Gramma says, tho', "Thes you
        wait,
    It's a-comin'— soon or late,
You'se the boys that's itchin' to
    be spanked."

Cats is funny creatures an' I like
    to make 'em yowl,
Gramma alwus looks at me with
    a awful scowl
An' she says, "Young gentlemen,
    mamma should be thanked
Ef you'd get your knickerbockers
    right well spanked."

PAUL LAURENCE DUNBAR

An' she says, "Now thes you
  wait,
It's a-comin'— soon or late,"
W'en a feller's itchin' to be
  spanked.

Ef you fin' the days is gettin'
    awful hot in school
An' you know a swimmin' place
    where it's nice and cool,
Er you know a cat-fish hole brim-
    min' full o' fish,
Whose a-goin' to set around school
    and wish?
  'Tain't no use to hide your bait,
  It's a-comin,— soon or late,
W'en a feller's itchin' to be
    spanked.

Ol' folks know most ever'thing
    'bout the world, I guess,
Gramma does, we wish she knowed
    thes a little less,
But I alwus kind o' think it 'ud be
    as well
  Ef they wouldn't alwus have to
    up an' tell;
  We kids wish 'at they'd thes
    wait,
  It's a-comin'— soon or late,
W'en a feller's itchin' to be
    spanked.

THE RIVER OF RUIN

Along by the river of ruin
They dally — the thoughtless ones,
They dance and they dream

By the side of the stream,
As long as the river runs.

It seems all so pleasant and
    cheery —
No thought of the morrow is
    theirs,
And their faces are bright
With the sun of delight,
And they dream of no night-
    brooding cares.

The women wear garlanded
    tresses,
The men have rings on their
    hands,
And they sing in their glee,
For they think they are free —
They that know not the treacher-
    ous sands.

Ah, but this be a venturesome jour-
    ney,
Forever those sands are ashift,
And a step to one side
Means a grasp of the tide,
And the current is fearful and
    swift.

For once in the river of ruin,
What boots it, to do or to dare,
For down we must go
In the turbulent flow,
To the desolate sea of Despair.

[265]

TO HER

YOUR presence like a benison to
    me
  Wakes my sick soul to dreamful
    ecstasy,
I fancy that some old Arabian
    night
Saw you my houri and my heart's
  ' delight.

And wandering forth beneath the
    passionate moon,
  Your love-strung zither and my
    soul in tune,
We knew the joy, the haunting of
    the pain
  That like a flame thrills
    through me now again.

To-night we sit where sweet the
    spice winds blow,
  A wind the northland lacks and
    ne'er shall know,
With clasped hands and spirits all
    aglow
  As in Arabia in the long ago.

A LOVE LETTER

OH, I des received a letter f'om de
    sweetest little gal;
  Oh, my; oh, my.
She's my lovely little sweetheart
    an' her name is Sal:
  Oh, my; oh, my.

She writes me dat she loves me an'
    she loves me true,
  She wonders ef I'll tell huh dat
    I loves huh, too;
An' my heaht's so full o' music dat
    I do' know what to do;
  Oh, my; oh, my.

I got a man to read it an' he read
    it fine;
  Oh, my; oh, my.
Dey ain' no use denying dat her
    love is mine;
  Oh, my; oh, my.
But hyeah's de t'ing dat's puttin'
    me in such a awful plight,
I t'ink of huh at mornin' an' I
    dream of huh at night;
But how's I gwine to cou't huh
    w'en I do' know how to
    write?
  Oh, my; oh, my.

My heaht is bubblin' ovah wid de
    t'ings I want to say;
  Oh, my; oh, my.
An' dey's lots of folks to copy
    what I tell 'em fu' de pay;
  Oh, my; oh, my.
But dey's t'ings dat I's a-t'inkin'
    dat is only fu' huh ears,
An' I couldn't lu'n to write 'em ef
    I took a dozen years;
So to go down daih an' tell huh
    is de only way, it 'pears;
  Oh, my; oh, my.

[266]

PAUL LAURENCE DUNBAR

AFTER MANY DAYS

I'VE always been a faithful man
  An' tried to live for duty,
But the stringent mode of life
  Has somewhat lost its beauty.

The story of the generous bread
  He sent upon the waters,
Which after many days returns
  To trusting sons and daughters,

Had oft impressed me, so I want
  My soul influenced by it,
And bought a loaf of bread and
    sought
  A stream where I could try it.

I cast my bread upon the waves
  And fancied then to await it;
It had not floated far away
  When a fish came up and ate it.

And if I want both fish and bread,
  And surely both I'm wanting,
About the only way I see
  Is for me to go fishing.

LIZA MAY

Little brown face full of smiles,
And a baby's guileless wiles,
    Liza May, Liza May.

Eyes a-peeping thro' the fence
With an interest intense,
    Liza May.

Ah, the gate is just ajar,
And the meadow is not far,
    Liza May, Liza May.

And the road feels very sweet,
To your little toddling feet,
    Liza May.

Ah, you roguish runaway,
What will toiling mother say,
    Liza May, Liza May?

What care you who smile to greet
Everyone you chance to meet,
    Liza May?

Soft the mill-race sings its song,
Just a little way along,
    Liza May, Liza May.

But the song is full of guile,
Turn, ah turn, your steps the
    while,
    Liza May.

You have caught the gleam and
    glow
Where the darkling waters flow,
    Liza May, Liza May.

Flash of ripple, bend of bough,
Where are all the angels now?
    Liza May.

Now a mother's eyes intense
Gazing o'er a shabby fence,
    Liza May, Liza May.

[267]

Then a mother's anguished face
Peering all around the place,
    Liza May.

Hear the agonizing call
For a mother's all in all,
    Liza May, Liza May.

Hear a mother's maddened prayer
To the calm unanswering air,
    Liza May.

What's become of — Liza May?
What has darkened all the day?
    Liza May, Liza May.

Ask the waters dark and fleet,
If they know the smiling, sweet
    Liza May.

Call her, call her as you will,
On the meadow, on the hill,
    Liza May, Liza May.

Through the brush or beaten track
Echo only gives you back,
    Liza May.

Ah, but you were loving — sweet,
On your little toddling feet,
    Liza May, Liza May.

But through all the coming years,
Must a mother breathe with tears,
    Liza May.

THE MASTERS

Oh, who is the Lord of the land of
    life,
  When hotly goes the fray?
When, fierce we smile in the midst
    of strife
  Then whom shall we obey?

Oh, Love is the Lord of the land
    of life
  Who holds a monarch's sway;
He wends with wish of maid and
    wife,
  And him you must obey.

Then who is the Lord of the land
    of life,
  At setting of the sun?
Whose word shall sway when
    Peace is rife
  And all the fray is done?

Then Death is the Lord of the
    land of life,
  When your hot race is run.
Meet then his scythe and pruning-
    knife
  When the fray is lost or won.

TROUBLE IN DE KITCHEN

Dey was oncet a awful quoil
    'twixt de skillet an' de pot;
De pot was des a-bilin' an' de skil-
    let sho' was hot.
Dey slurred each othah's colah an'
    dey called each othah names,

W'ile de coal-oil can des gu-gled,
po'in oil erpon de flames.

De pot, hit called de skillet des a
flat, disfiggered t'ing,
An' de skillet 'plied dat all de pot
could do was set an' sing,
An' he 'lowed dat dey was 'lusions
dat he wouldn't stoop to mek
'Case he reckernize his juty, an' he
had too much at steak.

Well, at dis de pot biled ovah, case
his tempah gittin' highah,
An' de skillet got to sputterin',
den de fat was in de fiah,
Mistah fiah lay daih smokin' an'
a-t'inkin' to hisse'f,
W'ile de peppah-box us nudgin' of
de gingah on de she'f.

Den dey all des lef' hit to 'im,
'bout de trouble an' de talk;
An' howevah he decided, w'y dey
bofe 'u'd walk de chalk;
But de fiah uz so 'sgusted how dey
quoil an' dey shout
Dat he cooled 'em off, I reckon,
w'en he puffed an' des went
out.

CHRISTMAS

STEP wid de banjo an' glide wid
de fiddle,
Dis ain' no time fu' to pottah
an' piddle;

Fu' Christmas is comin', it's right
on de way,
An' dey's houahs to dance 'fo'
de break o' de day.

What if de win' is taihin' an'
whistlin'?
Look at dat fiah how hit's
spittin' an' bristlin'!
Heat in de ashes an' heat in de
cindahs,
Ol' mistah Fros' kin des look
thoo de windahs.

Heat up de toddy an' pas' de wa'm
glasses,
Don' stop to shivah at blowin's
an' blas'es,
Keep on de kittle an' keep it a-
hummin',
Eat all an' drink all, dey's lots
mo' a-comin'.
Look hyeah, Maria, don't open
dat oven,
Want all dese people a-pushin'
an' shovin'?

Res' f'om de dance? Yes, you
done cotch dat odah,
Mammy done cotch it, an' law!
hit nigh flo'd huh;
'Possum is monst'ous fu' mekin'
folks fin' it!
Come, draw yo' cheers up, I's
sho' I do' min' it.
Eat up dem critters, you men folks
an' wimmens,
'Possums ain' skace w'en dey's
lots o' pu'simmons.

ROSES AND PEARLS

YOUR spoken words are roses fine
and sweet,
The songs you sing are perfect
pearls of sound.
How lavish nature is about your
feet,
To scatter flowers and jewels both
around.

Blushing the stream of petal beauty
flows,
Softly the white strings trickle
down and shine.
Oh! speak to me, my love, I crave
a rose.
Sing me a song, for I would pearls
were mine.

RAIN-SONGS

THE rain streams down like harp-
strings from the sky;
    The wind, that world-old
    harpist sitteth by;
And ever as he sings his low refrain,
    He plays upon the harp-strings
    of the rain.

A LOST DREAM

AH, I have changed, I do not
know
Why lonely hours affect me so.

In days of yore, this were not wont,
No loneliness my soul could daunt.

For me too serious for my age,
The weighty tome of hoary sage,
Until with puzzled heart astir,
One God-giv'n night, I dreamed
    of her.

I loved no woman, hardly knew
More of the sex that strong men
    woo
Than cloistered monk within his
    cell;
But now the dream is lost, and hell

Holds me her captive tight and
    fast
Who prays and struggles for the
    past.
No living maid has charmed my
    eyes,
But now, my soul is wonder-wise.

For I have dreamed of her and
    seen
Her red-brown tresses' ruddy
    sheen,
Have known her sweetness, lip to
    lip,
The joy of her companionship.

When days were bleak and winds
    were rude,
She shared my smiling solitude,
And all the bare hills walked with
    me   .
To hearken winter's melody.

And when the spring came o'er the
   land
We fared together hand in hand
Beneath the linden's leafy screen
That waved above us faintly
   green.

In summer, by the river-side,
Our souls were kindred with the
   tide
That floated onward to the sea
As we swept toward Eternity.

The bird's call and the water's
   drone
Were all for us and us alone.
The water-fall that sang all night
Was her companion, my delight,

And e'en the squirrel, as he sped
Along the branches overhead,
Half kindly and half envious,
Would chatter at the joy of us.

'Twas but a dream, her face, her
   hair,
The spring-time sweet, the winter
   bare,
The summer when the woods we
   ranged,—
'Twas but a dream, but all is
   changed.

Yes, all is changed and all has
   fled,
The dream is broken, shattered,
   dead.
And yet, sometimes, I pray to know
How just a dream could hold me
   so.

A SONG

THOU art the soul of a summer's
   day,
Thou art the breath of the rose.
    But the summer is fled
    And the rose is dead
Where are they gone, who knows,
   who knows?

Thou art the blood of my heart o'
   hearts,
Thou art my soul's repose,
    But my heart grows numb
    And my soul is dumb
Where art thou, love, who knows,
   who knows?

Thou art the hope of my after
   years —
Sun for my winter snows
    But the years go by
    'Neath a clouded sky.
Where shall we meet, who knows,
   who knows?

THE CAPTURE

Duck come switchin' 'cross de lot
    Hi, oh, Miss Lady!
Hurry up an' hide de pot
    Hi, oh, Miss Lady!
Duck's a mighty 'spicious fowl,
Slick as snake an' wise as owl;
Hol' dat dog, don't let him yowl!
    Hi, oh, Miss Lady!

Th'ow dat co'n out kind o' slow
    Hi, oh, Miss Lady!
Keep yo'se'f behin' de do'
    Hi, oh, Miss Lady!
Lots o' food'll kill his feah,
Co'n is cheap but fowls is deah —
"Come, good ducky, come on
        heah."
    Hi, oh, Miss Lady!

Ain't he fat and ain't he fine,
    Hi, oh, Miss Lady!
Des can't wait to make him
        mine.
    Hi, oh, Miss Lady!
See him waddle when he walk,
'Sh! keep still and don't you talk!
Got you! Don't you daih to
        squawk!
    Hi, oh, Miss Lady!

WHEN WINTER DARKENING ALL AROUND

When winter covering all the
        ground
    Hides every sign of Spring, sir.
However you may look around,
    Pray what will then you sing,
        sir?

The Spring was here last year I
        know,
    And many bards did flute, sir;
I shall not fear a little snow
    Forbid me from my lute, sir.

If words grow dull and rhymes
        grow rare,
    I'll sing of Spring's farewell, sir.
For every season steals an air,
    Which has a Springtime smell,
        sir.

But if upon the other side,
    With passionate longing burn-
        ing,
Will seek the half unjeweled tide,
    And sing of Spring's returning.

FROM THE PORCH AT RUNNYMEDE

I stand above the city's rush and
        din,
    And gaze far down with calm
        and undimmed eyes,

[275]

To where the misty smoke wreath
grey and dim
Above the myriad roofs and
spires rise;

Still is my heart and vacant is my
breath —
This lovely view is breath and
life to me,
Why I could charm the icy soul
of death
With such a sight as this I stand
and see.

I hear no sound of labor's din or
stir,
I feel no weight of worldly
cares or fears,
Sweet song of birds, of wings the
soothing whirr,
These sounds alone assail my
listening ears.

Unwhipt of conscience here I
stand alone,
The breezes humbly kiss my gar-
ment's hem;
I am a king — the whole world is
my throne,
The blue grey sky my royal
diadem.

EQUIPMENT

WITH what thou gavest me, O
Master,
I have wrought.

Such chances, such abilities,
To see the end was not for my
poor eyes,
Thine was the impulse, thine the
forming thought.

Ah, I have wrought,
And these sad hands have right
to tell their story,
It was no hard up striving after
glory,
Catching and losing, gaining
and failing,
Raging me back at the world's
raucous railing.
Simply and humbly from stone
and from wood,
·Wrought I the things that to thee
might seem good.

If they are little, ah God! but the
cost,
Who but thou knowest the all
that is lost!
If they are few, is the workman-
ship true?
Try them and weigh me, what-
e'er be my due!

EVENING

THE moon begins her stately ride
Across the summer sky;
The happy wavelets lash the
shore,—
The tide is rising high.

PAUL LAURENCE DUNBAR

Beneath some friendly blade of
grass
The lazy beetle cowers;
The coffers of the air are filled
With offerings from the flow-
ers.

And slowly buzzing o'er my head
A swallow wings her flight;
I hear the weary plowman sing
As falls the restful night.

TO PFRIMMER

(Lines on reading " Driftwood.")

DRIFTWOOD gathered here and
there
Along the beach of time;
Now and then a chip of truth
'Mid boards and boughs of rhyme;
Driftwood gathered day by day,—
The cypress and the oak,—
Twigs that in some former time
From sturdy home trees broke.
Did this wood come floating thick
All along down " Injin Crik?"
Or did kind tides bring it thee
From the past's receding sea
Down the stream of memory?

TO THE MIAMI

Kiss me, Miami, thou most con-
stant one!
I love thee more for that thou
changest not.

When Winter comes with frigid
blast,
Or when the blithesome Spring
is past
And Summer's here with sunshine hot,
Or in sere Autumn, thou has
still the pow'r
To charm alike, whate'er the hour.

Kiss me, Miami, with thy dewy
lips;
Throbs fast my heart e'en as
thine own breast beats.
My soul doth rise as rise thy
waves,
As each on each the dark shore
laves
And breaks in ripples and re-
treats.
There is a poem in thine every
phase;
Thou still has sung through all
thy days.

Tell me, Miami, how it was with
thee
When years ago Tecumseh in
his prime
His birch boat o'er thy waters
sent,
And pitched upon thy banks his
tent.
In that long-gone, poetic time,
Did some bronze bard thy flowing
stream sit by
And sing thy praises, e'en as I?

THE COMPLETE POEMS OF

Did some bronze lover 'neath this
    dark old tree
  Whisper of love unto his Indian
    maid?
And didst thou list his murmurs
    deep,
And in thy bosom safely keep
  The many raging vows they
    said?
Or didst thou tell to fish and frog
    and bird
The raptured scenes that there
    occurred?

But, O dear stream, what volumes
    thou couldst tell
  To all who know thy language
    as I do,
Of life and love and jealous hate!
But now to tattle were too late,—
  Thou who hast ever been so
    true.
Tell not to every passing idler
    here
All those sweet tales that reached
    thine ear.

But, silent stream, speak out and
    tell me this:
  I say that men and things are
    still the same;
Were men as bold to do and dare?
Were women then as true and
    fair?
  Did poets seek celestial flame,
The hero die to gain a laureled
    brow,
And women suffer, then as now?

CHRISTMAS CAROL

Ring out, ye bells!
All Nature swells
With gladness at the wondrous
    story,—
The world was lorn,
But Christ is born
To change our sadness into glory.

Sing, earthlings, sing!
To-night a King
Hath come from heaven's high
    throne to bless us.
The outstretched hand
O'er all the land
Is raised in pity to caress us.

Come at his call;
Be joyful all;
Away with mourning and with
    sadness!
The heavenly choir
With holy fire
Their voices raise in songs of glad-
    ness.

The darkness breaks
And Dawn awakes,
Her cheeks suffused with youthful
    blushes.
The rocks and stones
In holy tones
Are singing sweeter than the
    thrushes.

Then why should we
In silence be,

[278]

When Nature lends her voice to
    praises;
  When heaven and earth
  Proclaim the truth
Of Him for whom that lone star
    blazes?

  No, be not still,
  But with a will
Strike all your harps and set them
    ringing;
  On hill and heath
  Let every breath
Throw all its power into singing!

A SUMMER PASTORAL

It's hot to-day. The bees is
    buzzin'
  Kinder don't-keer-like aroun'
An' fur off the warm air dances
  O'er the parchin' roofs in town.
In the brook the cows is standin';
  Childern hidin' in the hay;
Can't keep none of 'em a workin',
  'Cause it's hot to-day.

It's hot to-day. The sun is
    blazin'
  Like a great big ball o' fire;
Seems as ef instead o' settin'
  It keeps mountin' higher an'
    higher.
I'm as triflin' as the children,
  Though I blame them lots an'
    scold;
I keep slippin' to the spring-house,
  Where the milk is rich an' cold.

The very air within its shadder
  Smells o' cool an' restful things,
An' a roguish little robin
  Sits above the place an' sings.
I don't mean to be a shirkin',
  But I linger by the way
Longer, mebbe, than is needful,
  'Cause it's hot to-day.

It's hot to-day. The horses stum-
    ble
  Half asleep across the fiel's;
An' a host o' teasin' fancies
  O'er my burnin' senses steals,—
Dreams o' cool rooms, curtains
    lowered,
  An' a sofy's temptin' look;
Patter o' composin' raindrops
  Or the ripple of a brook.

I strike a stump! That wakes
    me sudden;
  Dreams all vanish into air.
Lordy! how I chew my whiskers;
  'Twouldn't do fur me to swear.
But I have to be so keerful
  'Bout my thoughts an' what I
    say;
Somethin' might slip out unheeded,
  'Cause it's hot to-day.

Git up, there, Suke! you, Sal, git
    over!
  Sakes alive! how I do sweat.
Every stitch that I've got on me,
Bet a cent, is wringin' wet.
If this keeps up, I'll lose my tem-
    per.

Gee there, Sal, you lazy brute!
Wonder who on airth this weather
Could 'a' be'n got up to suit?

You, Sam, go bring a tin o' water;
Dash it all, don't be so slow!
'Pears as ef you tuk an hour
'Tween each step to stop an'
blow.
Think I want to stand a meltin'
Out here in this b'ilin' sun,
While you stop to think about it?
Lift them feet o' your'n an' run.

It ain't no use; I'm plumb fe-
taggled.
Come an' put this team away.
I won't plow another furrer;
It's too mortal hot to-day.
I ain't weak, nor I ain't lazy,
But I'll stand this half day's loss
'Fore I let the devil make me
Lose my patience an' git cross.

IN SUMMER TIME

WHEN summer time has come,
and all
The world is in the magic thrall
Of perfumed airs that lull each
sense
To fits of drowsy indolence;
When skies are deepest blue above,
And flow'rs aflush,— then most I
love
To start, while early dews are
damp,

And wend my way in woodland
tramp
Where forests rustle, tree on tree,
And sing their silent songs to me;
Where pathways meet and path-
ways part,—
To walk with Nature heart by
heart,
Till wearied out at last I lie
Where some sweet stream steals
singing by
A mossy bank; where violets vie
In color with the summer sky,—
Or take my rod and line and hook,
And wander to some darkling
brook,
Where all day long the willows
dream,
And idly droop to kiss the stream,
And there to loll from morn till
night —
Unheeding nibble, run, or bite —
Just for the joy of being there
And drinking in the summer air,
The summer sounds, and summer
sights,
That set a restless mind to rights
When grief and pain and raging
doubt
Of men and creeds have worn it
out;
The birds' song and the water's
drone,
The humming bees' low monotone,
The murmur of the passing breeze,
And all the sounds akin to these,
That make a man in summer time

Feel only fit for rest and rhyme.
Joy springs all radiant in my
    breast;
Though pauper poor, than king
    more blest,
The tide beats in my soul so strong
That happiness breaks forth in
    song,
And rings aloud the welkin blue
With all the songs I ever knew.
O time of rapture! time of song!
How swiftly glide thy days along
Adown the current of the years,
Above the rocks of grief and tears!
'Tis wealth enough of joy for me
In summer time to simply be.

A THANKSGIVING POEM

THE sun hath shed its kindly
    light,
  Our harvesting is gladly o'er
Our fields have felt no killing
    blight,
  Our bins are filled with goodly
    store.

From pestilence, fire, flood, and
    sword
  We have been spared by thy de-
    cree,
And now with humble hearts, O
    Lord,
  We come to pay our thanks to
    thee.

We feel that had our merits been
  The measure of thy gifts to us,
We erring children, born of sin,
  Might not now be rejoicing
    thus.

No deed of ours hath brought us
    grace;
  When thou were nigh our sight
    was dull,
We hid in trembling from thy
    face,
  But thou, O God, wert merci-
    ful.

Thy mighty hand o'er all the land
  Hath still been open to bestow
Those blessings which our wants
    demand
  From heaven, whence all bless-
    ings flow.

Thou hast, with ever watchful eye,
  Looked down on us with holy
    care,
And from thy storehouse in the
    sky
  Hast scattered plenty every-
    where.

Then lift we up our songs of
    praise
  To thee, O Father, good and
    kind;
To thee we consecrate our days;
  Be thine the temple of each
    mind.

With incense sweet our thanks
    ascend;

Before thy works our powers
    pall;
Though we should strive years
    without end,
    We could not thank thee for
    them all.

NUTTING SONG

THE November sun invites me,
And although the chill wind smites
    me,
I will wander to the woodland
    Where the laden trees await;
And with loud and joyful singing
I will set the forest ringing,
As if I were king of Autumn,
    And Dame Nature were my
    mate,—

While the squirrel in his gambols
Fearless round about me ambles,
As if he were bent on showing
    In my kingdom he'd a share;
While my warm blood leaps and
    dashes,
And my eye with freedom flashes,
As my soul drinks deep and deeper
    Of the magic in the air.

There's a pleasure found in nut-
    ting,
All life's cares and griefs outshut-
    ting,
That is fuller far and better
    Than what prouder sports im-
    part.

Who could help a carol trilling
As he sees the baskets filling?
Why, the flow of song keeps run-
    ning
O'er the high walls of the heart.

So when I am home returning,
When the sun is lowly burning,
I will once more wake the echoes
    With a happy song of praise,—
For the golden sunlight blessing,
And the breezes' soft caressing,
And the precious boon of living
    In the sweet November days.

LOVE'S PICTURES

LIKE the blush upon the rose
    When the wooing south wind
    speaks,
Kissing soft its petals,
    Are thy cheeks.

Tender, soft, beseeching, true,
    Like the stars that deck the skies
Through the ether sparkling,
    Are thine eyes.

Like the song of happy birds,
    When the woods with spring re-
    joice,
In their blithe awak'ning,
    Is thy voice.

Like soft threads of clustered silk
    O'er thy face so pure and fair,
Sweet in its profusion,
    Is thy hair.

PAUL LAURENCE DUNBAR

Like a fair but fragile vase,
  Triumph of the carver's art,
Graceful formed and slender,—
  Thus thou art.

Ah, thy cheek, thine eyes, thy
      voice,
  And thy hair's delightful wave
Make me, I'll confess it,
  Thy poor slave!

THE OLD HOMESTEAD

'Tis an old deserted homestead
  On the outskirts of the town,
Where the roof is all moss-cov-
      ered,
  And the walls are tumbling
      down;
But around that little cottage
  Do my brightest mem'ries cling,
For 'twas there I spent the mo-
      ments
    Of my youth,— life's happy
      spring.

I remember how I used to
  Swing upon the old front gate,
While the robin in the tree tops
  Sung a night song to his mate;
And how later in the evening,
  As the beaux were wont to do,
Mr. Perkins, in the parlor,
  Sat and sparked my sister Sue.

There my mother — heaven bless
      her! —
  Kissed or spanked as was our
      need,
And by smile or stroke implanted
  In our hearts fair virtue's seed;
While my father, man of wisdom,
  Lawyer keen, and farmer stout,
Argued long with neighbor Dob-
      bins
    How the corn crops would turn
      out.

Then the quiltings and the
      dances —
  How my feet were wont to fly,
While the moon peeped through
      the barn chinks
  From her stately place on high.
Oh, those days, so sweet, so happy,
  Ever backward o'er me roll;
Still the music of that farm life
  Rings an echo in my soul.

Now the old place is deserted,
  And the walls are falling down;
All who made the home life cheer-
      ful,
  Now have died or moved to
      town.
But about that dear old cottage
  Shall my mem'ries ever cling,
For 'twas there I spent the mo-
      ments
    Of my youth,— life's happy
      spring.

ON THE DEATH OF W. C.

Thou arrant robber, Death!
Couldst thou not find
Some lesser one than he
To rob of breath,—
Some poorer mind
Thy prey to be?

His mind was like the sky,—
    As pure and free;
His heart was broad and open
    As the sea.
His soul shone purely through his
        face,
And Love made him her dwelling
        place.

Not less the scholar than the
        friend,
    Not less a friend than man;
The manly life did shorter end
    Because so broad it ran.

Weep not for him, unhappy Muse!
His merits found a grander use
Some other-where. God wisely
        sees
The place that needs his qualities.
Weep not for him, for when Death
        lowers
O'er youth's ambrosia-scented bow-
        ers
He only plucks the choicest flow-
        ers.

AN OLD MEMORY

How sweet the music sounded
    That summer long ago,
When you were by my side, love,
    To list its gentle flow.

I saw your eyes a-shining,
    I felt your rippling hair,
I kissed your pearly cheek, love,
    And had no thought of care.

And gay or sad the music,
    With subtle charm replete;
I found in after years, love
    'Twas you that made it sweet.

For standing where we heard it,
    I hear again the strain;
It wakes my heart, but thrills it
    With sad, mysterious pain.

It pulses not so joyous
    As when you stood with me,
And hand in hand we listened
    To that low melody.

Oh, could the years turn back,
        love!
    Oh, could events be changed
To what they were that time, love,
    Before we were estranged;

Wert thou once more a maiden
    Whose smile was gold to me;
Were I once more the lover
    Whose word was life to thee,—

[284]

O God! could all be altered,
  The pain, the grief, the strife,
And wert thou — as thou shouldst
    be —
  My true and loyal wife!

But all my tears are idle,
  And all my wishes vain.
What once you were to me, love,
  You may not be again.

For I, alas! like others,
  Have missed my dearest aim.
I asked for love. Oh, mockery!
  Fate comes to me with fame!

A CAREER

"Break me my bounds, and let
    me fly
To regions vast of boundless sky;
Nor I, like piteous Daphne, be
Root-bound. Ah, no! I would
    be free
As yon same bird that in its flight
Outstrips the range of mortal
    sight;
Free as the mountain streams that
    gush
From bubbling springs, and down-
    ward rush
Across the serrate mountain's
    side,—
The rocks o'erwhelmed, their
    banks defied,—
And like the passions in the soul,
Swell into torrents as they roll.

Oh, circumscribe me not by rules
That serve to lead the minds of
    fools!
But give me pow'r to work my
    will,
And at my deeds the world shall
    thrill.
My words shall rouse the slumb'r-
    ing zest
That hardly stirs in manhood's
    breast;
And as the sun feeds lesser lights,
As planets have their satellites,
So round about me will I bind
The men who prize a master
    mind!"

He lived a silent life alone,
And laid him down when it was
    done;
And at his head was placed a
    stone
On which was carved a name un-
    known!

ON THE RIVER

The sun is low,
The waters flow,
My boat is dancing to and fro.
The eve is still,
Yet from the hill
The killdeer echoes loud and shrill.

The paddles plash,
The wavelets dash,
We see the summer lightning flash;

[285]

While now and then,
In marsh and fen
Too muddy for the feet of men,

Where neither bird
Nor beast has stirred,
The spotted bullfrog's croak is
heard.
The wind is high,
The grasses sigh,
The sluggish stream goes sobbing
by.

And far away
The dying day
Has cast its last effulgent ray;
While on the land
The shadows stand
Proclaiming that the eve's at hand.

POOR WITHERED ROSE

A Song

POOR withered rose, she gave it me,
Half in revenge and half in glee;
Its petals not so pink by half
As are her lips when curled to
laugh,
As are her cheeks when dimples
gay
In merry mischief o'er them play.

Chorus

Forgive, forgive, it seems un-
kind
To cast thy petals to the
wind;

But it is right, and lest I err
So scatter I all thought of her.

Poor withered rose, so like my
heart,
That wilts at sorrow's cruel dart.
Who hath not felt the winter's
blight
When every hope seemed warm
and bright?
Who doth not know love unre-
turned,
E'en when the heart most wildly
burned?

Poor withered rose, thou liest
dead;
Too soon thy beauty's bloom hath
fled.
'Tis not without a tearful ruth
I watch decay thy blushing routh;
And though thy life goes out in
dole,
Thy perfume lingers in my soul.

WORN OUT

YOU bid me hold my peace
And dry my fruitless tears,
Forgetting that I bear
A pain beyond my years.

You say that I should smile
And drive the gloom away;
I would, but sun and smiles
Have left my life's dark day.

PAUL LAURENCE DUNBAR

All time seems cold and void,
  And naught but tears remain;
Life's music beats for me
  A melancholy strain.

I used at first to hope,
  But hope is past and gone;
And now without a ray
  My cheerless life drags on.

Like to an ash-stained hearth
  When all its fires are spent;
Like to an autumn wood
  By storm winds rudely shent,—

So sadly goes my heart,
  Unclothed of hope and peace;
It asks not joy again,
  But only seeks release.

JAMES WHITCOMB RILEY

(From a Westerner's Point of
View.)

No matter what you call it,
  Whether genius, or art,
He sings the simple songs that
    come ·
  The closest to your heart.
Fur trim an' skillful phrases,
  I do not keer a jot;
'Tain't the words alone, but feel-
    in's,
  That tech the tender spot.
An' that's jest why I love him,—
  Why, he's got sech human
    feelin',
An' in ev'ry song he gives us,
  You kin see it creepin', stealin',

Through the core the tears go
    tricklin',
  But the edge is bright an'
    smiley;
I never saw a poet
  Like that poet Whitcomb Riley.

His heart keeps beatin' time with
    our'n
  In measures fast or slow;
He tells us jest the same ol' things
  Our souls have learned to know.
He paints our joys an' sorrers
  In a way so stric'ly true,
That a body can't help knowin'
  That he has felt them too.
If there's a lesson to be taught,
  He never fears to teach it,
An' he puts the food so good an'
    low
  That the humblest one kin reach
    it.
Now in our time, when poets
    rhyme
  For money, fun, or fashion,
'Tis good to hear one voice so clear
  That thrills with honest passion.
So let the others build their songs,
  An' strive to polish highly,—
There's none of them kin tech the
    heart
  Like our own Whitcomb Riley.

A MADRIGAL

DREAM days of fond delight and
    hours
  As rosy-hued as dawn, are mine.

Love's drowsy wine,
Brewed from the heart of Passion
    flowers,
  Flows softly o'er my lips
And save thee, all the world is
    in eclipse.

There were no light if thou wert
    not;
  The sun would be too sad to
    shine,
  And all the line
Of hours from dawn would be a
    blot;
  And Night would haunt the
    skies,
  An unlaid ghost with staring
    dark-ringed eyes.

Oh, love, if thou wert not my love,
  And I perchance not thine—
    what then?
  Could gift of men
Or favor of the God above,
  Plant aught in this bare heart
  Or teach this tongue the sing-
    er's soulful art?

Ah, no! 'Tis love, and love alone
  That spurs my soul so surely on;
  Turns night to dawn,
And thorns to roses fairest blown;
  And winter drear to spring—
  Oh, were it not for love I could
    not sing!

A STARRY NIGHT

A CLOUD fell down from the heav-
    ens,
  And broke on the mountain's
    brow;
It scattered the dusky fragments
  All over the vale below.

The moon and the stars were anx-
    ious
  To know what its fate might be;
So they rushed to the azure op'n-
    ing,
  And all peered down to see.

A LYRIC

My lady love lives far away,
And oh my heart is sad by day,
And ah my tears fall fast by night,
What may I do in such a plight.

Why, miles grow few when love is
    fleet,
And love, you know, hath flying
    feet;
Break off thy sighs and witness
    this,
How poor a thing mere distance is.

My love knows not I love her so,
And would she scorn me, did she
    know?
How may the tale I would impart
Attract her ear and storm her
    heart?

Calm thou the tempest in my
   breast,
Who loves in silence loves the
   best,
But bide thy time, she will awake,
No night so dark but morn will
   break.

But though my heart so strongly
   yearn,
My lady loves me not in turn,
How may I win the blest reply
That my void heart shall satisfy.

Love breedeth love, be thou but
   true,
And soon thy love shall love thee,
   too;
If Fate hath meant you heart for
   heart,
There's naught may keep you
   twain apart.

HOW SHALL I WOO THEE

How shall I woo thee to win thee,
   mine own?
   Say in what tongue shall I tell
    of my love.
I who was fearless so timid have
   grown,

All that was eagle has turned
   into dove.
The path from the meadow that
   leads to the bars
Is more to me now than the path
   of the stars.

How shall I woo thee to win thee,
   mine own,
   Thou who art fair and as far as
    the moon?
Had I the strength of the torrent's
   wild tone,
   Had I the sweetness of warblers
    in June;
The strength and the sweetness
   might charm and persuade,
But neither have I my petition to
   aid.

How shall I woo thee to win thee,
   mine own?
   How shall I traverse the dis-
    tance between
My humble cot and your glorious
   throne?
   How shall a clown gain the ear
    of a queen?
Oh teach me the tongue that shall
   please thee the best,
For till I have won thee my heart
   may not rest.

CPSIA information can be obtained
at www.ICGtesting.com
Printed in the USA
LVHW052118300423
745716LV00002B/36